FIRST SALIK WAR

THE V'DAN

JEAN JOHNSON

ACE BOOKS, NEW YORK

ACE

An imprint of Penguin Random House LLC
375 Hudson Street, New York, New York 10014

THE V'DAN

An Ace Book / published by arrangement with the author

ACE® is a registered trademark of Penguin Random House LLC.
The "A" design is a trademark of Penguin Random House LLC.
For more information, visit penguin.com.

ISBN: 978-0-425-27693-8

PUBLISHING HISTORY
Ace mass-market edition / January 2016

PRINTED IN THE UNITED STATES OF AMERICA

10   9   8   7   6   5   4   3   2   1

Cover illustration by Gene Mollica.
Interior text design by Laura K. Corless.

Penguin
Random
House

AUTHOR'S NOTE

Welcome to the second novel of the First Salik War, a trilogy set in the same universe as my military-science-fiction series, Theirs Not to Reason Why. Like the previous book, this one is all about First Contact . . . only this time, as events unfold, we see more of the other side of the equation coming into view.

In other words, this is Act II. This story should be enjoyable enough on its own, but to help readers new and old catch up on what happened before, I'll be giving you a little recap of what happened in the first book.

If you'd rather not risk any spoilers about what happened in the previous book, now is the time to turn to Chapter One and begin reading. If you're curious about what happened before, or just need a refresher after having been away for a while, read on.

———

Jacaranda MacKenzie, ex–Special Forces psychic and polyglot translator, had been requested by former Premiere Rosa McCrary to resign from being the Councilor for Oceania Province, representing hundreds of islands and their multitudes of cultures on Earth. Once she did, however, she found her military commission being reactivated and herself given orders to report to the Tower on Kaho'olawe Island, at the heart of the Space Force.

There, Jackie learns that because of a spate of precognitive visions both benign and potentially violent, she and a select handful of others will be involved in making First Contact with hopefully friendly aliens. This is good news, as the only true extraterrestrial sentients the Terrans have faced so far are the Greys, vastly superior in technology, vastly inscrutable in motives, and only thwarted by those with strong psychic abilities. But it is not the Greys that

Humans will be facing; instead, there seem to be many new races out there.

With her knowledge of the military and her familiarity with politics from her years as a Councilor, as well as her outstanding skills as a telepathic translator, Jackie has been selected to join one of the *Aloha* exploratory missions into deep space, traveling on ships that use OTL, other-than-light methods to traverse the vast interstellar distances in mere seconds. She is promoted to the rank of Major and given the authority to become an ambassador should First Contact actually happen. However, she immediately gets off on the wrong foot with the copilot for the mission, Lieutenant Brad Colvers, who, as it turns out, has a personal reason for distrusting psis.

Within a month, contact is made, but not with a friendly species as hoped. The *Aloha 9* is grappled and dragged into a huge starship manned by strange beings who look like a cross between a frog and an octopus, with vaguely ostrich-like legs. These, they learn, are the Salik, and they prefer to take live prisoners. Jackie, attempting to make contact, discovers there are five other Humans on board the bigger ship. Among them is a fellow psi, albeit a very poorly trained one, a psi who does not speak any language she knows.

Managing to communicate in rough picture-thoughts, she grasps that these alien captors will treat her own people like prey-prisoners, too. Determined to rescue the five who are on the alien ship, Jackie emerges, fights her way to the brig with a combination of telekinesis, holokinesis, and telepathy, and brings all of them back. Pushing her abilities, she gets the command codes from the Salik's minds, shuts down their ship's weapons, power, and the force field holding the *Aloha 9* in its hangar bay, and they take off for hyperspace.

Emerging on the far side, with no signs of pursuit, Jackie and her crewmates are free to begin communicating with their unexpected passengers. The newcomers seem human, but they have a distinct visual difference: Each one is spotted, striped, or spiraled in strange blotches of color, affecting everything from skin and hair to the iris of an eye.

Jackie attempts to communicate with the psi, to exchange languages psychically so they can begin communicating in earnest, but his poor training requires her to change plans. Forced to take control long enough to show him how to discipline his thoughts, she teaches him what the Psi League taught her. Once he is reasonably disciplined, she manages to make the language transfer, learning quite a lot about him, while he in turn learns quite a lot about her, exchanging his language, V'Dan, for hers, Terranglo.

Leaving the burgundy-striped blond man—who has identified himself as Captain Li'eth Ma'an-uq'en—to sleep off the psychic transfer, she begins to converse with the other four oddly marked humans. Their next-in-command, a green-spotted blonde named Leftenant Superior Shi'ol Nanu'oc, a countess in civilian life, takes offense at being rescued on a ship crewed by "juveniles." Jackie manages to smooth over the moment, calming things down, and gradually, in stages, the ship of Terran and V'Dan Humans makes its way back to its home base, MacArthur Station. There, they go into quarantine since it has become obvious that both groups are genetically Humans, albeit separated by nearly ten thousand years of disparate evolution.

While the crew's medical doctor and station medical staff work on producing antigens and vaccines for all the various microflora each side carries, Jackie continues to transfer languages and attempt to learn who these people are, where they come from, and what their war with the Salik is all about. Astronomers work with the V'Dan in an attempt to identify their homeworld, and members of the United Planets Council prepare their questions for their unusual guests. But the problem of being viewed as juveniles—simply because the Terran Humans lack the same skin-coloring *jungen* marks the V'Dan bear—continues to mount.

In an effort to prevent Countess Shi'ol from attempting to take over the role of highest authority among the V'Dan, Li'eth reveals himself to the Terran Council as Imperial Prince Kah'raman Li'eth V'Daania, thirdborn offspring of the Empress of V'Dan. From the shock of his own crew, they hadn't known this fact either; Li'eth reveals that he had been maintaining a physical disguise as well as a name-based one while serving in the Imperial Army simply so that the Salik and any other enemies would not know they had been facing such a high-value prize.

Though the Terrans accept Prince Li'eth's rank and ability to make preliminary promises for his people, there are still misunderstandings afoot over the Terran lack of *jungen*, which all V'Dan Humans acquire in puberty, marking the transition from childhood to adulthood. After a confrontation between Li'eth, Shi'ol, and Jackie in his quarters in quarantine provokes the prince into using his fledgling, untrained pyrokinetic powers, Jackie orders Shi'ol to her quarters and tries to figure out a way to avoid the prince being charged with the very serious crime of assault with psychic weaponry.

Eventually, she and he agree that his powers simply are not trained, and that Jackie herself doesn't have the right combination to help him gain control. Since there is a provision in psi-based law to let such charges slide for those who are as yet untrained but remorseful and willing to learn, Jackie arranges for a psychic instructor to be brought into quarantine, along with two doctors who specialize in virulent pathology to hurry along the efforts to isolate and create immunization programs for all the various pathogens being exchanged, V'Dan and Terran alike.

Under the guidance of Master Sonam Sherap, Li'eth slowly gains control over his powers. Using the Buddhist monk's sharp inner eyes, Sonam discerns there is more between Jackie and Li'eth than just frequent telepathic explanations of unusual or strange cultural concepts. He is convinced the pair have begun forming a Gestalt bond, a very rare but not unknown situation where the minds of two psis become quantum entangled to the point where they can boost and share their various abilities . . . at the cost of becoming emotionally bound.

Realizing this puts both of them into a very awkward political situation, Jackie heads to Earth to speak with the Terran Premiere while the V'Dan are escorted on a tour around the Sol System. After experiments to confirm that the bond is genuine, the Premiere asserts that he cannot decide whether or not to allow Jackie to continue being the first ambassador the United Planets has had in many decades. He turns the decision over to the Council itself to decide, leaving Jackie's fate in their hands.

Meanwhile, first audio, then visual contact is made with the V'Dan home system; the Terrans get to see the Empress of V'Dan, War Queen Hana'ka V'Daania for the very first time . . . and gain an inkling of V'Dan culture when she speaks very formally, almost distantly to her own son, a son presumed captured for dinner by her people's current enemy. Still, diplomacy wins the day, as arrangements to start learning each other's units of measurement and exchanging basic (nonproprietary) technological information begin, and arrangements are made for the Terrans to set up an embassy on the V'Dan homeworld once they have put together an expedition to make the hundreds-of-light-years voyage between the two systems.

A special Council session is convened to discuss whether or not Jacaranda MacKenzie should remain Ambassador of the Terran United Planets to the V'Dan people. Li'eth is questioned by the Council. When it looks like they aren't even going to ask the most important person in the debate any questions, he challenges the Council on trying to make decisions about Jacaranda Mac-Kenzie's life without even consulting her—a treatment he likens to slavery.

After a bit of debate, the Council interrogates Jackie, and their decision is rendered. Despite not knowing how the V'Dan will feel about—or even if they will believe in—the Gestalt bond between the pair, the Council members vote, voicing their confidence in Jackie's ability to be an honorable, ethical, moral ambassador despite the potential difficulties her Gestalt might have on the situation.

Li'eth knows that his return to his people means that their difficulties have only begun, not ended. His culture is very different from hers, and the world of V'Dan politics even more so. Rosa McCrary later approaches him, informing him that she has been included on the ambassador's expedition to V'Dan as Jackie's apprentice. The prince knows this is very different from the V'Dan way of things, where those in high positions of power almost never get demoted to a subordinate position without some source of disgrace being involved.

Once everything has been gathered, a fleet of ships carrying guards, embassy personnel, and supplies—including inoculation supplies for the V'Dan to culture and distribute to their own people—are launched from Earth. The book closes as Jackie and company leave the Sol System, bound for a new adventure among a new people who may be Human but are definitely not Terran:

The V'Dan.

———————

One more thing: For those of you familiar with my previous series Theirs Not to Reason Why, you may already know this, but for those who do not, I would like to explain something that has been overlooked by certain readers, which in turn has caused some of them unintended discomfort.

The soldiers in this book, members of the Terran United Planets Space Force, are all exactly that. Soldiers. Regardless of which Branch they serve, Navy, Marines, Army, or Special Forces, they are all considered to be soldiers serving in the Terran Space Force. While there are several similarities to the various militaries of the real world, many members of which I have had the honor of interviewing over the decades . . . *my* fictional soldiers are not meant to be viewed as actual members of the U.S. Marines, or of the British Navy, the Canadian Air Force, et cetera, ad nauseam.

They are their own thing, and the whole system has been made up out of a combination of knowledge gained from all of those interviews and the author's imagination. I have a great amount of respect for the very real men and women who serve in their national militaries, regardless of which nation that might be, because they are willing to lay their lives on the line for their fellow citizens, and chose not to copy any single real system.

I have not served in any military personally, but I have invested multiple decades in my research of militaries both modern and ancient. So, at times things may feel "very real" to many of you who have actually served . . . and then at other times you might think, "Wait—that's not right!" Some of these differences come from military sources found in other nations, and some of it is just fabricated out of whole cloth. Or at least some nice ribbon trim to weave it all together. I am, after all, an author of fiction, not nonfiction, and thus I ask that you keep in mind that this is my own creation, even as it is my own way of honoring those who have served in the real world by trying to get at least some of it right.

With all that said, welcome to Act II of the First Salik War, where newly made friends might be the most foreign of strangers out there, when unseen cultural differences can twist everything out of proportion . . . and where the only way to survive in high-stakes politics is either to cave in to gain what is needed immediately—thus losing everything—or to stand out, maybe even be shut out, and hope that someone will be smart enough to open the door once again.

And sometimes, it's all too easy to forget that there is still an enemy out there, an enemy bent on galactic conquest and lunch, when there are other, friendlier foes far closer to home, hiding themselves behind pleasant smiles and polite bows.

Enjoy,
Jean

CHAPTER 1

Getting changed in zero gravity was not easy. Clothing did not "fall naturally into place" but had to be tugged this way and that. Hemlines remained rumpled unless pulled straight and tucked into waistbands and so forth. And a skirt? Forget it. Forget all skirt-like objects in the weightlessness of insystem space. Jacaranda MacKenzie might wish to dress in a formal outfit to properly represent the people of the Terran United Planets, and she had brought skirts for wearing when they were in a gravitied environment, but she was not doing so in zero G.

That meant donning her military uniform. No longer a mere Major, equal in rank to their pilot, Commander Robert Graves, she had been promoted to the rank of Colonel. It was an awkward promotion, but the new, revised regulations on how an embassy should be conducted included the fact that all military operations within that embassy's jurisdiction had to have civilian oversight.

Just as the highest-ranked officers of the Space Force reported to the Secondaire and the Premiere of the Terran United Planets, all of the military personnel headed to V'Dan space had to report to the Ambassador. Which meant she had to outrank all of the personnel who were already assigned, and who possibly could be assigned, to her jurisdiction. By preference, she would defer as quickly as possible to Secondaire Pong and Premiere Callan . . . but should circumstances isolate the embassy, they had to have a clear-cut leader.

Jackie didn't feel like she was qualified, but Rosa McCrary had confided to her in private that she, too, had never felt like she was qualified to lead the military during her tenure as Premiere. Jackie, at least, had military experience. Still, Jackie only had to don her shirt with its silver eagles on the collar points and shoulder boards. She wasn't the Commander-in-Chief, and she never would be at the rate things were going, and that was just fine by her.

They did have an illusion of microgravity on board the *Embassy 1*, but only because the ship was gradually slowing down in its approach to the planet V'Dan. That meant anyone or anything unsecured had a habit of "drifting" forward into bulkheads and doors. Jackie was somewhat used to zero-gravity maneuvers and could sort of brace herself telekinetically, but that did nothing for hemlines. Or fellow travelers.

"Ah, sorry!" Ayinda muttered for the third time as she swayed and bumped into Jackie's back. "Sorry, Jackie . . . At least we won't have to deal with this for much longer. Right?"

"They did promise us quarantine facilities with full artificial gravity," Jackie replied, adjusting her pant cuffs. Today's outfit was a white shirt, black slacks with gray and blue stripes down the outer sides, black socks, and black shoes. Lace-ups, which meant having to fuss with the ties.

"*Sí*," Maria de la Santoya agreed, speaking in Spanish. "*But from what I learned from our guests, the facilities are military-grade at best. No paintings, no cushions, no artworks, no colors . . .*"

Jackie gave up after a halfhearted try sent her twisting awkwardly. She focused her thoughts while Maria spoke, lacing them telekinetically. Still, the doctor's words had to be addressed. Sort of.

"Speak in V'Dan, Maria," she reminded the doctor. "We all have to speak it from now on unless we're talking to the folks back home."

Everyone on this expedition spoke V'Dan, the language of their forthcoming hosts. She and a handful of other telepathic polyglots had spent hours and days transferring the language over and over just to ensure that everyone who came along would be able to speak, read, and write in their host nation's tongue. Perhaps not with complete fluency, which would only come with practice, but Jackie was good at psychic language transference.

They also all spoke Terranglo, obviously, but Jackie had wisely suggested a third language. Maria would have preferred Spanish—Terranglo was predominantly English with some Spanish mixed in—but for security reasons, Mandarin had been selected. Mandarin was not in the least bit related to the European languages underlying Terranglo. The phonetically written form of Mandarin had been transferred in its full to each embassy member, but so had a good chunk of classic ideographic Mandarin as well. That would give them a shorthand way to pass messages with a minimum of writing.

"Sorry," Maria apologized. "I think first in Spanish, not in Terranglo, let alone V'Dan. I'll be very bored in quarantine when I am not working if the quarters are as dull as we were warned. Unless they exaggerated."

"From what I gathered, they are indeed that dull. We will have the equally dubious joys of learning V'Dan etiquette while stuck in cramped quarters," Jackie added, sorting through her bags of jewelry. "But I've conferred with Rosa on some ways to keep us constructively occupied. Games and such that'll engage bodies and minds, and our new vocabularies . . ."

Adding a necklace was also not a good idea in zero G, but Jackie did have a pin formed from the ideogram for Double Happiness crafted from silver and a rich blue cloisonné. Deciding it would suit the neckline of her blouse, Jackie started to pin it on. An inbound blob of brown and black warned her in time to quickly angle the pin in her hand out of reach even as she flung up her arm to physically cushion the woman drifting her way.

"Sorry!" Lieutenant Jasmine Buraq apologized, quickly twisting and grabbing at the nearest handles. "My toes slipped out of the grips when the ship altered speed."

"No harm done, but everyone hold on just in case, while I pin this thing on my shirt," Jackie said. "I don't need to go into this first meeting bleeding."

Jasmine twisted around, orienting herself upside down to the other woman. "Let me get that for you, since we don't have a mirror in here. Centered, right? Got it . . . It goes a little weird with the silver eagles," she added, her fingers working deftly. "But not too badly. There, centered. At least, upside down."

"I have to remind the grunts somehow that I'm still a civilian

as well as their superior officer," Jackie joked mildly. Her own
toes were firmly lodged under a set of handgrips. The ship
braked again, though this time to the side, making everything
first sway, then feel briefly heavier as their bodies pressed
against the ship. She quickly pushed against the bulkhead, then
clung to a handgrip when they shifted direction yet again.

Commander Robert Graves' voice came over the speakers
in the crew cabin. *"Sorry for the rough maneuvers, folks.
We're getting some last-minute changes in our approach vectors from our hosts. ETA to buckle-up time, ten minutes."*

"Lock-and-Web, ladies," Jasmine reminded the others in
the crew. There were five guards on this ship, not including
herself, three of them women. All of the females floating in
the cabin, Jackie included, started packing away everything
that was floating and bumping against the cabin walls. It
wasn't as if there was anyone else available to do it; while they
were a fairly large expedition compared to the usual skeletal
scoutship crews, everyone had to be their own janitor as well
as whatever other role they were meant to fill.

For safety's sake, the embassy staff, guard contingent, and
their V'Dan guests had been broken up across several ships.
Rosa McCrary, former Premiere and Jackie's backup for the
post of Ambassador, was on a different ship specifically in
case one of their vessels emerged from hyperspace and
smacked into an as-yet-untracked asteroid or something. It
was a very, very small possibility given the vastness of space
and the fact that they had done some previous astronomical
surveys along the route, but nobody wanted to take chances by
placing all their important people on one ship.

The last time that had happened . . . it had been on the *Councilor One*. Thanks to the efforts of a criminal with a serious
grudge and too much technical knowledge, Jackie's own grandfather had died, along with a lot of other Councilors, crew members, and even some Advisors. Several safety laws had been
enacted since then, some of them common sense, and some of
them perhaps a bit redundant and old-fashioned, but ones that
had saved lives.

The only exception to that rule was placing Imperial Prince
Kah'raman Li'eth V'Daania on the same ship as the premiere
Terran ambassador, Jacaranda MacKenzie. That was a neces-

sity because Li'eth and Jackie were in the earliest confirmed stages of forming a Gestalt bond, a sort of psychic quantum entanglement of their minds and mental powers.

Separating a Gestalt pair brought on mental, emotional, and even physical distress, something the Terrans had learned over nearly two centuries of scientific study of verifiable psi phenomena. It could be done for short distances and for short durations, but that was it. Putting the thirdborn child of the Empress of V'Dan through unnecessary torment was not considered diplomatically appropriate, and so onto the *Embassy 1* he went.

He, of course, was changing in one of the other long, rectangular cabins, bumping elbows with some of the men. Just as she turned to pull herself out of the crew quarters, Jackie heard with both her ears and her mind his exclamation of pain.

"*. . . Ai!*" (*Saints take you!*)

(*. . . ?*) Jackie queried. She got an impression of someone's foot having shoved—accidentally—against his face. At least he knew it was an accident; the soldier's quick, almost babbled apology was sincere.

(*I will be deeply grateful for the day when your people install artificial gravity on all your Saints-be-damned ships,*) Li'eth groused. (*No offense meant; I know you lack our tech, just as we lack yours.*)

Jackie, mindful of the others waiting for her to move, pulled herself through the doorway and hovered in the middle passage out of the way while Ayinda and the rest scattered to find their assigned docking seats. She had to wait for Li'eth, since she had the aisle seat for their place in the cockpit. Waiting patiently, she could sense him putting away a few last items and latching the cupboards. (*None taken, don't worry. Even I could wish for artificial gravity—whup!*)

The ship swayed again, and she had to clutch at the handgrips, steadying herself with her mind. The others yelped, and there was at least one thump of flesh into bulkheads that she could hear. Luckily, no one seemed hurt.

"*Again my apologies, folks,*" their pilot called out over the intercom. "*Apparently, they're having to calibrate the automated defenses to accept us as 'friendlies' on their Friend-or-Foe targeting programs. That means a lot of quick responses to course changes, to prove we're willing to go wherever they tell us.*"

(*I could wish your people weren't at war, so such things wouldn't be necessary,*) Jackie sighed.

(You *wish it?*) he challenged dryly. Pulling himself through the hatchway, he reached out a hand to her. She touched it in brief physical reassurance, then caught his lightly shod foot and helped him angle his way into the cockpit. "Swimming" after him, she pulled herself into the foremost cabin, waited for him to strap himself into his seat, then followed suit.

The intercom activated again after three more minutes and two more course changes. "*Lieutenant Buraq to Commander Graves; all cabins are secure. I repeat, all cabins are secure. I am the last thing Locked-and-Webbed.*"

"*Understood, Lieutenant. ETA to docking . . . roughly fifteen minutes at this rate,*" Robert stated, checking his instrument overlays on the main viewscreen. "*But better slow than sorry.*"

"*Better secured than sorry,*" Jasmine returned. "*Buraq out.*"

Li'eth, peering through the viewports beyond the transparent piloting screens, pointed. He leaned in close to Jackie, gripping their shared console so that he didn't twist the wrong way in his seat. "There it is! V'Dan, Motherworld of the Empire . . . if no longer the Motherworld of our race," he allowed. "That's the nightside, and . . . from the outlines of all the city glow . . . that's Ashuul, the main continent of what we call the eastern hemisphere.

"The Autumn and Winter Temples are located there. The Winter Palace, too, which is where we'll be headed after quarantine. Winter came early this year, so you'll miss out on the autumn holy days, but by the time we get out of quarantine, it should be in time to see the winter festivals getting started."

Ayinda, strapped into the navigator's seat, pointed slightly to the right of dead ahead. "There it is, people. *Dusk Army* Station. Our home away from . . . embassy, I guess, since we're already away from home."

"It's big," Brad murmured, peering out the front window. "Very big."

The only reason Brad Colvers was with them was that he had finally agreed to a telepathic language transfer. That the copilot could speak V'Dan was thanks to one of her fellow telepathic translators, Lieutenant First Class Darian Johnston, stepping up to do it for Jackie. Neither she nor the copilot had wanted to merge minds for two to five hours. To his credit, Brad had only taken three and a half hours to make the transfer, half an hour longer than average, and far less than the strenuously resisting five that the V'Dan woman Shi'ol had taken.

"Unfortunately, the actual quarantine quarters are going to be cramped," Jackie reminded the others. She settled her headset over her ear and turned it on to the channel Robert was monitoring. She had already announced their presence in the system two hours ago, when they had been about fifteen light-minutes out from the planet, and had confirmed among themselves the safe arrival of all fifteen *Embassy* Class ships. Nothing but traffic-lane course corrections reached her ears.

The Terran version of quarantine had only needed to deal with just over a dozen people at most: five V'Dan guests, six original Terran crew members, and three additional guests, two pathologists and a psi trainer. Then again, they had primitive wheel-spun space stations that were rather small compared to the bulk of the station that lay almost directly ahead. The V'Dan had more than four hundred years of space exploration and colonization, plus artificial gravity.

Dusk Army looked like a hamburger to Jackie. A giant metal hamburger, nothing more than a cylinder ridged and ringed along the sides with sensors and shuttered observation ports in place of the bumps and ridges of meat patties and vegetables, with domes at either end representing the buns. Tiny oblongs of light were windows; even tinier pinpricks were external sources of light. "Anyone know where we'll be parking?"

Her quip was taken seriously. Robert lifted his chin at their destination. "I had a bit of a chat with Docking Control while half of you were still waking up from your prejump nap and getting a meal. They're not used to so many small ships needing to go into quarantine all at once. They have enough space for this ship and two more of our more normal-sized ships in the quarantine section's hangar bay, but the rest will have to stack and rack on three docking gantries."

(*Stack and rack?*) Li'eth asked, glancing at Jackie for enlightenment. (*I didn't even think to ask where all these ships will park, but what does he mean by that?*)

(*These ships have dorsal and ventral airlocks—the ones*

on the topside and the underbelly normally aren't used save in an emergency, or for stack and rack parking,) she explained, dredging the details out of her memory. It was from her training days shortly before the *Aloha 9* had encountered the Salik warship holding Li'eth and his crew. *(In the event of an emergency, a line of ships can be linked up airlock to airlock, each one parking at a right angle to the one below it, belly to back. You can stack them left-right-left-right, or in a left-hand or right-hand spiral, or even nose-to-toes, alternating the opposite way. The tail fin just clears the wings.)*

(Why do I get the feeling there's a story behind that design?) Li'eth asked her.

(Because you're getting better at reading subthoughts?) Jackie offered. Her eyes were on the station they were approaching, but her inner thoughts were on her training lectures. *(There was a bad case of carbon-dioxide scrubbers on three of the earliest* Aloha *models. One of them went to the rescue of the other . . . and then* their *atmo-scrubber broke down, which required calling in a third ship. There was a lot of awkward maneuvering, of coupling and decoupling. None of the hulls were damaged, but all three sets of pilots and copilots complained so much to the design teams that they pulled production on the original models and immediately modified the next generation to include stackable airlocks.)*

(Don't worry,) she added in reassurance, catching his own subthoughts. *(All of those scrubber models were replaced and all of the replacement parts as well, with the new ones triple-checked before being installed. The last of the current* Aloha Class *came into use round about the time I was recalled to active duty; the rest have been coming off the production line with several other upgrades, too.)*

(And your people put together fifteen new ships in just a couple of months?) Li'eth asked her, impressed.

(It didn't take that *much to redesign the hulls,)* she countered. *(The airlocks were already a long-proved design left over from modular supply-depot construction. The exact same type of depots we stopped at for resupply on the way here, in fact. Even the 1, here, was already under construction when the hatchways were added for modification. The body's thicker, the wings a little broader, but it's still modular construction.*

The hardest part was rerouting the conduits, and that wasn't all that difficult.)

(*Duly noted. I suppose I should remind myself that your ships are a fraction of the size of ours. Ours can take anywhere from half a year to two years to build,*) Li'eth admitted. (*But then again, they're a lot bigger, and they don't make you feel sick each time they travel from star system to star system.*)

(*Plus you get an actual private cabin, rather than a shared one,*) she agreed. That in turn conjured up a strong subthought of his, of how cramped the quarters were no doubt going to be.

(*One hundred ninety-five people are a lot of people to put into quarantine, even if some of them are going to be manning some of those docked ships,*) he pointed out. Even he knew that much, that the Terrans were going to keep some of their ships fully crewed and prepared for departure at a moment's notice during the quarantine period. As soon as they were cleared to depart quarantine and had ferried their personnel to the surface, several of those ships were going to deliver precious telecommunications gifts to other worlds in the known galaxy, while the embassy staff set up and got ready for a formal introduction to the Alliance.

(*At least we convinced them to put all the psis into their own shared quarters,*) Jackie said. Then wrinkled her nose. (*At least, I think we got it through to them.*)

Jackie had brought four other polyglot telepaths with her on this expedition. That had taken away almost half of her people's most powerful psychic translators. It was deemed necessary, though. With their new potential allies embroiled in an interstellar war, the faster both sides could communicate with each other, the better it would be for everyone involved.

Two of them were even xenopaths. Unlike Darian Johnston, whose military commission—like Jackie's—had been reinstated for this mission, Aixa Winkler had never actually touched a fully sentient alien mind before. Johnston had served for ten years, and had faced down the Greys five times. Winkler didn't have that kind of experience; instead, she had served for decades as an animal-rights advocate, communing with a wide variety of subsentient minds.

Min Wang-Kurakawa was a newly minted junior-grade officer. She had expected to be sent on patrol ships to pay for her secondary career in engineering, being a technosentient psi as well as a polyglot telepath. Clees—Heracles Panaklion—had been included in the embassy not only because he was a polyglot psi, but a Psi League instructor. His official job would be to assess and offer training to any V'Dan psis, being certified for basic instruction in all known branches of abilities with two decades of practice at training and teaching.

He had also declared he would be the embassy's chronicler, hauling along a variety of camera equipment, ". . . to capture the behind-the-scenes history in the making!" Jackie had a hard time imagining where the fifty-two-year-old got all his energy and enthusiasm. He hadn't been one of her instructors—a case of her living all around the Pacific Ocean, while he had lived and taught around the Mediterranean Sea on the opposite side of the planet—but she had read the glowing recommendations from many of his students, appended to his personnel file.

The lowest-ranked telepaths were Johnston and Winkler, but low was comparative. At Rank 9 each, they were sensitive enough to pick up thoughts at a mere touch. Bunking with nonpsis could lead to tensions and troubles whenever roommates might bump into each other, as they invariably would. Fellow psis could shield their own thoughts, true, but even if the mental walls weren't up, they would be far more understanding and forgiving of any accidental touches leading to accidental eavesdropping.

Robert spoke, though not to her. Still, it drew Jackie's attention back to the actual docking as he chatted with the station's traffic managers. Dead ahead, the *Dusk Army* now filled most of the view through the forward windows. Not just the station, but a large, rounded, rectangular set of doors that were sliding slowly open, revealing a well-lit interior.

Terran and V'Dan docking technology were not yet compatible, so Commander Graves was having to dock and land manually. Jackie suspected that the "course corrections" on approach were not only for the sake of the insystem defense grid, but to reassure the station's traffic control center that he would heed verbal directions swiftly and accurately.

Her comm station pinged. As the chief pilot, Robert was in constant communication at this point with *Dusk Army* Traffic Control. That meant this was something else. Jackie noted that it was a video link, and opened the channel. The man who appeared on the screen had both mint- and forest-green stripes along each cheek and a stripe down the center of his scalp, tinting his brown hair. He wore a dark shade of green for his jacket, with grass-green lapels, cut vaguely along the lines of Li'eth's Imperial Army uniform and decorated with gleaming silver buttons molded in a pattern of some sort of beast, but it was not an actual uniform.

She offered him a smile. "Greetings. You've reached the communications officer for the *Embassy 1*. How may we help you?"

Hazel eyes narrowing, he frowned at her. ". . . Aren't you the Ambassador? You look like her."

"That is correct, but until I have disembarked from this particular ship, I am also its comm officer. How may I help you?" she repeated. On her left, Li'eth shifted a little closer, peering at the screen.

He gave her a look somewhere between puzzled and dubious. ". . . May I speak with your protocol officer?"

"That would be me as well. How may I help you, *meioa . . . ?*" she asked, using the Alliance term for addressing someone politely. Without a suffix, it was gender neutral and thus considered very polite.

"That, Ambassador, is Imperial First Lord Mi-en Ksa'an," Li'eth stated, leaning in even closer to Jackie. (*I know him by sight,*) he added quickly, telepathically, (*but we rarely moved in the same social circles, for all that he's a First Tier relative by four generations, if I remember correctly.*) Out loud, he added, "Greetings, Ksa'an. Are you still working for the Protocol Ministry?"

"Yes . . . Your Highness. It is good to see that you are well. We will need to speak with these Terrans about the proper protocols for welcoming them into the *Dusk Army*'s containment quarters," the green-striped man stated.

Jackie eyed him. "I am confused as to the need for protocol, Imperial First Lord."

He gave her a skeptical look in turn. "How so, Ambassador?"

A sudden shift of the nose of their ship made everything sway forward and down. Robert cursed under his breath and corrected, compensating for the transfer from weightlessness to artificial gravity. It felt like Mars, lighter than it should be.

Jackie swayed and clutched at her console, then breathed deep to adjust to the sudden need for supporting her own weight after fourteen days in space.

"Please remember that I am not V'Dan and do not understand nor grasp your customs . . . but I would think at this point we are medical patients. Where we come from, all patients are treated equally, save that their needs are based on a triage of who is in need of the most immediate attention. Since we are all healthy as we enter quarantine confinement, the only protocol that should then be followed is a security matter."

". . . Security?" the V'Dan on the other end of the linked screens asked.

"Yes. My head of security wishes for one of our doctors and some of his troops to tour and assess the quarantine facilities before I disembark," Jackie told him. "This was outlined in the notes we sent through the hyperrelay node at your system's edge—speaking of which, we have a satellite node ready to deploy. Your people have not yet indicated where you want it."

"That is not my department, meioa," the protocol lord demurred.

"Well, it will give me something to discuss with someone else while we wait for the team to make its assessment sweep. You can arrange that, yes?" she asked him.

". . . Yes." He didn't look entirely pleased about that.

Jackie chose to address that skepticism with a dose of pragmatism. "My people have a saying. 'Trust is earned, respect is given, and loyalty is demonstrated. Betrayal of any one of those is to lose all three.' I believe the speaker was a fellow named Abdelnour from around three hundred years ago . . . This is the 'trust is earned' stage, meioa," she clarified, using the Alliance's preferred form of address, since she was still a bit unclear on what an Imperial First this or that Lord meant. "My people would like to trust yours, that your facilities are adequate for containing pathogens, and safe for us to live in for the duration of our quarantine stay. However, as this is an incredibly important meeting, my people need direct reassurance that everything is indeed safe.

"We would have extended the same courtesy to our guests, save that there were so few of them that it was simply easier to view and demonstrate everything in person, with no security chiefs demanding that their checklists of procedures and requirements be met," she finished lightly. "There are 195 of us Terrans, and Captain al-Fulan takes his responsibility as our chief guardian seriously."

Indeed, Captain al-Fulan had literal checklists of everything security- and safety-wise that he intended to mark as acceptable or inadequate. She had rolled her eyes when he had first showed them to her, but the captain had explained patiently that *he* had twelve years of working high-profile security details, including in areas that were dangerous. The Terran United Planets worked hard at representing everyone they could, but there were still pockets of humanity who insisted on rioting, rebelling, and committing acts of violence against each other.

Dr. Du would be accompanying him. The pathologist was now familiar with space-station quarantine containment procedures, and intended to study the V'Dan version to make sure they were adequate for her checklists. Jackie had a few checklists of her own, but all of them were in languages other than Terranglo. It wouldn't be diplomatic to let the V'Dan know what she really thought of the things she observed, right now.

As it was, she observed the Imperial First Lord sighing. ". . . Very well. What is the proper protocol among your people for welcoming aboard a military security team?"

That, she could handle easily. "As is our military custom, they will ask permission to come aboard, and when it is given, they will expect an introduction to the officer on deck, meaning the person in charge of the hangar bay. Captain al-Fulan will offer a salute in the Terran fashion, since he is a visiting officer. Your people may use the V'Dan version in return, as His Highness has agreed with me that both are meant as a similar symbol of respect. After that, he will introduce Dr. Jai Du, who will accompany his team as they investigate.

"They will then expect to be shown all over, have all the basic procedures for safety drills demonstrated, their questions answered, and when the captain says it is safe, the rest of us will begin disembarking and off-loading supplies. At that point, the only thing you need do is have whoever is in charge of the quarantine procedures welcome me aboard as an Ambassador—literally, just say 'Welcome aboard, Ambassador,' or however you wish to phrase it—and welcome the others aboard.

"At that point, we'll just expect you to run our people through the safety drills and explanations, show us where to stow our equipment, that sort of thing. Simple and efficient. This is quarantine, after all," she finished, "not a grand introduction to your Empress. That comes later, and can be conducted with full ceremony at that time."

Ksa'an hesitated, then dipped his head to the side a little. "I will admit I have not done any formal greeting ceremonies under quarantine situations before. It has not been needed in decades. But if you will find no offense in such an . . . abbreviated greeting as you outline," he allowed, "then that could be acceptable."

"We Terrans will take no offense so long as we are all polite to each other," she reassured him.

"Ambassador, if you are done speaking with their protocol officer," Robert called out in the pause in their conversation, "we are now safely parked, and *Embassy 2* is coming in for a landing behind us."

"Thank you, Commander. Meioa, if we have satisfied the preliminary needs of protocol, I shall contact Captain al-Fulan to let him know he will be free to board the station upon his arrival."

"Of course, meioa—welcome aboard, Grand High Ambassador Maq'Enzi," he added politely, giving her name a V'Dan twist to its pronunciation . . . and not quite the same one Li'eth had used. The transmission ended.

Sighing, Jackie shook her head to clear it and typed in the link to the *2*. "Time to let al-Fulan know he can start checking off the items on his lists."

(*It's only going to get worse from here on out,*) Li'eth comforted her, in a backwards jesting way. (*Our military's protocols aren't that much different from your own because so many even of our officers are commoners by birth and etiquette . . . but the civilian sector . . .*)

She reached over and squeezed his hand gently, letting their intertwined fingers rest on the edge of the console. The gravity was still less than Earth Standard by about two-thirds, but that was understandable, as it no doubt allowed the incoming ships to maneuver with less wasted fuel. On one of her tertiary screens at the bottom of the main trio, she could see an analysis of the molecules on board, more of the same sort of highly complex, potentially toxic petrochemicals the Salik had used. Not exactly an abundant fuel source when compared to clean, pure water, let alone a safe one. She knew that Maria, their chief doctor, was worried about their exposure to those long-abandoned chemicals. Petrochemicals on Earth were synthesized strictly for lubrication and hydraulic needs, not as a fuel source.

Aside from certain basic needs, everything was different here. Everything was going to be different in how those needs were met. Some of them were needs the V'Dan simply hadn't considered but might be able to supply once they were addressed. Some were going to be things they hadn't even dreamt of, yet . . . or might even balk at providing.

(*We'll try to be ready for it,*) she reassured him. (*And try to be understanding whenever a conflict comes up.*)

———

"And this," their contamination-suited guide stated, gesturing at a door painted a paler shade of gray in the shades-of-gray halls around them, "will be your quarters, Ambassador. Now, if Your Highness will come with me, I will show you to your own suite."

Li'eth frowned at the man. "I was told in our communications that the *Dusk Army*'s quarantine sector only has twenty cabins, two bunks apiece. Between the V'Dan of my surviving crew and the numbers of the Terrans, we have two hundred people in need of places to sleep. I thought I made it clear that we were all willing to share to ensure the comfort of our guests."

". . . Yes, Your Highness," the masked, enclosed figure stated after a brief but palpable hesitation. "We have arranged for the Grand High Ambassador to have a private room, and for you to have a private room, as is proper for your station. The rest will all share quarters in rotation, or sleep on their ships. As was indicated."

"Then why are we wasting space with two of us having separate quarters from the rest?" he asked. It was hard to see the other man's face through the silvered plate of his protective suit, but Li'eth could sense that the man's aura was the sort of dull, muddy gray associated with a blank, uncomprehending stare. Jackie's aura was mostly calm tinged with a touch of impatience, and the Terran soldier behind her had an air and aura of alert boredom. He returned his gaze to the quarantine worker. "At the very least, I should be sharing my quarters with Leftenants Superior Ba'oul Des'n-yi and V'kol Kos'q."

"They . . . are Leftenants Superior, Your Highness. You are Imperial Tier, and they are Second Tier. It would not be appropriate," the other man finally stated, his tone cautious, as if he was trying not to offend someone who had lost his wits.

"I am *also* a Second Tier officer," Li'eth returned. "If it will ensure that two sleeping schedules are freed up on one bed so that two more Terrans do not have to sleep on a floor or in zero gravity, I will share my cabin with my fellow officers."

(*Wait, you picked the wrong people,*) Jackie cautioned him, while the other man processed that suggestion. (*If they've changed this, then they may have changed something else.*) She addressed the quarantine aide aloud. "On a related note, I specifically requested that the *telepaths* who accompanied us—what you would call holy ones, with the ability to speak mind-to-mind—be given separate quarters from the rest. Did you set aside a cabin for them?"

"Ah . . ." That, too, was a question that seemed to faze him.

"If he is indeed willing to share with others, technically His Highness and I should share our cabins with the other holy ones. Two males and two females," Jackie clarified. "It is a point of Terran protocol that *psychics*—what you call holy ones—be given quarters separate from those without such gifts whenever they will be confined in close quarters with many others for more than just a day or two."

The quarantine worker eyed her, then turned to look at Li'eth, his flexible suit twisting slightly. Li'eth nodded. "I am willing to share with my fellow holy ones."

"Your Highness, that would be highly—"

"—The Terrans' understanding of holy ones and holy powers is vastly advanced compared to our own," he stated, interrupting the inevitable, protocol-based protest. "In anything relating to holy powers, they *are* the authority. Arrange things as the Grand High Ambassador directs. I will share my quarters with the two male holy ones, and she with the two females. That will free up four sleeping shifts for four more Terrans."

The man hesitated like he wanted to protest, but sighed and gestured for the prince to follow him. Li'eth sighed mentally. (*I think I have been in the military too long . . .*)

Pressing the button on the doorframe, Jackie stepped into a cabin only slightly larger than the previous ones she had seen her fellow Terrans being guided into, with two bunks built into one wall, a narrowish long couch along the other, a door at the back for the bathing facilities, and two square-and-beam arrangements on the wall behind the couch that could swing down as a pair of tables. More shades of gray were livened by beige bedding and beige cushions with the same sort of easily wiped surfaces as the Terrans used, though she had no clue what kind of material it was.

(*Why do you think you've been in the military too long?*) she asked.

(*Because while the military does have a Tier system, it's considerably more practical and pragmatic in how it handles various matters than V'Dan civilian life tends to be. I had forgotten how rigid and confining it could be, to be near the top of the Imperial Tier instead of near the bottom of the Second,*) Li'eth explained, moving away from her cabin door. His guide hadn't gone far, just around the corner and down a short distance.

At a gesture from the suited guide, he stepped inside his own quarters and shared the awareness that the only differences between his and hers were that his quarters had an actual desk with a workstation between the door and the bunk, the sofa had three individual tables that could be pulled down, and the cushions and bedding were light blue, which blended in more pleasantly than beige, given the dull pewter gray of the walls.

(*So that's the difference between our suites? An extra table and a desk?*) Jackie asked, reading his subthoughts.

(*And blue blankets and cushion covers.*)

(*I'll be booted if I'll ask permission of our hosts—mind if I move in with you, and relegate the other psis to this room?*) she quipped. (*I like orange, not beige, but blue will do in a pinch.*)

(*It . . . wouldn't be diplomatic. We cannot appear to be living together. At least, not until my people grasp the fact that your people are indeed adults,*) he reminded her.

(*Yes, yes, the inherent visual prejudice of your people toward the* jungen*less,*) she sighed. Finding a locker, she stowed her kit bag. (*I'm going to contact the other four. Thank you for being willing to share your quarters with Darian and Clees. Just gently remind Clees he is* not *allowed to take any pictures whatsoever while you're in your shared quarters. I'll do it from my end, too.*)

(*You Terrans and your nearly compulsive need to record every moment of your lives,*) Li'eth teased lightly. (*Why do you do that, anyway?*)

(*You've mostly seen the government side of things; civilian life is a little bit more circumspect,*) Jackie explained. (*The government has to be transparent and open for everything but security secrets. We dealt with . . .*)

(*. . . Too much corruption in your past. Yes, I paid attention to the history overview lectures,*) Li'eth returned. (*You will be recorded here, but it will be like your quarantine, for medical and safety reasons. Those reviewing the footage will be reluctant to do so particularly in the privacy of your quarters because of the lack of* jungen.)

(*And again, we get back to this simple, singular difference. I'm hoping it won't be that bad, Li'eth,*) she told him. (*But I'm not holding my breath.*)

He found a similar cupboard for his own gear. (*I wouldn't advise it, no. We're supposed to be able to overlook such things, but I'm not going to hold my breath, either. I suspect no one will know how good or bad our reactions will be until they are put to the test.*)

An alarm blared, startling both of them. A voice came over the intercoms, belonging to Dr. Du, speaking in swift but crisp V'Dan, then again in Terranglo. "*Emergency! Dr. Maria to the kitchen immediately, and bring your* epi kit! *Emergency! All Terrans report to the hangar bay immediately! All Terrans report to the hangar bay immediately!* Code Blue! Dr. Maria to the kitchen with an epi kit, stat! All Terrans report to the hangar bay immediately!"

(*?!?*)

Dashing out of her quarters, Jackie cast out her mind as she ran. She sorted through the babble of confused, startled, and worried minds, and zeroed in on a desperate, panicked set of thoughts, strong enough that Jackie could *feel* the clogging of her lungs, making it seem like she had to struggle to breathe even as she sucked in full lungfuls of air. Behind her, she could hear another set of running boots and sensed Li'eth catching up.

They entered the large kitchen area and skidded to a stop, Jackie bumping into a counter and Li'eth grabbing onto her. The prince blinked down at the sight of a group of Terrans huddled around one of their members, a youngish woman with curly brown hair and almost V'Dan golden skin. Her face and throat were blotchy and swollen, her body contorting as she wheezed with wild-eyed desperation for air. Maria de la Santoya, the first Terran doctor he had ever met, skidded into the galley from a different doorway, a silver-sided case in her hand. She scrambled to the fallen girl—woman, Li'eth corrected himself—and quickly flicked open the latches. A babble of words spat from her mouth, words he didn't understand.

Jackie did; it was Spanish. She quickly translated it into V'Dan, knowing that the doctor was too focused on her patient, checking pulse, eyelids, testing the puffiness swelling her face. "What did she eat? Does anyone know if she ate or drank anything?"

"The corporal said she was hungry, sir," one of the men kneeling by the patient responded. Li'eth realized both were in very similar brown or mottled brown-and-beige uniforms, as were the other six in the room. "She tried one of the fruits. I tried it, too, and it tasted good, but kinda hot and peppery—that red one, like a red pear but with the three lobes at the bottom?"

Jackie eyed the bowl he pointed to, and shook her head. "That's a V'Dan fruit. I've seen just about every kind there is on Earth, and that's not one of ours."

The soldier started to speak, then widened his eyes . . . or tried to. His own face was starting to swell. Li'eth felt his hands starting to heat up. (*Jackie, I think my holy—my* biokinesis *is activating. It does that when it's needed!*)

She looked quickly between him, the soldier, and grabbed his hands, dragging him over to the soldier. Li'eth moved willingly. With her palms on top of his, she pressed his hands to the man's face (*Concentrate . . . breathe deep . . . imagine the swelling and the airway constriction reducing . . . imagine his blood pressure holding steady instead of dropping . . . there! I can feel it working . . . Thank goodness biokinesis doesn't require a medical degree.*)

Maria looked up from where she had injected epinephrine into the corporal's outer thigh at the midpoint. Her hand continued rubbing the muscles to distribute the drug, but her gaze fell on the pair of psis. *"What are you two doing?"*

"He ate the fruit, too," Jackie replied in Spanish, lifting her chin. She could feel a bit of heat in her own fingers. *"Li'eth's biokinesis triggered. We're trying to clear the anaphylactic shock from their systems."*

"Mother of God! I thought the booster shoots we developed would have stopped *this. Jackie . . . we only have twenty days' worth of food for two hundred people,"* the doctor stressed. She put the epi injector aside and pulled out a breather mask with a small ampoule of compressed oxygen. Fitting it together, she placed it over the wheezing woman's mouth and nose, and pressed the button, forcing oxygen into her lungs. *"Stupid primitive location—I don't even know what sort of medical facilities these people have. They insisted on showing me to a* cabin, *first!"*

"What is going on in here?" a silver-suited figure demanded. This voice was female, not male, but the V'Dan words were flavored with a touch of annoyance. "This isn't a play-place! Get off the floor!"

Li'eth couldn't move since his hands still felt hot; he had to stay crouched and continue to stave off whatever weird infection the other man had. But Jackie could. In quick mental consultation—almost faster than thought—she stood and faced the speaker.

"We are experiencing a medical emergency," she stated clearly in V'Dan. After several months of speaking it, with Li'eth's help in correcting her pronunciation, she knew she would be understood. "Please clear the area of all nonessential personnel. This includes you. If you wish to be useful, assist in guiding all the Terrans not in this chamber back to the hangar bay and *politely* ask them to wait for further instructions."

For a moment, the quarantine-suited figure lingered, as if

uncertain whether or not to argue, then the V'Dan woman left. Li'eth felt his hands fall cold and pulled them away, rubbing at them. A moment later, they started heating again. (*What do I do now?*) he asked Jackie, looking up at her. (*I can feel the holy fire—nonpyrokinetic fire, I told you how it's a different kind of heat—and I'm not very practiced at using it.*)

(*Ask Maria if you can touch her patient,*) Jackie directed him. (*Actually, I'll do it.*) "Maria, let Li'eth lay hands on the corporal. I'll go tell . . ."

She broke off as a trio of silver-suited figures hurried into the kitchen. "Out of the way!" the lead figure ordered. All three of them carried cases that, while not exactly like Maria's, undoubtedly carried a number of similar things. "Clear the area! What's the emergency?"

Maria remembered her V'Dan vocabulary. "The emergency is for something *your* people do not even have the words to describe. Back off and let me do my work. Here, you hold this mask over her face. Keep her breathing."

"Excuse me, child, but you do not—"

"Meioas!" Jackie snapped, halting the lead figure as the . . . man? . . . stooped to reach for Maria's shoulder. The voice could have been contralto or tenor, and the frame was slender. "Allow me to introduce *Doctor* Maria de la Santoya, chief medical officer of the Terran embassy. Apologize, and *move back.*"

The crouching figure hesitated, then slowly rose and stepped back. Maria finished examining the male soldier, then reached for her epinephrine equipment. Swapping out the needle and adding a fresh ampoule, she injected the male in the thigh and began massaging the muscle, no doubt under the theory of better safe than sorry, though his face was no longer quite so blotchy even if it was still a little puffy. Jackie explained for her, since she was busy with her patients.

"Our doctor is medicating and monitoring two patients who are apparently suffering from medical conditions which your people have not suffered in over ninety-five *centuries*. At least, according to your holy texts," Jackie added. That caused the trio to exchange awkward looks, thanks to the limited fields of view in their silvered quarantine suits.

(. . . *The heat is gone. Either they're going to die anyway, and there's nothing more I can do for them,*) Li'eth half joked grimly, removing his hands from the corporal's knees, the closest part he had been able to touch, (*or my holy gift isn't needed anymore because they might actually recover. Saints certainly know, because I don't.*)

(*A lot of biokinetics work that way,*) she reassured him. (*Nobody has to use their psychic gifts if they don't want to, not even medical gifts—it falls under the heading of "bodily autonomy"—but ones like that often trigger anyway when needed.*)

". . . Is this condition contagious?" one of the silver-suited V'Dan asked.

Jackie shook her head. "It is caused by exposure to certain foods, insect bites, flower pollens, and so forth. It can also vary from person to person. In this case, they ate one of the local fruits. Their bodies went into shock, with itching, stinging, rashes, swelling, and loss of blood pressure. The medicine applied by Dr. de la Santoya is usually very effective at managing the symptoms, but the onset was rapid, and they will require careful monitoring over the next day or so. You will assist our doctor, but *she* is in charge of these cases, as this is something you are not trained to manage."

"Under *no* account is anyone to be allowed into any places where plants are growing, nor are they to be allowed access to *any* V'Dan food supplies," Maria added sternly, done with checking the soldier. She moved back to check on the corporal, and nodded. "You six, you are their squad mates?"

"Doctor, yes, sir," one of the remaining Marines confirmed. "We were to report to the galley for K.P. as soon as our gear was stowed in our cabins. Are Corporal Chaluley and Private Thompson going to be alright?"

"Yes, they should be alright for now," Maria confirmed. She lifted her gaze to Jackie's and swapped languages back to her native tongue. *"Twenty days of food, my friend. That is not good."*

"It's worse. It's space food," Jackie said. *"It's going to taste overseasoned for everyone in a gravitied environment."*

Her attempt at humor earned her a wrinkled nose. *"Laugh all you want, but we are in serious trouble. Do we turn around and head home, or stay here and order more food?"*

"Ordering food is a temporary solution, but I don't want to give up just yet. We have a few day's leeway in that twenty.

Let's ask a few questions." Switching to V'Dan, she lifted her chin at the trio. "You're all doctors, yes?"

At their nods, she tipped her head at Maria.

"Your counterpart has several questions. Mostly to do with your *jungen* virus," Jackie clarified. "Because of it, your people are naturally immune to what we call a *histamine* reaction—the immune system overreacts to a foreign substance and causes the symptoms I described. The amount of *histamine* triggers in your food must be overwhelming to have reacted so fast. Are any of you an expert in the *jungen* virus and its effects on your genetics?"

All three shook their heads. Jackie lifted her chin at the door. "Pick two of you to go prep the infirmary for two patients, then start figuring out whom to call. We need the foremost authorities on *jungen*, and preferably an expert on holistic genetic therapy. One of you remain behind to guide the patients and their handlers to the infirmary."

"You know your medical terms well," Maria muttered in Spanish, her tone lighter than usual with humor.

"I'm required by law to be up-to-date on a high percentage of science, technology, engineering, arts, mathematics, and even some general knowledge of first aid and current medical advances, remember?" she quipped back.

"What is that language you are speaking?" one of the suited doctors asked.

"Spanish. *Try to remember to speak in V'Dan wherever possible,"* Jackie added to her medical officer. *"I'll find someone who is knowledgeable and willing to sit down with you for a transfer of medical terminology and equipment understanding."*

"That would be deeply appreciated." Switching to V'Dan, Maria pointed at the patients. "You three, lift the corporal; you three, lift the private. Keep their heads and necks straight, and do not compress their chests. Doctors, one of you lead the way to the infirmary. Jackie, I need you to go explain to the others and the incoming personnel—"

"—That we're not to eat any of the local food. And then I'll go get a direct line back to home to start discussing how to get enough food out here. *Doctors,"* she added firmly, realizing the trio still stood there. Jackie pointed at Maria. *"She* is the expert in this particular medical emergency. *You* will get

the infirmary ready, and start contacting experts in the fields
of *jungen* and genetic therapy."

They moved. Jackie shifted out of the way of the soldiers,
who had been quietly conferring on how to lift their companions. Being trained military personnel, they managed a credible lift and side-shuffle carry. Jackie could have lifted both
easily enough, but she needed to go to the hangar bay.

(*Li'eth, will you stay with them, and watch over them?*) she
asked. (*Keep the doctors cooperating? I have to go handle the
nonmedical side of this.*)

(*Of course,*) he agreed promptly. Rising from the floor, he
dusted off his knees and followed the shuffling, brown-clad
warriors.

Jackie used the door behind her, trying to dredge up a
mental map of the sector. Since there were a good seventy or
eighty people all streaming toward or clustering in one zone,
she let the weight of their mental presences guide her.

Her mind raced over what was needed as she moved. They
hadn't brought all that many provisions, thinking that they
could rely on V'Dan food, since the V'Dan had eaten Terran
food with little problems. They had discussed the need for
antihistamine booster shots to counter whatever the world of
V'Dan might throw their way, but it was clear those shots were
inadequate for the local onslaught of histaminic triggers.

That meant they had to make some hard decisions. First,
she would have to reassure everyone that everything was relatively okay, that the station wasn't going to blow up or whatever. Second, she would have to explain what the emergency
was—no V'Dan food could be trusted, and even the V'Dan
version of Terran foods couldn't be trusted because it had been
evolving on the local planet for nearly ten thousand years.
Third, she would have to direct that a single day's rations be
removed from the incoming ships, but no more; if they had to
return home, it would be best to keep all the food on board so
that it wouldn't have to be repacked onto each vessel.

Dead end, Jackie realized, blinking at the supply closet on
the other side of the door she had just opened. *Okay, back-
track and go around . . .*

Her fourth task would be a chat with the incoming crews
on what they thought the best solution might be, either having

more Terran ships bring food directly from Earth while everyone stayed put here in V'Dan home space, or to have some of their *Embassy* Class ships off-load their gear to make room, and head out to meet the *Aloha* Class vessels midway for cargo transfer. Both had their pluses and their minuses; waiting for ships from Earth to get to V'Dan meant waiting fourteen days out of twenty, but they'd have their own ships on hand in case they had to leave in a hurry.

If they sent out *Embassy* ships to meet the fleet halfway, that meant the Terran fleet—limited still in number—could have a faster turnaround time to head back, pick up more food, and come back with it for the next cargo run . . . but they couldn't keep up cargo runs indefinitely, and fewer ships here at the station meant fewer available seats for getting the Terrans away should things go wrong. *I'll have to ask them what the maximum safe transport capacity is for each ship. It might be a rough ride in some of those jump seats, but I know we weren't maxed out on capacity for personnel. Cargo, yes; personnel, no.*

I was so *hoping those booster shots would work,* she thought ruefully, reaching an airlock with a thick-glazed window looking onto the hangar bay. *I don't know if these V'Dan even have genetic resequencing therapy. We do, but all the equipment's back home, and it doesn't always work, particularly on anyone who suffers from chimerism . . . We'll give the V'Dan three days to ship up their experts and the necessary equipment,* Jackie decided.

That gives us three further days to determine if anything can be done, before we have to decide if we can stay and try for some sort of gene-therapy solution, or if we have to say "Sorry—but feel free to come visit us!" and pack up to go home.

Unfortunately, there are a lot of variables that are beyond our control right now. As far as First Contact scenarios went, having two of her people nearly die from anaphylactic shock was not the sort of "first" she'd wanted anyone to experience. *Definitely nowhere on my list of Things To Experience, here.*

CHAPTER 2

Doctors To-mi Kuna'mi and Mi'en Qua were not quite what Jackie had expected. The fact that they were able to come up to the station so quickly and had agreed to enter quarantine was a blessing, but for two V'Dan women from the same planet, they were not exactly ordinary.

Dr. Qua was tall and thin, with dark blond or perhaps light brown hair pulled back in a bun, and a smattering of roughly fingernail-sized lavender dots that outlined the edges of her face and striped the topside and underside of each arm. She wore clothes in shades of purple cut in the current V'Dan style, somewhat Napoleonic and somewhat modern, and her lavender eyes were a bit strange but not too disarming.

Jackie had seen several pictures of V'Dan citizens as part of the preliminary exchanges of information between the two nations, and spot patterns like that were not common. Nor was the way she held herself, taut with energy inside, seemingly calm on the outside. This moment was important to Mi'en Qua; Jackie wasn't nearly as good at reading auras as Li'eth, but she could sense some grasp of the importance of this moment in the other woman's energies. Like a babbling brook, she wasn't a rushing tumble of emotions going through white-water rapids, but did have motion disturbing her otherwise clear depths.

The other woman, Dr. Kuna'mi, was a still, calm pool by comparison, the kind of pool on a clear day that mirrored the sky, the land—the space station, technically. To-mi Kuna'mi wore her hair loose, letting it fall over and around her shoulders in thick, dark waves. She actually kind of looked Asian, rather than a blend of indeterminate Terran-style ethnicities, and her skin had that golden-brown look to it that wasn't too far off from Jackie's own. The exception were her eyes, which were blue, not brown.

Like Jackie, her figure was a bit fuller than on the thin side, though not quite as plump as Jackie's had been back at the beginning of all of this. The woman showcased it with a suit of strong contrasting navy blue, sapphire blue, and white, making the outturned lapels look almost Art Deco, not just Napoleonic. It took the Terran Ambassador several seconds past the rounds of greeting bows, and even past waiting for the two women to receive vaccination shots versus Terran diseases, before she realized the other unusual feature of Dr. Kuna'mi's appearance. Mainly because Dr. Qua mentioned it.

". . . And of course, my colleague is *the* authority on the *jungen* virus and all its effects," the genome specialist stated. "Please don't be fooled by her lack of marks; she's been working in this field for well over fifteen years."

Lack of . . . Jackie blinked and focused on the other woman's face. Dr. Kuna'mi smiled slightly at the praise. Slightly, but wryly. On impulse, Jackie admitted, "To be honest, I hadn't noticed. Terrans simply don't notice those sorts of things. Please, come this way. You'll be bunking together for a sleeping shift in the same cabin as myself and two of my own specialists—thank you, by the way, for being willing to endure the crowded conditions with us while your colleagues outside quarantine work on cross-checking our antigens and vaccines with V'Dan medicine for compatibility."

"Your willingness to not only undergo such precautions, but to offer solutions to the potential health problems you bring is very admirable," Qua told her, as a handful of Jackie's soldiers hefted the bags and boxes the two women had brought into quarantine with them. "Very mature," she added, moving to follow the Ambassador.

Jackie glanced over her shoulder at that, one brow arched. Was that another case of V'Dan bias against the unmarked, or just a comment on their foresight ability. "Of course it is. We tried to consider in advance your people's good health and medical needs as well as our own. It takes a little more effort, but only a little, to ensure that the people of V'Dan stay healthy.

If we make sure your people have a chance to stay healthy, then there's a chance they will stay happy about meeting and making treaties with my people."

"Yet you were unable to anticipate the impact of the breath-stealers inherent in our food," Dr. Kuna'mi pointed out calmly, her tone matter-of-fact.

Maria, her injector tucked back into its case, her legs pacing the space between the two local doctors and the guards with their belongings, addressed that question. "Since we had no actual samples of your food on hand, *señora*, we went with what looked like the baseline *histaminic* response capability of our guests' biologies. We miscalculated due to a lack of information, not a lack of mature foresight."

"True," Kuna'mi allowed, dipping her head.

"What does *sen'yor-ah* mean?" Dr. Qua asked as they entered the airlock between the hangar bay and the rest of the quarantined sector of the station.

"It's in a language called *Spanish*, which shares some words with Terranglo, our main trade tongue," Jackie explained for her, falling into the role of translator with ease, since it was her longest-running career. She tapped the controls on the airlock door—fairly simple to use—and helped fill the time as they waited for the air to cycle with a bit more information. "The closest equivalent would be calling you by your commonly used female-gendered honorific, meioa-e, which I am told is actually a Solarican word, not V'Dan."

"That is correct," Dr. Qua agreed. "Everyone but the K'Katta can pronounce it and understand its meaning."

"In Spanish, *señora* is used to address an older woman, an honored or respected woman, a married woman, or, in its most archaic sense, a noblewoman. In this case, Dr. de la Santoya is using it as one highly educated colleague to another out of respect."

"What she said," Maria agreed, flicking a hand at Jackie.

Dr. Kuna'mi eyed Jackie with an ongoing hint of amusement. "You fill the role of a translator very smoothly, Grand High Ambassador. You must have had practice."

"I've been a translator for longer than I have been an Ambassador, a politician, or even a soldier," she replied. "I speak over eighty Terran languages, and now I speak V'Dan as well.

With luck, I will find those among the other sentient races who will be willing to attempt language transfers, and add those to my list."

"Over eighty languages!" Qua exclaimed softly, disbelief coloring her tone, and her aura when Jackie glanced her way. "You expect us to believe that?"

"I will admit that I do not speak all of them *fluently* at the moment," Jackie said, correcting herself physically as she almost took the wrong corridor to her quarters. These V'Dan military-style quarantine quarters were very . . . alike. Very gray-painted. She wished they had artwork hung on the walls to make them more memorable. "But it only takes me a short while in the company of a native speaker to regain that fluency.

"The 'trick' to it is that I can learn a language very quickly via what you call holy powers, the ability to speak mind-to-mind without words. Ask any of our five guests, and they will tell you that I learned V'Dan in just three hours and could teach Terranglo to them within three to five, depending on how quickly they cooperated. I have since had ample cause to continue to use it, which further sets it in the mind."

Something in the air shifted at her words. Jackie slowed, unsure what it was. *No, not the air . . . the aether.* She glanced behind her, at Dr. Qua's ruffled brook of an aura, at the matching one of Dr. Kuna'mi . . . almost matching. Jackie still had the odd sense of a mirror-smooth surface, but it was now deep below the ruffled stream. An *unnaturally* mirror-smooth inner core, she realized, facing forward with a blink. With an aura-based illusion of a more normal mind on top.

It *was* an illusion of normalcy. How she knew that, she wasn't sure; her ability to sense auras was still fairly new. But it was more than that. Her *telepathy* told her it was an illusion. The other woman, Dr. Kuna'mi, was mirroring the normal turbulence of a normal, nongifted mind, the mind of the woman next to her, and Jackie had rarely sensed two minds being so closely alike. Even when a group of people were focusing strongly on an identical group task, there were always subcurrents of differences.

In Dr. Qua, there were subcurrents that riffled the waters of her mind, like rocks at the bottom of the stream, save that the "rocks" of the mind came and went. In Dr. Kuna'mi . . . a smooth glass bottom lined the streambed, reflecting all above it but revealing nothing beneath that polished surface. It was the *weirdest* set of mental shields Jackie had ever sensed. Very strong, very practiced . . . very un-V'Dan, if what she had learned from Li'eth was the V'Dan measuring stick.

There was no way that Dr. Kuna'mi could be Terran, or Terran-trained. That left . . . exactly what, Jackie did not know. She had yet to encounter actual V'Dan psis other than His Highness, and until she did, she could not say for certain that Li'eth's initial nearly nonexistent training was normal for these people. *I'll have to wait until I can meet with the priest-hood of their Sh'nai faith before I can be sure. Which will have to wait until quarantine is over, when we can linger lon-ger than our own food supplies can last, and when all the formal greetings and initial, important meetings are over.*

So many things had to wait until then. For now, though, they had reached her assigned quarters. Mindful of the fact that Aixa and Jasmine were inside sleeping, she stopped in front of the door and faced the two ladies. "Since we will be sharing quarters with two others, Aixa Winkler," she said, pronouncing the last name *Vinkler* in the proper German accent, "and Min Wang-Kurakawa, we have moved things so that the other two female *psis*—holy ones, in your culture—are on the same sleep schedule with each other, and that the two of you will be on your own sleep schedule.

"Terrans have certain rules of etiquette which we have de-veloped for the comfort and safety of interactions with our holy ones," Jackie continued. From a pocket, she pulled a sketch of the Radiant Eye, a simple circle-within-an-oval de-sign with eight bars radiating from the pupil point. "This is the mark of what we call the 'Radiant Eye' in your language. It is the symbol of the largest school for training holy gifts, and though there are other major and minor schools for training such things, because of its popularity, our military has been granted permission to use a variation of this symbol.

"There are five of us among the Terrans, two males and three females including myself, plus, of course, His Highness, who is sharing his quarters with the other two men," she con-tinued. "Grouping us together has nothing to do with rank, but everything to do with courtesy. Touch, we Terrans learned long ago, increases *psychic* abilities. *Telepathy*, the ability to read others' thoughts, is definitely one of those increased by touch . . . and the stronger a *telepath* is, the stronger that ability will be influenced by touch. In fact, if you accidentally touched me and I was not aware and thus guarded against such things, I would be able to hear whatever you are thinking. Not just the strongest thoughts, but even some of the subthoughts.

"*Most* people with these abilities do *not* like reading others' thoughts," Jackie stated firmly, while the two doctors exchanged wary looks. "This includes myself and the four *telepaths* I have brought along to be assistant translators. We strongly believe that thoughts are meant to remain private, and we have a whole series of classes which each *psychic* must take in regards to ethics and ethical behavior in such matters. One of those things is a phrase, 'What was yours is still yours,' and it means that if we do accidentally pick up something, we are bound by laws of ethics not to reveal it to anyone else . . . barring only thoughts of having completed a major crime such as murder or grand theft."

Kuna'mi twisted her mouth into a wry sort of smile on one side of her face. "That's an interesting way of putting it, that of having *completed* a major crime."

Jackie shrugged, lifting her hands. "We are all *Humans*. Our species is known to have fits of rage and thoughts of murder from time to time. The difference is whether or not we *act* upon those urges. The law cannot punish a man or a woman for a mere thought, however violent or awful. It can only punish a deed that has been committed, or been attempted.

"With that said, if you do accidentally brush up against me or one of the others, we may learn things about you," Jackie stated. She lifted her chin at Maria, waiting patiently behind the other two. "And *when* I and others assist Maria in translating between her knowledge of medical terminology and yours, we will learn things about each of you because the translation process leans heavily upon context based on your memories. But we are pledged to keep personal information to ourselves, and to not make comment upon it without permission or absolute privacy with you alone."

"Basically, the Ambassador's five-minute lecture on ethics and etiquette boils down to 'do not touch, poke, or annoy the *psychics*, and they will not touch, poke, or annoy you,'" Maria translated dryly. "Are we almost done? I should like to get to work. The sooner we can figure out things, the sooner we can eat food that is prepared, not packaged. What is crafted for the weightlessness of space, where smells are difficult to sense and thus enjoy, will taste overseasoned and odd in a gravitied environment."

"Quite. Inside this room, ladies," Jackie explained, "there are four cupboards to the immediate left of the door. You may use the two bottom drawers. Aixa and Min are using the top two, in deference to Aixa's age—Aixa is also using the bottom bunk. The two of you can sort out who sleeps where when your sleep shift arrives. My own gear is stored under the sofa bench nearest the washing facilities. If you need more room, use the ones to the far right as you face the bench, not to the left.

"I requested that they leave a light on since there are privacy curtains that can be pulled across the bunk openings, but as they are asleep, please stow your gear quietly. I will stay out here because it is too crowded inside with three people moving around all at once." Touching the door controls, she opened it up, showing the dimly lit cabin. The curtains were indeed pulled shut, and one of the women inside was snoring softly.

Since the door slid sideways into the wall, the two women were able to access the lockers easily. Each doctor paused to sort a few belongings, stuffed most into one of the two lower cupboards, and picked up the small bags and sturdy cases that no doubt contained personal versions of the tools of their trades.

Once the door was shut again, leaving the two women inside to sleep in peace, and the group was following Dr. de la Santoya, Dr. Qua eyed Jackie. "So what is the verdict on what you will do about the medical reaction your people are having to our food? You said you had less than twenty days of food."

"We've already shifted cargos and dispatched six of our ships to head out to meet other vessels from the Terran fleet at the midpoint, which are being stocked and sent under way with extra packs of preprocessed foods," Jackie revealed. "We're still in negotiations on shipping fresh foods other than meats, eggs, and dairy, since we don't want to contaminate the V'Dan agricultural system with plant matter that could potentially resprout before it finishes composting."

"What about frozen or canned foods?" Kuna'mi asked.

"Those have been given clearance because they fall under preprocessed; it's all been blanched or cooked so that it cannot germinate," Jackie clarified. She rubbed at her brow briefly. "All these things are topics that I never really thought I'd have to consider. I've assigned staff members to track dietary needs versus what we can ship, versus what we cannot yet ship due to quarantine requirements . . . They're doing a wonderful job of being both flexible and willing to take up whatever task needs managing, so I don't have to do it all myself, but since I'm the person in charge, they want to run everything past me to make sure it's a good idea."

"Will you be running off to handle all of that, then?" the markless V'Dan asked. Her inner aura was still a mask, an illusion similar to Dr. Qua's, but her expression hinted at a touch of hope, if not her tone.

Jackie shook her head. "Since it's easier for two *psis* to share quarters at the same time—since if we bump into each other, we know it's an accident if we sense anything and thus it's more quickly forgiven and forgotten—it's their current sleep cycle. That means if you want to get to work, I'm the telepath on duty. The two gentlemen, Darian and Clees, are on a different sleep cycle from each other, as well as from the two ladies, but I'm not sure yet which one of them picked to be on duty at this hour."

They reached the infirmary. Maria led the way inside. Her two patients had been let go after extensive observation, so the interconnected cabins were empty of bodies though they were full of strange equipment . . . and a lot of signage in V'Dan explaining explicitly how to use each piece of equipment. The signs themselves were actually poster-thin monitors with displays that rotated slowly from manual to manual, alternating with lists of items found in cupboards and drawers behind each one. Jackie thought it was incredibly clever since there was never any guarantee that a medical professional would be caught in need of quarantine, or in a healthy enough shape to manage such things.

"I'd hate to bore you with highly technical matters," Kuna'mi said, tipping her head a little. "We should be fine without you."

"This is also the single largest stumbling block to us setting up an embassy on your homeworld," Jackie pointed out. "It makes sense for me to be involved, or at least to be on hand to observe and thus be more likely to understand what's going on, should any decisions need to be made right away."

She hesitated, then deliberately reached out with a mental set of knuckles and "rapped" on the other woman's illusions and inner shield. That got her a slight but swift narrowing of Kuna'mi's blue eyes.

(*I'm guessing that you're capable of hearing this,*) Jackie sent privately, meeting the other woman's gaze with nothing more than a mild blink of her own eyes. (*I meant it when I said that my people's ethics insist that I not spill any mental secrets of those around me . . . including the fact that you are far better trained than anything I've heard to date on how V'Dan mental abilities should be. You're not getting rid of me . . . and if it is determined that an additional translation session is necessary to impart the proper understanding of our disparate medical lexicons, I will perform that task . . . and whatever I may learn of you of a personal nature, I will refrain from sharing with Dr. de la Santoya, nor ever mention to anyone else that I have learned it.*)

". . . You seem to be quite dedicated," Kuna'mi replied out loud, though from the unchanged mental placidity, she could have been replying to Jackie's verbal words. "I hope you are equally trustworthy."

Jackie did not take offense. "I am aware that trust only builds with time, through a measuring of how well one's words and one's deeds match. I look forward to the chance for both our peoples to build that trust, as well as extending respect to one another."

That made the blue-eyed doctor snort. "I'll wish you the best of luck in that. Markless adults have to be five times as good as anyone else just to get an equal amount of respect. I'll presume you'll want some sort of mark-free version of *jungen* though, given how you are not V'Dan."

"That would be correct," Maria stated, lifting her chin a little. "I am not going to inject any genetics-altering virus that will change the way they look into any of our people. We stopped judging each other based on the color of our skin well over a century ago. We will not go back to such an immature system."

Jackie stepped in verbally. ". . . What the doctor means to say is that we are not V'Dan, and our cultural viewpoint on such matters is therefore different. It will be easier if the V'Dan people simply keep repeating that to themselves, that we Terrans are different, and that we should be judged as you would judge other non-V'Dan."

"Well, it wouldn't do you, personally, any good to get the virus *with* the marking ability intact," Qua said. "You're past the age of puberty, when the virus makes its changes. You'd only get marks out of children caught just before puberty or earlier, and it'll still take a few generations before everyone has them."

"Which we don't want to do, as it would run contrary to Terran values," Jackie said. She gestured at Maria. "Doctors, if you'll give Dr. de la Santoya your full attention, I'm quite sure she's impatient to start getting familiarized with your V'Dan version of genetic-sequencing machines. Once we've gotten everyone up to speed on Terran versus V'Dan machinery and terminology, you'll be able to get to work right away."

APRIL 26, 2287 C.E.
DEMBER 20, 9507 V.D.S.

His Imperial Highness, Kah'raman Li'eth Tal'u-ruq Ma'an-uq'en Q'uru-hash V'Daania, thirdborn child of Empress Hana'ka, stared into the mirror in his semiprivate cabin and acknowledged that he did not feel like himself anymore.

It was a strange thing to admit, but over the last five years, ever since shortly after joining the military at the age of twenty-seven, Li'eth had slowly grown used to *not* being an Imperial Prince. Yes, the officers of the Second Tier were considered technically equal with the lesser nobles, but when one was off in a ship for months on end, the social lines blurred. There was some distance, some formality . . . but the best crews in his experience were those whose officers weren't rigidly strict on fraternizing only within their "own kind" as it were.

Captain Li'eth Ma'an-uq'en could mingle just fine with his

bridge officers, his wardens, his sergeants, even the enlisted, though mingling with the lowest ranks was a rare thing. Imperial Prince Kah'raman . . . *I don't even think of myself as Kah'raman anymore,* Li'eth admitted.

Li'eth, which meant *Year of Joy,* was a fairly common name actually, popular around the time of his birth. He'd encountered a good ten, twelve men during his years in the Imperial Army that shared the name. Most of those encounters had been good, leaving him feeling comfortable *being* a fellow "Li'eth."

Kah'raman, which meant *King of Starshine,* was not a common name. It was literally a regal name, a name reserved for the Imperial Tier, a name with a royal title embedded in it right from birth. Thirdborn, but still royal, Imperial, distinct from all others.

I'm glad I had those years of getting used to being "just plain Li'eth" in the military before encountering Jackie's people, he decided, reaching for the complimentary shaving stick tucked in the mirrored cabinet. *They have very little in the way of a caste system. A much wider variety of cultural backgrounds—vastly wider,* he acknowledged, activating the stick with a touch of the upper button. Carefully, he rubbed the glowing end over his right cheek, removing the hints of light brown and burgundy stubble that had grown there overnight. *But fewer social strata.*

Thinking on how loose and fluid social climbing or sinking can be in the Terran system . . . I think I can understand how adrift Shi'ol must have felt. No automatic deference once she pointed out her civilian title, and no automatic looking to her for leadership. No sense of "you're allowed to do that because that is the way of your Tier" or the equally important "you'd never do that because it's just not the way your Tier behaves." Such as the cleaning they'd all had to do.

He'd gotten used to the more relaxed ways of the military . . . and the greatly lessened expectations laid on a youngish man presumed to have been born of Third Tier parents—highly educated but not ennobled. Captain Li'eth Ma'an-uq'en had been a commoner. One with a close resemblance to His Imperial Highness save for the bit of burgundy stripe he had concealed on his cheek.

But he wasn't Captain Ma'an-uq'en anymore. He didn't have the freedom to mingle with the lower Tiers with impunity, even just casually. An Imperial Prince was almost never *casual*. It went against the order of things.

So why am I thinking back to that looh-ow *picnic we had on the beach of her home island, with her family and important locals and their friends?* He eyed his image in the mirror, half-shaven, and sighed. *I know why. I'm not used to being an Imperial Prince anymore. Even when I went home on Leave for celebrations . . .*

The real reason? He hadn't seen the Terran way of life back then. The way they flowed from formal to casual with graceful ease. How their welcoming warmth was the grease that made those transitions look so easy. They had social strata—in giving their V'Dan guests a sampling tour of their world and insystem colonies, the Terrans had *not* avoided showing them slums, poverty-stricken regions, the homes of the wealthy, or menial labor versus the work of the highly educated.

They weren't apologetic in the sense of being embarrassed; on the trip around the Sol System, the V'Dan had been shown archived documentaries of a selection of worst and best moments in Terran history, including genocide on a scale seen only a few times in the Empire's very long history. The Terrans had simply said, "These are some of the worst things in our history, things we have recordings for, whereas with others we do not have as much. We teach ourselves and remind ourselves of these things, of the evil in them, in the hopes that we will continue to avoid repeating these mistakes."

Matter-of-fact. That was how they handled their mistakes. No stammering denials, no overly dramatic breast-beatings. Just a simple, straightforward message of, "We have bad things and good things in our history, we are aware of it, and we aren't going to pretend they never happened."

Like the Massacre of the Valley. Men, women, elders, children . . . even the infants. Cross-bound and gutted alive, among other horrors. Not my ancestor's brightest nor most blessed hour. That Emperor had been slain by those who were horrified at what he had ordered done, along with the troops who had done the deeds alongside him. The War Crown had passed to a collateral line, a cousin of the First Tier . . . but though the civil

war had been won by the right and just side, it could not erase
the horrific crimes committed against a people whose only
transgression was that they wanted no nobles set over them, that
they wanted their people to be deemed equals with each other.

Eventually, the Valley of the Artisans had been repopu-
lated with both survivors and newcomers and deemed a pro-
tectorate of the Empire. The lessons learned had gone into the
history books and never been taken out. Sometimes softened,
but never removed. Of course, he had no control over what the
Terrans would be shown of V'Dan history, its highlights and
its lowest points such as the Valley. He had no idea if those
who were in charge would be quite so open. Not that it could
be kept secret; eventually, they would get their hands on unex-
purgated historical accounts. But would his own people be
so . . . so *comfortable* with themselves?

Somehow, Li'eth doubted it. Finishing up his shaving with
a touch of the wand to neaten his left sideburn, he checked his
image, then shut it off and tucked it back into the cabinet. A
splash or two of water washed off the little scraps of stubble,
along with a swipe from a cloth to dry his face. He had already
showered, then dried and braided his hair. It was time to don
one of his uniforms.

These were true uniforms, properly tailored and properly
styled, not the approximation the Terrans had managed. Properly armored against most handheld weapons, too. Not that he
expected to be attacked, but without the plasflesh painting his
cheek, hiding the distinctive length and hue of the *jungen*
stripe extending beneath his right eye, he couldn't hide who he
was. Imperial Prince Kah'raman V'Daania and not merely
Captain Li'eth Ma'an-uq'en. Someone always had a grudge
against the Imperial Family. Sometimes, they tried to express
that grudge physically.

For that matter, the Salik could strike at any time. There
wasn't a prophecy guaranteeing his survival if he became a
Salik captive a second time. That meant staying out of their
tentacles. He'd fight to the death if that happened again.

(*I'm getting some grim, unhappy subthoughts from you,*)
Jackie's mental voice interrupted. Her *telepathic* touch felt
like a warm ray of sunshine slipping down between the clouds
spreading gloom throughout his mind. (*Is something wrong?*)

(*Just thinking,*) he tried to dismiss, leaving the washroom. A prod from her, however, told him she wasn't going to let the subject go until he aired it. Pulling out his clothes, Li'eth replied while unwinding the towel from his hips. (*I had bad dreams again, this morning. About the Salik. On top of that, today is your semiformal introduction through the windows. I'll be expected to be on hand as the highest-ranked anyone inside quarantine. There is always someone in any large crowd who has a grudge against the Imperial Family.*

(*Your people constrained themselves to just shouting an occasional, "Go back wherever you came from!" and "Earth for the Earthlings, not for the weirdlings!" but I didn't feel physically threatened. Then again,*) he allowed, threading a belt through his pant loops, (*your people had no idea anyone else of our race was out here, away from your home system.*

(*I'm not sure how my own people will react, though. Knowledge that we came from another world is a major religious foundation stone. It's sort of been expected that if anyone survived the cataclysm of the Before Time world, they'd have grown up to be wise and mature and . . . not what your people actually are, which is very V'Danic . . . ahh . . . what's the word in Terranglo . . . Humanistic? Very Human, at any rate. Mortal and fallible and prone to the same lows and highs in every direction . . . which may be disappointing for many, and outright mind-shattering for some. Concerns for our safety are therefore making my thoughts grim.*)

While she mulled that over, he pulled on undershorts and socks, then reached for the dark crimson trousers with their hard-to-puncture meshweave interfacing. Cream-colored shirt, bright red jacket with golden lapels and matching meshweave interfacing. Jacaranda did not press the point as he continued to dress but changed the subject somewhat.

(*Part of me isn't thinking grim thoughts about that, so much as I'm busy thinking this is going to be like seeing a new species of animal in a zoo,*) she told him. ("*Come, watch the rare polar bear through the bars of the cage! Throw peanuts at the albino elephant! Watch out, for that monkey will try to fling its own feces at you! Step right up, it's just ten credits per visit to see the new Terrans at the Alliance zoo!*")

A snort escaped him. Mouth involuntarily twitching up at

the corners, Li'eth straightened from tugging on his boots and checked his image in the mirror on the inside of the washroom door. Blond hair damp but neatly braided, with streaks of burgundy here and there, the one long tendril of burgundy angling down across his right eye, the broad side lapel, the frogging neatly . . . no, that one was twisted. He unbuttoned it, smoothed out the braiding, and reattached it.

(*Which is just silly, a touch of nervousness at the unknown,*) Jackie continued, (*with no idea how everyone will react to us. Or even if they'll like our version of "pageantry." I know that Lord Ksa'an is a bit dubious on how little we have for the moment.*)

(*Imperial First Lord Ksa'an,*) Li'eth corrected her, checking over his image carefully from head to feet, even turning to check the Imperial posterior to make sure the coattails lay smooth and perfect. (*It's very important not to skip the Imperial First bit. He's very proud of his status.*)

(*Duly noted . . . though I think your people are going to be shocked by how casual we Terrans tend to be. Or at least by how short our titles are. I keep trying to turn and check to see who this "Grand High" Ambassador is. We don't have different degrees of Ambassadorship, you know.*)

(*Yet. You may find it useful as you send more and more to the various worlds out here.*) A tug and twitch of his trouser leg made the dark red fabric drape properly over his left, calf-length boot rather than bunch up on the cuff edge. He even had replacement medals, brightly enameled metal disks on pins rather than dangling from colorful ribbons like the Terran ones. The solid steel triangles of his captain-rank pins gleamed at the collar, on the shoulder boards, and at the cuffs of his military coat, large and visible . . . which made him wonder if he was going to retain the lowly Second Tier rank of a captain.

It wasn't as if he could hide his true identity anymore, after all. The Terrans in their negotiations had mentioned his identity freely. He couldn't blame them for doing so, however; Li'eth understood that such things were their way of showing trustworthiness, of honor and integrity.

That thought made him wonder if he should assert his rank a little, and not the military one. A mere captain couldn't dictate where a leftenant superior should serve—they were placed in command of them, not allowed to pick—but an Imperial Prince *could* command that, say, a certain Leftenant Superior V'Kol Kos'q should serve him directly.

And didn't Empress Kah'nia-sun instruct her son, Hi'a'gon, that, "A prince should always strive to have two good friends about him, good enough to be honest and tell him 'no' when he needs to hear it," back in the seventh millennium? Wait, eighth. It was in the mid-7600s . . . somewhere . . . When exactly did Great-plus Grandmother rule . . . ?

He shook it off as unimportant. With forty-five centuries' worth of ancestors to keep track of, surely even an Imperial Prince could be forgiven the sin of forgetting exact dates of specific reigns now and then. That, and the clock set in the wall by the door said it was nearly time for the semiformal viewing. No time to look it up on the workstation.

The meeting would take place in the observation lounge, which had a nearly floor-to-ceiling viewing window. Reporters would be few and carefully vetted. Officials would also be few and carefully selected. Questions would be few and carefully prepared in advance. In archaic hydrofluid terms, this was an interview meant merely to "prime the pump" with a splash of information, sharpening the curiosity of the currently available public, and setting things up for a hopefully smooth broadcast to the other worlds. Either by slow mail courier, or by those Terran hyperrelay things.

It was kind of exciting simply to *be* here and now, at this place and time, knowing that they were making progress on bringing the Terrans into the Alliance and into helping them win the war.

Entering the observation lounge, Jackie selected one of the center seats in the double row of chairs lining the chamber. With her were nine others selected from the Terran delegation to be the first to meet and converse with locally based representatives of the other sentient races in the Alliance. Rosa took a seat to her left, and Li'eth picked a spot near the broad, floor-to-ceiling window that filled most of the forward wall.

That window was shuttered at the moment. The others filed in, ranging from Captain al-Fulan and two Marines who were free at the moment in their duty shifts to attend, to Clees and his ever-present hovercameras, a couple nurses, and a handful of embassy personnel. The Imperial Prince subtly tugged his uniform jacket straight as they took seats, and began.

"Today, you will be meeting the Choya. They are an amphibious race, preferring temperatures and humidities warmer than customary for . . . our joint species," he amended, carefully not calling anyone a V'Dan. "Under previous conditions, you would have met representatives from both the Choya and the Salik at the same time, as they both prefer humidity and heat . . . but obviously that is no longer possible. For reasons of comfort, the others will be introduced in their own pairings."

He paused, lifting his head a little. Jackie glanced over her shoulder to see that one of the two Marines had lifted her hand. Upon being acknowledged by their host, she stood, shoulders and chin level, arms at her sides. "Imperial Prince, I am wondering why you would introduce the aliens in pairs, sir!"

Jackie felt a touch of humor in Li'eth's underthoughts. They colored his aura with bits of gold, making her reflexively blink the vision away. She wasn't used to *seeing* auras; that was his ability, and a distracting one for the Gestalt to give to her. Seeing things from a distance—more like sensing but with some inner vision—yes, she could see things via clairvoyancy, when it related to wanting to merge a holokinetic illusion with its surroundings, but not auras.

"Please relax . . . Private, yes?"

"Sir, Private First Class Jay Krimmer, sir!"

(*The words you want in Terranglo are "At Ease,"*) she offered.

Dipping his head, Li'eth switched languages briefly. *"At Ease, soldier, and be seated. This is not a formal meeting, and I am not in your chain of command."* Switching back to V'Dan, he gave her an explanation. "Introducing alien races in pairs was suggested by the K'Katta as sound psychology. Indeed, experiments have proved that the alien races, when introduced in pairs, are more likely to be perceived as allies. Alone, they seem friendless and thus less friendly. Together, they can be viewed in terms of 'If those two can get along with each other in the same room, then we should be able to get along with them, too.'

"This has not only proved to be effective among . . . *Human* mind-sets, but among their own kinds as well. For the most part, the Salik being the current notable exception," he stated. Returning to the subject of introductions, he gave them some information about the species they were about to meet. "The Choya, being amphibious and preferring saltwater to freshwater habitats—though they can occupy freshwater with the right provisions—are fairly unique. Even the Salik rely more upon lung power once they become adults, but the Choya remain in possession of fully functional gills as well as functional lungs from birth.

"The females tend to be slightly smaller than the males, and have multiple front-to-back crests, usually no less than three but most often four or five; males tend to be slightly larger and usually have only one, or at most, two crests. Male crests are further distinguished by being taller than female ones by a couple size factors—in measurement terms that don't require you to try to translate between Terran and V'Dan systems, it's roughly the difference between a single finger-bone versus an entire finger," he offered. "There is, of course, no shame in not being able to tell them apart right away, and you can always refer to them by the honorific meioa, or in third person by the pronouns for 'they,' 'them,' and so forth.

"This, of course, goes for any of the beings you are about to meet, including our fellow V'Dan . . . who are *Humans* like you." He paused, eyed the gathered Terrans, then nodded at Jackie. "Are you ready, Grand High Ambassador?"

"Yes. Is everyone else ready?" she asked, twisting to look around her. Every member of the Terrans save for Clees had taken a seat; the telepath-cum-reporter hovered at the back of the room, peering through a camera hovering directly in front of him and guiding two more into clinging to the walls, one behind and to his left, the other up at the front of the room, where it attached itself to the ceiling and angled its lenses down at everyone. At the nods of the rest and with no signs of dissent, she turned back to the shuttered window. ". . . You may begin when ready, Your Highness."

Nodding, he turned to the room controls. *"Is everyone ready on the other side?"*

A familiar voice came back across. *"Everyone is ready; thank you for being settled on time."*

Nodding, Li'eth tapped the button that unlocked the window shutters. They split horizontally, rising into the ceiling and sinking into the floor on both sides of the glass, or whatever served as a transparent substance for V'Dan observation ports. On the other side, standing off to the left side of the round-cornered window, Jackie could see Imperial First Lord Mi-en Ksa'an, with his two-tone green stripes and his dark brown hair. His outfit today was a deep blue with overtones of purple, cut in a style similar to Li'eth's military uniform.

Behind and beside him were three more V'Dan. Filling the right half of the chamber sat the Choya delegation, a total of five aliens. Jackie knew that two in each party were reporters, news collectors for transforming the account of the meeting into packets that would be sent off on each starship leaving the local system, in the hopes that someone would get this information back to their home governments or to colonyworlds. One of those reporters for each group was easy to determine, too, for they were doing things with objects that seemed to be used for guiding and checking on hovering gizmos. Cameras, most likely, small and vaguely similar to the ones being wielded by their own makeshift reporter.

The V'Dan were, well, V'Dan. Humans with colorful marks on their bodies, clad in outfits similar to the Imperial First Lord's. One fellow, sitting next to the camera-tending woman, had chosen a shirt and braid-frogged vest that bared his arms so that his yellow lightning stripes could be seen on his mahogany skin.

It took Jackie a few moments to realize that the reason for his bare arms wasn't the heat, since the other V'Dan were dressed conservatively despite the sweat forming on their faces. It was, she realized, because none of the randomly placed, wobbling, forked *jungen* marks turning his dark chestnut skin a vibrant gold on those bared arms reached up past his collarbones. Nothing on neck, nothing on face, nothing visible in the dark brown of his eyes or the short-trimmed, tight black curls of his hair. Though the much-lighter-skinned woman seated next to him, playing with her camera controls, had medium blue blotches irregularly scattered over her limbs, somehow his branching, golden streaks look more intriguing, more prominent, thanks to the sheer amount of skin exposed.

Jackie didn't have much more time to contemplate that; they were already being introduced to the foremost V'Dan aside from the Imperial First Lord. That was the Admiral Superior Jes-na Tal'en-qua, a formidable-looking woman with honey-gold skin, brown eyes, dark hair liberally streaked with gray and patches of burgundy, and, of course, burgundy-hued crescents a little bit larger than Ba'oul's aqua blue ones scattered over her skin, about the size of finger and thumb arched in a large curve.

"Welcome aboard the *Dusk Army*, Grand High Ambassador," the admiral stated. "I am aware the accommodations of our quarantine sector are not exactly First Tier, but I hope they are adequate."

"Thank you. They are indeed adequate," Jackie returned politely. She stifled the urge to suggest paintings on the walls and potted plants tucked into corners. As things stood, the paintings might be a good idea, but the potted plants would probably put out too many histamines via pollen and perfumes. "Thank you for being willing to accommodate so many of us at once."

"The life-support systems are managing adequately, without strain," Admiral Tal'en-qua stated politely.

"Behind her are News Collator Ar-med J'shouran, and his technician, Pel Sa-min," Ksa'an introduced next. "They are attending mainly to record these events for posterity, though Honorable J'shouran will be asking a few questions. Is there any business which you wish to discuss with the Admiral Superior at this time, or with Honorable J'shouran?"

Jackie glanced around her at her fellow Terrans before replying. She got a response to her silent inquiry, but not a verbal one. It was a telepathic one, and came with a polite mental knock and a physical flutter of Clees' fingers. (*Any chance I could discuss technical aspects with their reporter crew?*)

Smiling, Jackie faced forward. (*I'll look into it.*) Out loud, she said, "Not at this moment, though our own News Collator would like some time at some point to discuss professional subjects with the Honorables J'shouran and Sa-min."

"Of course. A suitable session will be arranged for a later time," Ksa'an promised.

Li'eth had explained to Jackie when this meeting was first being arranged that introducing the familiar V'Dan first was a way to give both sides a bit of time for studying each other's unfamiliar biology . . . save that the Terrans were the same as V'Dan, more or less, so the Choya shouldn't need quite as much time. Still, it was a courtesy to allow the Terrans to look their fill before introductions were made. With the initial greeting finished, the Imperial First Lord gestured at the Choya seated in the front row.

"Grand High Ambassador Ja'ki Maq'en-zi, I present Ambassadorial Adjunct G'nneal, Forearm of Grand High Ambassador Terrlog."

(*What the . . . ? Forearm?*) Jackie wasn't the only one to think it; Clees shared his own exclamation at the same moment.

(*Sorry,*) Li'eth apologized quickly. Jackie quickly passed along his explanation when he continued, reassuring Clees as well. (*I forgot to explain that the Choya like to name themselves after important feats, functions, and features. Landscapes, body parts, deeds, that sort of thing. The Grand High Ambassador himself is called the Thumb of the Son of Cho—thumbs being very important body parts for most sentient species to possess. Even the K'Katta have their own version of thumbs, since a part of the definition of sentiency includes tool-wielding abilities.*)

(*Right.*) She refocused her attention on the greeting the Choya was giving her. She had to concentrate to understand his accent, since he spoke with more liquid vowels and consonants than the firmer, more glottal-stop-riddled sounds the V'Dan tended to make. An idle corner of her mind pondered which Terran language V'Dan sounded like. *Possibly Urdu or Sanskrit, though there is some African interior influence, and a touch of . . . pay attention, Jackie.*

The Adjunct was asking her a question. "You arrre the same ssspecies as the F'Dann?"

"As far as science and medicine can tell, yes," she replied. "We, the *Terrans*, evolved on our world. We call our species *Human*, or *Humans* for the plural form. At some point, the V'Dan were removed from our mutual world and brought here. We have no record of their migration, however."

Adjunct G'nneal ruffled his double crests briefly, narrowing his eyes. The paired flaps of skin were apparently controlled by thin ribs, which raised and lowered two, three times. "Very fffew of usss have records lonnnger than sssix thousannd yearss. The VV'Dan being an exsssceptionn. They sssseem to have been borrrnn with pennnss grrripped."

(*The thing he's doing with his crests and his eyes is a sign of humor,*) Li'eth murmured in the back of her mind.

(*I'm glad to know that.*)

(*Remember, don't smile back with bared teeth,*) he added, sensing her incipient reply.

(*I remember,*) Jackie agreed. That had been among the protocol lessons given to them before they had even left Earth, let alone the Sol System. She smiled with closed lips. "Our potential new allies are exceptional in many ways. We brought three historians in our embassy delegation to study the histories of the various Alliance races, as well as specifically studying V'Dan history, including its earliest records, to try to make sense of how our joint species came to be separated."

Twisting in her seat, she indicated a figure in the next row back. The woman, her face more squarish than oval, her brown hair neatly styled and falling to her shoulders, realized Jackie meant her, and stood, smoothing the skirt of her sleeveless, light blue dress.

"This is Meioa Adelle Mariposa, one of our historians," Jackie introduced. "She has expressed interest in your people. Another kind of historian, similar to your news collectors, is also one of our primary translators, Heracles Panaklion; he is at the back of the room, and is an amateur reporter, someone more interested in current events."

Clees lifted his hand at the introduction, then returned it to his control tablet. Adelle sat down again. On the other side of the window, the Choyan Adjunct lifted a hand, spreading his digits with the palm toward himself. The move stretched the webbing that had hung slack until that moment. "Ssharinng your obserfations would be appreciated. Lllooking in the mirror of annnother's eyess can be faluablle for ssself-examination."

"I would be happy to share copies of my recordings, meioa," Clees stated. "For now, we have only the ability to translate our programming languages into V'Dan formats, but we hope to improve that, soon."

"We will share our recordings, too, in F'Dan format," the Adjunct agreed, and looked to Ksa'an, then beside him to the two females seated to the right.

"Next is Military Consultant Fifth Rank Cheru, Knuckle of the Embassy Guard here on V'Dan," the V'Dan nobleman enlightened them.

The female—five crests streaking her skull from the brow backward—blinked slowly, then lifted her chin. It wasn't quite as prominent as on a Human, and her teeth were a bit sharp in front, not quite the incisors of a Human, but she didn't seem overly threatening. Jackie knew that appearances could be deceiving, however; the rest of the alien's body was quite muscular under the straps wrapped around her torso and throat, and she had what looked like weapon holsters and ammunition pouches strapped to thighs and arms, both forearms and upper arms.

"I am currriousss about your millitary capabillities," the Consultant stated. Her accent was a little bit different than Adjunct G'nneal's; she seemed more capable of pronouncing Vs and such, and easier for Jackie to understand overall. "Your ssships are small, and nnnot impressive on first llook, save for one thing."

"And that would be?" Captain al-Fulan asked.

Jackie quickly introduced them. "Meioas, this is the head of our embassy guard, Captain Hamza ibn Tariq ibn Iosef al-Fulan. You may call him Captain al-Fulan. Commander Robert Graves is in charge of our ships and their crews, but it is currently his sleep cycle, and the captain is authorized to communicate on his behalf."

"A plleasurrre it is to meet my counterparrt," the female Choya stated. "You may call me Consssultant Fifth Cheru. The irrrregularity in your ssships is a currious inability to dissscernn what llies behind theirrr hulls."

A swift look away and down by Ksa'an focused Jackie's attention on him. She tried to view his aura, but it swirled with too many colors for her to discern any useful meaning. A glance at Admiral Superior Tal'en-qua showed that her own aura was agitated.

"Imperial First Lord Ksa'an, Admiral Superior Tal'en-qua . . . my apologies if this is a breach of etiquette concerning sovereign military capabilities, but have the V'Dan had problems as well at scanning through our hulls?" Jackie asked.

Li'eth's cousin didn't meet her gaze. The head of the space station cleared her throat, squared her shoulders, and clasped her hands in her lap, legs crossed. "At *this* time," Tal'en-qua stated, "we have not been able to discern the depth of detail we normally can through other Alliance vessel hulls. I will state, however, that the *Dusk Army* is not quite as efficiently equipped for such things as a typical military—"

"—Please, Admiral Superior," Li'eth interrupted. She blinked and leaned forward in her seat, peering at him as he shifted more into view through the observation port. Li'eth held up his hand, palm toward himself. "If our technology cannot scan accurately through their hulls, then *admit* it. The different technologies these Terrans could bring to the negotiation table could alter the course of the war. But they will not bring what they do not know could be useful."

She arched a brow at him. "Is this advice from a *captain*, or from the Imperial Prince?"

He didn't flinch. "Both, Admiral Superior."

Sighing, she didn't hesitate more than a heartbeat or two before she faced Jackie again. ". . . We can't tell a Saint's spit of information through those polished hulls of yours. We've gotten minor readings through the viewports, but the angle has to be just right, and the ship has to be stationary."

"Which is good information to know, Admiral Superior. If *we* cannot sense anything through them, and the Choya cannot," Li'eth stated, "this means that it is a potential new armament to thwart Salik scanners, too."

"I woullld be happier to knnow how well they survive direct damage," the Consultant stated. She looked at Captain al-Fulan. "Would you have anny spare hull segmennts for testing?"

"None that we can spare at the moment, Consultant Fifth," al-Fulan replied calmly. "But I could arrange to have some shipped as soon as negotiations begin."

"Nnnegotiationss?" G'nneal repeated. His crest rose and stayed up.

"Some things we may choose to share freely, but we will retain control of the technology, such as our *hyperrelay* communication systems," Jackie told him and the others on the opposite of the observation window. "Other things, such as our hull material, may be negotiated for direct purchase or even for production formulas."

"Mmmmay, but not *willl*," Adjunct G'nneal pointed out, flattening his dual crests.

Jackie nodded in confirmation. "Those are things that must be determined through negotiations and fully shared data. I suspect our military analysts would insist upon seeing how your weapons measure up against your own hulls as well as ours, along with tests of our weapons against yours as well as our own. Such things require transparency among allies, but such things require trust."

"Trrrranssparenncy?" G'nneal asked, looking at Ksa'an for clarification.

The Imperial First Lord blinked. "Ah . . ."

"Forgive me for using a Terran phrase. I meant everything needs to be revealed, not concealed," Jackie restated. "Honesty on both sides, open sharing, nothing hidden. Transparent like this window, as opposed to opaque like that wall," she added, pointing off to the side. "It is a word used for when you need to see through the barrier to what is happening on the other side."

"That mmmakes senssse," the Adjunct said. "Let uss rrremember to discuss what nneedsss to be accomplished rrer these nnnegotiationss to begin."

Jackie nodded. "Agreed."

The meeting with the Choya had been held before lunch, and Jackie felt it had gone well. Rosa had, too, pointing out in a quiet conversation in Mandarin all the things she thought had been handled well and a few things she thought Jackie should consider for future reference. As confident as Jackie felt about making negotiations—part and parcel of being a translator for the government, as well as being a Counselor—it felt good to know she had the older, more experienced woman's praise and advice.

It also felt a little weird for Rosa to be in the junior position, after having looked up to the older woman as the seniormost stateswoman in their entire nation for five long years. But that was the way of Terran politics these days; once a person stepped down from an office, they ceased being that office. Rosa was entitled to a small pension supplement at retirement age, and every former top-level Counselor had security teams watching over them even after they stopped being a Counselor, but that was it. Including one who had served as a former Premiere.

Not everyone agreed with a particular Counselor's policies, nor a Premiere's leadership, not even one as well liked as McCrary had been. But little more than that had been expected to be retained by McCrary in compensation for her years of service. Nor for Jackie, when she had been asked to step down. No huge perks, no lavish postoffice income, though it was expected that they should remain in touch with their successors, and that if they were recalled to the capital for any reason, or sent anywhere on official business, the government would pay for the trip.

This was one heck of a trip, being asked to be one of the first Ambassadors the Terrans had seen in decades, and the two women spent most of their lunch break talking—in Mandarin, for relative privacy—about some of the interests of the Choya, some of the things that had been openly revealed, and some of the things that, cautiously, might be inferred from which subjects they had discussed freely and which they had discussed reluctantly, or even avoided. Cautiously, because the Choya were *not* Humans, for all they spoke V'Dan reasonably well.

It did mean that Jackie couldn't sit with Li'eth at lunch, but she could feel him engaged in multiple video conversations in his quarters. Somewhere in there, he managed to snatch enough bites to count as a meal, and returned to the observation lounge looking composed and neatly uniformed as usual.

The meeting with the Solaricans and the Tlassians was held after lunch, after a break long enough to cool down and dehumidify the other side of the observation lounge. As with the Choya, Li'eth had prepared a speech to explain the next two races before opening the window. There was a different mix in the Terran audience this time; Captain al-Fulan had been replaced by his second-in-command, Lieutenant First Class Jasmine Buraq. Clees was still on hand with his cameras at the back, but the historian was now a Thai man, Surat Juntasa.

He sat in the front row to Jackie's right at a politely murmured request, and peered at the shuttered window through a pair of archaic-style glasses. Seated next to him, when he turned his head away a little, she could see the heads-up display on the inner side of the lenses and realized he was using a piece of personal recording equipment more discreet than Panaklion's hovering equipment.

Catching her looking his way, he smiled and spoke in Thai, tapping the metal frame of his glasses. *"I inherited these from my great-grandfather. Twenty-first-century interface equipment, reprogrammed to communicate with modern equipment. They still work. Not everything that is old is obsolete."*

Her Thai was a little rusty, but she managed to reply in kind. *"I'm glad your eyesight is fine, Juntasa. I was worried for a moment as to why you needed them."*

He shrugged. *"As the body ages, the eyes that wax in youth will wane past middle age. Besides, I can pick up thermal images from these things. The whole thin bar across the top doesn't just provide stability; it's a sensor input like the old gaming systems of . . ."*

He had to break off when a voice came through the comm unit in the wall. *"We are ready on this side."*

"Ambassador?" Li'eth asked her, while the others fell quiet, ending their own conversations. He waited while she looked around, then at a gesture from her, he replied through the pickups. *". . . I will give them the introduction now, then open the shutters when all is ready."*

"Acknowledged."

This time around, Jackie resolved not to be as distracted. She would pay attention to every little thing. Oddly, it wasn't easy. Her body wanted to shift in her seat, when she knew she had to stay respectfully, attentively still.

"The next two Alliance races you will see are the two who get along best with our fellow V'Dan," Li'eth stated, gesturing at the shutter-covered wall. "In your language, they would be described as *felinoid*, for the Solaricans, and *saurian*, or *reptilian*, for the Tlassians. Amusingly enough, there are evolutionary patterns that have created creatures similar to your *monkeys* on the Solarican and Tlassian motherworlds . . . but they are not related to each other, nor to your monkeys, just as your cats and lizards are not related to either of these races.

"For all that they evolved on separate worlds, the Solaricans and the Tlassians can consume several of the same foods, live in the same general conditions and climate ranges—the Solaricans prefer temperatures that are a little bit cooler," he allowed, "but they can tolerate heat, just as the Tlassians can tolerate cold conditions."

"They are warm-blooded?" Maria asked from her seat at the far end of the front row. "The Tlassians regulate their body temperature biologically, rather than assisting it with external temperatures?"

"Yes," Li'eth confirmed. (*I am glad she explained what that meant,*) he added in a brief aside to Jackie. Continuing out loud, he dipped briefly into the backgrounds of each race. "The Solaricans have several pockets of colonies scattered around the galaxy, and admit as much, but they prefer not to invoke cross-regional trade since they claim that once you know five or six interstellar visiting races, they are similar enough not to bother with such things. Out of politeness, we have chosen to believe them . . . but the Empire secretly suspects it is because the cost of transporting trade goods is prohibitively expensive. Particularly as the hub of all their travel, their homeworld, lies well above the galactic plane.

"The Tlassians, on the other hand, are the nearer of the two, and are our closest neighbors. They occupy a swath of the galaxy that lies 'upstream' of the V'Dan Empire—'downstream' is toward the black hole at the center of the galaxy," he clarified, "as everything slowly drains in that direction—and have happily allowed pockets of the Empire to settle on their colony-worlds, just as we have allowed some of their settlers to build homes on our own. The Solaricans have a few enclaves here and there, but tend to strive to be self-sufficient wherever possible."

"Just like cats," someone in the back row joked under his breath. The Imperial Prince frowned.

"No, *not* just like cats. Their political structure requires them to be self-sufficient. Based upon the felines we brought with us to V'Dan, most cats tend to be modestly social at best, and often are loners. Solaricans tend to form strong social bonds. They are in a precarious position, however, as there is only so much of the resources of the Empire overall that can be dedicated toward any one particular clutch of Solarican settlements," he informed them. "That means they must limit the potential for conflict, and one of the easiest ways to do that is not to get into situations where problems and misunderstandings between species could escalate into open aggression and combat."

Jackie was pleased when the man muttered a soft but sincere, "Sorry, I didn't think."

"Please do think," Li'eth stated earnestly, looking at each of the Terrans seated before him. "You may not meet many Choya, but you will meet a lot of Tlassians and Solaricans, many Gatsugi, and on average more K'Katta than the Choya. Please think in advance about what you might say, how you would gesture, and even the way that you smile."

"Diplomacy 101," Rosa stated.

Li'eth, who had been given a chance to study some of the classes offered in Terran learning institutions, nodded at her, understanding the reference. "Exactly. Basic diplomacy rules. The Solaricans, because of their rules on not evoking any conflicts, tend to be a little reserved around strangers. Once they get to know individuals, they can be warm and welcoming. Tlassians, on the other hand, are much more open in their lives. Which brings me to a warning about interspecies . . . relationships."

"A warning?" Jackie asked, glancing at the others. They, too, looked curious.

"Yes, a warning. Tlassian attitudes toward things which most V'Dans, and presumably most Terrans, find private and personal . . . tend to be more open and direct. Additionally, they find the scent of certain of our kind to be . . . intriguing. If I may be blunt and direct, rather than diplomatic," he added, and switched languages to Terranglo, "*a typical Tlassian might find one of you sexually attractive, based on how you smell in person . . . and they might make an offer to engage in sexual activities. They will make this offer even if you are in public, surrounded by others, though the actual act is expected to take place elsewhere. They are not pushy about it, however.*"

Jackie felt her face heat a little. Glancing to either side, she saw she wasn't the only one; even the unflappable Rosa was looking a bit pink in the cheeks. "*How should we handle this, diplomatically? How could it even work, if they're a completely different species?*"

"*Tlassians and V'Dan—Humans—have similar, ah, equipment,*" Li'eth explained. He was grateful it would take a while for the interpreters to catch up on their language and translate this part. It wasn't entirely proper for a member of the Imperial bloodline to discuss such things, let alone so openly. *"There are no known diseases that can cross between the two, though of course that is based solely upon V'Dan information. In terms of function and capacity for pleasure, both species work in similar ways. And, of course, it should be obvious that there is no way to crossbreed between the two species. Only the Feyori can do that, and only by becoming the same species as their intended target."*

"So it's acceptable to simply say 'No, thank you,' when turning them down?" Jackie asked. Receiving a nod, she asked next, *"What is the proper protocol if one is instead intrigued by such things? That is, after there have been reassurances that our pathogens won't harm them."*

"Jackie," Rosa murmured, her tone quelling.

"I am not going to tell anyone they have to explore in those directions," Jackie countered firmly. *"But I am equally reluctant to say they cannot, either, as it is their body and their life, not mine. Nor yours, for that matter. The only instance in which I could is if there is a sound reason, such as interspecies pathogens, or who knows what. Similar methods doesn't necessarily mean the exact same."*

Li'eth reassured them quickly. *"Like us, they do not copulate in public but will offer to make arrangements for a date, then see how things go from there, which is very similar to V'Dan custom, save that we're a bit more discreet,"* he told the listening Terrans. *"As for differences in, ah, expectations, actions, and reactions, it is advisable to do a lot of research beforehand. There are resources in our data matrices, which can be made available. It's not common, but neither is it unknown for V'Dan and Tlassians to . . . indulge.*

"Both nations' viewpoint on the matter is, so long as everyone involved is fully adult, fully willing, and have done research beforehand . . . it isn't anyone else's business. As in any relationship with one of our own kind, casual or otherwise, I would advise getting to know a particular individual as well as the mechanics of the subject in general before exploring in such directions."

Seeing the Terrans nod impatiently, Li'eth figured the subject had been covered sufficiently. It wasn't something he was personally familiar with, being from the Imperial Tier, but he could have named five people of the First Tier who he had heard had indulged in such things. He continued in V'Dan.

"Above all else, even if it offends your personal preferences, please consider it a compliment if a Tlassian makes such a suggestion. They will not take offense if you say a simple 'No,' and they will respect your decision. In fact, they will not bring it up again with you in particular if you do say 'no' . . . so there is no need to *remain* offended. And if there is no need to remain offended, there is no need to be offended in the first place. Agreed?" he asked.

"Agreed," Jackie replied, nodding. "We will make sure it gets put into any protocol handbooks involving *Human*-Tlassian interactions."

"Excellent. One other thing," Li'eth added. "Don't worry about not being able to tell genders apart. They do not have as much overt gender dimorphism as our species does. Tlassian females tend to be a little larger than most males, but they are comfortable with being called by neutral terms. With all that said, are you ready to meet them?"

At a nod from the gathered Terrans, he turned to the controls, contacted the other side to let them know the Terrans were ready, and, upon receiving clearance, retracted the shutters.

This time, the same two V'Dan reporters were there, but a different officer occupied the front seat. It was a red-uniformed male with his pale cheeks and ash-blond hair spotted in dark purple rosettes, similar to Shi'ol's grass-green markings. Next to them were seated two vaguely feline figures in the front row, two more in the back, and to the right of them, closest to Li'eth's side of the observation window, a trio of Tlassians all seated in the front.

The Tlassians were more eye-catching in a way; the one on the left had purplish, rugged skin shaded to light brown and beige, with a purple-and-beige crest stretching across the skull, sort of like a halo. The center Tlassian had a mottled, banded greenish hide, and the last one had a yellow face, fading to blue toward the back of the head and along the almost triangular sides of the neck. The two-part coloring extended down into blue on the backs of his or her hands, with yellow on the inner forearms, palms, and fingertips.

Their eyes were more forward-facing than a typical lizard's, and their limbs looked like they had more freedom of movement. Their garments were sleeveless and cross-folded in front, sort of like a *jinbei*, a sleeveless Japanese jacket, and their trousers were made from gathered folds, each leg almost as broad as a skirt, gathered at the knee. The one with the yellow-and-blue coloring wore sandals baring claw-tipped toes, while the other two wore boots. Their tails could be seen tucked under the stools they used, or curling around to the side, though the limbs didn't look quite as flexible as the tails of the Solaricans in the middle seats.

Those four, the two Solaricans seated in the foreground and the two in the back, were more humanoid in their general build than the Tlassians, though otherwise they were quite felinoid in appearance. The slope of their brows to their noses were different than expected, more lionish than house cat, and their jawlines gave them a sort of heavy-jawed, muzzle-like air, but weren't nearly as pronounced as the Tlassians, with their forward-thrusting snouts and large nostrils. Both species had taller than expected skulls, too, given how they did look vaguely like Terran lizards and cats.

Fur colors and coat lengths varied quite a lot among the Solaricans. The first one to catch Jackie's eye, seated just to the left of the Tlassians, bore a very short, plush, almost velvet-length coat of fur in a soft cloud silver, outlining a whipcord body. The second one she focused on, seated closest to the V'Dan on Jackie's left, was a shaggy-maned felinoid with a hide of predominantly thick cream fur with brown and ginger blotches that had apparently been trimmed short on the limbs with the alien equivalent of barber clippers, save for an almost decorative "ruff" at his or her wrists and ankles. The color of that trimmed, neatly combed, long fur was a rich cream blotched here and there with solid ginger-spice and coffee-brown patches.

Seated behind them were two more felinoid aliens. The first had a variant of Siamese fur coloring, where the cheekbones as well as nose and chin were accented, plus the jawline as well—looking more Human in outline than catlike, as a result. The ears, the shoulders, elbows, and backs of the hands were coated in a medium short fur probably no longer than thumb joint in length, brown for accent, cream for the main color. The hide of the fourth alien was a deep, mottled brown, the fur longer than a thumb from the looks of things but shorter than the very fluffy mane of the tricolor one.

Those that had long fur were clad in sleeveless upper garments and knee-length lower ones. Those that had short fur had longer sleeves and leggings, though the sleeves themselves were slit down the front edge, allowing the wearer to either shrug the arm back under its cover or push it forward for freedom. *Very much like old medieval . . . what were the names of those coats . . . I know this one . . . I . . . boot me, I do know it . . .*

Gard-corps? Houppelande? I wish I'd paid more attention when my cousins babbled about it . . . Pay attention, Jackie, stop fidgeting mentally. Li'eth's cousin is about to begin the introductions.

"First, we have War Lord Krrrnang," Ksa'an stated, indicating the fluffy-maned Solarican closest to him, "who is acting as an adjunct of the local Solarican Fleet under Ambassador Trrrall." He rolled the Rs and almost swallowed the NGs. "Meioa War Lord, I present Grand High Ambassador Ja'ki Maq'en-zi, representative of the *Terran* Empire . . ."

CHAPTER 3

APRIL 27, 2287 C.E.
DEMBER 21, 9507 V.D.S.

(*When* will *your people release the communications satellites?*) Li'eth asked Jackie, closing the door to his quarters. As soon as the third interview was over, the camera-happy Terran telepath, Clees, would be claiming the upper bunk for his sleeping shift. Heracles, that was his full first name. *So many things to track and remember.*

(*After we have received permission from each government,*

including a recorded broadcast of introduction that we can use in each system, ones with appropriate security codes, and reassurances that their people will take seriously the warning not to tamper with or attempt to open or move the relays,) Jackie told him. *(The tampering is obvious since they're primed to explode if opened, to ensure the technology stays out of enemy hands, but the movement is because it's still very much a new technology, and we're not sure just how much stress the aiming algorithms can be put under.*

(We've done our best to compensate for intragalactic motion, but each star system moves at its own speed relative to the rest, and to the movement of the galaxy as a whole, and to the movement of the universe overa—AAAAH!)

Li'eth stumbled, startled by that scream, loud inside his head, faint but still audible through his ears. Jackie shrieked again. He bolted down the hall, wondering who or what was attacking her.

(AAAAH!—GETITAWAYFROMMEEE!!)

A moment later, her mind stopped screeching, only to fall into a jumble of Terranglo and what sounded like Hawai'ian maybe, and a couple other languages on top, all of it flickering and tumbling and muddling too fast for him to make any sense. He hooked his hand around the frame of the open doorway to help throw him into the observation lounge, and found her with her back pressed up against the left-hand wall, her limbs drawn in tight, her hands pressed over her face, shuddering with rapid, struggling breaths.

Alarmed, Li'eth looked all around the room. There were a handful of others who had left their seats, including three more who looked equally terrified, huddling against the wall, shielding their gazes or staring fixedly at the left-hand wall, muttering to themselves. A half dozen more looked upset; they weren't huddled at the edges of the room, but they were looking *anywhere* but at the observation window. A final three didn't seem to be reacting adversely to the view but still looked a little perturbed.

He wasn't the only V'Dan in the room, he realized. Shi'ol was there, too. The countess stood by the control panel for the observation window, her mouth compressed in a tight little smile. A smug, almost triumphant smile. Beyond the window stood three delegations of viewers. The majority were fellow V'Dan, being officials from the station, a couple of the reporters, and his distant cousin, Imperial First Lord Mi-en Ksa'an. Three of the bodies on the other side of the window were the four-armed Gatsugi, their skins flushed in muddled hues of uncertainty, but they weren't the cause of the fear in the room.

That could be attributed to the two K'Katta already present on the other side of the observation glass. That explained Jackie's mental shout, the other Terrans' upset expressions, the way half a dozen had abandoned their seats.

Shi'ol had exposed them to the K'Katta with absolutely no warning. And Shi'ol *knew* that Jacaranda MacKenzie was arachnophobic. She had been there in the Terrans' quarantine sector when a tiny little eight-legged bug had frightened Jackie out of her seat. The appearance of a ten-legged, somewhat similar-looking version enlarged to a leg span as broad as Li'eth himself was tall would be horrifically startling without a chance to mentally prepare for it in advance.

Which, by V'Dan law, *should* have taken place before that shutter was opened.

"Shi'ol Nanu'oc," he stated crisply as he faced the Second Tier countess. "You are stripped of your noble rank for the duration of this quarantine. You are stripped of your officer rank for the duration of this quarantine. Your rank is now *lowest* of the Fifth Tier. You will *apologize* to each and ever single Terran in this room. *Individually.* And you will apologize to the K'Katta, our oldest allies, for the grave insult you have given them as well as to our newest potential allies."

"I did nothing wrong!" she tried to protest. "I was simply trying to—"

Lifting his hand between them, Li'eth cut her off. "—As a *former* Countess of the Second Tier, you *know* what the proper protocols are for introducing new V'Dan—new *Humans* in specific—to the K'Katta," he warned her, each word as hard as a knife even when he had to correct himself. He stabbed his demand at her, his tone an ice-cold blade. "You. Will. Apologize. *Now*, Private Nanu'oc."

Her slight smile and its hint of triumph had faded into a tight line at his words. At her demotion. Stiffly, the green-spotted woman saluted, fist formally thumped over her heart.

Turning, she took a step forward, turned again, and began apologizing to each person on the other side of the window, to the Imperial First Lord, the Ambassadors, and then the other observers. Satisfied for the moment with Shi'ol's obedience, Li'eth reached out to Jackie's mind.

He was relieved to find she was no longer shaken and cowering, though he could sense her flinching away from looking anywhere near the right-hand clutch of sentient beings on the far side of the large observation window. (*Will you be alright?*)

(. . . *Yes.*)

(*I think I am finally mastering telepathy,*) Li'eth stated lightly. That made her glance at him, shifting her gaze from the left side of the room to where he stood by the right-hand doorway. He dipped his head slightly in acknowledgment. (*I do believe I am beginning to sense exactly what constitutes a lie, mind-to-mind.*)

She coughed at that, clearing her throat with a sound that was not quite a laugh. (*Yes, well, if I keep telling myself that, eventually it won't be a lie, now will it? Li'eth . . . how am I going to get through this? I can't even look at them without being frightened. My heart races, my hands sweat, and I keep wanting to push them far, far away with telekinesis. That would* not *be diplomatic, and I* know *it would not, and I am carefully* not *doing it . . . but if they had been a meter closer, I would have. I can't . . .*)

(*You were* supposed *to be introduced carefully. Most subcultures within the Empire are educated from an early age on the fact that the K'Katta are polite, friendly, and our allies, and thus must be treated with respect and courtesy. But for those pockets of aboriginal culture where they choose to stay separate from interstellar life, they are encouraged to contact the Department of Protocol, who appoints a protocol officer familiar with their culture to help them transition, should they need to travel to regions where the K'Katta visit, or even need to conduct commerce or other interactions with that race.*

(*In that tradition, you and your companions were supposed to see a soothing, encouraging visual presentation first, before the window shutter was to be opened. I know for a fact that you did* not *see such a thing because I could not sense you seeing it.*)

(*No, that* modo *pretty much raised the shutter as soon as I entered the room,*) Jackie growled mentally, her underthoughts carrying currents of pointy, stabby, overly hot but only half-formed ideas of retaliation. (*I'm not sure of their body posture, but I think the others were startled,*) she added, her subthoughts meaning the people beyond the window. (*The ones with four arms all shifted to similar shades of creamy beige with gray undertones, though they look like they're recovering.*)

(*Gatsugi colormood for shock and surprise,*) Li'eth confirmed. A glance at Shi'ol showed she had finished apologizing to his distant cousin. "And now apologize to each and every *Terran*, Private," he directed aloud. "Starting *and* ending with two apologies for the Grand High Ambassador, who represents billions of sentient beings."

The demoted countess faced Jackie. She didn't look directly at the other woman, just in her general direction. "I apologize . . . Grand High Ambassador." Shifting, she eyed the next woman. "I apologize, Assistant Ambassador."

Rosa McCrary lifted her hand, forestalling the younger blonde from moving along. "Countess," she stated, "I suggest you remind yourself for the rest of today that it was your choice to alter protocol. Of course, I cannot say what your motives for doing so were. Only you might know that. But I suggest you set those motives aside. A mature person does not choose to make others look or feel bad. A mature person strives instead to make others feel welcome and strives to make them feel comfortable in all situations. You are in command of your own destiny. I should like to see it be a mature and thus responsible one from now on."

Shi'ol curled her lip, looking down her nose at the older woman. "Who do you think *you* are, to talk to *me* like that?"

Rosa stared her down without bothering to lift her own chin. "I am a mature woman offering a *less* mature woman some good advice. Here is another piece of good advice: Try to match your words and your deeds more closely, young lady. It is, of course, up to you as to whether or not you will do so. Rest assured that, either way, we will know what kind of a person you will be in the future by what *you* choose to do. We already know what kind of person you *are*. Do keep in mind that you can change . . . so that, hopefully, you will."

Staring at the woman, Shi'ol finally moved to the next person in the line without saying anything more than a terse "I apologize" to each of the others. When she reached Captain al-Fulan and murmured her apology, he, too, lifted his hand, forestalling her from moving on.

Unlike Rosa, he chose to speak in Terranglo, no doubt as a moment of diplomacy. *"If I catch you causing problems for anyone in the Terran delegation again, I will have you arrested and removed from our vicinity on grounds of disorderly conduct and disturbing the peace. And if you resist that arrest—"*

"Thank you, Captain," Jackie interjected smoothly, her tone both simultaneously supportive with a touch of chiding. *"We hope that it will not be necessary."*

Shi'ol moved on. When she had finished with the others, she dragged in a deep breath and marched back to Jackie. Li'eth moved up, intercepting her. "Your apologies to the others were barely adequate, Private. Please state to the Grand High Ambassador *what* you did wrong, and apologize for that."

This close, he could see a muscle working in her jaw, shifting one of her grass-green rosette marks. But she did comply after a moment. "It was wrong of me to expose you and your people to the K'Katta without ensuring you first went through the proper protocol procedures. I apologize."

Jackie studied her a moment, then simply said, "Apology accepted."

". . . Do I have the Captain's permission to leave?" Shi'ol asked, staring past Jackie's shoulder.

"You will go straight to the supply quarters and search for the insignia of a private; if you cannot find any, you will requisition it for delivery. I expect to see you wearing that ring-and-bar for the remainder of your time in quarantine," he instructed her. "You shall wear it on your civilian clothes as well, as a reminder that your obligation to behave with the *courtesy* expected of an officer of the Imperial Army does not end when you don the attire and rank of a civilian, Second Tier or otherwise.

"That courtesy and its required forethought is still expected from a noblewoman, and it always will be. Dismissed, Private," he directed her, and stepped aside so that she had a clear path through the doorway.

Without a word, though her lips were pressed together, Shi'ol left. Mindful of his duties, his obligations, Li'eth stepped up to the window. He did not apologize to each individual, but he did apologize.

"I regret the actions of my subordinate and extend apologies on behalf of the V'Dan government and the V'Dan military. If you are willing to wait, I will close the shutter now and deliver the introductory program to our foreign guests."

One of the K'Katta curled up a foreleg. The comm unit between the two chambers picked up a bit of clicking and whistling, then the alien's translator box came on, speaking in a soothing male V'Dan voice. "It is a bit like erecting a retention wall after the rising water has already flooded the home, but we are content to wait. It is imperative to reassure our newfound allies that we are friendly, peaceful, and have no intent to cause harm."

The Gatsugi had returned their colors to calm light blues with only hints of cream and touches of green. Their chief spokesperson gestured with three hands, the fourth one remaining in its owner's lap. "We/The Collective concur/agree/will abide with this/our esteemed/honorable K'Kattan delegate/representative. It/This situation is hoped/desired to be recovered/restored to a point/potential for peace/cooperation/regained trust/respect."

Imperial First Lord Ksa'an bowed his head as well. "I will also make a personal note to revoke two grants of merit from House Nanu'oc for the countess' deplorable behavior, Your Highness. In the meantime, we will wait while you reassure our guests that our allies are peaceful and trustworthy."

"Thank you, meioas," Li'eth agreed, and tapped the controls to close the shutters between the two chambers. Sighing, he turned to face the Terrans, wondering how to begin recovering from this protocol disaster.

There had been four of the dozen-plus who hadn't been scared into looking away, and three more had gradually peeked at and faced the K'Katta delegates. Or at least looked at the Gatsugi, doing their best to ignore the shorter aliens. But three remained with their gazes averted from the now solidly shuttered window, and one of them was the Grand High Ambassador. That would not do.

"Ambassador, meioas, if you will direct your attention to the *closed* shutter, it is also a display screen. The video you are about to see was designed to allay the understandable concerns and instinctive fears of aboriginal cultures—those who do not normally participate in the modern ways of the Empire, and thus have little to no knowledge of who and what the K'Katta are," he continued, pitching his voice to be soothing, friendly, and reassuring. "You may not be aboriginal, but your fears are still natural. There is no shame in being afraid of seeing something so different when it evokes instincts buried deep within our minds.

"However, it is also a fact of modern life that the K'Katta are our allies and have been closely involved in helping us to develop advanced technology, including the artificial gravity weaves allowing us to occupy this station under normal living conditions instead of being forced to float around, as you experienced on your journey here," he stated, and gestured at the shuttered window behind him. "They are kind, they are patient, they are honorable, and they *very* much prefer cooperation and trade over any other activity. In short, they are the best allies a peace-preferring nation could want."

Jackie looked at him a long moment, then edged away from the wall. One step, then two, she moved back toward her seat, putting her trust in him. So did the other three, another woman and two men. One of the ones who had *not* flinched away was her assistant, the older woman, Rosa. The former Premiere.

That was a concept which continued to confuse him a little. Rosa McCrary was a woman who had been the equivalent of his mother, the Empress of V'Dan. She had been the Premiere of the Terran United Planets, their foremost leader, for several years . . . but was now *below* Jackie in her rank? Jackie had been the equivalent of an Imperial Advocate while Rosa had been an Empress of sorts, but now things were flipped, and the older woman was now junior to the younger.

The dynamics of their past and current ranks made for almost *too* much fluidity in their social structure for him to comprehend. He wondered if any among his own people could possibly comprehend it.

". . . If you are all composed and ready, and if you will take the seats set out for you," he added, gesturing at the padded chairs set in two rows, "I will begin the presentation. Please do not take offense at how it is aimed at those who are from presumably low-tech cultures. Given how each of our advanced nations is still learning about the other side, it was decided to simply use the presentation we already have, with the assumption that you do technically know little about the Alliance and its allies."

Drawing in a deep breath, Jackie squared her shoulders and moved forward. Her outfit was similar to Rosa's in that each wore a calf-length skirt, a jacket that fell to her hips, and a low-necked shirt underneath. Jackie's outfit came in shades of peach and pale pink, and the other woman wore shades of blue and pale green. The Grand High Ambassador—Li'eth could see her pulling that side of her personality into place with each step—carefully moved to the front row. She took her seat between Rosa and the captain of the *mah-reens*, soldiers who were serving as the bodyguards and security specialists for the embassy.

Her movement, dignity visibly regained, prompted the others huddled along the wall to uncurl and return to their own chosen seats, their expressions somewhat more embarrassed than unsettled, now. As everyone was situated, Li'eth tapped in the commands for the presentation, which filled the upper half of the window.

It was, as warned, designed for introducing the K'Katta to aboriginal cultures who did not pay much attention to modern society or modern technology, so it explained things in very simple terms. But it did give a general history of K'Katta/V'Dan relations, narrated by a V'Dan professor of xenoprotocols. The woman, standing to the left of the projected images, was accompanied at first by vague sketches of what the K'Katta looked like, then with still photos on the right.

He knew the histories, but Li'eth had never needed to see this particular, watered-down version of them. Three times, wars were nearly started over misunderstandings, but in each instance, diplomacy finally won, and trade began. Those stories were intermixed with tales of K'Katta crews helping to rescue stranded V'Dan ships, the offering of supplies and parts, the cautious, painstaking learning of each other's languages . . . only to find that syntax and grammar were remarkably similar to High V'Dan, even if neither side could physically pronounce each other's words.

Once the two sides could communicate, the K'Katta earnestly sought new sources of vegetables, fruits, nectars, and a very few flesh-based proteins. They eagerly exchanged artworks—particularly sculptures and musical compositions— and in general were interested in improving lives on all sides rather than harming them. Overall, the K'Katta were happiest when exchanging information and goods. Some of the most reassuring exchanges had come once enough of each other's languages had been learned to allow translations of literary and entertainment works, though for the visual arts, most of that had flowed from the V'Dan to the K'Katta and not the other way around at first, for obvious reasons.

The sketches of the stiff-furred spiders became animated as a brief discussion of K'Katta anatomy was given; the most unique feature was their dual skeletal system, with bones inside and chitin-like armor outside; the second-most-unique feature was how they could see into both the ultraviolet and infrared ranges, depending on which sets of eyes were being used.

A video appeared on the screen of a K'Katta chitter-whistling shrilly and the translator box—programmed for words but not much in the way of inflection—cried out, "Oh I am in pain! I have agony! This hurts very badly!" while V'Dan medical personnel attempted to calm the alien and splint a bloodied, compound-fractured leg, while one of the medics apologized over and over for not having any K'Katta-compatible anesthetics on hand.

Li'eth sensed several underthoughts in turmoil in his Gestalt partner. They were linked by a sort of quantum entanglement of their minds, and he could feel her fear of the giant, spiderlike beings mixing awkwardly with her compassion for the injured, shrilly whistling and swiftly clicking alien. He didn't reach out to her; he didn't want to interrupt the message being delivered.

There were more scenes of fuzzy miniature K'Katta playing and rolling and climbing—no doubt the images were provided in the belief that the children of most species were considered cute by V'Dan aesthetics, which surely wasn't too different for the Terrans—and pictures of slightly older ones learning in the K'Katta equivalent of a school. Images of K'Katta creating art, of playing chime-and-drum music that was slightly atonal to V'Dan ears but still breathtakingly beautiful . . . and then the news of the Salik War. That pleased Li'eth, to know that someone in the Protocol Department was keeping these presentations reasonably up-to-date, if not necessarily tailored for their newest friends.

The K'Katta, the film explained, had been hard-hit by the Salik because the K'Katta preferred negotiation over conflict. That meant the Salik had decimated five colonyworlds before the aliens had regretfully stopped trying to negotiate and started fighting back. They were hard to motivate to fight and did not like to press a battle when a foe turned to flee. But once they were committed, they did fight hard when defending themselves and their allies.

The film concluded with a speech by the V'Dan professor of xenoprotocol stating that, ". . . Though we may instinctively find these beings fearsome in appearance, and though your fears will not fade today just because you have learned several important facts, I hope you can now acknowledge with honesty that these are indeed gentle, worthy allies.

"They are beings who have a lot more in common with the average V'Dan's thoughts, feelings, wishes, and needs than the Salik, who are bipedal and monoskeletal, ever could have with our people. The K'Katta are sentient beings the Empire is proud to call our friends. And the more we openly acknowledge it and repeat it to ourselves, the less fearsome they will appear, until we can see them for what they truly are: one of the best allies the Empire could possibly have."

The presentation ended with neatly scribed vertical characters, V'Dan characters, suggesting several keywords to use when searching for more information in their data matrices.

Li'eth ended the program and waited to see if anyone had a comment to make. The other woman who had been frightened—one of the captains of the fifteen ships that had ferried everyone here, if he remembered right—spoke up in the silence. "I think I would have been a lot more reassured if I had seen that *before* seeing those . . . alien beings."

Jackie dragged in a deep breath and let it out. "I myself find it reassuring to hear that they are more gentle than fearsome . . . but I am also still unnerved by even just the memory of their appearance. Not as much as I was to begin with, but . . ."

"*I* feel sorry for them," Captain al-Fulan said. That earned him several bemused looks. He shrugged, glancing around at the others. "They have no racial fear of *us*, yet must deal with our fear of them . . . and as *our* people say," he added, looking over at the prince, "'What we do not understand, we fear; what we fear, we hate; and what we hate, we destroy.' I may be in the military, but I would rather not get to the hating stage, let alone the point where we destroy. That would not be polite of us, at the very least."

Discussion, Li'eth knew, was an important part of the desensitization process. He pointed at the man who had refused to look. "What about you, meioa-o? How do you feel now, having learned these things?"

The Terran looked around at the others, then touched his chest, brows lifting in silent inquiry. At Li'eth's nod, the dark-skinned man spoke. "I'm a nurse practitioner, and . . . I want to get a degree in xenobiology. Real xenobiology, not just the animals found back on Earth; that's veterinarian medicine. I want to learn about new sentient races, and how to cure their ills, how to make them feel better. But . . . Don't mistake me, I felt really bad for that . . . poor broken leg, that was a nasty compound fracture. But they still look creepy and scarier than a *moggofroggo*."

(*Jackie, what is a . . . ?*)

(*I believe it's similar to a* modofrodo,) she replied quickly. The subthoughts that came across involved unpleasant epithets and socially unacceptable personality slurs. Out loud, she said, "Don't worry, Arthur. There are several friendly alien races to choose among for your studies."

Arthur . . . Jackman, that's his family name, Li'eth reminded himself. He was used to keeping track of hundreds of courtiers, advisors, officers, and soldiers, but it wasn't nearly as easy memorizing names and faces among the Terrans. Their lack of *jungen* made that task a bit difficult for him, particularly if there was more than one person with a similar set of skin tone and hair color in a group. For that much, he envied Jackie's easier time in telling them apart, but he wasn't surprised that she had memorized all those names and faces.

"I know, but I feel guilty, feeling squeamish about this

particular race," the nurse, Arthur, said. "Guilt compounded on top of fear. My oaths as a medical professional are in conflict with my abhorrence of . . . of things with that many legs." He shuddered, and the man next to him touched his shoulder in sympathy.

"Well, if it will help," Rosa stated, "*I* will volunteer to interact with the K'Katta. I find their appearance a little disturbing because it's so unusual, but not frightening. I believe I can get used to it quickly enough."

"That . . . might be the best idea, Rosa," Jackie admitted slowly. She shook her head, standing so that she could face the large, shuttered window. "But for now, I must find the nerve to greet them calmly, rationally, and politely. Just as I will greet their foremost ambassador when we move on to the planet. It isn't their fault I'm afraid. Now . . . is everyone ready, or do we need a few more moments?"

A hand raised, one of those whose reaction had been in the midrange, so she nodded and changed the subject. "Arthur, how are Dr. Du and the others coming along?"

He looked relieved to be talking about his work rather than the aliens on the other side of the shuttered window. "Quite well, actually; they've been running tandem gene-splicing sims on both our and their machines, and the results have been matching within a 0.2 percent variance with the normal strain. But that's down from over 5 percent found in yesterday's experiments, so things are proceeding rather quickly.

"That is to say, we're talking about an insertion on a single chromosome pair; there's pretty much zero risk of the splice's happening on any other pairs," the nurse practitioner added. "So it's a larger improvement than that sounds. A few more runs, a little bit more tweaking and they should have the viral delivery agent perfected. Dr. Kuna'mi has been working on setting up a markless version of the *jungen* virus, but she'll still need at least two more days of hard biocoding, plus an extra day to free up enough machines to begin running the sims."

"I hope somebody else understood all of that," one of the others muttered, a quip that provoked a few chuckles.

"Bottom line, Arthur?" Rosa asked, craning in her seat to look at him.

"One week to live testing, and we already have a list of

volunteers," he stated confidently. Then amended with a shrug, "Provided nothing huge goes wrong, of course."

"Let's hope it doesn't," Rosa agreed. "I'd like to try some of the local foods without risking anaphylactic shock."

"Alright," Jackie stated, as the others nodded. The general expressions of her fellow Terrans had calmed from the fright of earlier. "On the other side of that shutter, we have three sets of allies. One set looks like us, but with funny, painted faces. One set doesn't look *that* much like us . . . and I've already envied their four arms long before we met them," Jackie added wryly. "Usually, whenever I'm trying to carry too much at once."

That earned her a few chuckles.

Dipping her head in acknowledgment, Jackie continued. ". . . And one looks like a nightmare, but which we are reassured are actually good friends. So . . . deep breaths . . . let it out slowly . . . deep breaths again . . . and out slowly . . . and a third deep breath . . . now breathe normally . . . good, good. Everyone braced and ready?"

She received several nods. No one shook their head. Turning to face Li'eth and the window, she squared her shoulders. "We are ready to meet members of the Alliance, and our future new allies."

(*Are you sure?*) Li'eth queried, hesitating. (*I can still "hear" your fear in your underthoughts.*)

She met his gaze levelly, brown eyes honest yet determined. (*Does it matter if I am still afraid or not? Greeting all of them politely is the correct thing to do . . . so I will do it.*)

(*You are a very brave, mature woman.*) Turning, he touched the controls. *"We will be opening the window shutters in just a moment. Please be seated, meioas. Thank you for your patience."* Turning back to the Terrans, he said, "Remember, there are no enemies here, only allies and friends. Not all of them are *Human*, but all of them are peaceful. They are here to speak with you out of duty, curiosity, the intent to welcome you to this world, and to introduce you to the Alliance a few nations at a time."

Gauging the auras of everyone in the room, Li'eth finally opened the shutters with a touch on the controls. They parted vertically, retracting into the ceiling and the floor. All of the Terrans save for their leader were seated; all of their viewers were seated as well. For a few moments, the two sides studied each other in silence, observing the differences.

The Terrans who were soldiers and ship crew members wore either a brown or a blue military uniform, both sets striped down sleeves and trouser legs in black with matching black boots and belts. The Terrans who were civilians were clad in a variety of colors, the cuts more varied, ranging from skirts to trousers, loose blouses to fitted shirts, most with a light jacket, as the station's ventilation system kept the air slightly on the cool side of comfortable. Footwear varied just as much.

The Gatsugi sat on chairs not much different from V'Dan furniture, save that they had a two-tier armrest style they preferred for supporting the upper and lower pairs of forearms. They were clad in gathered trousers and bell-sleeved tunics dyed in shades of blue and green and things of clear pale yellow, wearing pale gray vests embroidered in cheerful shades that in both the Gatsugi and the V'Dan languages denoted their names, ranks, and general importance. Their skin tones were complementary shades of blue with hints of peach-gold, with the two reporters at the back the peachiest of the quartet.

The K'Katta sat on slightly bowl-shaped objects similar to rather tall footstools; that height allowed them to sit more or less with their eyes at the shoulder level of the V'Dan and the Gatsugi. The padded edges supported their upper knee joints, and a padded rim midway down the sides supported their feet-claws. Li'eth knew that their truefeet and midfeet claws were clad in fitted sheaths that protected the floor surfaces from those sharp tips. The handfeet claws were left bare, since those weren't the ones kept sharp for climbing or self-defense.

Those claw sheaths blended into their brown and tan bodies—female K'Katta were lighter in color than males—but the sashes tied around their abdomens and upper thighs did not. The ones wrapped around their torso equivalents were broad and pastel; those that were attached to their legs were darker and thin, barely ribbons. Out of deference to being paired with the Gatsugi for this initial interview, they had selected compatible colors, light and clear, mostly in the cool tones instead of the warmer ones.

All things considered, when they relaxed like that, legs drooping down and outward a little, they didn't look like actual spiders. Considering how many of his own people were still instinctually unnerved by such things, Li'eth had no idea why the Immortal High One had thought it a good idea to allow spiders to make the crossing along with pollinating insects, birds, frogs, so on and so forth. Unless it was purely to ensure that the insects brought across didn't outbreed the local versions before the native predators could develop a taste for them. That was just speculation, however; it wasn't as if the Immortal would ever show up, reveal herself, and allow him to ask why allow spiders to come along during the *d'aspra*.

The silence was broken by the chief K'Katta delegate curling up his leg toward his mouthparts. Whistling and clicking as those parts moved were quickly translated by the device riding on the top of his neck, and the comm system between the two chambers obligingly transmitted all of it. "We apologize for appearing like monsters from the depths of your subconscious minds—"

Jackie lifted her hand, palm out, then quickly flipped it palm toward herself, V'Dan-style. "—No, please," she interrupted, facing them on her feet. "*Never* apologize for the way your people look. That is simply how you were born, how your people evolved. You should not feel bad, or be made to feel bad, simply because of an accidental reaction from someone else. We Terrans pride ourselves on looking beyond surface appearance. That some of us have failed is our shame, not yours. My shame, not yours. Never yours."

Li'eth could feel the sincerity in her words, a bright earnest yellow in her aura, a feeling of cream riding on the top of milk in her mind. Curdled milk, for the fear was still there, and it was larger than her sincerity, but she had it under tight control. Locked down.

"It is I, as the representative of my people, who must apologize to you. To all of you. Please forgive our reactions." She managed a closed-mouth smile in Li'eth's direction before looking back at the others, his fellow V'Dan, and the Gatsugi seated in the middle. "After having seen the protocol film, my fellow Terrans and I believe we would not have reacted quite so badly. It was not your fault that the shutters were opened before any context could be given to us to help soothe our subconscious minds."

(*You're doing very well,*) Li'eth praised her as she paused for breath.

(*Creepycreepycreepycreepy,*) was her reply. It wasn't even really aimed at him, but at least it was intermixed with, (*I will not freak out . . . They* are *sentient beings . . . Creepycreepy-creepycreepy . . .*)

"Nor was it any fault of yours," the K'Kattan envoy graciously allowed, bringing up a handfoot to gesture toward the window. "We are accustomed to witnessing unease among some of our V'Dan allies. If there is anything we can do to reassure you that we are friendly and not fierce, please let us know."

"At the moment . . . I shall be honest and say that if you simply refrain from sudden or swift movements, we should be reasonably alright," she returned.

Li'eth sensed a rising tide of fear and reached for her mind with his own. Clasping her mental hands, he held her firmly. (*They will obey, they will be slow, they will be graceful and not abrupt . . .*)

(*Thank you.*)

"As you wish, Grand High Ambassador. We shall be like thickened honey before you," the envoy assured her.

". . . With that said," Imperial First Lord Ksa'an stated, rising to his feet, "I shall introduce the K'Kattan delegation first. Grand High Ambassador Maq'en-zi, please be seated for your comfort."

Nodding, Jackie sat down. Li'eth moved away from the side of the window, taking one of the spare chairs at the back of the room. When they were settled, his distant cousin began.

"The one who speaks is the First Protocol Advisor to Grand High Ambassador K'kuttl'cha of K'Katta. For the sake of pronunciation and convenience, his name and title—and those of the others—have been translated into V'Dan as First Protocolist Ch'chik. Seated to his far side is Commander-of-Hundreds Twee-chuk-chrrrrr," Ksa'an continued, rolling the Rs with the tip of his tongue. He gestured with his hand at the front of the two tan-furred aliens. "She is an officer in their Guardian Army and is the head of security for the Grand High Embassy of K'Katta to the V'Dan Empire. She may be addressed as Commander Twee, Commander-of-Hundreds, or Guardian Twee.

"Behind them is Honorable Twer-chih'chik," he continued, shifting his outstretched hand to indicate the final tan-furred, not-a-huge-spider entity sitting on the third stool in the back, "who represents the K'Katta news collectors for the V'Dan System . . ."

APRIL 30, 2287 C.E.
DEMBER 24, 9507 V.D.S.

"And then *I* said to the mathematics professor, 'But you yourself said zero isn't nothing; zero is *everything*, so how could I have gotten a failing grade on that paper just because I proved it?'" V'kol quipped as he and Li'eth entered the entertainment lounge. "Which was only parroting what he himself had said when he assigned that lecture!"

Li'eth laughed. "Did you at least get the . . . grade . . . corrected?"

He trailed off, looking around the nearly empty chamber. It was large enough to hold eighty or so people, and should have held around eighty, but there were only two people inside. In specific, a certain demoted, green-marked private, who sat in one of the padded chairs, switching entertainment channels in a slow, desultory fashion, and a certain blond Terran seated at the opposite end of the broad couch. But the off-duty hours of Lieutenant Brad Colvers wasn't his concern. Shi'ol's on-duty hours were.

"Private Nanu'oc, aren't you supposed to be cleaning the hangar-bay floor right now?" he asked, keeping his tone mostly mild. The disappearance of the Terrans was important, but merely a matter of curiosity, not of missed duty.

"I *cannot*, sir," Shi'ol stated without turning her head or getting up. Colvers glanced their way even though she did not; the markless man's expression was somewhere on the borderline of mildly annoyed, no doubt by the interruption and conversation. The privilege-suspended countess continued with a slight edge to her tone, one that was also mildly annoyed. "The Terrans have taken it over. I am therefore taking a break now, sir, because floor-cleaning is the last of my duties for the day. Sir."

Li'eth and V'kol exchanged looks. V'kol finally shrugged, and said, "Carry on, then, Private."

Gesturing with a pink-marked hand, the leftenant superior nudged Li'eth out of the lounge. By unspoken accord, they turned down the corridor toward the hangar. V'kol eyed the prince a couple times before finally speaking.

"Did *she* tell you what they were planning to do?" V'kol asked, meaning the Terran Grand High Ambassador.

Shaking his head, Li'eth headed into the observation hall, overlooking the hangar. The Terrans—two-thirds of them, the ones not actually asleep at the moment—had sprawled out over the floor, some sitting, some lying on their backs or their stomachs, all of them with what had to be every single spare writing tablet in the quarantined section of the space station in their hands. Three of the five Terran telepaths were seated on crates. Jackie sat at one end of the trio, her body perched at an angle to the window up on the second floor. She and the other two telepaths present did not have tablets in their hands, however.

About a dozen people were still on their feet. One of them, a man with brownish hair and freckles—one of the brown-clad soldiers, a *mah-reen*—started reciting something from his tablet, while everyone else . . . Li'eth wasn't sure what they were doing, but as they watched, a couple more of the dozen or so who were standing sighed and sat down. Then one of the women who was still standing checked her tablet and recited from it as well . . . and then some sort of conversation took place.

The other anomaly in the room was a set of five giant grids spaced around the edges of the group. They sat vertically, like a set of cubbyhole shelving, and were filled with large cubes. Each of those cubes had a different set of V'Dan characters painted boldly on their surfaces.

"It looks like they're marking off lists," V'kol murmured, shading the windowpane with his hand to prevent reflections from the corridor's lighting. "But where they got the giant letter-cube shelves . . ."

The woman shouted and threw her hands up in the air, while the *mah-reen* and the others sighed and sat down. They applauded, but it was clear she had come out the victor in whatever they were doing. When everyone settled on the deck plates again, the cubes in the shelving grids vanished. It happened, Li'eth noted, at the exact moment that Jackie MacKenzie picked up a transparent cube about the size of her head and . . . shook it?

She rattled it vigorously, pale objects tumbling this way and that inside the box, then she sort of gave it a trembling shake that settled the cubes inside into their slots. Next to her, one of the Terran telepaths—clad in gray, the Special Forces color for their military—held something in his hand, recited something in a steady rhythm—and the cubes on the shelves were back, this time with a different jumbled combination of letters.

"Oh! Oh, I *know* this game. *Quon-set!*" V'kol exclaimed, pointing at the observation window. "I don't know what *they* call it, but that's the game of *Quon-set*."

Li'eth gave him a confused look. "I haven't heard of that one."

"It's a vocabulary search game—look at the cubes. First column, second row, go right three cubes, and then down two, and it spells the word *p'vink*. Minus the punctuation, of course."

P'vink was the word for skipping in sets of two, trading off which foot was the lead foot every two sets. It was a popular dance step for the more vigorous dances. Nodding slowly, eyes wide, Li'eth discovered more words. He pointed. "There, diagonally from just below the top right corner, you can see the start for the word *b'gonnan*."

"Yes, but that wouldn't actually count because you can't double up on letters," V'kol argued lightly. "You've already used the two *N*s, and there's no third one in the grid. But it's a good first try—why don't we go down and join them?"

Blinking, Li'eth eyed his friend. "Join them?"

"*Yes*, join them." V'kol pushed on his shoulder, moving him toward the airlock door. "Ba'oul is busy giving stellar coordinates to the Fleet and the astrophysicists, Dai'a is working with the doctors to help gauge the severity of the . . . what did the Terrans call it?"

"*Histamines*," Li'eth supplied, moving only a step. He wasn't sure if he should join, because now that he was back, with his face and his identity uncovered . . .

"Yes, the *histamines* in our plant life, and Shi'ol is busy watching nothing on the entertainment casts. That leaves us either each other for company, or the Terrans, and they're all either asleep or in the hangar bay, playing a vocabulary game. Or sitting on a couch in Shi'ol's presence. *I* say, why not pit these Terrans against two native speakers?" V'kol offered. He smacked Li'eth lightly with the back of one pink-spiraled wrist and grinned. "Come, it'll be fun!"

Bemused but willing to give it a try, Li'eth joined his friend and fellow officer in heading for the nearest stairs down to the hangar-bay floor.

CHAPTER 4

(*Honestly, Li'eth, you have a perfectly valid reason for how you performed,*) Jackie consoled him. (*You've never played that kind of game before. It takes a lot of effort to pick out a word from a jumble of letters, particularly ones that could be turned sideways or upside down. And you found three words no one else did.*)

(*Three words total out of five rounds,*) he retorted glumly, and poked at the food on his plate with his *umma*, the standard V'Dan military-issue utensil. He wasn't the only one poking at his food, but he was one of the few who had a freshly made meal to eat.

Even though they had to eat packet foods for now, with dubious names like *peppernoodle hash* and *Mongolian beef stir-fry*, the Terrans had settled into using the dining hall within hours of their arrival. They had done so by sharing a rotation of eight different mealtimes throughout the day, including four snacking hours, moments where they could gather and trade preferences with each other, and used the local utensils and plates and such.

Of course, the Terrans had undergone a round of laughter and merriment, calling the Fifth Tier V'Dan utensil—the one

most commonly employed by the military—a *spork*, a cross
between their words for *spoon* and *fork*. The exact same sort
of utensil they had provided for eating while on board their
strange ships, from the very first day Li'eth and his remaining
officers had been rescued.

He poked the one in his hand at the vegetables on his plate.
V'Dan vegetables, of course; those of his people in quarantine
were still free to eat whatever they liked, and indeed were expected to eat it rather than deprive the Terrans of their carefully stockpiled resources. That, and a lot of the food had
come in through quarantine in the expectation that it would
feed two hundred people. Most of it could be kept refrigerated
or frozen until they had a successful inoculation, but in the
meantime, lots of fresh vegetables had to be eaten. They were
cooked and seasoned reasonably well, but he was still feeling
a bit down from the end of the cube game.

(*V'kol got over twenty unique,*) he pointed out.

(*You had five rounds played against roughly a hundred
people,* including *V'kol, who has played this sort of game
many times before. He had the familiarity of* how *to play the
game,*) she reminded him, using her left hand to pick up her
mug of water, which had been flavored with some sort of fruit-
smelling powder. Her right hand was busy clasping his left
under the cover of the table. (*The rest of us had the familiarity
of the Terran version—though not all had played it before—*
and *they were working hard to exercise their newly implanted
vocabularies. Which was the point of playing the game for us.
But for you, it was just supposed to be a fun pastime. So . . .*
did *you have fun?*)

He had to admit that he did. (*It was enjoyable, yes. Kind of
thrilling to get those three words no one else got. I just wish I
had more. I'm supposed to uphold the honor of the Empire,
and all that.*)

(*Take comfort in how the game fulfilled its foremost purpose: to have fun. You had fun; therefore, it was successful. If
you like, we're playing it again tonight, so that third shift can
have a chance at picking unique words no one else has. You're
not in the tally for the chores list, so you can put in more than
ten rounds total if you want. You can try to get more unique
words if you do come. Twenty hundred V'Dan time,*) Jackie told

him. (*We'll be in the hangar bay again because the game pieces Sergeant Nhieu manufactured before leaving Earth are awfully noisy, and we don't want to ruin the rec room for anyone else.*)

(*How many unique words did you get?*) Li'eth asked, chewing on a mouthful of pan-fried vegetables. (*You did play, didn't you?*)

(*Polyglots are not allowed to play. One of the hallmarks of being a telepathic polyglot is either a photographic memory, or one close enough to being eidetic as to not make much difference. That, and we sometimes confuse which language we're speaking. But as a compensation, we make excellent arbiters on whether or not a word is real, particularly us telepaths.*)

(*That's . . . a little bit sad, actually,*) he decided. (*Not getting to play that game? It* was *fun. You should be able to enjoy it.*)

She shrugged. (*We have other games where it's more fair for everyone. I like* checkers, *but I'm bootless at it. Total failure.*)

The subthought images that came with the game's name almost belied her words; it was a fairly simple strategy game. She simply didn't have a mind that worked well in those ways. At least, not quite as well as other minds did, or so she felt. Li'eth squeezed her fingers briefly in sympathy. She released his hand, needing two for the next mouthful of her meal, the dreaded *peppernoodle hash*. This, she had told him, was "slightly better than the so-called Hawai'ian pork" which, she informed him firmly, tasted nothing like the tender, flavorful, fruit-stuffed roasted boar they had enjoyed that day on the beach of her family's island home.

The smell of it was a bit strong, and he could see her eyes gleaming from the need to water. That was the problem with food designed for zero gravity; without gravity to provide thermal convection currents, food literally did not smell as good as it should have, rendering its taste less than perfect. That meant everything in the packets the Terrans were eating was overseasoned to compensate.

(*I'm getting subthoughts of how awful that stuff is, even when we're not touching,*) he told her.

(*I've been shielding my opinions from you, so as not to ruin your own meal,*) she admitted. Lowering her *umma*, she returned her hand to his where it rested on his thigh. As promised, only a tiny bit of gustatory disgust came through her mental walls. Gamely chewing her way through another mouthful, Jackie looked at the clock on the wall. (*We'd better hurry. I want a few moments to tidy up and compose myself before meeting with the priesthood representatives.*)

An odd thought crossed her mind. One odd enough, Li'eth found himself twisting and diving mentally after it, trying to track it down. Jackie sucked in a breath, startled, and began coughing, choking on a bit of her food. For a moment, the thought-trail was lost. The prince readied an apology when she could concentrate on things other than breathing. (*Sorry. I didn't mean to startle you.*)

She pinched the back of his hand, making him flinch. (Ask *before you go diving through someone else's thoughts, Li'eth! Even if it's your Gestalt partner's thoughts.*)

(*I apologize, I am sorry,*) he repeated. (*But you have some . . . doubts . . . about V'Dan psychic training and abilities? Or doubts as to my explanation of them? That line of thought does concern me.*)

Coughing again, she cleared her throat with a sip of her fruit water, cleared it a second time, and sighed. Mentally as well as physically. (*What do you know of Dr. Kuna'mi?*)

(*Less than you. She* is *acknowledged as the Empire's foremost authority on the* jungen *virus,*) he stated, (*but that is all I know.*)

(*Well, she is psychic to some degree. And she was* not *trained by the same people who trained you.*)

Li'eth knew she didn't mean her own training, or the training which that elderly fellow, Master Sonam Sherap, had given to him in the midst of enduring the Terran version of quarantine. She meant V'Dan training. Training that was wrapped in religious mysticism and couched in religious terms, and which was inadequate in the way that only religion could be, when compared against the methodical, thorough, exacting ways of using science to accomplish the same tasks with far superior results. All of that floated in the subthoughts underlying the meaning of her words.

(*I know I did not receive the best of training; I would have had to join one of the Temples to receive that,*) he reminded her. (*There are many mysteries which only the initiated members of the Sh'nai priesthood are allowed to know.*)

(*Well, she's good enough to be a* Terran *psychic,*) Jackie told him. (*Today's meeting with your priesthood is going to tell me how good they are . . . and yes, I can do that without directly reading their thoughts. Of course, if we open up telepathic conversation, I'll do that, too.*)

(*What a delightful idea. Because if you can read their thoughts, then they can read yours, and if they can do that, there goes the privacy of your people,*) Li'eth pointed out.

Jackie shook her head slightly, smiling at her packet. He knew it wasn't for the food. (*You underestimate me, and you underestimate my government. I am the bold, honest face of my people, but I am also trained at keeping people* out *of my mind, and out of specific corners of my thoughts. Including you, I'll have you know.*)

(*Well, we have gone for hours without contacting each other from time to time,*) he agreed, picking up his mug of *chalba-a'pa* juice.

Her smile became a smirk. (*You've never once picked up on the times where I've speculated on what you looked like when naked, back on that enemy ship, have you? Such as, what happens to the shape of that one stripe on your penis when you're excited?*)

Juice sprayed over his plate. Li'eth grabbed for his napkin, coughing hard to clear the liquid from his lungs. (*You Saint-swearing agitator! You timed that deliberately!*)

(*Nope, but I will say it was fortuitously accidental. Sorry about the water in the pipes.*) She solicitously offered him her own napkin, untouched throughout her meal.

(*The water in the what . . . ? Oh, the* breathing *"pipes," got it.*) Li'eth accepted it and coughed into it a few more times before blowing his nose.

(*Ever since I saw how much of your body* did *have stripes, beyond what shows on your face and hands . . . well, I've been curious about that,*) she confessed. (*I'm an adult, I'm a female who is interested in males, and I find you attractive.*)

(*Why did you hide it?*) Li'eth asked her, glancing her way while he mopped at the table next.

She shrugged and scraped at the last bits of her food. (*It wouldn't have been polite or diplomatic to bring it up, and I didn't want you to feel uncomfortable, so I suppressed it. I still wondered, but I kept it locked behind tight walls.*)

(*So why reveal it now?*) he asked her.

Jackie smirked again. (*Because it was funny. And it made my point. You're my Gestalt partner. Our brains are intertwining, telepathically. You're harder to keep out of my thoughts and subthoughts and underthoughts than anyone else. But we're taking the inevitable conjoining slowly . . . and until I can talk with your mother, the Empress, on what exactly a Gestalt pairing is, what it means . . . I cannot in good conscience push that bonding process any faster than absolutely necessary.*)

(*Your willpower must be legendary among your people,*) Li'eth observed, clearing his throat roughly.

(*Possibly, but it's not the sort of thing a public servant boasts about, so I've never competed in any way. Well, beyond training exercises,*) she allowed. Scraping the last bite from her packet, she washed it down with the rest of her juice, then unwrapped the mint-flavored chocolate that came with the meal. (*I'll be glad when we can get back to eating real food, but I do believe I'll miss these little mints . . .*)

He wanted to talk about how the stuff seemed remarkably like a sweet made from the fruit of a tree his people had, *klahsa,* a known nonnative, but a different thought crossed his mind. (*Jackie, when I have had . . . thoughts . . . about you as well . . . did you sense them?*)

(*A little bit. I tried not to pay attention, though. I know that Gestalt pairings don't bother with total mental privacy. It takes time to grow accustomed to the other person's thoughts, and sometimes a pair has to adjust their personal worldviews to make their ideas and ideals more compatible, but at the same time, you learn a lot about tolerance, compromise, and cooperation. Besides, most of your thoughts about me have been complimentary, even the intimately aligned ones,*) she finished. (*Who wouldn't feel good about that?*)

(*I have tried to accept you as you are,*) he told her. Since he had sprayed spittle over his food, the last few bites didn't appeal to him. Draining his juice glass, he mopped the table again with the napkins, then gathered everything up to take to the galley space for cleaning. The Terrans were thriftily storing their packaging on their ships to be taken back to their world for "reprocessing," since their *plexi* was some sort of thoroughly recyclable polymer. (*I will admit I had problems in the beginning, but I set my mind to accept you as the different beings that you are.*)

(*I know.*) Mentally, Jackie hugged him. Physically, she was busy gathering up those wrappers so she could take them to one of the bags that would be hauled back to their ships by whoever had that chore for the day.

(*You shouldn't hug me like that,*) Li'eth reminded her, only half teasing. (*It just makes me want a real one.*)

(*An awkward thing to do when we're constantly being watched by all the surveillance cameras. I am aware that without* jungen *marks, I look younger than I really am.*) She washed her hands at the cleaning station. (*I do think that today's meeting with your priesthood will help clear that up, though. The fact that we* are *in a Gestalt pairing, that I'm an adult, and that physical contact is a necessity for maintaining optimal mental and emotional health.*)

(*Your clinical discussion is exceedingly romantic,*) he retorted dryly.

(*If I talk in terms of romance, they'll never take the Gestalt seriously,*) she replied calmly, not fooled by his sarcasm.

(*True.*) He started to say more, but Dr. Qua entered the galley from a side door. She stopped for a moment, blinking, then hurried toward him, hands outstretched.

"Your Highness, you should not be scrubbing dishes!" she told him, distress coloring her tone.

Li'eth started to retreat, since she was right, he shouldn't have to . . . but Jackie was lurking in his mind, and he stopped himself. Stepping back up to the sink, he shook his head and continued rinsing his plate.

"The Terrans have the right attitude toward these things, Doctor," he told her. He even blocked her hands with his elbow and a pointed look. "*I* made the mess; therefore, I should be the one to clean it. Besides, who *would* do it if I do not? We are all Third Tier or higher, here in quarantine. And at the moment, your skills are far more important than mine. I am merely a son and a soldier. You are a doctor who will help save these Terrans' lives."

"Well, one of the Terrans could . . ." She trailed off, brow furrowing in thought. Finally, the lavender-spotted woman shook her head. "They shouldn't handle the food. Their daily medicines are keeping them from reacting to the toxins in the air, the *histamines* as they call them, but direct contact makes everything worse."

"With some things, direct contact makes everything better," Li'eth murmured, thinking of Jackie for a moment. He reached for the detergent and started scrubbing his rinsed tableware to get them fully clean. "But in this case, no. They should not be handling our food, even just our food waste."

"But you are of the Imperial bloodline; your blood alone excuses you from menial tasks," Qua pointed out.

"I also have a duty to lead by example," Li'eth countered, rinsing the plate and setting it in a drying rack. He moved on to his glass, saving the *umma*, the *spork*, for last. "These Terrans believe one of the signs of maturity means accepting responsibility without flinching or hesitating. Even for unpleasant tasks."

Qua frowned at him, brows drawn together and teeth nibbling on her bottom lip. He could tell by her aura that she was thinking things through. Finally, the geneticist said, "What would the Empress say about her son's washing dishes?"

"That I am acting in ways our guests think are proper, and thus it will help them regard me as someone worthy of their time and attention."

Actually, he wasn't completely sure what his mother would *think*, but that was what she would *say* after giving it careful thought. After all, she had contacted his first commanding officer when he was a newly graduated ensign and had told the woman not to go easy on him just because of his bloodline.

"I learned to wash dishes in the military, Doctor, after my mother instructed my first commander to treat me the same as anyone else . . . and there, even the utensil is clean, and far faster than it would be if I tried to call someone else to do it." Setting it next to the glass and the plate, he rinsed his hands and dried them. "If you'll excuse me, I have a meeting to attend in the observation lounge."

"Of course, Your Highness." Bowing slightly, she moved aside so that he could exit the galley through the same door she had used. He could sense her watching him as he left, and almost reached out to try to read her thoughts but stopped himself. That would be inappropriate, he knew.

Instead, he turned just past the doorway, and said, "Please, call me Li'eth while we are in quarantine together." Lifting his hands, he gestured at his cream-shirted, red-trousered, coatless body, the casual equivalent of officer wear. He had not been perfectly tidy in washing his dishes, which meant his shirt was spotted here and there with water. "Particularly if the moment is not formal."

Dr. Qua eyed him dubiously. "I think you may have been overly influenced by these Terrans, Your Highness."

"Or perhaps I have been overly influenced by military life, first and foremost. I am, after all, a mere captain, not even a captain superior, and have been a mere Second Tier officer for the last few years." Dipping his head politely, he left. He hadn't planned to visit his quarters to pick up his jacket, left behind so that his meal would not run the risk of staining his uniform. But the geneticist's words were a possibility to consider.

Deciding that he could afford to be a little bit late, he turned right toward his quarters, instead of left toward the observation lounge. (*Dr. Qua brought up a good point. I shouldn't act too casual or too Terran in my behavior for fear of being seen as "overly influenced" by your customs.*)

(*Oh, what rot and nonsense. Everyone is influenced by every single person they meet. Plus, if they get along—and are the same species; I don't know enough about interalien reactions— they are going to "mirror" each other's speech, mannerisms, posture,* everything,) Jackie retorted. Her subthoughts were sympathetic toward him. (*Take as much time as you like. I'm not afraid to meet the local priesthood on my own.*)

(*You're a strong woman,*) he praised her, before turning his attention to the task of making himself look like a proper officer. (*I'll be there soon.*)

Glad that Li'eth was no longer feeling morose over his performance in the game, Jackie headed for the observation lounge.

After meeting the K'Katta, the other races seemed almost

normal by comparison, but at the same time, Jackie had to admit that it did make the spiderlike·race seem a bit less alarming. Not completely normal but less frightening. She had heard that there were psychics among the arthropodic species, same as there were among the Solaricans. The silver-furred one had been introduced as Seer Laiyang, and if she had correctly interpreted the word choices being used, the alien psychic was a telepath and a clairvoyant, among other things.

And, of course, there was an entire caste of psis among the Tlassians—she had met their representative, Priest-Envoy Chelleug, along with Worker-Envoy Tarik and Warrior-Envoy S'ssull, the one with the yellow-and-blue hide—but now it was time to meet the V'Dan version. So today's meeting was to be strictly with V'Dan gifted, fellow Humans, all of whom were members of the majority religion, the Sh'nai faith.

A cluster of robed Humans were already gathered on the other side of the unshuttered window when she entered the lounge. The comm speakers weren't active, but she could see five figures, what looked like two women and three men. Most of their layered clothes were variations on cream, but the hemlines of the long, bell-like sleeves and the cross-folded, scallop-edged overrobes were decorated in a series of embroidered and appliquéd motifs ranging from pale blue and white snowflakes on two of them, to autumn leaves, flowers, and sprigs of greenery.

As much as the life-support officer wasn't a die-hard follower of the Sh'nai faith, Dai'a Vres-yat *was* heavily interested in all the stories and lores of the major religions of her people, and had regaled the Terrans with some interesting—if at times confusing—stories of their main religion during their time together in quarantine, back in the Sol System. With at least some of those snippets of information in mind, Jackie was able to tell exactly who was in "control" of the Sh'nai faith right now.

Li'eth's comment about winter coming early wasn't about weather or temperature. It was about how they only have nine holy days a year, not twelve. Dai'a said that once a year, one of the four season-based factions of the faith gets to take command for six months, not three, with the season preceding it being "skipped" for that year. That's why there are five representatives here. The Winter Temple is in ascendancy—Autumn is being "skipped" this year, with Winter taking over its duties, rites, and some of its privileges—and so they get to have two representatives. She eyed the woman with the golds and browns and peach hues decorating a palm-wide swath of her hemlines. *Autumn still has power, though, for all its rites are being overlooked, and as the skipped season, it can still band together with the other two to overrule Winter in its ascendancy.*

An awkward system, from my point of view, but I suppose there are some nice checks and balances in it, she decided as they noticed her entrance and turned to face her through the window. Behind her, more of her own people entered. Turning her attention to them, she gestured for the men and women to take some of the seats. Today's session would have a smaller number of participants, not quite as many members of the military, and a couple more historians.

A rattling sound in the corridor grew louder, resolving into a transport cart. Maria, taking a break from her medical work, helped Heracles push the cart into the room. A few of the others rose to shift the chairs, making room for the sled, which contained one large, bulky object, one smaller, chest-sized machine, and a silver-sided case filled, no doubt, with the diagnostic tools of her trade.

"Ambassador, what are those objects?"

Jackie hadn't even realized Imperial First Lord Ksa'an had entered the other half of the observation lounge. Moving over to the controls, she checked to make sure the comm system was open on her end, and addressed his questions. "The smaller of the two machines is a *KI* monitor, what we call *kinetic inergy. Kinetic* means movement, and *inergy* is a combination of the words for 'inner' and 'energy' in Terranglo. This is meant to differentiate it from the physics definition for kinetic energy, which is the measurement of potential energy, such as is found in a coiled spring waiting to be released, or expressed energy, such as a hammer striking a nail.

"Kinetic *inergy* on the other hand," Jackie explained, using V'Dan words wherever she could, since the people on the other side of the window did not speak Terranglo, "is the measurement of how much *psychic* energy—what you would call holy energy—is being expended. I was told that the honorable representatives of your Sh'nai faith would be discussing holy powers today, so I arranged to have a KI machine on hand. Dr. de la Santoya has agreed to help monitor the proceedings so that your people will have some hard biological facts to go along with any, ah, 'holy' demonstrations.

"The larger of the two machines is a portable hydrogenerator. Whenever we're not using solar power, we're using purified water deconstructed into hydrogen and oxygen through a special catalyst my people have developed. Since we're still in the process of figuring out how to convert from one power system to the other, there are as yet no ways for us to plug our machines into yours," she explained. "So it just made sense for us to bring along a few portable generators for our needs, for now."

"A generator in quarantine?" the woman in the autumn-edged robes asked. She turned enough that Jackie could see that the right side of her jaw had a deep blue blotch on it, one that ran up into the hairline of her short-cropped gray hair. "Isn't that dangerous?"

Jackie shook her head. "So long as no one hits the case with a giant hammer, or tries to disassemble it, I don't see how it could be. There are far too many safety features installed to fear anything bad happening, otherwise."

"She means the fumes, child," the elder of the two males in winter-edged robes stated.

Child.

Jackie carefully quelled the urge to frown beneath the weight of a patient, diplomatic smile. "I am not a child, meioa, and have not been one for many years. Every single Terran who came here, every single member of our embassy, is also an adult. Please remember that and address us accordingly. As for our generators, they only produce a modest amount of oxygen as a waste product. All of the hydrogen and most of the oxygen are carefully converted into energy.

"Even waste heat is conserved and converted back into energy through various means, leaving the outer casing cool and comfortable to the touch. It's a very efficient design," she added. A few more people trickled in through the door. Jackie paused to count heads. Just as everyone accounted for on the Terran side of things finished taking their seats, Li'eth strode in, looking formal and calm. "Ah, good. Welcome, Your Highness. I believe we are ready to begin."

Nodding, he moved over to take her place by the controls, allowing her to settle into the center seat in the front row. "Excellent. Meioas, are you ready?"

The priests took their seats, and Ksa'an took his place by the far side of the window, diagonally from the prince. "We are ready," the protocol officer stated. "I am not certain how much of the Sh'nai faith you know—"

Li'eth raised his hand, gently interrupting his kinsman. "I have explained that the Sh'nai leadership consists of four 'seasonal' Temples, and that due to the rotation of holy days in a year, one of the Temples has ascendancy once a year in rotation. At the moment, Winter Temple is in ascendance and Autumn Temple is in abeyance, though they, of course, still have most of their rights and privileges. They simply do not have their holy days celebrated this year."

Ksa'an bowed his head. "Then I shall begin. Our visitors today, meioas, are the highest-ranked members of the Sh'nai faith. I present High Priestess Be'ela of the Holy Eye, leader of the Autumn Temple."

The woman with the blue *jungen* mark along her jawline inclined her head politely. Jackie nodded back.

"Next is High Priest Sorleth-ain, leader of the Summer Temple." That introduction came with a nod from the brown-skinned male with the shaved head and light golden rosette clusters dotted here and there over his skin. Ksa'an moved on to the next. "And the High Priestess Tar'eth Truthspeaker of the Spring Temple . . ."

That nod came from the woman with deep brown skin and pink borderline spots similar to Dr. Qua's lavender ones. Unlike the short-cropped salt-gray strands of the other priestess, High Priestess Tar'eth had no signs of gray in the intricately braided strands of her dark hair. Interestingly enough, the pattern of her hair was repeated in the next man introduced. That was a fellow also in his late forties or early fifties, his pale golden skin streaked with brown squiggles, his long hair also interlaced and pinned in looped and latticed braids.

"Next is Superior Priest De'arth of the Open Mind. He is here as the Winter-Ascendant assistant to the Grand High Priest Suva'an of the Winter Temple, who graces us with his presence," the Imperial First Lord finished, bowing to the man with the golden-brown skin, shoulder-length gray-and-burgundy hair, his skin boasting occasional burgundy crescents scattered here and there. Including one that caught the corner of his left eye, turning it half dark red, not just brown. In turn, the Grand High Priest lifted his chin slightly, acknowledging the introduction.

Li'eth took up the Terran side of things, now that his cousin had finished. "Your Holinesses, I present to you Grand High Ambassador Jackie MacKenzie, third-highest member of the Terran government. Beside her is Assistant Ambassador Rosa McCrary . . ."

Jackie lifted her hand slightly and nodded at the introduction, then sat still while Rosa and the others were introduced one at a time. This meeting was a little bit more formal in its introductions than the previous ones, but then these weren't adjuncts or assistants or protocol officers and news reporters. These were the movers and shakers of the most prominent religion in the V'Dan Empire.

For all that her body was quiet, her mind was active. Jackie looked with her inner eye at the three with the fanciful names, the chief priestesses and the junior priest from the Winter Temple. None of them had the mirror-smooth mental shield of Dr. Kuna'mi. It was interesting to note that the two who did not have names suggesting the presence of holy gifts had similar shielding to the other three. Unfortunately, all of their psychic walls were the equivalent of walls made out of scavenged, unmortared rubble by comparison.

More than that, the powers of the three flared unevenly. *Not grounded, just like Li'eth. They have no concept of centering themselves, no understanding of grounding, and without those for a very necessary level of conservation of energy and effort, plus a solid foundation from which to brace everything and a way to shunt aside energy spikes from both within and without—what the . . . ?*

The assistant Winter priest, De'arth, moved on the psychic plane. She blinked and stared, switching her focus to an attempt to evoke the auras that Li'eth could far more easily see. It took her effort, but she was learning, catching up to him . . . and she could see the orange-and-greenish-blue tendrils following the priest's glance. They wound through the glass or whatever it was the layers of the observation window were made of, and pressed against Li'eth's shields.

Li'eth faltered a little in his introductions. He cleared his throat and continued but didn't seem to realize he was being probed. Annoyed, Jackie debated what to do. In Terran terms, what the priest was doing was illegal, unethical, and immoral. In V'Dan terms . . . she had no idea what the laws were. There was one thing, however, she could guess: It probably was not politically correct to probe at the mind of a member of the Imperial Family unasked . . . and she knew perfectly well that none of the V'Dan on the other side of the glass had asked.

(*Li'eth,*) she interjected softly as he faltered again. (*The High Priest of the Winter Temple, De'arth, is trying to probe his way into your mind. Do you want me to smack his mental fingers, like I once di—*)

(Yes, *please!*) he returned swiftly, breaking off his introductions to fix the other man with a glare.

Reaching out with her own much stronger telepathy, Jackie *smacked* that tendril of thought. Superior Priest De'arth jumped in his seat, eyes widening.

"Holiness De'arth, in the Terran culture, attempting to probe the thoughts of another person without their clearly expressed permission is beyond rude." Li'eth held the startled priest's gaze. "It is, in fact, considered illegal. Do I have to remind you that to probe the mind of a member of the Imperial Tier without our permission is *also* considered illegal?"

". . . I was simply attempting to ascertain the strange aura your mind now carries, Your Highness," Superior Priest De'arth replied carefully. "Your mind appears to have been influenced by whatever it is that also covers the minds of some of these . . . Terrans."

"These Terrans," Li'eth stated carefully, "are vastly more experienced in training and managing their holy abilities. They are as far in advance in their abilities as this space station is from a mud hut in the Q'oba region."

"Oh, come now!" Grand High Priest Suva'an protested. He gestured at the windowed view of the Terrans in question. "You expect us to believe these children possess holy secrets that far in advance of our own? When by all logic, they'd never even heard of the Immortal and Her teachings before meeting you?"

"I *remind* you, Grand High Priest, that we are *not* children," Jackie stressed, cutting through their argument. "Please stop thinking of us as V'Dan. We are *not* V'Dan. In some ways, your people are more advanced; we do not deny this, and are mature enough to know that if we set aside our cultural pride, we will be able to learn from you. In *other* ways, *we* are the ones who are more advanced. The sooner you in turn acknowledge this, the sooner your own people will be able to benefit from our vast experience.

"We. Are. Not. V'Dan," she repeated firmly when the older man drew in a breath to speak. "Please take a deep breath, and consider us to be on a par with the Gatsugi, or the Solaricans. We are not V'Dan, we do not share your culture, and we will only be patient with these inadvertent cultural insults for so long before they will start to have a negative impact on Terran-V'Dan interrelations.

"I, for one, would like to avoid letting things deteriorate that far." She managed a small smile. "I'm certain your people would like to avoid such a simple mistake as well. As for our skill in what you call holy gifts, where your people have continued to deal with such things from a religious standpoint, my people have long since turned them into a science.

"As with all science, such things can be questioned, qualified, measured, quantified, and trained. I myself studied for several years at a special boarding school for the highly gifted, starting at the age of fourteen and concluding with an advanced education certification in what we call *para*linguistics, the ability to communicate via *telepathy*, which is what we call speaking mind-to-mind. We have a ranking scale to indicate strengths of various holy abilities. My rank as a *telepath*, a mind-speaker, is 15, and my rank as a *xenopath*, a speaker-with-alien-minds, is 14," she explained. Gesturing to her far right, she added, "Aixa Winkler, here, has a similar advanced certificate, specializing in *xenopathy* at Rank 11, the ability to communicate with non-Human minds."

Aixa raised her age-wrinkled hand. She had been deemed physically fit for the trip to V'Dan, but she was the oldest member of the embassy staff at fifty-nine, edging out the next oldest by four full months plus a few days. Jackie flicked her hand over her shoulder, not bothering to look; she could sense

Clees' position with her mind by the presence of his shields, and that was good enough for her.

"Behind us stands Heracles Panaklion, who is busy with the hovering cameras, recording these events, and who has also specialized in mind-to-mind communication. His strongest gift is telepathy at Rank 13, though he also shares the gift of *auramancy* with His Highness, the ability to see auras of energy and emotion, focus and awareness. That's Rank, what, 7?" she asked Clees.

He nodded. "I am a Rank 7 *auramancer*, as well as a Rank 7 out-of-body practitioner, a Rank 9 in *clairvoyancy* and *clairaudiency*—the ability to see and hear things at a distance when there is no physical way to actually see those things," Clees explained in an aside, "—and a Rank 13 telepath, as the Ambassador has said."

"Yes, and Darian Johnston, here—his military rank is equivalent to your military's leftenant superior—has a degree, an education certification," Jackie explained, gesturing to the other side behind her, "in cryptography and stenography based on his abilities as a polyglot telepath. Next to him is Min Wang-Kurakawa. Her military rank is the equivalent of a leftenant, her telepathic rank is 12, and like the leftenant superior, she has engaged in mind-to-mind combat with our enemy on the far side of Terran space from your Alliance, a highly advanced race we call the Grey Ones.

"The *only* thing keeping the Greys from assaulting our worlds and kidnapping our people is the mental strength imparted by our training programs. Those programs," Jackie continued briskly, "come with a great deal of responsibility, including a heavy set of ethics, a code of honor if you will, which all psychics must abide by under Terran law. Those ethics include *not* probing or scanning anyone else without their permission, save only by sheer accident . . . as physically touching someone has been known to trigger abilities inadvertently.

"Despite its existence, that exception does not qualify for this moment . . . as it is obvious His Highness is beyond your physical touch." She dipped her head politely. "Perhaps it *was* inadvertent. You do not, after all, have the benefits of our rigorous Terran training. But now that you are aware that *we* are aware, please try to consciously avoid probing anyone in our presence. We take our vows very seriously when it comes to our ethical mental behavior.

"I apologize for startling you, High Priest, with my telepathic slap . . . but it is our first and foremost instinct to watch and warn each other in such ways, in order to make *sure* those ethical behaviors are maintained."

"If she hadn't done it first, I was about to do it myself," Clees stated from the back of the room. "Pushing your way into someone else's mind uninvited is as legal in our society as breaking into someone else's house. Which is to say, it isn't legal. It's breaking the law."

"Only it's worse than just breaking into someone's house," Min added, joining the conversation. She tucked a lock of her chin-length black hair behind her ear. "Our minds are our last refuge of privacy, the only place where we can think anything and everything without being condemned or censored for it. Only when thought and action are combined to commit a crime can a mind be probed, and *only* to ascertain whether what is being said in a court of law is a truth or a falsehood."

The High Priestess for the Temple of Spring nodded. "That is how my own holy powers are used. I can discern if someone is speaking a truth or a falsehood—I do not need to go into the mind's depths to see the truth or the lie in a person's aura. And you are all telling the truth . . . though I cannot sense anything deeper than that."

"Of course we are. We are adults, ethically trained and highly experienced in such matters. Only the youngest of children barge into another person's home uninvited," Aixa stated shrewdly. "Such things might be forgivable once, perhaps twice if the person is very young. But we Terrans are adults. We presume politely that you are also adults. Now that you know such things are beyond rude . . . you will refrain from doing it again in our presence, yes?"

The Grand High Priest, Suva'an, smiled in a benign sort of way. "We would not presume to do it to one of your people. But His Highness is—"

"—His Highness *agrees* with the Terrans," Li'eth said flatly. "My thoughts are my own. They belong to no one else and are entirely my property. I will treat anyone attempting to steal into my mind and read them the same as I would treat a thief breaking into my chambers."

"My point, Highness, is that these Terrans have unknown motives and unknown methods. How can you possibly trust them?" Suva'an asked, flicking his hand at the Humans seated across from him.

"I trust them because I have spent months living among them, seeing for myself how well their words and their actions match. They are honorable, they are ethical, and they are vastly superior in their holy training than even the best of us can claim," Li'eth told the Grand High Priest. "More than that, I have been blessed through a holy pairing with the Grand High Ambassador, a bond that at times brings us closer than thought. But even with that for permission, *she* does not invade my thoughts carelessly or casually."

That caused a stir among the V'Dan on the other side of the observation window, a mix of startled coughs and disbelieving splutters. High Priestess Be'ela narrowed her gaze, sitting up even straighter in her chair than before.

"You expect us to believe that *you* and *she* are a Holy Pairing?"

"My people call it *Gestalt*," Aixa stated, speaking before Jackie could. "The word means 'the end result is greater than the sum of its parts.' We have tested the Ambassador and the prince, and they qualify on all measurable counts."

"I was informed that you, Ambassador, were among the crew members of the ship that rescued His Highness and his fellow officers," High Priest Sorleth-ain stated, nodding at Jackie. "Do you really expect us to believe that one of the first holy ones of your people to meet one of the first of our own were somehow spontaneously blessed by the Saints in a Holy Pairing?"

(*I was hoping to avoid bringing up this subject this early,*) Jackie sent to Li'eth.

He answered the high priest instead of her. "Is it not written in our own holy books that when the Motherworld reaches out to our people, that there will arise a Holy Pair of exceptional power, who will save one of the cities of the Chosen People? Our meeting was foretold . . . and I was forewarned that I would be involved in a different prophecy, a warning that prevented me from the sensible choice of committing suicide when my ship was boarded," Li'eth stated bluntly. "Because I obeyed *that* prophecy, I was in a position to be rescued, which in turn allowed me to make peaceful contact with the Terrans, here.

"One prophecy has led to the next, resulting in my still being alive and thus able to stand before you today . . . but those are only *our own* prophecies. The Terrans have foreseers of their own, and were able to predict not only that they would encounter that same Salik warship, but were able to see the Ambassador's face as one of the prominent players in that First Contact encounter."

"I myself thought the odds were astronomical," Jackie offered when he finished. "But one of our teachers of *psychic* abilities, holy gifts, reminded me that between the prophecies of your faith and the precognition of my own, those odds were not so much astronomically huge, as *guided* into taking place."

"Is that how you got this position of Grand High Ambassador?" Grand High Priest Suva'an challenged her. "Purely by prophecy? Or is it simply a means to assert undue influence upon Her Eternity through leveraging the moods and thoughts of her son?"

Jackie wasn't the only one to stiffen. For a moment, Heracles and Min and Aixa and Darian all tried to voice their protests to Jackie, wanting to give her support and— (*Quiet, all of you,*) she ordered. Out loud, Jackie stated in a calm, measured tone, "That is a serious accusation. It is, however, one born from complete ignorance of Terran ways.

"To reassure you, our highest levels of government studied that exact possibility. They determined that it would not happen. If you wish to press the matter, we will make the Council session in question available to everyone. *After* you have learned more of Terran values, Terran customs, Terran laws, and Terran ways. But *not* before," she warned firmly, letting her expression turn a bit stern, even chiding. "A half-informed opinion is just as bad as an uninformed opinion. Until you know us better, you will have my personal word that I have zero interest in influencing the thoughts of Imperial Prince Kah'raman Li'eth V'Daania, and the word of my government that they place their faith in me to behave ethically in all such matters."

"You insist that we are supposed to take the word of a foreign government on how their representative will behave around the son of our leader?" Suva'an challenged.

Rosa addressed that question. "The penalty for crimes committed via *psychic* abilities—your holy gifts—involves something we call *lobotomy*. It is a surgical procedure that scars, destroys, or even removes sections of the brain. It is done in stages as needed until the person ceases to be able to use their abilities." She paused, then stated softly, "Naturally, this tends to leave the person mentally and even physically crippled for life. It is, I assure you, a penalty that all sane psychics strive to avoid, including the Grand High Ambassador. Her rank would not save her from that punishment if she were to ever lose her wits and commit such a crime."

(*Should I mention . . . ?*) Li'eth asked Jackie, hesitant.

Knowing he meant his own near brush with the law, she negated it. (*Not at this time. That would be too much for them to understand; they would misread the severity and the salvation of it and focus on the wrong things. They just don't understand us yet.*)

(*It will eventually have to be addressed. Your Terran psychic system is vastly different from V'Dan expectations,*) he pointed out.

(*We won't lower our high standards for ourselves.*) Jackie smiled faintly. (*But we will try to be patient while your people bring themselves up to our level.*)

"How can you prevent such a thing?" the Truthspeaker was asking.

"Through yearly, and in some cases, twice-yearly, psychic examinations by neutral parties. Enough strong telepaths working in concert can overcome the natural defenses of even a very-high-ranked telepath such as the Ambassador," Rosa explained.

(*Looks like Rosa has this in hand. Except we meant to discuss the religious aspects first.*)

(*I also failed to introduce the last two people.*) Clearing his throat, Li'eth stepped into the conversation again. ". . . As much as these things need to be discussed, I was not finished with the introductions on this side of the observation glass. If you will please be patient and polite, I will return to doing so. The Terrans have their protocols, and we have ours."

"Of course. Our apologies, meioas," Ksa'an stated. Beside him, the five priests settled back in their chairs, some looking a little impatient but all willing to acknowledge that the interruption had been somewhat rude. Grand High Priest Suva'an nodded to the Imperial First Lord, who gestured in turn at his protocol counterpart. "Please continue introducing them to us, Your Highness."

Dipping his head slightly, Li'eth did so. Jackie made more mental notes. It would be wise to plan out how to reveal the various psychic differences, as well as what and when. Half-answered questions could lead to the wrong conclusions all too easily. *Everything starts with our political processes, I think, and the history underlying our choices in being this way. Once they grasp how much we revile corruption and revere personal accountability,* then *maybe these people will grasp why we insist on being so ethical.*

CHAPTER 5

MAY 3, 2287 C.E.
DEMBER 26, 9507 V.D.S.

"So, that's that?" Jackie asked Maria, Qua, and Kuna'mi. All three doctors nodded. They had requested that Jackie and Li'eth meet them in one of the conference rooms, but no one had bothered to sit down, since Maria had said in her message that the meeting would be brief. "There's nothing left to test?"

"That is that," Maria confirmed aloud. "The vaccines and antigens have passed medical testing and are being replicated for distribution . . . and the first of the modified *jungen* recipients have passed the initial forty hours of close observation with flying colors. A bit of fever as expected, and general aches and pains, but those are subsiding right on schedule."

"We'll inoculate the rest of you in waves, wait a week for caution's sake after the last of you gets a batch of my modified virus, then you should be free to leave quarantine," Dr. Kuna'mi confirmed.

"Have you told Imperial First Lord Ksa'an?" Li'eth asked.

Qua shook her head. "It's still night down at the Winter Palace—remember, our days are slightly longer. You've been trying to lengthen yours, but you're still offset by a few hours at the moment. He wouldn't be able to reach anyone important for another four, five hours, so I thought we'd tell you the good news first. You Terrans have been keeping yourselves carefully occupied, but we know these are tight quarters. If you have a goal to wait for, it should help ease the constricted feelings."

"Rosa and I have been doing our best to keep everyone occupied and not thinking of all that, yes," Jackie said. "The recreational facilities in your quarantine facilities weren't meant to keep two hundred people physically occupied, but we've at least kept everyone mentally on the move."

"At the rate of processing thirty of you a day—with monitoring assistance from your own medical staff—we should get the last of your people through their fever danger zone by the eighth day, then just add seven days to that," Qua agreed. "As soon as Ksa'an can arrange things with Her Eternity's Court, you'll be able to head down to the capital by day sixteen, if all goes well, get settled into your ambassadorial quarters, and be introduced formally with full ceremony on day eighteen."

"It's just as well replication and distribution will take roughly two weeks," Kuna'mi mused, her tone thoughtful. At Jackie's quick look, the calm, composed, markless doctor explained. "It's only three days to Janva 1, which is the start of the new year. Everyone will be celebrating the turnover, and they won't have room in their schedules to add you to the lists—no insult is intended, of course, but New Year's Day is the day when many worthy souls gather up their family's merit certificates and petition for placement among the lowest of the nobles of the Second and First Tiers. But it'll be well before Janva 29, which is the first official holy day of Winter."

"I still don't really get that," Jackie told the *jungen* specialist. "I understand in theory what a caste system is, but Terrans evolved beyond that over a hundred years ago. We learned to acknowledge that all kinds of work can be worthy of doing, whether it's being a Councilor, or being a janitor. The idea of being stuck in a Tier is incomprehensible to me."

"There is some mobility," Qua reassured her. "Most everyone in the Fourth and Fifth Tiers can move upward to the Third. That is, if they have the intelligence to master the high education levels and expert trade skills required. My family has more Fifth Tier workers—unskilled labor—than Fourth Tier, but here I am, clearly a member of the Third. Ambition, skill, and intelligence is all that is needed."

"I think the Ambassador grasps all of that," Kuna'mi told her companion, eyeing Jackie sideways. "I believe what she is looking for is the historical basis for the system, yes?"

"Yes, and why it's held together so long," Jackie said, grateful the markless woman understood what she really wanted to know. Then she wondered if the tightly shielded woman understood *too* well. She didn't *think* her mind was open to general skimming . . .

"Part of it lies in the fact that the Empire has taken pains for millennia to express its appreciation for all of its members," Kuna'mi told them. "There have been a few times when an emperor or empress—or even nobles serving as regional governors—have failed to do so, and the eventual uprisings of discontent have been stressed ever since as something to be avoided by a smart ruler. Acknowledging that every job is important in its own way, whether it's skilled or unskilled, certainly helps. And each month gets one day to celebrate the hard work and accomplishments of the Fifth Tier, one to celebrate the Fourth, one to celebrate the Third, and one to collectively celebrate the efforts of the Second, First, and Imperial Tiers."

"Those always take place on Firstrest Day," Qua explained.

"*¿Sábado, sí?*" Maria whispered to Jackie.

"*Sí,*" she confirmed. At the bemused look from the two doctors, Jackie explained. "We call Firstrest Day *Saturday*, or *Sábado* in Dr. de la Santoya's native language."

"Thank you for explaining. The other reasons for the system's working include that, for a very long time, those who earned the rank of noble became governors and overseers of regions," Kuna'mi continued. "Even the most alien of governments understands the sheer inertia of bureaucracy. To keep it from bogging down in nepotism, official government positions require a competency test, and as a corollary, noble parents are encouraged to pick the child that *best* can handle being their heir, and not just whoever is firstborn. That helps ensure the likelihood that an heir will make a competent head of the bloodline."

"That would reduce the number of *idiotas* being put in charge, yes," Maria agreed.

"I'm not certain what *idiotas* is, but I think I can guess the context," Qua quipped. "And yes, it does help. Even in the Third and lower Tiers, we pick heirs we hope will be trustworthy."

"One of the things that helps the lower Tiers accept the superiority of the higher Tiers is that those of even the highest Tier can fall to the very bottom of the heap," Kuna'mi said next. "There's nothing like a chance to feel superior to someone who used to be higher ranked than you, to help stroke the ego in our species." She tipped her head to the side, acknowledging, "A cynical observation, but still a truthful one for many."

"It's said that the High One's reign was free of castes, that everything She did when rewarding a subject was based upon their merit," Qua offered. "Whereas the War King came from a culture with a caste system—two castes, warriors above, workers below. Somehow, the merging of the two eventually evolved into the five Tiers we have today—technically, six; no insult was meant, Your Highness."

"None taken," Li'eth reassured her.

"Well, while it is interesting to learn more about how your culture is arranged, I have 'cultures' that need to be watched," Maria stated. The other two doctors gave her blank looks.

Jackie came to her rescue. "In our language, the word *culture* means not only the social rules and expectations for a specific group of people, but also refers to cultivating bacteria and so forth, taking samples and figuring out how to make them grow, that sort of thing. It's a pun."

"Ah, right. Puns. I didn't realize the word could be used like that since you said it in V'Dan. I should go help you as well— To-mi, if the Ambassador has some time right now, why don't you get her to give you one of those language transfers everyone is talking about?" Qua offered to her colleague. "I've already had one from that nice older woman, Aixa. It's been very helpful."

"I don't think that will be necessary," Kuna'mi demurred, smiling.

Oh, this is interesting, Jackie thought. She smiled back. "I would think that it *would* be very necessary. You are the foremost authority on the *jungen* virus. My people will want to interview you thoroughly to reassure us that we won't get stripes or spots if we don't want any."

"Oh, I don't think they'd go that far," the markless woman tried again, shaking her head. "You'll have plenty of people exchanging all sorts of knowledge, soon. And I'll be needed to stay here, to monitor the version we're giving your people."

"I don't invoke my social rank very often these days," Li'eth stated. "But I am going to order you to sit with the Grand High Ambassador, Doctor. Learning Terranglo will only add to your authority and your ability to convey information. It will also increase the prestige of the Empire—you do have the time for it right now, Jackie?"

"Of course—if you'll excuse us, Doctors?" she added to Qua and de la Santoya. Both women nodded and took themselves out of the conference room. Jackie sent privately to Li'eth, (*I take it you're having some of the same suspicions as I am?*)

(*Yes. She's most likely a Feyori in disguise,*) he said.

(*I'm not a Feyori,*) a third mental voice stated. Kuna'mi's voice. She met their brief, sharp looks with a polite, mild smile. (*Or, not exactly. I was* also *hoping to simply smooth things over, but otherwise stay out of the spotlight.*) Gesturing at the chairs of the conference table, she said out loud, "If we're going to do this, perhaps we should sit down? Will you be joining us, Your Highness? I'm sure it might turn out to be helpful someday if you learn, or at least can observe, how language transfers work."

"I don't have anything else to do," he murmured, and moved to take a seat.

Since the table in this room was reasonably narrow, Jackie seated herself at one end, and the two V'Dan flanked her in the nearest chairs, Li'eth to her right and Kuna'mi to her left. "Join hands, please, and relax your minds. Breathe deeply four times with me, to help clear stress and open up your thoughts to contact . . ."

Kuna'mi breathed deep, let it out . . . and chuckled mentally. (*I haven't heard those words in a very long time. I've said them, but I haven't heard them.*)

(*You're the Immortal, aren't you?*) Li'eth asked the doctor, suspicion crystallizing sharply in his subthoughts. (*If you're not a Feyori shaped like a V'Dan, then you can only be the Immortal. She was said to be the child of two half-breeds.*)

(*Very clever of you to remember that. It's an obscure bit of history. And yes, I am, which is why I wanted to help the Terrans transition through this meeting with the* jungen *virus but did not want to catch royal attention,*) the woman confessed.

Jackie was still a bit skeptical, but she could feel the awe and reverence in her Gestalt partner. (*So what does that mean, you're Immortal?*)

(*It means I cannot be killed. Not by accident, not by old age. I can appear to age . . . if I put some thought and effort into it,*) she allowed. (*But slay me, and a handful of seconds later, I pop back to life. Since I really do not enjoy the whole painful dying part, that usually puts me in a bad mood, so I wouldn't recommend testing the theory empirically.*)

(*Of course not—and you wish to remain unacknowledged because you made a promise to my ancestor to stay out of V'Dan politics,*) Li'eth said next. (*Correct?*)

(*Correct. When I originally created the* jungen *virus, it was not the one I already had within me. That one was based on the version I gave* your *people, Ambassador,*) the doctor told them. (*The original was a viral agent endemic to V'Dan.*)

(*Call me Jackie, please,*) Jackie said.

(*Call me To-mi, then. Don't call me Shey, young man,*) she added, cutting off the rise of Li'eth's subthoughts. (*Discretion is key. As I was saying, the original one given over ninety-five centuries ago was a native beast. My equipment was primitive at best when it came time to genetically manipulate it so that it could alter the genes of a Human host appropriately. That's how it got a little messed up, adding in the marks. I knew that would happen, though, so I wasn't overly concerned about it. The current version is based on tweaking that followed the version I was given, roughly four hundred years into the future.*)

Jackie and Li'eth exchanged looks. They returned their gazes to the woman on the left side of the table, both with arched brows.

(*Mind your physical reactions, children,*) the Immortal chided. (*Remember,* everything *we do in quarantine is being recorded, and* will *be analyzed. I don't need a transfer of Terranglo because I already speak it, but we will have to sit here for a handful of hours.*)

(*I should've visited the washroom,*) Li'eth quipped dryly. (*If that is so, isn't the version you speak four hundred years out of date? A linguistic anachronism?*)

(*Not by that much. I only left Earth a few months after the* Councilor One *tragedy,*) To-mi told them. (*I knew from my history lessons that moving back to V'Dan at that time would give me the chance to set myself up for the single most vital First Contact moment in the Alliance. That was in 2265 Terran Standard, which gave me twenty-two years to establish an identity, slog through biology and medical lessons, gain my certificates, and become the foremost expert on* jungen *in the entire Empire. In other words, the person that would be tapped to help adapt Terran biology to handle V'Dan histaminic overloads.*)

(That *is what you think is the most vital part of this whole First Contact situation?*) Li'eth asked, somewhat incredulous. (Allergies?)

(*I have learned over the millennia that what is truly important is often seemingly insignificant. Without this very real biological hurdle being negated, Terrans will not be able to attend most Alliance meetings—which are held in V'Dan-friendly spaces. They will not be able to colonize other worlds—again, with the aid of previously established colonial knowledge thanks to the V'Dan—and so on and so forth. Your soldiers won't be able to serve on V'Dan ships or V'Dan planets, you won't be able to communicate in person . . . I see you get my point, yes?*)

(*I see the merit in it, yes,*) Jackie agreed. (*Our booster shots have kept us ahead of histaminic reactions to the pollen in the air here in quarantine, but that's in a relatively sterile environment. We get some exposure through the life-support bays where food is grown and carbon dioxide recycled into oxygen*

*through the plants. But on your homeworld, where there are
no artificial controls throttling down the pollen counts . . . it
would be a medical nightmare.)*

(*That, and I am the authority on* jungen,) To-mi agreed.
(*On the bright side, most allergic reactions will be quelled to
a very bearable, even ignorable level, if not outright eradi-
cated. The common cold will rarely induce runny noses or
sneezing fits—at the cost of increased fatigue and fever risks,*)
she allowed. (*But that's endurable. And both worlds will open
up a host of new trade venues for spices, herbs, vegetables,
meats, all manner of new foods, as well as plant-based
objects. And you'll find some M-class worlds where the local
agriculture will flourish under a combination of V'Dan and
Terran sources and efforts. Eventually.*)

Jackie wasn't completely convinced. (*You say you're the
Immortal. But how—*)

(*—Can I prove it?*) To-mi finished for her. (*I am not going
to kill myself to prove it. Nor can I tell you all that much about
the future—no, I cannot, for two important reasons.*)

(*Oh, really?*) Li'eth challenged her, lifting a brow.

(*Yes, really. The first is obvious. I really shouldn't interfere
too much. This is* your *timeline. Your* galaxy-shaking First Contact *and all its associated events. Besides, you're both grown-
ups,*) the Immortal added. (*You're smart enough to make good
decisions. I'll only step in if things start to get out of hand.*)

(*And the second reason?*) Jackie asked. (*Or was that it?*)

(*The second reason is that I am carrying around over fourteen thousand years of memories in my head. I was taught a
lot of Terran and V'Dan history—with what I thought at the
time was a rather odd emphasis on certain events,*) she added
in an aside. (*The people who helped raise me are, or rather,
will be followers of the Prophet of a Thousand Years. I didn't
know what I was when they started educating me. But they
could only do so from* known *historical records. A lot of this
stuff is unknown, even by me, because history often gets
reduced to what the Terrans call* sound-bites, *little snippets of
information only so large, and no more.*

(*Some of this, I know exactly what will happen. Some of it,
I have only a thin veil of information. Some of it, I know*

nothing about. I'm sorry if that disappoints you, children, but that is the way things are.)

(*. . . I don't know how anyone could keep fourteen centuries' worth of memories straight, let alone fourteen thousand,*) Jackie mused in the quiet that fell between them.

(*It isn't easy. There's a special way I can kill and revive myself that brings all the memories flooding back, but . . . it takes a long time to sort through all those memories, so I try to do it only once every fifty or so years,*) To-mi confessed. (*At this point, it takes me almost two weeks to sort through everything, and add to my records. Eventually, I hope to share everything I know . . . but it'll be after my original life span ends. I don't know what will happen to my body when "I" am born in the future. The closer I get to that era, the more nervous I get. Two objects cannot occupy the same point in space at the same moment in time. I don't know if one sentient being can occupy the same span in the timestreams, even if I take pains never to encounter myself.*)

(*I hope you'll forgive me if I don't feel too much sympathy for that problem,*) Li'eth told her. (*I'm still trying to accept the idea that I am holding hands with the Immortal High One, First Empress of V'Dan.*)

(*It's about as likely as your holding hands with your Gestalt mate, so try not to let it slow you down,*) To-mi told him tartly. (*And yes, I did know about that in advance.*)

(*Tell me something. If you are the Immortal, why reveal it to us? Li'eth said that when his ancestor won, you agreed to step down from V'Dan politics,*) Jackie asked next. (*Why reveal it to a member of the Imperial Family?*)

(*Because you aren't the sort of woman to let something like this go. I realized I had forgotten to disguise my training from you when you reminded me of your abilities—again, millennia's worth of forgetfulness, here,*) To-mi said, sighing. (*And when I did remember, I could tell that you saw through my attempts. Which meant once you compared it to the expelled shit they call training in this era, you'd question me. I waited until you brought it up, however, to see if you even would, and in particular, how you might bring it up.*

(*This version is reasonably discreet . . . and I do admit it will allow me to speak Terranglo right away. As long as you don't tell everyone who and what I am, I'll be fine,)* she concluded.

(*Something is bothering me,*) Li'eth stated. (*Your mental voice . . . your tone, the words you pick . . . they're different from when you speak aloud.*)

(*Of course they are. When I speak aloud, I am playing the role of Dr. To-mi Kuna'mi. And when I speak telepathically, I am playing another role. The weight of my true thoughts would unnerve both of you.*)

(*I am not sure I completely believe her,*) Li'eth sent to Jackie as privately as he could. It didn't seem to help.

(*If I were you, Highness, I wouldn't believe me, either. If you want proof, I'm afraid you will have to wait until we are not being watched by security equipment,*) To-mi pointed out. (*Your physical reactions would be at odds with what you'd normally display during a language transfer.*)

(*How strong a telepath are you?*) Jackie asked.

(*I haven't been tested in ages, young lady. Eons, technically. I've spent the last couple hundred years avoiding KI machines and painstakingly learning how not to set them off by sheer proximity for those times when I do have to use my gifts.*) To-mi paused, then offered, (*I could teach you the trick of it, if you like.*)

(*That would be unethical,*) Jackie declined. She didn't even have to think about it. (*And I would rather you didn't teach it to anyone else . . . though for security's sake, you should tell me what its weaknesses are.*)

(*It's just a particular sort of mental shield, a way of concentrating that cages kinetic-inergy waves and reflects them back toward the center. It's not easy to maintain for great lengths of time, and the smaller the shield, the shorter the duration because of that reflected pressure, but it has gotten me in and out of Psi League training facilities,*) To-mi said.

(*That begs the question of why, if you have such exacting, Terran-style training,*) Li'eth asked, (*haven't you taught it to my people?*)

(Your ancestor.) That rather flat, mental assertion came with a distinct overtone of dislike, disappointment, and distaste. (*The stubborn, goat-brained, anti-anything-Immortal did his best to try to wipe out the Sh'nai faith, starting with my very-well-trained priesthood. His own psis weren't nearly as well trained. It was all I could do to preserve the majority of the history books, the rituals. By the time I realized he was specifically targeting the gifted and destroying their training scrolls first and foremost, it was too late.*

(*All I could do was try to save the core of the religion, knowing that those prophecies would need to be remembered for this very moment. So to speak—don't think at me in that tone of subvoice, young man,*) she added to Li'eth. (*No matter what legends may have sprung up around me, I am still just one person. I am unable to stop thousands of angry, bitter, stubbornly prejudiced warriors on a self-righteous rampage. I had given him my word I would not interfere in his choice of government . . . though I did step in a few times to politely remind him that if he wanted to retain his power over my people, he would have to bend in a few areas or risk a full revolt.*

(*Since he was determined to separate government from religion, I was free to salvage the religion as best I could . . . but again, just one person. You're lucky you even have as much as you do, in regards to Sh'nai beliefs and books,*) To-mi concluded.

Jackie wasn't so sure about that. She attempted a private sending of her own, much more skilled than Li'eth but aimed at the self-proclaimed Immortal. (*You could have taught them in person, as part of their strictly religious rites. You're clearly quite accomplished. So why didn't you?*)

(*Because of you. I knew from my history lessons that the Terrans would bring in their highly skilled psychic discipline, and that such things would help turn the tide of this particular war,*) To-mi answered.

Jackie knew both sendings were private because Li'eth asked over the top of their thoughts, (*I'm still trying to figure out how you, a renowned Imperial expert, who doesn't have a birth record, managed to escape being caught up in the lie of your current fabricated identity. How did you pull that off?*)

(*Easily. The Valley of the Artisans was created not only as a refuge for the arts, sciences, and literacy needs of free-minded people, saving them from the brutal savagery of one of your other, slightly more recent ancestors,*) she told him, (*but also as a refuge for me to visit and integrate myself into the world through their records system. They're pledged to provide me with an identity every time I need one. And no, they don't give identities to criminals,*) To-mi stated firmly, no doubt reading Li'eth's underthoughts on that topic. (*No, you are not going to investigate Dr. Kuna'mi's background, either.*)

(*And why not?*) he challenged her.

(*That could lead to my being exposed, and* that *would be detrimental to the Empire. Think it through. If the Immortal is proved to exist, then it will cause huge religious upheavals at a time when the Empire needs to remain united and thus strong. I am willing to prove in private that I am who I say I am, at a time and place when we are* not *under surveillance, but you're just going to have to wait. Exercise both discretion and patience, Prince. This meeting doesn't have to become a part of history. It isn't important enough.*)

Jackie was not completely convinced. There was more to To-mi's offer than just proving her words were true. (*You want to influence this meeting between the Terrans and the V'Dan. Not just smooth over the whole histamine problem. You want access to me, because I'm the Ambassador . . . and access to him, because he's Imperial Family. All of it behind the scenes.*)

That earned her a slight smile, one felt more mentally than seen physically. (*History has judged you well. Seemingly sweet, seemingly innocent . . . but not naïve,*) To-mi replied. (*I'm looking forward to watching it unfold firsthand, so to speak. As for your accusation . . . it is true insofar as I wish to avoid mucking up time. But I only know the grand-picture details, and I cannot interfere too much.*)

(*Time travel shouldn't exist, period, because of predestination paradox,*) Jackie pointed out. That earned her a mental snort. As their conversation went on, the awareness of the room around them was starting to fade, turning into a table in the vast, quiet warehouse where she liked to cleanse and center her mind. The physical woman, To-mi, didn't move, but the one inside their joint vision rolled her eyes.

(*If you go back in time to slaughter your own grandfather, there is no paradox; you just end up having your motivation shifted to a different reason for killing that particular person because someone else becomes your grandfather at that point. Your actions do not destroy your own existence. They* can, however . . . destroy others.) There was a stark sobriety to her gaze in the aetherspace where their inner selves sat. A moment later, and the blue-eyed, Asiatic-looking woman blinked, banishing it. Her neutrally polite look returned in its place.

Either this woman was the universe's greatest actress, or she'd had a very long time to practice such things. Jackie was beginning to believe it just might be the latter. Every one of To-mi's thoughts was genuine, but organized, with no stray sub-thoughts roaming around. Very well shielded, even internally.

(*Well, then. What shall we talk about for the next two hours or so?*) Jackie asked. (*If you cannot tell us much about the future, and not much about yourself . . .*)

(*Actually, I was hoping to catch up on the happenings back on Earth in the last couple of decades. I never got to find out what happened in the entertainment series* Alexander the Great. *They deviated a few times from the original stories, but they were getting most of the historical daily-life details fairly accurate.*)

(*I suppose this is where you tell us you lived through that era?*) Jackie asked, skeptically.

To-mi grinned at her. (*I was on Earth, yes, but I was in China, actually. With this face, I could go almost anywhere in the temperate zones. By the time I heard about Alexander's conquests reaching India, I was thousands of kilometers away. And by the time I got to Babylon, he was dead and his putative heirs were squabbling over their inheritance rights. But the daily life, they got mostly right.*)

(*Well, I could see if the series is in our entertainment files,*) Jackie offered. (*I was more interested in other shows at that age, so I've never seen it. We haven't put together any packages for entertainment-show exchanges yet, because we haven't enough speakers in each language yet, never mind translators.*)

(*If it helps, I could offer suggestions—not precognitively directed, just some ideas—on various things you can trade for, and in what order for priority,*) To-mi offered. (*I do have a fairly good grasp on what the two sides could offer, and peaceful trade agreements are definitely something I'd like to see negotiated.*)

(*I'll listen to your advice,*) Jackie agreed.

(*And I'll take mental notes for our side as well,*) Li'eth confirmed. (*I don't know if I'll be given many chances to act as a liaison just yet, but I should be prepared.*)

(*Mm, yes, the Gestalt pairing. That's going to be interesting. Some will believe, and some will refuse to believe—and that, I can tell you, has as much to do with your lack of jungen as anything,*) she added to Jackie. (*But I'm sure you're beginning to be aware of that. You're also from a culture where anyone can become anything, a very fluid hierarchy of social status. The prince is not . . . but I'm pleased to see you do seem to have gained some mental flexibility in recent years, yes?*)

(*Through the military, yes,*) he admitted, flushing a little. (*Are you reading my thoughts?*)

(*It can't be helped at my strength, particularly as we're touching. But as the Psi League says, what was yours remains yours. I would no more share your secrets with anyone than I would my own,*) To-mi told both of them. (*And since I fully intend to walk away from this meeting with my anonymity intact, so will your privacy . . . Yes, that's a wise decision, deciding to wait until after we're no longer in proximity to each other before the two of you discuss this whole session.*

(*I suggest we get back to the topic of trade goods,*) the odd woman continued. (*It's safest. Obviously, you will want to prioritize artificial gravity in exchange for something, but I'd suggest trading ceristeel plating for it. Hyperrelay communications is your biggest point of leverage, so don't—sorry, Your Highness—give it away.*)

(*We had already considered that,*) Jackie replied smoothly. She could feel a touch of annoyance from Li'eth but couldn't tell if it was from stating the obvious or withholding a huge advantage. (*The military advised the Council not to give that one away. Ceristeel, though . . . are you sure it'll be of interest? What about whatever the Alliance uses for ship plating?*)

To-mi shook her head. Not in reality, just in the virtual telepathic space Jackie had created for them. (*Ceristeel is better at resisting damage from impacts, and vastly better at a combination of absorbing, dissipating, and deflecting energy weapons. With very minor modifications, an exterior hull of ceristeel can be retrofitted to most ships in a fraction of the time it would take to build new ones. Particularly fighter craft, as those above all others tend to be standardized and thus uniform in shape anyway.*

(*Your lasers are okay, but right now, Tlassian designs are vastly superior, with more calories per kilo of fuel. Which means that hydrogenerators are going to be the big bargaining chip if you keep the hyperarrays and hyperrelays to yourselves for a while. That's going to revolutionize everything on its own, even though it won't be integratable into the military for a few years yet, since engines are harder to redesign and replace than just adding an extra layer of hull plating. For now, I'd say focus that more on the civilian bargaining side of things.*)

Jackie shook her head. (*The catalyst is a proprietary item, same as accessing hyperspace.*)

(*Oh, they won't be able to manufacture that for years, don't worry. But portable generators that run on water? It'll shake up the biofuel farmers,*) To-mi allowed, (*but it'll be a boon for insystem haulers to start amassing ice for processing. Cheap fuel means that a lot more off-world mining can be done, which will preserve the environments of a lot of colonyworlds, M-class or otherwise.*)

(*Ehm—what?*) Li'eth asked.

(*M-class, what we call Earth-like planets, suitable for sustaining Human life,*) Jackie explained. (*The designation came from an old entertainment program. Astrophysicists balked for years over whether or not to use it, but it was so prevalent in nonscientific culture that they eventually caved in. We're still classifying the other letters of the alphabet, but I know that the V'Dan geophysicists who shared their technological definitions for such things have been giving Lars no end of thrills on trying to match their versions with the theoretical classifications built up around the alphabet structure.*)

(*When did he do that?*) Li'eth asked, distracted.

(*It was while you were being grilled at the Tower on Kaho'lawe, in the week or so before we left. Lars sent me a message bubbling over with sheer joy on the findings, and asking me to ask your people if they knew of any planets near our space which we could begin colonizing. The faster we can get our mining and such out of the Sol System, the happier our environmentalists will be.*) She paused and rolled her eyes mentally, virtually. (*Not that they won't complain about mucking up the ecology of* other *worlds, but they're less concerned about airless planets and asteroids, so on and so forth.*)

(*Speaking of colonizing, that's going to be an important one, but don't rush it, either,*) To-mi cautioned them. (*The most efficient way to colonize would be to jointly colonize a planet, since the V'Dan have the know-how and the resources, while the Terrans have the heavy population pressure at the moment. But it'll have several cultural hurdles to get past first.*)

(*The biggest being the perception of anyone without* jungen *being nothing more than a child,*) Jackie muttered.

(*At first, yes, but the biggest is actually something of a much more long-term consequence,*) To-mi cautioned. (*By that, I mean, who is* in charge *of the Human race. Do you join the V'Dan Empire? Do you have the V'Dan Empire join you? Do you remain separate entities? Think about it, Ambassador. If most of your worlds are jointly colonized, particularly at first, it's going to cause a lot of pressure in the Empire to take you under their wing . . . again, with the perception of* jungenless *being juvenile,*) she allowed. (*But Earth is the Motherworld of your joint species. Should it be relegated to a junior role?*)

(*I . . . can't deny that most of the Empire will look down on your people for having just one system settled,*) Li'eth agreed reluctantly. (*Particularly when we have several. You're an insystem empire, but we're an interstellar one.*)

Jackie, thinking, asked, (*Would hydrofuel technology be worth bartering for assistance in colonizing our own worlds, do you think? Not joint colonization, but just . . . hiring ships and equipment and experts to train our own people how to do things efficiently?*)

To-mi nodded slowly before turning her attention to the prince seated with them. (*Possibly . . . What do you think, Highness?*)

In reality, he kept their hands linked, but telepathically . . . he sat back and rubbed his chin, thinking. (*Possibly. We've had problems balancing the environmental needs versus our economic needs through using biopetrochemicals. Particularly as only two of the V'Dan-style—your M-class—worlds have had massive deposits of archaic petrochemicals—I asked Meioa Thorsson about what your fuel history was like, and he explained about the ancient forests, the lack of bacteria and such that could digest cellulose for millions of years, and the eventual conversion of the fallen forest materials into oils and so forth.*

(*That was not too dissimilar to what V'Dan experienced, and Beautiful-Blue, and Chchchch—those are the Gatsugi and K'Katta homeworlds, respectively,*) he explained in an aside to Jackie. (*Compared to that, water ice is abundant in many systems, including moons and planets that aren't comfortably inhabitable, as well as comets and other fragments. Plants raised to be processed into petrochemicals require a great deal of space that could be put to other uses though they're quite useful for helping convert carbon dioxide into oxygen for life-support needs while the plants are growing.*)

(*You'll always need some form of oil for greasing machinery,*) To-mi dismissed. (*The point is, Earth needs to expand onto other words to alleviate its massive population-density problems, and hydrofuel-energy generation should be strong enough to balance the ledger for assistance with your basic colonization needs. I'm not saying it's supereffective and will pay for everything—your skills at bartering will be put to the test, I'm sure—but it is a very strong bargaining chip when you consider the environmental needs, the prevalence of it, and the considerably faster and cheaper process of purifying water versus creating biodiesel-style fuels. Not to mention how environmentally friendly it is by comparison. Solar power can handle stationary needs for houses and businesses, but large vehicles and heavy payloads require a much more powerful, more consistently reliable energy source.*)

(*I'll keep all of that in mind,*) Jackie promised her. Since they had at least a couple more hours to go, and a lot that could potentially be discussed, she moved on to the next topic. (*What do you think about trading food? Dr. Qua was talking about waiting at least a full year of in-depth research and genetics information being exchanged, studied, and tested, to make sure everything can be digested, and all possible pathogenic contaminants can be accounted for and controlled . . .*)

MAY 5, 2287 C.E.
DEMBER 28, 9507 V.D.S.

The plain, metal-encased pen rolled back across the table for a full meter and came to a stop in front of His Rather Bored Highness. It stopped precisely on a row of triangles embedded under the clear lacquer; the table had triangles, squares, and rectangles beneath its polished surface, giving it some visual artwork in an otherwise bland and boring conference room sized only for six people at most.

"Again," Jackie directed patiently, releasing the object from her mental grasp. "Focus on moving the pen away from you, exactly the length of your hand from wrist to longest fingertip, but no more than that."

(*This is boring!*) he protested. (*Well, not boring, but . . . I am feeling so restless right now. Can we do something else?*)

"Control is essential. Move the pen precisely, Your Highness." She felt it, too, an itch under her skin to be doing something, anything. Something physical, at any rate. But they were now on a countdown to being released from quarantine, and that meant she wanted Li'eth's powers firmly under control. The others could teach him some control over his pyrokinetic and auramantic abilities, but she was the best person to get him to work on his telekinetic control. (*Once you can do that three times in a row, I promise we'll move on to something else.*)

(*You feel it, too, don't you?*) Li'eth asked. He didn't bother with the pen. (*The longer we've been cooped up in quarantine, the worse it has grown. It . . . I feel like we aren't touching enough?*)

She pondered that. (*Possibly. We may need more than just arms against arms or a simple hug. That's worrisome, though.*)

He picked up her underthoughts. (*They're going to have to deal with it sooner or later,*) Li'eth reminded her. (*We're a holy pairing. To separate us is anathema. If we can prove it to the Temples' satisfaction.*)

(*I'm not sure how cooperative they'll be after my fellow psis and I sort of trounced their holy beliefs with our very scientific demonstrations,*) Jackie reminded him. (*We tried to keep things factual and impersonal, and just strictly, "We decided to approach everything from a scientific standpoint when we finally had a machine that could measure the strength of these abilities when they were being used," but . . .)*

(*Being told by* children *that the children know better than the adults . . . yes, they weren't too terribly happy. If nothing else, the* important *person to consult is Her Eternity. She has final say over everything,*) Li'eth reminded her. (*If you can get her to understand, her word is literally law, when she commands something.*)

(*That will probably have to wait until we are in person, when it is easier to explain such things and be judged sincere and truthful.*) She realized after a moment what he was doing, and gave him a chiding look. (*No more stalling, Li'eth. If you can move that pen, rolling or lifting and gliding, your choice, exactly a handspan three times . . .* then *we will sit and cuddle. And see if a bit more intimacy than merely holding hands will stifle our restlessness.*)

He sat up a little in his seat. Not that he had slouched, exactly; princes did not slouch. But her offer was a good incentive. (*You promise?*)

(*I promise. Three times. Hand length. Go,*) Jackie urged him. Then quickly caught the pen as he flicked it too hard. (Gently! *The object is* control, *not distance.*)

(*Yes, teacher.*) He sighed, watching her bring the pen back to its starting place. Focusing more carefully, he very gently nudged the pen. It rolled about a fingerlength. So he patiently nudged it again. Another fingerlength, or about the length of his hand from wrist to longest fingertip. (*Does that count?*)

(*Yes, I'll let it pass. But only this one time. Either lift it and move it, or roll it in one take.*)

Nodding, he tried a slightly harder nudge. The pen rolled . . . almost long enough. The table had a pattern embedded in its smooth-lacquered surface, and . . . he was off by half a finger. A tiny nudge, and he looked at her. (*. . . Yes?*)

(*Try again. I know you're frustrated, but control is important. Control may one day save your life, or the life of another. Lack of control will endanger everyone.*) She brought the cylinder back to its starting point, a row of triangles. To prove her point, the pen stopped precisely on the points of those triangles. (*Remember, this isn't just about pushing the pen. It is about stopping it, too. And not just as a hard wall that would*

*make it bounce back. Try to think about the problem, and how
you would shape the forces you are wielding.*)

Sighing, he focused, and thought. Finally, instead of a solid
bump . . . he cupped it in a curve, pushed to the edge of the
rows of squares that marked the proper length on the table,
then tilted the cupped shape of force downward, pressing the
pen into place with just enough force to stop it. (*Ha!*)

(*Excellent—and a very clever way to shape the telekinetic
forces. Now, bring it back to the starting position yourself,*)
she said. (*And do it three times exactly like that.*)

(*Yes, meioa.*) Carefully, he rolled the metal pen back and
forth three full times. Almost. It got away from him twice. Sighing, focusing, Li'eth stared at it and carefully shaped, and . . .
managed two more good rolls. The trick of it required constant
vigilance in his concentration.

"Well done!" Jackie praised out loud when the pen reached
the squares and stopped right on the line. "Time to let your mind
rest, and for the two of us to ease the bond of our holy pairing
through some physical contact. If you are willing, please move
your chair back."

Nodding, he scooted it back . . . and quickly brought up an
arm to support her back as she settled sideways on his lap. Today,
she was in pants and shirt in that plebeian military gray, a few
shades lighter than the walls around him. Not particularly flattering, but he didn't care. She was warm, she smelled wonderful,
and he cradled her close against his cream-and-scarlet frame.

Jackie felt good, being held like this. But she needed more.
Twisting a little, she wrapped her arms around his ribs and
snuggled his head against the side of his neck. His hair was
loose today, giving her a place to bury her face. Hers was up
in a bun. Wanting to give him some privacy, too, she reached
with her mind for the wooden pin skewering her curls in place.
Setting it on the table with her telekinesis—neatly aligned
next to the pen—she cuddled closer.

(*Yes. I need this,*) she whispered mentally. Her lips grazed
the side of his throat, and she inhaled his warmth, his unique
male scent. A touch of soap, but no cologne, no perfume, just
clean, warm male. It required filling her lungs a second time,
and a third.

(*You smell even better,*) he told her, nosing his way to her own neck for a slow, satiating sniff. (*Whatever that Terran stuff is you use for cleansing yourself . . . mmmh. It has a delicious perfume.*)

The move scraped a faint hint of beard stubble against her skin. She tried to ignore the goose bumps that raised. (*Shampoo. I don't like soap on my body, so I've been using a no-scent shampoo. It doesn't leave much of a residue, and almost no smell.*)

Li'eth breathed deep, nuzzling her a little. (*Then all this delicious scent is pure you.*) He nuzzled her again, then held himself still. A thought raced through his head. Hoping her hair concealed his intent, he parted his lips just a little bit against the side of her throat, and licked. (*. . . Delicious, indeed.*)

(*Li'eth . . .*) It came out more *lieth* than *li'eth* in her mind. *Beloved* instead of *year of joy*. She knew they had to remain circumspect. She knew it but couldn't quite bring herself to stop him. It felt good. It felt like what she needed, like a cat that needed to purr. (*You have . . . thirty seconds to enjoy all that . . . before it's my turn.*)

(*Give me a full* mi-nah, *not thirty* se-nah,) he bartered, tasting her again.

(*I'd give you five full minutes, if I could,*) she murmured. Contentment soaked through her skin, into her muscles. It didn't have a chance to reach her bones, though. Someone activated the small conference room's intercom system.

"*Grand High Ambassador Maq'en-zi, why are you sitting on His Imperial Highness? That is not acceptable behavior.*" The voice was in that nebulous zone of either contralto or tenor and slightly distorted by the broadcasting unit, which was over by the doorframe.

Hiding the urge to roll her eyes, Jackie shot back, "It is perfectly acceptable if both His Imperial Highness and I decide it is acceptable. Which we have, meioa. We are both mature adults, and we both clearly consent to this. Furthermore, whoever you are, I am certain you have zero authority over either of us. Should you go *looking* for that authority, all I can say is that such an act would be considered petty at best and an insult at worst. In the light of these facts, your inquiry under Terran rules of protocol is, in a word, *rude.*"

"I must agree with the Grand High Ambassador," Li'eth

stated, removing his face from the side of her neck for a few moments so he could speak. "You are being rude. Keep your opinions behind your teeth and do not comment. If the sight of the two of us embracing offends you so deeply that you feel you must stop it because you cannot bear to see it . . . then I suggest you do not look. We are not hugging *you*, thus you have no right to try to stop it. *That*, meioa, is what makes your actions rude."

(*Definitely rude,*) Jackie agreed, irritated. She buried her face against his throat and licked him, then snuggled closer and tilted her head a little, giving him room to nuzzle her neck again. Nuzzle, and discreetly lap at her skin in tiny, slow strokes. (*My people certainly wouldn't have flapped their mouths as if they were God's own arbiter of the social rules! I ought to lodge a complaint against a* voyeur . . . *if I could just . . . figure out . . . You know, those little licks are very soothing . . .*)

He nipped her with his teeth. Jackie sucked in a breath, startled. She struggled to keep her expression calm but sent him a subthought with a little sting of her own, to remind him he shouldn't do that.

(*Nonsense. They're supposed to be pleasurable, not* soothing,) he chided, gently tonguing the spot his teeth had stung. (*I was trying to turn your anger into arousal.*)

(*They are doing that; trust me, they are. It's just that your touch soothed me right out of my anger,*) she pointed out. (*And now you're trying to make me squirm?*)

(*Perhaps. But I have decided just now that I don't give a Saint's* shakk. *Yes, I know how crude that is,*) Li'eth added. He nuzzled her throat again, nibbling with his lips. (*This feels good. Soothing, as you say, but also in a stimulating way. You just . . . You smell so* good, *Jacaranda-Flower. I don't feel quite so restless, cuddling with you like this. We haven't done this since leaving your ship.*)

Squirming a little, she managed to tuck her face into his own neck and shoulder. (*Exactly. This is exactly what we need.*)

A soft chuckle escaped him. (*Not* exactly *what we need. To feel better, I'd rather do this without all these layers of clothing in the way—nothing indecent, just the outfits we wore on that beach. For now. Maybe later . . .*)

(*Yes, for now . . . and yes, that would be great,*) she agreed. (*You and me in a warm spring wind, the scent of sand and seaweed, the sun blanketing us with its heat, the ocean spray helping to keep us cool . . .*) Part of her mind still wanted to race with other thoughts, as it always did. But for the first time in her life, the scent of the man she snuggled with was more important. Warnings, customs, lists . . . not nearly so important as this. Rather than being pushed away by each other's subthoughts, like random ball bearings careening around and crashing into each other, it was more like their thoughts were attracting each other. *Like magnetic ball bearings.*

(*An amusing thought,*) he agreed . . . and shivered a little when she licked along the flat neckline of his uniform. (*Careful, I'll need to be decent when I stand up at some point.*)

(*I'll be careful. Ish,*) she teased. (*Don't worry. Five solid minutes of gentle cuddling and necking, and we'll go back to practicing your gifts.*)

(*At least I get this as an incentive. Also, "necking" . . . ?*) he asked. There was a lot more behind her strange phrase than just discreetly nibbling on each other's necks. (*That's an odd designation for something involving far more than necks.*)

(*True. Unfortunately, we cannot involve more than lips and necks, and just plain hugging, until everyone understands what we are, and that it can be possible for me to do my job even while I'm involved with you.*)

(*That is a disappointment,*) he agreed. (*But I won't stop holding you, just yet. If I could . . . if we could get away with it . . . I'd sleep curled up together with you.*)

She nuzzled him, enjoying the faint rasp of the stubble beneath his ear as it rubbed against her own. (*I'd do that, too. We may need to, at some point . . . may? No. Will. We will have to transition into living together at some point.*)

(*If it helps, the diplomatic wings are actually fairly close to the imperial quarters. Your walk to work wouldn't be too onerous,*) he offered.

Jackie grinned and quietly kissed his neck. (*Or maybe I'd just have you move in with me.*)

(*. . . That might not be a bad idea. Has it been five minutes yet?*) he asked, thinking more of wanting to stay like this than of the need to continue practicing control with his gifts.

(*We have a little bit more time,*) she reassured him, not wanting to think too much about anything else, herself.

(*Good.*)

CHAPTER 6

MAY 6, 2287 C.E.
JANVA 1, 9508 V.D.S.

The V'Dan, the Terrans discovered, didn't put as much emphasis on their version of New Year's Eve, so much as how much they celebrated New Year's Day. In fact, the handful of V'Dan among them kept themselves quite busy putting up makeshift decorations, folding almost origami-style paper hats, and wishing everyone a "Blessed New Year" and a "Happy Winter's Day!" Plus, "Happy Saint Gedred's Day," whoever that was.

The Terrans, game for any sort of party, got into the spirit of decorating and asked for stories about the holidays—plural—celebrated on "Janva First." And, of course, they mulled over how similar *Janva* was to *January*, and *Dember* to *December*, debating just how many words between Terranglo and Imperial High V'Dan crossed over. They couldn't partake of any of the traditional foods their hosts assembled—or even be in the kitchen at the same time as all that cooking, for safety's sake—but most everyone was eager to explain in histaminically neutral spaces about their favorite holiday treats and memories from various celebrations from childhood on up.

So it struck Jackie as a bit odd to see Dr. To-mi Kuna'mi rise and walk away from one of the crowded, heavily chatting tables in the dining hall with a very flat, very masklike expression. Rigid, or at least unmoving. Everyone's face moved, normally. By a blink, by an eyebrow shift, a lip twitch. The way how one's eyes shifted, what they focused on. But . . . in that one moment, not hers.

Curious, Jackie drifted over to the table. Lars held the attention of everyone there; he had brought out a Terran data-pad and used it to display something familiar. Childish sketches in washed-out, almost watercolor shades, paired with neatly penned discussions. She had to hear Lars saying the name of it to grasp what it was.

The Voynich Manuscript. The moment she heard the geo-physicist mention it, several things clicked into place in her mind. Moving away from the table without a word, she crossed to the other woman, the markless V'Dan *jungen* specialist. The youngish-looking woman stared blindly at the entertainment screen, but from the lack of movement in her eyes, she wasn't seeing the live broadcast of New Year's Day celebrations taking place down at the plazas in front of the Winter Palace.

(*You know that manuscript.*) She shaped the sentence gently, like a tentative knocking on a door that had been slammed shut a few minutes before.

(*Her name was Mishka.*)

Jackie staggered under the weight of those four words. She clutched at the back of the V'Dan-style couch between her and the entertainment screen. A couple of her fellow Terrans glanced up at her in curiosity but returned their attention to the show. Two of the five crowded onto the couch were taking notes on what they were observing. Three were sharing snack packets brought all the way from Earth. None of them had any clue of the weight of grief and wistfulness inherent in the words of the other woman behind their cushioned perch.

Standing there with such seeming calmness. Such casualness, save for the set mask of her blue-eyed, lightly tanned, dark-haired face.

(*Do you want to tell me about her?*) Jackie asked tentatively.

An image unfurled in her mind. Richer than words, more nuanced than a whole orchestra, a spool of memories uncoiled and scrolled past. A girl-child persecuted because of a combination of her bloodline and a lack of *jungen* marks. The prejudice that kept trying to have her killed. A family line that had been friends to the strange, markless lady who sometimes came to visit. Prejudice that boiled over into anger and action against both of them, when *she* had innocently come back to update . . . something . . . and had lingered for a visit to see how the family was faring.

Prejudice that sprang from the hatred of outworlders, not just local V'Dan. Meddlers. Feyori, who thought the child's existence was an abomination and that she should die rather than let . . . something called a Rite of Simmerings? Rather than let such a thing unfold, they wanted to slay the child. The pawn-thing, in their minds, that had been endowed with too much in the way of potential power.

To-mi's decision to flee that world, taking the girl-child with her, streamed through Jackie's thoughts. At first, they lingered in a pleasant climate . . . somewhere in Europe. Mediterranean-ish, but with mountains. But then trouble reared its head, and To-mi and the girl fled, relocating to a much harsher, or at least colder, climate . . . Russia, Jackie realized. The moment she thought *that*, To-mi spoke again, mind-to-mind.

(*Yes, that Mishka. The Mishka bloodline. That's where the name comes from. I called her Isa or Isabella for those few years in northern Italia. I created backgrounds for both of us, dug up some gold to pay for everything—child's play, in those days; no bureaucracies keeping track of everything—and first sought refuge with a family near Verona. I hoped the Renais-sance would make for a good place for her to be raised, some-thing close to the sophistication of the V'Dan Empire in that era . . . It didn't last.*

(*After we had to flee, I carved out a little manor of sorts. Raised her with a good, solid education, and helped her pick out the right kind of man for a husband . . . You must under-stand, she had no gifts. No psychic abilities manifested during her lifetime, or her children's lifetime, or theirs. That was in part the bargain I made with the Meddlers on Earth. No one could touch her family line for ten generations, in exchange for keeping her half-breed inheritance suppressed.*)

Jackie wanted to seize on that word, *half-breed*, and ask a thousand questions, but tightly quelled the urge. She had invited To-mi to share, not to be interrogated. To-mi noticed her courtesy.

(*Thank you . . . By that point, the bloodline had been*

*thinned out that it only ever resurfaced as vague abilities—
Rank 4 or 5 at the absolute strongest, but most were barely
registerable by KI-machine standards,)* To-mi explained. She
shrugged subtly. (*There was a certain Russian mystic who had
flashes of insight, clairsentiency tied to biokinesis, forming
biokinesience. That's the very rare form of—*)

(*—The very rare form of being able to sense biokinetic
activity and even diagnose it instinctively, even in others,
without directly healing, yes,*) Jackie agreed. (*It's rare, but
I've heard of it. But . . . Lars was saying just now that the
manuscript was likely made in Italy, not Russia.*)

That shifted the other woman's mask. Her mouth twisted
in a wry smile. (*I found her writing in it after we'd been on
Earth for about a year. I chided her, pointed out all the
dangers—being accused of witchcraft was a serious thing,
back then—and she agreed to let me take the book away. I
didn't want to destroy it, but I wasn't quite ready to go to the
Vault to store it yet; she was smart but too young to be left
alone with strangers, you see. We were staying at a* villa *along
the shores of the Lago di Garda—about halfway between
Venezia and Milano, just west of Verona—when there was a
fire in the middle of the night.*

(*Ironically, even without having shown anyone the book—
it was safely tucked into my baggage—I was accused of starting the fire with witchcraft, and Isa and I had to flee. Most of
the northern cultures of Earth have been rather patriarchal
and misogynistic for far too long, so any woman who was
clearly well educated, who didn't bow to male authority, who
wasn't a proper piece of chattel-property, was therefore
looked upon with suspicion and accused of witchcraft for dar-
ing to have original thoughts and exercise free will. I
thought . . . I thought the book had burned in the fire, and if it
hadn't, it would've surely been considered witchcraft and thus
burned anyway if found . . .*

(*. . . I guess whoever did find it decided to save it and hide
it rather than destroy the thing. She did eventually get better
at drawing and coloring . . . but confined herself to cataloging
local herbs and legends and the like.*)

(*If the bloodline was diluted after ten generations,*) Jackie asked cautiously, (*how did they rise to prominence several centuries later? Lars has also said that manuscript was carbon-dated to roughly nine hundred years ago.*)

(*Easy. The Feyori created another half-breed in the area. When the two bloodlines met and commingled, it woke the dormant abilities—psychic abilities are not natural to your species,*) she added in a rather casual aside. (*They're not natural to any matter-based species. They are only naturally found in the Feyori themselves because they are energy-based, and manipulate matter via what we call psychic abilities.*)

(*If they're energy-based, and we're matter-based . . .*) Jackie frowned softly, thinking to herself. *Wait, hadn't Li'eth mentioned . . . ?*

(*They transform from energy to matter that is shaped like a particular species, mate with it, and create half-breed bloodlines. In some species, nothing happens—we are all very lucky that psychic abilities do not breed true in the Salik, for instance,*) To-mi pointed out. (*In other races, the change is radical enough to form a permanent subspecies, as found in the Tlassian priest caste—you'll find their training methods almost compatible with your own once you burrow beneath the religious mysticism. But none of the other races have your KI machines, not even the saurians, and so they haven't been able to nail anything down with solid, scientific accuracy. Terran training is going to reshape the face of "holy abilities" all across the Alliance, not just among the V'Dan, you know.*)

That . . . was a lot to wade through. An awful lot to think about. Psychic abilities . . . ? Her own bloodline was a result of . . . ? Jackie didn't know what to think.

(*Based on what I'm reading in your subthoughts, you're most likely the result of two or more bloodlines crossing and spiking in your specific combination of genes,*) To-mi told her. (*But not all such creations are the result of seemingly random breeding programs. One of your progenitors, Jesse James Mankiller, was "redesigned" from the cellular level on up. The act saved her from death, and apparently paid off a debt incurred long after you'll be dead and long before I will be born. If I remember my, ah, unusual history lessons right.*)

Jackie winced, lifting a hand to shield her brow. This was *too* much information. (*Please . . .*)

(*Yes, I suppose that is more than enough for now. But I sense you now believe me . . . ?*)

(*It's possible you could have picked up names of places and bloodlines and such from the other members of my staff, but . . .*) Jackie sighed and lowered her hand, looking up at the ceiling. A lighter shade of plebeian military gray than the walls around them, but only by so many shades. Counterpoint to the darker gray of the floor. The very blandness of it did help to ground her, enough that she asked flippantly, (*Any other revelations from Earth's history you think I should know about?*)

(*I was Ludwig's "Immortal Beloved,"*) To-mi stated.

Jackie blinked and slanted her companion a sidelong look. The entertainment screen was now showing advertisements. Hundreds of light-years from home, and some things just did not change. (*Ludwig . . . ?*)

(*Ludwig van Beethoven. The composer? The incredibly famous composer of that name who went deaf?*) To-mi prodded her.

This was something Jackie knew a bit about, thanks to her grandmother on her father's side. (*That was considered to be Josephine, the countess who was out of his reach.*)

(*He loved her, too, and loved her deeply. But she was not his* immortal *beloved,*) To-mi stated. (*He loved me because I understood him and his music, and could* share *his music with him even as his hearing started to deteriorate.*)

(*Telepathy,*) Jackie realized, and received a faint nod.

(*Exactly.*)

(*So . . . if you've been going around, changing identities, keeping your immortality hidden . . . ?*)

She wrinkled her nose. (*Vienna, 1809. Bonaparte had been bombing it. Ludwig went out for a walk a few days after the bombing had ceased, and was therefore the only eyewitness to a half-bombarded wall falling onto me.*)

(*A wall,*) Jackie repeated dubiously.

(*A stone wall. Squashed me flat, with what looked like a chest-sized block dropped right on my head. Because he was so wrapped up in the music inside his head, I thought he was still in his brother's home nearby, composing, not walking along the street. So I popped back to life on the spot, rather than being discreet about it, and scared him spitless. It took me almost a full hour to get him calmed down and convinced not to mention it to anyone, ever, since no one would believe him, and would instead think he had gone mad. The sanitoriums of the day were ghastly, and he knew it, so he did eventually agree.*

(*It helped that he could hear me fully and clearly . . . and that I helped him "hear" his music on the occasions I could visit. He fell in love with me . . . and for a while, for the time that he lived, I loved him back,*) she finished simply. Her sub-thoughts were closed off, however, unlike the grimness of her opening statement in this conversation.

Jackie considered the other woman's statements for a long moment. (*Either you have giant-sized brass boots as a liar, or you are telling the truth. I . . . can't entirely tell at this point,*) she finally sent. (*You're very good at keeping your thoughts crisp, clear, and contained.*)

(*Thank you. Practice does make perfect,*) To-mi quipped. (*I do have a few of his conversation books carefully preserved. Eventually, when Humans are ready, I'll open up my Vaults and show them whole new glimpses of histories long forgotten. Ideally, that was what was supposed to happen to Mishka's journal.*) A slight frown pinched her brows a little closer together. (*If I'd known, I would have gone back and preserved it properly. That is one piece of history I was never told about. I find that fact mildly annoying.*)

(*Either way, it's definitive proof of contact between Earth and V'Dan in the last one thousand years . . . I think one of my colleagues might have given a language transfer of V'Dan to an historian interested in the Manuscript,*) Jackie confessed. (*I was kept busy giving it to telepaths who could then give it to other people, along with transferring it to various members of my own embassy staff.*)

(*That, and Mandarin? All the translator telepaths in the whole of the League and the Order must've been busier than the proverbial one-legged man in a gluteal-kicking contest,*) To-mi stated dryly.

(*Something like that, yes. Add in on top of that my practicing my holo- and telekinesis for the Merrie Monarch Festival, worrying over my career path, providing cultural-liaison translations on demand for His Highness . . .*)

(*Dealing with the Imperial and First Tiers will be almost a breeze, compared to that,*) To-mi quipped. (*Except you'll also have to deal with Second through Fifth. Mostly Imperial, First, and Third, though.*)

(*Yes, about their Tier system . . .*) Jackie began, only to have their conversation interrupted by a beeping from a device on the other woman's body, some sort of paging tool.

To-mi checked the flat little device and smiled apologetically. "Looks like someone's having a slightly higher fever than usual. A doctor's work is never done. Please excuse me, Ambassador. Your medical staff are good, but I am the resident expert."

"Of course," Jackie allowed graciously. (*Unless this is just a ruse to get out of answering?*)

(*I cannot win all of your battles for you, youngling. Or even just one of them. But I may answer a few questions in due time.*)

———

Li'eth studied both the Terran tablet propped up to one side and the V'Dan workstation screen directly ahead, reading the original Terranglo side by side with the translated V'Dan. Rosa McCrary and a young man named Maraq Sawhney had called him into the matrix lounge, a chamber filled with workstation cubicles. While the two dozen other Terrans in the chamber quietly searched and studied various niches of V'Dan information and entertainment, the three of them worked on something a little more important, in his opinion.

The fellow, Maraq, had been assigned to the embassy for his nonpsychic skills in translation and information retrieval. Whether it was an actual language or figuring out a foreign computer program, Maraq was good at it. He had managed to master the V'Dan data matrices early on—similar to the Terran Internet system—and had been kept quite busy working on various projects Rosa had deemed necessary.

They had reached the point where the most recent "necessary" translation was an in-depth explanation of what a Gestalt was, how it functioned, how to ascertain it was a true mental bond, and how to get the V'Dan people to realize it was a real thing between him and their appointed Ambassador. Li'eth himself had spent some of his own time researching everything he could about the V'Dan versions. They had been stuck in quarantine for weeks now, and it was something useful to do.

"Well, meioa? Is it accurate?" Maraq asked. He was a natural polyglot, not telepathic, so it wasn't as if he could just ask the prince directly, mind-to-mind, and pick up all the subtle nuances that mere speech alone could not always convey. "Or are there any ambiguities that still need to be explained?"

Considering that the translation into V'Dan was almost five times the length of the original, thick with annotations and sidebar explanations . . . Li'eth flicked the text back to the beginning and pointed with a finger. "Shorten up these two sentences in the summary. I believe there's a V'Dan quote you can use instead, one found in the notations I culled from the fortieth century era, pre-Reformation."

"Yes, yes, I know that one," Maraq agreed.

"The more of your own people's experiences we integrate into this presentation, the more they hopefully will accept it," Rosa murmured.

"There you are, Your Highness," a familiar voice called out. Li'eth straightened, turning to face Dr. Jai Du. The pigmentation differences mottling her tan-and-pale face had looked vaguely like *jungen* back in Terran territory, but now that he had been around his own people again, they didn't quite look right.

"Dr. Du," he stated politely.

She nodded in return. "I've already reported this to Ambassador MacKenzie, but she said I should also report it to you . . . and it's good to see you again, Honorable McCrary, since you should know it, too."

"Know what?" Rosa asked.

Du dragged in a deep breath and switched to Terranglo. *"These crazy idiots of yours—and I do normally respect your people, Highness—are insisting that I need to tell you and Jackie that you are not allowed to cuddle. Why are they coming to me with this* yi dwei da buen chuo roh?" she exclaimed, thumping her chest with her fingers. *"And this isn't the first time, either. They have this . . . this* fuhn pi *that I have some sort of authority over all of us. I don't have any authority over you, and I certainly don't have it over the rest of the embassy, save for a few lab assistants. I'm a viral pathologist, not the lao buhn ni'un!"*

"I . . . *don't know those words,*" Li'eth stated cautiously in Terranglo. A glance at McCrary showed that the older woman was blushing.

"*You don't need to know them,*" Rosa told him, her expression grim. "*Du, I don't know why they're coming to you, either. Is it just you, or do you know of anyone else being approached?*"

Du spread her hands, then let her arms and shoulders drop, shaking her head. "*They might be pestering some of the others, but I haven't heard anything. As far as I know, it's just me.*"

"*What do you think we should do about it?*" Li'eth asked her—and got a finger poked at his face.

"*See? That's exactly it! You have the Assistant Ambassador standing here, right next to you, and you are asking me what to do about this?*" Du challenged him. "*This is completely wrong! I'd understand it if it were a question of sanitation or health concerns, but this is . . . this is an* administration *problem. Your people are not grasping who is in charge here. I'm sorry to say that includes you.*"

Li'eth opened his mouth to reply . . . then shut it. Realization flushed heat through his face. His marked face. He studied her marked—if naturally, not *jungen*-based—face, and bowed his head. "*You are right, Dr. Du. I apologize. And I think I figured out why everyone is trying to turn to you. Your, ah, skin colors . . . they aren't exactly* jungen, *but they are much more like the mottled features* my *people expect to see in adults. So . . . your presence here, as the only one possessing anything close to* jungen, *makes you seem like the adult in a crowd of children.*"

"*Even those of us with silver streaks and burgeoning wrinkles?*" Rosa asked dryly.

He was forced to admit it. "*I apologize, meioa, but . . . yes. Your signs of age carry about as much weight as the doctor's younger but mottled face . . . but still, my people will assume she has a tiny bit more authority. Perceived maturity leads to perceived authority.*"

"*This has to stop,*" Du insisted, cutting her hand through the air between them. "*I do not have the authority your people*

*are assuming I have, and they are going to get in deep trouble
if they keep coming to* me *to fix their perception problem."*

"*That's just the way we are,*" Li'eth tried to soothe her. "*If
you could just make allowances—*"

"*That's not—*" both women snapped. Du bowed a little,
gesturing at McCrary to answer for both of them.

"*. . . That is* not *acceptable to us,*" Rosa stated, hands going
to her hips as she stared him down. "*The only allowances we
are willing make is in trying to remember not to take offense
at your people's archaic, skin-based prejudice. But if you think
we are going to* accept *your people trying to force onto Jai Du
a level of authority she* does not have *in the Terran embassy,
your people need to have another think!*"

Li'eth quickly raised both hands, palm toward himself.
"*Please! That first one was the* only *one I meant. Just . . . Dr.
Du, please just tell them plainly that you do not have the
authority they are assuming you have, and direct them to speak
to Rosa or Jackie. If you keep telling them that, they* will *eventually remember it.*"

"*They had* better *start remembering,*" Du snapped, and
turned on her heel to stalk out.

Rosa sighed. "*I was hoping it wasn't so prevalent. I was
hoping that Leftenant Nanu'oc's behavior would be found in
only a small fraction of your people. But I think it really is an
endemic problem.*" Pausing, she switched back to V'Dan. "It
took our own people almost two hundred years to reduce our
own prejudices against skin color and other silly peripherals
to nearly nothing.

"Nearly one hundred years of that was spent in carefully
crafted education programs to help the new generations grow
up with open minds and open hearts, to supplant the bigoted,
close-minded ones as they died off." She looked at Li'eth, her
blue-gray eyes sober, her expression just a touch stern. "I'm
afraid your people won't have nearly that much time to get
over it, Highness. They need to know that treating us like children is unacceptable, and they need to know it right away.

"I am going to recommend to the Grand High Ambassador
that this needs to be the very first issue addressed to your
people," she told him.

Li'eth nodded slowly. "I think it might have to be, Assistant Ambassador."

MAY 10, 2287 C.E.
JANVA 4, 9508 V.D.S.

"¡Buenas tardes, Jackie!"

Jackie struggled up out of her exhausted, fevered sleep at the cheerful greeting from their chief doctor. Prying open her eyes, she saw what looked like Maria de la Santoya directing a troop of Space Force Marines who had already gone through the Terran-adapted *jungen* fever. Under the doctor's command, they assisted her infirmary roommate, Lieutenant Buraq, into a hoverchair and wheeled her off to somewhere, then efficiently stripped the linens off the bed, wiped down all surfaces, and applied fresh sheets and blanket.

Eyes feeling hot, skin tight, head aching and everything sheened in sweat, she managed to prop herself up on an elbow and croak, "What . . . what's happening with Jasmine?"

"She's being relocated to another bed. We have a special patient to share this end of the bay with you. *Señores, se mueven ese equipo, por favor* . . . Yes, the equipment, *gracias.*" As soon as the diagnostics equipment was moved to the other side, she had them pull the bed at the end of the room up close to Jackie's. "*Sí, sí,* touching distance. Just like that . . . wait, lower the side rails so they aren't in the way. Good, now put them back together. *¡Excelente!* Now, bring in our new patient . . ."

Slumping onto her back, Jackie didn't even have to ask who it was. She might be spending most of her time sleeping her way through the virus-induced aches, pains, and heavy fever, oblivious to the world of late, but there was only one reason to put both beds close enough to touch, with no barriers between them. Sure enough, Li'eth came gliding in on a hoverchair guided by yet another soldier drafted for infirmary duty. He looked about half as miserable as she did, flushed and sweating, his attention somewhat distracted, even dazed. The one thing he did display that she was certain she did not was that he looked a bit disgruntled.

Then again, he'd been stripped out of his clothes at some point and tucked into what passed for hospital gowns among the V'Dan. The garments were over-the-head affairs that were sort of like tabards, only they fastened down each side. Thankfully, they came with shorts . . . which also fastened down each side, but at least it added a modicum of modesty.

"I could have walked," he groused as the hoverchair drifted to a halt by the newly moved bed.

"Nonsense. You were wobbling all over the place," Maria countered. "I have no intention of meeting any V'Dan injury lawyers, just because you wanted to be stupid. Onto the bed now, meioa. As I explained in the exam room," she continued, while a pair of muscular Marines assisted him out of the chair and onto the infirmary bed, "the *cause* of your symptoms does not exist. Technically, that makes them 'phantom' symptoms, but the symptoms themselves *are* very real.

"When you are feeling dizzy from Jackie's fever spilling into your brain, *you are* dizzy. You are not suffering from the *jungen* fever that she is, but you *are* suffering from a sympathetic fever. That fever is real, and your V'Dan medical guides on taking all fevers seriously is why I am insisting on putting you into an infirmary bed. The reason why it is a bed next to the Ambassador's is because this is being caused by your Gestalt link, which means the *cure* lies in the Gestalt link.

"And the reason why I am repeating all these points is because *your* people don't know more than three things about holy pairings, whereas *our* people have been scientifically studying them for generations," Maria added tartly. "Now, because this is a side effect of the holy entangling of your brains, you are under *doctor's orders* to hold hands as much as possible while you both recover. But not when you have to go to the washroom. Two fever-weakened people trying to support each other are two people who are too close to falling down and injuring both of themselves.

"Keep the monitoring bracelets on you at all times. I want both Terran and V'Dan medical equipment scanning the two of you at all times. With luck, your presence will trim a day or two off the Ambassador's recovery, so get to it, lie back, and relax," the doctor ordered.

Jackie, having already anticipated the order to hold hands, slid her fingers against Li'eth's the moment he reached for her. His skin felt extra warm, and the pressure of those fingers entwining with hers hurt her joints, but she bore it without complaint. Any pressure was enough to make her body ache; that was a side effect of the virus propagating through the cells of her body, rewriting her genetics. Even the blanket draped up to her waist hurt her hips and legs, not to mention her toes.

"And how are *you* feeling?" Maria asked her, moving to Jackie's side of the conjoined beds. Her eyes were busy reading the monitors, but Jackie knew the older woman was listening.

"Achy, overly hot, exhausted, and more than ready for this to end," she muttered. "Beyond ready. This is far worse than the mild discomforts of acquiring and suffering each other's versions of the common cold—and yes, I know it's because it's rewriting my body."

"Good. You are only allowed to whine once per day about it. Focus instead on your partner. See if the two of you can speed up the process and alleviate your joint fever." She leaned over Jackie's bed, peering at Li'eth's bank of monitors, and nodded. "¡Muy bien! Already I am seeing biometric movement in all the right directions. Subtle, but it is there. I will be back after supper to check on both of you. Behave."

With that, the dark-haired doctor bustled out again, shooing the last of the Terran guards ahead of her. Tired as she was, Jackie couldn't quite get back to sleep just yet. She peeked at Li'eth, feeling how warm he was, seeing the exhaustion in his face. As much as she wanted to reach out to him with her mind, she was aware of how much they were being monitored in this moment. "Couldn't sleep?"

"I'm actually suffering from an excess of it. I suspect it's the bond that has been making me so sleepy," he added. He lifted his other hand to his mouth, stifling a yawn behind it.

"They gave me medicine to help me sleep my way through this," Jackie pointed out. "That's undoubtedly spilling over onto you, too, along with the fever."

He nodded sleepily, then sent privately, (*Maria was thinking very, ah . . . "loudly" . . . when she examined me.*)

(*Yes?*) Jackie prodded him when he hesitated.

(*I picked up from her thoughts that the reason why she waited two full days before insisting on examining me . . . was to ensure there would be plenty of medical evidence to back up the realities of our Gestalt. I think she wanted me to hear those thoughts. Was it wrong to read them, if her permission was unspoken?*) Li'eth asked.

(*Not at all.*) Curling onto her side, she tugged that hand free, switching to the other one so that her right arm could tuck under her pillow. (*She knew in advance that you're a telepath, she knows that touching someone at our level of strength increases the likelihood that you'll overhear her thoughts, and that is something the crafty woman* would *do. This way she can extemporize an excuse, such as, "Oh, I wasn't sure the Gestalt was strong enough that her fever would resonate onto him. But clearly it did, so there's another proof of their holy bond for you, I guess . . ."*)

He smiled faintly. (*Devious Terrans. Plots within plots. Such a doubt would be very reasonable to my people, even generous in the face of their own doubt. And she's not lying about it, either. She's telling the specialists monitoring our every move what she's doing, but doing it in a way that will invite everyone to look at the proofs without forcing them to look.*)

(*Her bedside manner is a bit stern and demanding, but she does know how to juggle reactions in her patients,*) Jackie agreed.

(*Those watchers aren't her patients,*) he dismissed.

(*Are you sure about that?*) she challenged him. (*Terran medicine addresses the mind as well as the body, you know. What she's doing is similar to a massage, I think. Jostling them out of their tight, closed positions, getting them to loosen up and open up to new ideas coming along. We all have our . . . 'scuse the yawn . . . our techniques for that.*)

"That was a big yawn," he murmured out loud. "Why don't you sleep? I'll stay awake awhile longer, and keep watch."

(*Heh,*) she chuckled sleepily. (*Good luck with that. I'm about to go out like a light . . . and I think you are, too . . .*)

(*Perhaps. It's frustrating that I finally get to* sleep *with you . . . and it's still under tight . . .*) He paused for a big yawn of his own. (*. . . surveillance.*)

She managed a mental snort before dropping off, both sympathetic yet realistic about their situation.

─────────

The call came while Jackie and Li'eth were chuckling over some of Dr. Qua's stories involving various different genetic-therapy patients over the years. Since both were lying in bed, snacking on fruit cups from Terran food packets that had been freshly delivered in the last few days, Qua broke off her story and moved to the commscreen when the machine beeped.

"Now, who could be calling you?" she asked. Glancing over her lavender-spotted shoulder, she gestured at the beeping screen. "Should I . . . ?"

"Go right ahead," Li'eth directed her, setting his dessert aside on the overbed table that had been pulled into place. It had been decided before supper had been served that he would eat from the Terrans' food supplies, so as not to contaminate the room with V'Dan histamines before the genetic changes had settled. Ever since the dispatched ships had come back from the halfway point laden with a plethora of packets, the Terrans had been happily selecting their favorites rather than being given random packets and having to find someone willing to trade.

Some were now quite able to have V'Dan food, and were carefully beginning their introduction to the local dishes, albeit with monitoring bracelets and food journals in which they were methodically writing down everything they experienced. "For posterity" and "For science" and "For potential trade" were all phrases being bandied about. But they still craved familiar flavors. More than that, this stuff wasn't space food, overly seasoned in an attempt to compensate for the perennially stuffed-up nose that troubled a traveler in zero gravity.

The screen snapped on, and all thoughts of food vanished from Li'eth's head. His mother, formally dressed in her War Queen regalia, stared sternly through the pickups. "We will speak with His Imperial Highness, Kah'raman—"

Qua quickly dipped her head and moved to the side. "—Of course, Eternity."

As soon as she was out of direct view, Qua tugged on the positioning arm for the commscreen, bringing it over to the bed and angling it just so, so that its pickups were aimed at Li'eth's head. The moment the monitor was in place, she quickly slunk out of the room. To his left, Jackie quietly set her own fruit cup on her own bedside table and leaned on her elbow to watch the screen.

"Imperial Prince Kah'raman," Empress Hana'ka stated formally. "It has been brought to our attention that you are acting inappropriately with a juvenile."

The what . . . ? Face flushing with rage, not just her fever, or even any sense of embarrassment, Jackie grabbed the edge of the monitor and jerked it so that it angled toward her, not toward the Empress' son. Between his presence and their meal, she had enough energy at the moment for some right-eous indignation and had no fear of unleashing it.

"That is *enough*! Pay attention, Empress: I am *four years older* than your son! If anyone is robbing the cradle here, as my people would say, *I* am as the older person. Furthermore, what we are doing is exactly what we *are* supposed to be doing. We are spending time in physical proximity to each other to ensure we both remain healthy, as is *required* of a *Gestalt* pairing."

(*Jackie, please—!*) Li'eth tried to interject, even as his mother narrowed her eyes in anger.

She ignored his mental plea and that affronted glare. "*Every* single time I and my people get called a juvenile by your people, it is an *insult* to our people. You call us juveniles because we are markless, despite our repeatedly telling you how, even in V'Dan time measurements, every single person in this embassy is a full adult. To constantly degrade our ma-turity and respectability is giving your people a very negative impression to my people. Frankly, meioa, I would think it pa-tently obvious that insulting the very allies *your own prophe-cies* say you need to win this war is the *stupidest* thing you could possibly do!"

Hana'ka's eyes widened far enough that the whites could be seen all the way around her gray irises.

"I can only assume you are, one and all, doing it out of sheer, mindless, unthinking ignorance," Jackie added, reining in her temper so that she could be diplomatic. Blunt, but dip-lomatic. "And I will *graciously* instruct my people to forgive and forget every single one of those many insults which have occurred up until this very moment. Your debt is therefore wiped clean, Empress. Be gracious enough to realize that this *is* the proper, diplomatic thing for me to do. But now that you *do* know how much your people are insulting mine, Eternity, I suggest instead that you take pains to start watching every single thing you and your people say to my people.

"We are not juveniles. We are adults. We are *not* V'Dan. We are Terrans. So please, stop *treating* us like juvenile V'Dan," she warned the red-faced, burgundy-striped woman on the other end of the commscreen. "As for how much time we are spending together, your son and I are bound together in ways that, if we are forced to stay separated, will negatively affect *both* our health. These negative effects include depression, anxiety, paranoia, despondency, agitation, spontaneous *teleportation*, and a distinct decline in health, up to and including possible death.

"All of these have been tracked and documented for well over a hundred years by Terran scientists. All of these have *also* been outlined, summarized, reported on in detail, cross-linked to *V'Dan* instances of similarity, and . . . that report *was* sent yesterday, wasn't it?" she asked Li'eth.

"The day before yesterday, about three hours V'Dan Standard after your injection with the modified *jungen* virus," Li'eth told her. (*And I have never seen my mother so speechless, before. I am not certain if this is a good thing or a terrible thing. I do know that no one has ever dared speak to her like this before, but she may simply be waiting to see how much you offend* her *before you are through.*)

"Thank you. All of that was reported to your people two days ago, Empress," Jackie continued, choosing to ignore her partner's cautionary sending. "I realize that may not have been enough time for even the briefest of summaries to have reached you, but I suggest very politely that you back off, find that report, *read it*, and only then—after contemplating everything in that report—you may request a polite conversation on how it might affect Terran-V'Dan relations. *My* government has already considered numerous questions to that effect, and they have chosen to continue placing their trust in me as their selected representative.

"I give you their reassurances as well as my own that I am

quite capable of keeping the needs of my nation separate from the needs of myself in this unexpected, inadvertent, and entirely accidental holy pairing. The strength of our Terran representational government lies in our honor and our honesty, and I have both. Now, if you choose not to believe me right away, I can understand that," Jackie allowed. "But my government requests that you give this situation time to see that my words *and* my deeds match in their integrity, displaying both honor and honesty in abundance.

"I trust, Empress, that I have satisfied the *polite* questions you no doubt had in mind when you called?" she asked.

". . . Are you finished?" Empress Hana'ka asked bluntly.

Jackie thought about it a moment, then stated, "No. Whatever idiot thought you should be so pestered and bothered by *their* prejudices and paranoia as to have to make this call should be chastised because they stirred up far too much trouble. All of which could have been alleviated immediately by stopping to think, to assess, to remember that I am *not* a V'Dan, and which should have been very easily smoothed over by the simple expediency of *remembering* I am not V'Dan.

"From our perspective, Empress, we Terrans stopped treating each other poorly on the basis of our skin color over a hundred years ago. To insult our palpable maturity based purely on our skin color—including our lack of marks—and to treat us as though we have no responsibility, no maturity, and no authority simply because of *skin color* is an archaic insult that we find both bewildering and deeply offensive. Particularly when your subordinates keep going to Dr. Jai Du as if *she* is the ultimate authority.

"I will state this very clearly: Jai Du is *not* a designated arbiter. She does not have any authority in this embassy outside of her specialization as a pathologist and a medical doctor. If your people have a problem with any of my people, they need to bring those concerns either to me or to Rosa McCrary. *We* are the only two with arbitration power in this embassy. Ideally, all such queries should be sent through McCrary, unless it deals with her specifically, then it should be brought to my attention. If at any point it is a matter in which I *do* need to be involved, it will be brought to my attention.

"This was outlined in the list of protocol questions we

answered. That your people should request such protocols be arranged only to ignore the proper, requested procedures does not leave a good impression, Empress. The same as how insulting us by ignoring our actual maturity in favor of some arbitrary skin marks does not give a good impression," Jackie stated. "Your people need to understand that we do consider such things insults and that we will only tolerate so much disrespect before we will be forced to take appropriate action." Her body felt tired and achy from the fever, her mind racing with energy from her meal. Pausing only a moment, Jackie said gravely, ". . . *Now* I am finished. I thank you for listening with such courtesy and patience, Empress."

Hana'ka stared for a long moment, her mouth pressed tight. When she spoke, it was in clipped tones—more clipped than the usual glottal-stop-filled V'Dan. "You speak to me as if you are my equal—"

"—I *am* your equal, Empress," Jackie asserted sternly. "My government is a representational government. I represent the Terran United Planets. *All* of it. My equals in the scope of representation are the Secondaire and Premiere. As an Ambassador, I have the right to propose legislation, *and* the right of the executive branch to see that any treaties are carried out as they pertain to Terran interests in the greater galactic community. I cannot single-handedly authorize a treaty, nor turn a proposed law into an actual law, but those are among only a very few limitations on my power.

"I am third-ranked, yes, but third-ranked in a government system completely *unlike* your own. I am *not* the equivalent of a child who stands to inherit. I am *not* a princess to any throne. *I am higher ranked* than any princess could ever be. Nor have I been given my great authority on a whim. My people have voted to grant me the power to determine all policies in regards to how your people are handled—they bestowed their confidence in me *knowing* of the holy pairing your son and I are now in. With that vote, I have the power to veto any suggestions you make about your treaties with us. I hold the authority to send our ships into battle at your side. I also hold the power to send them into your face. I am *responsible* for all such orders, and I must report my reasons to the Council as a whole and be judged accordingly, but that does not make me a *subordinate*.

"I say it again, and I hope you carve it into your brain this time: I am *not* V'Dan. My people are *not* V'Dan. Our government is *not* V'Dan. Terrans are *not* V'Dan. We are the same species, but we are *not* the same culture," Jackie asserted. "Your son is attempting to remind me *telepathically* not to insult you, but this is *not* an insult. This is information you clearly need in order to be able to accept, assimilate, and access it each and every time you address one of us. In a representational government, when I say I represent the *entire* Terran United Planets when I stand before you . . . or lie here in an infirmary bed," she amended wryly, "then that means I *am* your equal.

"So yes, I can and *do* speak to you as a peer, Empress Hana'ka V'Daania," Jackie told her. "I realize you are not accustomed to considering very many people your equal, and none of them a fellow *Human*, a member of your same species, before now. But until the Secondaire or the Premiere stand here with me, outranking me in person, I *have* that level of authority. There is nothing you can do or say to remove that power from me. Only an act of the Terran Council can do so. You are *not* Terran and have no vote in such matters. Just as I have no say in your being Empress of V'Dan.

"I apologize for diverting your planned speech, but it is clear that there are a lot of preconceptions and misconceptions that need to be clarified between us. I admit that I have an advantage in that I have been able to ask His Highness many questions about your government structure, and that you have not had any similar opportunities of your own. One day, we will both hopefully know enough about each other that such interruptions will no longer be necessary."

"You seek to correct me?" Hana'ka asked, lifting a blond brow. Unlike her son, none of her burgundy *jungen* stripes, small and more frequent than his, crossed her eyes. None came farther onto her cheeks than their edges, in fact.

"I seek to save you from making costly diplomatic mistakes out of ignorance. My people have a saying, Eternity," Jackie said. "There is a difference between ignorance and stupidity. Ignorance can be cured through education and enlightenment."

Her eyes narrowed. The Empress lifted her chin slightly. "You said earlier that to continue to . . . insult . . . your people would be an act of great stupidity."

"In light of your apparent prophecies proclaiming you will need our help, yes," Jackie agreed. "Insulting someone over and over makes it that much less likely they will want to assist you in any way. My oaths as a member of the Terran government require that I offer assistance to your government to ensure our interactions are mutually beneficial. But I cannot behave properly *for* your people. Neither am I a rug to be walked upon by everyone in the room. If they or you insist on continuing to treat us in ways that we find insulting, after we have informed you that they are insulting to us, then *that* would be an act of stupidity, not an act of ignorance.

"Mature people cease performing the actions or speaking the words that insult another person, once informed of the transgression. Only the young think they can get away with such things indefinitely even after they've been enlightened. Neither of us are *that* young, Empress," she finished dryly.

Hana'ka lifted a brow, her own voice just as dry. "You think you are as old as I am?"

"I am told that V'Dan and Terran years are very close to each other in length, to within less than a single day. The age of adulthood in Terran society is eighteen. I have been told that the age of legal adulthood in V'Dan is, coincidentally, also eighteen. For your people, this means the age at which they have most likely passed through the *jungen* fever, plus have acquired a sufficient level of education to function as an independent adult. My people don't have the virus, but we also expect our youth to be educated and behave with maturity and responsibility by the time they turn eighteen.

"I am thirty-six, Empress Hana'ka, which means I am *twice* that age." She could feel her headache from the fever coming back, and hoped the conversation would end soon. Or rather, the hammering home that she was not a juvenile and would not stay quiet at being insulted like that again. "I may not be sixty-two, like you, but I have not been treated like a child in a very long time. Just like you.

"I have served for five years in our military, with the responsibility—the burden—of fending off a technologically vastly superior foe with just the power of my holy gifts. I have served for years as a government translator, with the weight of ensuring that no mistranslations lead to costly misunderstandings among literally hundreds of different cultures. I have served as a Councilor, responsible for the safety and well-being of millions of people. I am now responsible for the safety and well-being of *billions* of people. Every single member of this ambassadorial delegation, staff and guard alike, has also long since been proved to be a responsible, mature *adult*. Just. Like. You.

"Now, do you have an actual problem, Empress? One which only I or your son can handle? Because I am sore, tired, feverish, I have a headache building, and I need to rest. As a consequence of our inadvertent holy bond, your son is *also* sore, tired, feverish, and in need of rest."

"Then you will break that bond. I will not have my son—"

"—Your *ignorance* is showing again, Empress," Jackie interrupted, rolling her eyes in a silent plea to her ancestors for patience. "The only way to break this bond is death. Long-term separation brings deep depression, anxiety, and a decline in health that leads to each partner's dying. Slaying one of us will cause the murder of the other as well. There is *nothing* that all of Terran science has been able to uncover that can stop this process. Your V'Dan mysticism is even less useful, given its sheer ignorance of *psychic* abilities. We can barely slow down the progression of this bond as it stands. I agree that it is inconvenient, but it is also not an obstacle."

"*I* believe that this bond is an advantage, Empress, not a disadvantage," Li'eth stated, asserting his own political opinion. "The Ambassador and I are being forced by it to see past shallow differences of skin color and cultural expectations. We are forced to find compromises that benefit us both. We are forced to respect each other as individuals as well as representatives of each other's culture."

"I do not recall appointing you as such," Hana'ka told her son.

"That is irrelevant, Empress. I *am* a representative of our people because of this bond," he told her.

"You seem confident that they understand holy pairings. Are you so certain they understand such things far better than we do?" she asked.

"I have zero doubt, Empress," he confirmed. "The Terrans are vastly superior to the V'Dan, the Solaricans, and even the Tlassian priest caste in their understanding of all such holy abilities, whether it is speaking mind-to-mind, seeing emotional auras, even to how to train the summoning of holy fire to appear *at will*, my Empress. I have absolute confidence in their understanding of holy pairings because they have spent *generations* of time in scientifically studying their holy pairs.

"I have spoken with many different holy ones. I have been given instruction by a *professional* trainer. It was just a few weeks' worth of training, but already I have so much more control over my abilities that I feel like the holiest of priests is a stumbling child by comparison, now that I can safely walk through the universe without feeling like I might accidentally set someone on fire . . . and I myself am *still* a stumbling child in turn, compared to the mental acrobatics and athleticism of someone like the Grand High Ambassador, who underwent years of formal training in her youth and who has been using her abilities consistently for decades."

"There is no shame in admitting to a point of ignorance," Jackie stated. That refocused Hana'ka's attention on her. "Doing so simply says, 'I know I do not know this subject, and I am ready to be enlightened on it.' There is, in fact, great honor in being willing to learn. I state freely that I am ignorant about artificial gravity. My people acknowledge our ignorance openly and agree that we have much to learn about it. If you want to know about artificial gravity, you go to someone who understands it. You find an expert in gravitics, you ask questions, and you listen to what they have to say. This is no different.

"Read the report we prepared," she repeated. Tired now, she let her eyelids drift shut as she spoke. "As His Highness has said, it is backed by decades of solid, observed-and-tested data, if not centuries. He has personally overseen its translation, and specifically its correlation to similar incidents reported in your *Book of Saints* on holy gifts and holy pairings. If you have more questions after having read it, you may come to me, or to any of our four holy-gifted translators. Particularly Heracles Panaklion, who is a certified instructor of such things." Struggling to get her eyes open again, Jackie eyed the woman on the commscreen. "Now, is there anything else you need to discuss at this time?"

"If my son's health is being affected by yours . . . how are *you* doing?" the Empress asked her.

Her inquiry sounded sincere. Jackie rubbed at the bridge of her nose and sighed. "Exhausted. Tired of feeling ill. Tired of aching all over. And I have no experience in managing *biokinetics*—what you call holy healing—and neither does your son, so neither of us knows how to speed this up. Nor do we know if it's safe to do so deliberately since I am having my genetic code rewritten in every cell of my body. And what I want right now, more than most anything else, is to just put my head on his shoulder and sleep, because touching each other alleviates some of the pains and the aches. But I am prohibited from doing so because of all this cultural *crap*."

"Crap?" Hana'ka repeated, uncertain of the Terranglo word.

"Shakk," Li'eth translated.

His mother colored a little but diplomatically ignored the blunt, inelegant word. "If it will alleviate your suffering . . ."

Jackie seized on that hesitant statement. "Thank you." Rolling off her elbow, she dropped her face against Li'eth's tunic-covered shoulder, tucked her arm around his waist, and closed her eyes with a heavy sigh. "Feel free to have a conversation. I'm going to rest, now."

Li'eth prodded her mentally into shifting just enough that he could unbury his arm from how she draped over his side. Tucking his biceps under her head, he stretched it out, then curled his arm back in. Fingers cupping her hair, he cradled her head on his shoulder and met his mother's stare. "This is the most physically intimate we have been, Empress. No matter what she may look like to ignorant eyes, neither of us are juveniles, to be ruled by unthinking hormones."

(*You tell her,*) Jackie agreed, snuggling into the warmth and faint musk of his chest. (*You tell 'er . . . we're not stupid kids . . .*)

(*You're putting* me *to sleep, with your sleepiness,*) he warned her.

(*Too bad. Comf't'ble.*)

"I am feeling tired as well, Mother . . . Perhaps it would be better to discuss this later, *after* you've read their report?" she heard him add pointedly. "That way, neither of us wastes your time in reviewing redundant information."

The Empress said something, but it was all nonsense now to Jackie's fever-tired mind.

CHAPTER 7

MAY 14, 2287 C.E.
JANVA 8, 9508 V.D.S.

Jackie eyed the three-lobed, reddish, pear-like fruit in her hand. Their combined food-and-medical crisis had started with one of these, and now she had the privilege of finally being able to taste one. Just as she brought it up to her lips, Dr. Kuna'mi came over with a tray of her own food—the kitchen was finally producing full meals for nearly everyone—and projected a thought her way.

(*Careful,*) the odd, markless woman stated, smiling at Jackie. (*That might taste good.*)

Jackie hesitated only a moment before biting into the rind, which was supposed to be edible. That, and a source of histamines. It was tangy, sweet, and slightly bitter, with a perfume reminiscent of mint and pears and a hint of lemon, but mostly pears. (*The V'Dan name for this translates as "red pear," doesn't it?*)

Shrugging subtly, To-mi picked up her *umma*, poking the local-style spork into her casserole dish. (*So I didn't have that much of an imagination. Its full original name was* ka-rousho'p'ari, *which means three-lobed-red-skinned-pear. Calling it a* roush-p'ari *just took out two syllables.*)

The two ate in silence a few minutes until Jackie set down the uneaten core. The seedpods were long, triangular things, almost shaped like canoes, and she had been warned in her language transfer not to eat them. In the V'Dan language, they were called *v'pou-da shova*, or the *seeds of explosive expelling*.

Not in the sense of inducing vomiting, but rather, it involved the opposite end of things. By comparison, Terran pear seeds were downright harmless.

Her mind wasn't fully on the inedible portion of the fruit, however. It was on a random thought. (*Why seven days?*)

(*Clarify?*) To-mi sent back.

(*I know why on Earth; the Moon's quarters can be broken up into approximately seven-day spans. I know the innermost moon here has a roughly one-month cycle, but . . .*)

(*The moons are only a small portion of the reason why. It's because of the Pleiades. They're often called the Seven Sisters, or Seven Puppies, or Seven Little Boys . . . lots of myths, but not really for that reason, either. The disaster happened when the Pleiades were high in the sky. Everyone on Earth remembered it as a Day of the Dead, the Day of the Flood, the Day We Were Saved from Our Doom . . . and the V'Dan remember it as the Day of the D'aspra, the Day of Salvation, the Day of New Life.*

(*Except the V'Dan don't have the same viewpoint of the actual Pleiades star cluster here that we had back home, nor do they have any knowledge of the "modern" legends from the last five millennia on Earth,*) To-mi added. She nibbled on a piece of herbed bread slathered in V'Dan butter, made from cattle that had evolved on V'Dan after having been treated with a bovine-friendly version of the *jungen* virus so that they, too, could feast on the local plant life without problems. (*There are legends of the Seven Saints, however, overseers for the various sections involved in the d'aspra.*)

(*Well, we are coming up on a V'Dan weekend equivalent. In two more days, we finish packing up and head down to the embassy and suites reserved for us; in three, we settle in . . . and on day four, the equivalent of a Tuesday, we get presented to the Empress.*)

(*I heard from my colleague, who lurked outside your infirmary room, that you gave Her Eternity a bit of a shocking setback, talking to her like a peer.*)

Jackie looked over at the blue-eyed woman with features that were more Asian than Caucasian. She wasn't about to back down from what she saw as the truth. (. . . *And?*)

To-mi smiled at that. Her face radiated warmth, approval,

and a hint of mischief that might not have been amiss on one of the *kupua*, the heroic tricksters of Hawai'ian legends. (*I'm not shocked. I do understand the Terran mind-set these days. I am wondering how she took it, however.*)

(*I think she's getting used to it. We had a polite conversation on how to handle the physical-proximity needs between His Highness, who will be quartered as usual in the Imperial Palace, and I, since I will be quartered with the other Terrans in the Diplomatic Palace.*)

(*. . . And?*) To-mi prompted when Jackie said no more, her tone lighter than Jackie's had been.

(*And it's still undecided. She wants to control all such meetings to be physically decorous. I don't think she gets why that isn't going to last,*) Jackie stated.

(*Well, he* is *a delicious-looking fellow,*) To-mi allowed. That earned her a hard stare from the Ambassador. She shrugged again. (*What? I'm only over fourteen thousand years old. That is* not *the same thing as being dead. He is both handsome and a good man, and I am pansexual enough to appreciate both qualities whenever they are found together, which means I find you* appealing *as well—but I am* also *polite enough not to poach, so you may relax.*)

"Grand High Ambassador," someone called over the galley hall's intercom. "Please come to the matrix room. You have a comm call from Imperial First Lord Ksa'an."

Sighing, she stood and started gathering the rubbish from her meal. "I'll be glad when we can set up our own communications system in the embassy zone and use our own commlinks. I don't blame the V'Dan for being cautious about foreign communications systems on a military station, but at least on the planet, we can set up our own network."

The *jungen* specialist held out her hand, palm toward herself. "You go and answer your call. I'll take care of your luncheon things when I take care of mine."

"Thank you. That's very kind of you," Jackie told her.

To-mi smiled wryly. "I'm just glad you *can* eat V'Dan food, now. Safely, that is."

"I'll be even more glad when we can send home shiploads of the modified virus and start curing all those *allergies*," Jackie stated, using the Terranglo word since there was no equivalent in V'Dan. *Histamines*, yes. *Antihistamines*, yes. But not *allergies* or *allergic reaction*, or any variant thereof. "Too many people have suffered and even died over something your people haven't known for nearly ten thousand years."

"You'll have some people wanting the marking version," To-mi warned her. "Those who will want to admire and emulate the V'Dan. But I think you are doing the right thing, requesting and requiring a nonmarking version—and not just because I'm getting my full due respect among you markless Terrans."

(*Understood,*) Jackie returned silently. Out loud, she merely said, "We like who we are, these days. Some days more than others . . . but still, we like who we are. Thank you for taking care of my tray, Doctor."

"My pleasure, Ambassador."

―――――――――

"And at that point, I swap outfits and introduce the military contingent as the local military commander-in-chief," Jackie confirmed. "The introduction includes the performance of a *haka*, at the, ah, rather enthusiastic request of the soldiers. Out of ninety-four of us, eighty-seven voted for it, and the rest abstained—my performance at a hometown festival was broadcast on a lot of news bands in our version of the matrix. A couple of the troops and I demonstrated a sample of it to Admiral Superior Jes-na Tal'en-qua just this morning, and she thinks it will be appropriate for the Imperial Court."

"That is good to know, but there is something in that which I do not understand," Ksa'an stated from his side of the monitor screen. "You're going to be there the entire time. How will you be changing clothes from your civilian garments as the Grand High Ambassador to the uniform of your role as the commander of your military contingent?"

"*Holokinesis.* I . . . one moment, meioa," Jackie said, breaking off their discussion when she realized one of the soldiers in question had entered the room and stopped next to her. She switched languages to Terranglo, facing the dark-skinned woman. *"Yes, Corporal?"*

"I'm sorry, sir," the corporal stated politely, if somberly. *Sir* was considered these days to be the correct term for a

superior commissioned officer, regardless of gender. *"I was instructed by Commander Graves to contact you immediately and give you this."*

She held out a datapad. Frowning, Jackie accepted it and flicked the button to turn it on. On the pad desktop, a large icon had been left prominently in the center. Tapping it, she watched it unfold into a recorded comm message. It was her brother-in-law, Maleko Bennington. He looked haggard, his hair a mess, clad in rumpled, dirty clothes.

"Aloha, Jackie. It's been twelve hours since Hurricane Thomas the Ninth hit the Isles. Just . . . just over two hours ago, your tutu, Leilani . . . she passed away. We think it was, ah, first a heart attack brought on by the strain of trying to help everyone get to the storm shelters and get themselves organized, and then a stroke. Ah . . . they weren't . . ." He looked away from the screen, and the lighting in whatever concrete-lined room he was in gleamed along the edges of his eyes. *"We have medics here at the shelter, but they weren't able to revive her. I know you can't make it back in time for the funeral . . . so Hyacinth is going to . . . she and your brother Jacques will stand in for you, together. He'll be flying up from Australia in a few days.*

"Your mother flew in on a government craft, and is out busy assessing the damage. Hyacinth is telling her right now. I stayed at the shelter with Tutu Leilani and the kamali'i . . . Alani is taking it hard; she was with her tutu when Leilani collapsed the second time. Hyacinth says half the south shore was flooded by a storm surge. The schools are going to be okay, but she hasn't gotten near the house, yet. But we'll be okay," Maleko stated, looking into the camera. *"Everyone had warning, we all shuttered our homes and got to the shelters.*

"We'll be okay," he repeated. *"I know Leilani wanted to meet the Empress, but . . . Maybe you can ask if a cupful of her ashes can be scattered on V'Dan?"* he offered, attempting a joke. It fell a little flat. He wiped at his cheek, then managed a second wavering smile. *"We've already had people coming up to us, swearing that if they survived in the houses, they'll be donating some of the bits of the na lei given to the off-worlders and left behind for souvenirs, to spread on the waves during her funeral.*

"Look, you don't worry about us, okay?" Maleko asked the camera recording his message. *"Aside from Leilani, everyone is* fine. *You take care of yourself, wahine makua. Aloha nui loa, a hui hou,"* he finished.

The recording ended. Jackie didn't remember when her left hand had left the tablet in the care of her right. It pressed now over her mouth while her eyes stung with grief.

"Ambassador, is something wrong?"

Blinking hard, she returned her gaze to the V'Dan screen. The green-striped face of Li'eth's cousin looked jarringly odd, but the expression on the nobleman's face was one of genuine concern. A moment later, she felt a tap on her mental walls, and the soothing touch of Li'eth's mind reaching out to hers.

(*Something has upset you. What happened?*)

(*Grandmother Leilani is dead . . . and I'm stuck here, hundreds of light-years away. I can't go back to pay my respects.*)

(*I'm sorry, Bright Flower,*) he soothed her, wrapping her in a mental hug.

The world around her faded into the background, leaving them mostly embracing on the beach in his memories. The beach in her memories, of seeing her grandmother lounging on that beach, running along it in laughter, hauling around a surfboard until her late seventies, celebrating many an occasion with a *lu'au* shared with friends and family and anyone who happened to be strolling along the beach in front of her house . . .

(*She was a wonderful woman. I think Mother would have liked her,*) Li'eth murmured.

Jackie struggled not to break down in tears. She knew she wasn't on that beach in reality. She had to maintain control. She had to be dignified . . .

"I'm sorry, meioa," she heard the corporal apologizing. "The Ambassador has just received word that her grandmother has passed away, the head of her mother's family. Perhaps it would be better to continue in a few hours, when she has had some time to grieve?"

"Of course. I offer our condolences for the Ambassador's loss. I will call again in four hours," Ksa'an stated.

Dragging her attention back to the real world, Jackie opened

her eyes in time to see the corporal shutting off the monitor.
". . . Thank you."

"I'm sorry as well, sir," the corporal stated gently. "The
comm system on the *Embassy 1* is ready and waiting for you
if you want to make a call back home immediately. If not, it
will remain on standby."

"I'm . . ." She wasn't ready for this sort of news. She needed
a few minutes of privacy in which to break down . . . but a part
of her knew it would be *good* for the V'Dan to see how a Terran handled her grief. "I shall go see someone, and . . . compose myself. Then I'll go to the ship. In a little bit. Thank you
for bringing this to me, Corporal," Jackie added, offering back
the pad.

"Of course, sir. I'm just sorry it had to be delivered. Will
you need an escort anywhere, sir?"

Jackie sniffed. "Ahh . . . somewhere that has some tissues
for my nose and eyes."

Smiling, the younger woman dug a small, wadded stack of
tissues out of her thigh pocket. "My drill instructor said a
good Marine was always supposed to be prepared, sir. So did
my grandmother, before she passed away."

"Thank you." Rising from her chair, Jackie wiped at her
eyes, blew her nose, and headed out of the communications
room. She could sense Li'eth headed her way, and decided a
detour to the hydroponics garden was in order.

There, among green growing things . . . and some things
that were yellow and blue and peach in hue . . . she would let
herself grieve. It was popular with the Terrans now that all but
the last handful of patients in the infirmary were safe to go
anywhere that V'Dan plant life grew. Someone had dragged
in chairs, setting up little lounging areas that annoyed the
V'Dan robots programmed to tend the plant life; the Terrans
moved their chairs from time to time whenever the machines
drew near but otherwise ignored the things.

There, in the only place that could even remotely be said to
be Hawai'ian in appearance, she would grieve. Jackie would
grieve, and do her best to get the urge to cry through her system
because they were on an increasingly short schedule between
this moment and the moment of full, formal presentation.

But maybe, just maybe, she *would* ask if she could have a small container of her grandmother's ashes shipped to V'Dan, to be scattered on the beaches of an alien planet. Her grandmother had loved their home isles fiercely, but even she had been caught up in the fascination of meeting Humans from another world. Leilani *had* wanted to come here. Someday.

MAY 16, 2287 C.E.
JANVA 10, 9508 V.D.S.
CITY OF THE WINTER PALACE
V'DAN HOMEWORLD, V'DAN SYSTEM

Seen from above, the various main buildings and interconnecting structures of the Winter Palace gleamed like a series of necklaces and pendants forged in slightly iridescent gold. They gleamed, filigree laid among a myriad of snow-dusted gardens, which in turn were surrounded by sprawling buildings of a hundred different styles of architecture, if not more.

"This city has been occupied for almost the entire span of recorded civilization," Li'eth told Jackie. He pointed at the monitor screen. "The Winter Palace has been remodeled multiple times, of course, but if you look past that escort ship, just beneath it, you can see the sunlight glinting on the bay. And right there, a finger in that bay, is the first of the three ancient lighthouses for the bay. That one has been standing more or less intact for almost ninety-five hundred years."

Maria, seated just ahead of them, peered at her own monitor. "It looks like it's made out of huge stone blocks."

"How else would anything last over nine thousand years?" Li'eth quipped back. "It's said the Immortal chose to build in stone because stone is the only thing that can outlast *her.*"

"Yes," Lars agreed. "But you have to pick the *right* stone. Pick the wrong kind, and it crumbles like sand. Even sandstone," he added on a soft chuckle.

"Imperial Landing Control to Embassy 1*, you are cleared for approach to Imperial Hangar 3 behind* Imperial First Escort. *Do not deviate from your flight path."* The voice came through Jackie's headset, distracting her. At this point in their journey, answering Landing Control was the pilot's job, however.

"This is Embassy 1. *Our flight path is acknowledged,"* Robert replied, *"and we are following* Imperial First Escort *to our landing site, over."* He tilted their ship to follow their lead escort's flight path in circling around the edge of those golden buildings.

". . . Over, what, Embassy 1*?"*

"It . . . means . . . my part of the speaking is over?" he replied hesitantly, while Jackie bit her lip in an effort not to laugh. *"It's a Terran call-and-response thing."*

Off mic, Jackie muttered, "So many little differences, so little time to remember, explore, and explain them all . . ."

"We'll get them learned and explained eventually," Li'eth reassured her. His cousin had wanted him to descend in a different ship until Li'eth had pointed out that it would be best to have a protocol officer on board for any last-moment explanations, and that it would be proper to honor their arrival by having one of the Imperial Tier escort them the full way to their new quarters.

"Those buildings are much bigger than I thought," Lars exclaimed softly. "It's one thing to gauge distances on Earth, because we know what the buildings are like in size, but this . . . ?"

"The First Empress did not build small," Li'eth agreed, eyeing the massive, pyramid-shaped structures. "There, between those two squared-off buildings; that's Imperial Hangar 3. It's assigned to the embassies, so it has the least amount of traffic."

"It's like flying over a surrealistic, modern Chichen Itza," Maria murmured.

"Only with far fewer trees, and many, many more buildings," Lars agreed. "Those plazas are also huge down there."

"Those are the celebration tiers," Li'eth told them. "The biggest two at the far end are for the Fifth and Fourth Tiers, then the Third Tier is fully upon the Imperial grounds—the stairs between each Tier's courtyard can be raised in case of rioting, cutting off access to anything higher."

"Here we go, people," Robert warned them. Their vessel straightened out under his hands, and aimed for a low opening tucked between two flat-topped, iridescent, gold-coated structures.

"You'll be in the building on the left. Because your embassy is so large to start with, we've moved the K'Katta to the building on the right," Li'eth said. "They were very gracious about it. Grand High Ambassador K'kuttl'cha said this also makes more sense; she wouldn't have to trot all the way over to the right-hand building to talk about joint-colony matters with her counterpart among the Gatsugi . . . and then she joked about how she might get fat from lack of exercise. The K'Katta *don't* get fat," he added. "They just either regurgitate or excrete more often. So it was a joke."

"If that was a joke, then your waste-management facilities would be the ones getting fat," Lars quipped, smiling. "A potbellied toilet would be funny."

(*Oh, great, here comes the bathroom humor. I guess he forgot that this is all still being recorded for posterity.*) Jackie sighed.

(*Well, the Imperial Family is not supposed to jest about such things, officially . . . but flatulence happens,*) Li'eth pointed out, smiling faintly.

They ran out of time for jokes. The gleaming winter sunlight vanished, replaced by artificial lights as all but the first of the escort vessels peeled off, and the string of Terran ships slowed and ducked into the hangar bay. There had been some concern expressed on the maneuverability of Terran vessels, since their design was clearly aerodynamic—gliding-flight capable—while the hangars were designed for vertical landings and takeoffs.

But as smoothly as if he had practiced and run this course a hundred times before, Robert brought the *Embassy 1* to a hovering stall via the thruster panels, turned the craft, and followed the portside tunnel under the huge building that was supposed to be their home. Terran embassies of the recent past had often been stand-alone affairs, with whatever patch of ground they occupied being considered a legal part of the nation represented in the building. V'Dan embassies were different, with their occupants being treated as honored guests in the local leadership's home.

Jackie knew privately that her fellow Terrans felt this guaranteed there would be listening devices installed in their quarters, no matter what the V'Dan might promise. But since they had yet to establish any sort of international currency exchanges, there was no way as yet for them to buy property and build an independent embassy upon it. The only thing right now that guaranteed them any privacy was the fact that every last one of her people, even the reluctant Lieutenant Colvers, now spoke Mandarin . . . and none of the V'Dan knew that language. Not even Li'eth. *Except maybe the Immortal, but I'm not sure if she counts, since she'd have to explain* how *she knows it.*

But there would be watchers and eavesdroppers. Openly visible as well as covert or denied.

While their escort vehicle tucked itself into an alcove, they in turn landed on a huge octagon as directed. As it began descending, more instructions came forth. "Embassy 1, *your assigned berth is North 5-10 through 5-13, due starboard of the descent elevator. Understand that in the event of an emergency, the lift will immediately descend to the lowest level and remain there, clearing the tunnel for direct escape by all vertical-ascent vehicles. All Terran vehicles have been assigned berths in hangars Bay 3 North 5 and Bay 3 North 6.*

"*Acknowledged, Hangar 3 Control,*" Jackie answered, since Robert was busy peering at the ships on the hangar floors they descended past.

While the city up above had looked clean and shiny, even under patchy scatterings of snow slowly melting in the winter sun, down here, the local version of concrete looked grimy from untold years of petrochemical exhaust. There were scratches and scrapes on the walls, fading bits of paint, and sections that had been freshened with brighter colors in recent days. And there were robots in view, sweeping the ground, toting toolboxes, and being of general use. More than the Terrans used, but then it had only been just over one hundred years since the AI War back on Earth.

The vehicles in the other bays—North 1 and 2 looked like they were reserved for Solaricans, North 3 and 4 for Tlassians, given the shapes of the sentient figures working among the various craft and support columns—came in a wide array of sizes and types, from a couple about the size of the *Embassy 1*, to a handful of the *Embassies 2* through *15*, to dozens and dozens of what looked like V'Dan-style hovercars. Some had panels open and parts strewn around. Others looked like they were being refueled.

Then North 5 came into view. It, too, was brightly lit, but most of the hangar-bay floor was barren, emptied of vehicles and equipment. To the left—portside—as the lift finished descending and jolted lightly, stopping flush with the floor, there were about forty hovercars parked in between the columns in the distance, and what looked like *Embassy 4* and *5* parked in the far corners on that side. Six brown-clad Marines stood on the ground dead ahead in front of six more V'Dan clad in red-and-gold uniforms, with cream trousers instead of the usual red.

Both sets of warriors stood there with their weapons holstered and bodies braced in somewhat similar versions of Parade Rest. A good score or more of what had to be V'Dan staff and hangar personnel stood behind them, save for two figures in bright reflective clothes waving lightsticks to the ship's right. Ground crew was ground crew, it seemed, regardless of which world one occupied.

The view of those vehicles and personnel out the portside windows shifted; murmuring more to himself than into his headset, Robert lifted them off the elevator pad. He glided the ship to the right and simultaneously turned it to the left, spinning slowly enough that when they landed, the nose of their ship pointed straight at the lift pad and the cluster of transports far beyond. As soon as they touched down, the lead Marine gestured; the other five snapped to Attention, turned, and moved toward the ship. The V'Dan followed suit, their red boots crossing the concrete floor in unison; the V'Dan hangar workers trailed cautiously behind.

Jackie checked the freshly painted V'Dan numbers on the columns surrounding them. *"Hangar 3 Control, the* Embassy 1 *has landed. Thank you for guiding us in. We look forward to the arrival of the rest of our fleet.* Embassy 1 *is shutting down . . . now."*

"Acknowledged, Embassy 1. *We hand control of your ship over to the ground crew in North 5."*

Robert and Brad finished shutting off the engines. "And that's that," the Texas-born Asian murmured, reaching up overhead to tap switches, shutting off the heads-up display overlaid on the forward-facing windows. "Welcome to V'Dan."

"I think that should be my line," Li'eth quipped. "As you say, welcome to V'Dan."

"Brad, would you go coordinate with the ground crews on fueling procedures?" Robert asked his copilot. "I can finish up in the cockpit."

"I'll get started on showing the others which cupboards and lockers to open," Lars offered, meaning the soldiers and staff tucked into jumpseats in the other cabins of the ship. Some they would know they could touch because those contained their personal belongings. Others were split between supplies that had to be kept on board and supplies that were meant to be off-loaded and carted to their new home.

"I'll go greet Captain al-Fulan and his troops," Jackie said. Li'eth unlatched his harness at the same time as she did, but they both waited for Lars to get out of the way since he was first out of his seat.

Brad rose to follow them, muttering half to himself. "Join the Space Force. Be an experimental vessel pilot. Meet friendly new aliens, and convince them, yet again, that we just need *water* for fuel, not liquid toxins . . . I hope these guys—these meioas," he corrected dryly, "will actually believe me when I say all we want is a garden hose."

"I reinforced your request when I heard the *Dusk Army*'s fueling crews complaining about it," Li'eth told him. "You won't have to jury-rig a funnel from the watering line to your tanks."

"Somehow, Your Highness, I doubt they've magically crafted Terran-style fuel pumps out of thin air," Colvers stated sardonically, staring him down.

"No, but they'll have several sizes of funnels available this time around, so no jury-rigging will be needed for that part, at least," Li'eth pointed out mildly. He offered a brief smile.

"Don't quit your day job, Highness . . . but thank you," Colvers acknowledged. He did not like psychics, and no doubt was staying back so that he wouldn't even accidentally brush against the prince, but at least he was acting a lot more cooperative and polite these days. Mostly polite. "Eventually, we *will* convince your people to cut out the dangers of petrochemicals."

(*Don't quit my day job?*) Li'eth asked Jackie, following her out of the cockpit cabin.

(*He means your attempt at humor wouldn't be good enough to make a living in the evenings, doing stand-up comedy.*) She sent him a series of mental images to explain it, too.

(*Ah. Well, I* cannot *quit my day job. No one is released from the Imperial military during wartime until the enemy is defeated and the war is declared ended,*) he remind her.

"*Ah-ah!*" Lieutenant Buraq squeezed ahead of Jackie, lightly slapping the other woman's hands away from the portside airlock controls. "You do *not* leave this ship until a Marine has determined it is *safe*, Ambassador."

Li'eth cupped Jackie's shoulders as the woman carefully checked the readouts for the exterior air. That took only half a minute, but she also checked a visual sweep of the wing area with the monitor, another half minute. Finally, she opened the airlock cautiously . . . and straightened once she was satisfied, stepping to the side.

"You may now safely disembark, Ambassador, Highness."

"Thank you, Lieutenant." Jackie didn't protest too much at the safety precautions. On their own world, most safety precautions were built into their infrastructure. Here . . . it all had to be manually checked until they could build their own embassy enclave, with their own materials, their own plans, and their own labor.

Outside, the steps had already been unfolded from the shuttle's underbelly. Captain al-Fulan awaited her at the bottom, his uniform crisp, his hand lifted to his brow. "Ten-*hut!*"

His five Marines snapped to Attention, lifting their hands to their temples as well. They stood just beyond the ramp on either side, clad in their Dress Browns like their captain, waiting for Jackie to descend. She did so. As soon as she reached the bottom, she lifted her hand in a brief return salute, fingers straight, hand and forearm angled just so. That permitted them to lower their arms. She turned to al-Fulan as soon as his arm was at his side once again.

"*How are things looking, Captain?*" she asked in Mandarin, aware of the V'Dan guards just a few meters away.

"*As clean as we can manage, given we don't know what we're supposed to be looking for,*" he replied in kind. "*The facilities are quite large, mostly self-contained, and most of the plumbing is brand-new. The sp . . . the K'Katta,*" al-Fulan amended politely, "*were the previous inhabitants, so apparently a few things had to be changed. They are polite beings, and were willing to minimize chances of unexpected daily contact by moving to the other building.*"

"Yes, that was very polite of the K'Katta," Jackie admitted in V'Dan. She still felt unnerved by the very idea of sentient giant spiderlike beings . . . but she would deal with it. "I trust you forwarded our thanks."

"To the two that I have seen in our pretour of the facilities over the last several hours," he agreed. "Apparently, the life-support systems in the two buildings are just different enough that it would be easier to house us here alongside the Solaricans and Tlassians, rather than the southern embassy building, and easier to house the K'Katta with the Gatsugi and the Choya.

"This also allows us to expand into a few extra, unused chambers, whereas we'd be short a few rooms in the other building if we ever wanted to expand the embassy's head-count." Sweeping his hand toward the patiently waiting guards, the captain changed the subject. "May I introduce you to the Imperial Palace Guard? They are also known as the Elite Guard, and are somewhat analogous to our Marines."

Nodding, Jackie moved with him, letting Li'eth trail after her.

"Grand High Ambassador, this is Grand Captain Nes Tes'rin. Grand Captain, our Ambassador and head of Terran military operations in Alliance space, Jacaranda MacKenzie. Her military rank in our tongue is *colonel*, which, if I understand the equivalency of our ranking systems right, means she is essentially your peer," al-Fulan introduced them. "But only in military terms, during military maneuvers."

The grand captain lifted his fist to his chest, thumping it over his heart in formal salute. A quick study of customs, Jackie managed a credible return salute. "Grand Captain."

"Grand High Ambassador," he replied briefly.

She eyed the neatly uniformed man. His outfit carried a lot more gold braiding and frogging than expected. With olive-golden skin, dark brown eyes, black hair neatly pulled into a queue that allowed his curls to form a single, thick ringlet, his cyan-blue marks were an odd contrast to his red-and-gold uniform. Still, he managed to look formal and somewhat formidable, and that had her respect. "I am told your people will be providing an extra security perimeter outside our embassy?"

"That is correct. Anything that takes place within your suites' walls will be yours to handle, unless there is structural damage, or your people or your emergency system call for our aid," he confirmed. "The moment you step outside those spaces, however, you are under *our* jurisdiction. Our rules will be obeyed."

"That was already understood, Grand Captain. Every member of my staff knows they must behave. However, we are not familiar with V'Dan laws, beyond those built on compassion, courtesy, and common sense," she warned him mildly. "We may accidentally transgress."

"We are aware of that, meioas," the Elite officer stated. "Our job is as much to facilitate, explain, and smooth over such things as it is to guard your safety, above and beyond maintaining the safety of the Imperial Tier and the Winter Palace. Speaking of which," Tes'rin stated, turning to bow to Li'eth, "welcome home, Your Highness. We were glad to hear you had survived your . . . incarceration by the enemy."

"Thank you, Grand Captain," Li'eth stated. "We should continue to the tour of the embassy facilities. The Terrans are not afraid of hard work, and they have a lot of equipment to move into the suites; they will be eager to get moving. Shall we lead the way?"

"Of course. If you are ready, Grand High Ambassador?" Tes'rin asked. Jackie nodded.

"First Platoon B Gamma, remain here and secure the shuttle," al-Fulan ordered, pointing at his handful of troops. "B Beta, Corporal Gammoor, remain on hand to escort each group. Hangar personnel, please line up your trolleys and cargo sleds where Corporal Gammoor directs."

Gammoor, a gentleman from the same province of Cameroon as Ayinda if Jackie remembered right, broke formation to approach a set of workers maneuvering a hose toward the Terran ship. "Meioa, that hose had better contain *drinking* water. You *will* be drinking it before a single drop touches the tanks of our ships as a demonstration that it *is* water. If you are not completely confident that it contains drinkable water, take it back now . . ."

"Gently," the captain murmured in Arabic, more to himself than to anyone on hand.

"Nice to know everything's in good hands," Jackie quipped in the same tongue, moving with him to follow the Elite Guards.

Two remained, she noticed, but they stayed back a little ways, clearly not there to interfere with the others on the *Embassy 1* disembarking. Lieutenant Colvers, seeing that the corporal was taking care of identifying the hose's contents, remained near the tail of the oversized ship. *"That's a good threat."*

"Gammoor thought of it when we first landed, and smelled the petrochemicals growing stronger. All of our troops have been adapting quite flexibly, but then we picked the best we could get," al-Fulan agreed. A whining rumble from the lift, which had ascended, warned them that the next Terran ship was coming into view.

"Might want to tell him not to actually make anyone drink biodiesel fuel," Jackie suggested. There were hints of such chemicals in the air, but they were relatively faint compared to the smells encountered in the quarantine docking bay on the *Dusk Army*. Then again, this place looked like it had been freshly scrubbed, smelling faintly of detergent-style compounds. *"As effective as it is as a threat, we are merely guests here."*

"It'll happen only if they insist they have the right hose and bring it within a meter of the ship. They almost pulled the wrong hose to ours," al-Fulan warned her. *"Threatening them seems to be the only way to get them to take our orders seriously."*

"Don't overuse the authority."

"Of course not, but petrochemicals in the tanks would destroy the engines. My job is to protect you and the others," al-Fulan warned her, brown eyes stern with his devotion to that duty. *"That includes securing our ships against any possible tampering and destruction, in case we need to leave at a moment's notice."*

She couldn't argue with that.

(*I take it that is yet another of the languages you speak?*) Li'eth asked her when their conversation fell quiet.

(*Yes, we're going over potential protocol versus security concerns,*) Jackie reassured him. (*He voiced them in his native tongue, so to show courtesy, I replied in it.*)

(*How do you keep all those hundreds of languages straight?*) he asked her.

(*It's only eighty or so, and practice. Lots and lots of practice. It helps that many of them are related to each other, though that can cause occasional bouts of confusion, too.*)

They were approaching a column larger than the rest, which was saying a lot; Jackie had seen houses back on Earth that were smaller than most of these support struts. This one had what looked like a bank of lifts attached, but all of them were apparently built to withstand quite a lot of weight. Even the stone-and-steel trusses overhead were interlocking arches, and every single arch and column shaft had repeating bits of equipment attached to it.

Li'eth caught her looking up and sent an explanation. (*Those are inertia dampeners in case of an earthquake, explosion, or other sort of stress or strain on the structure. Earthquakes are very rare here, but there have been two in the last nine thousand years.*)

(*And the explosions?*) Jackie asked, eyeing the Elite Guards flanking what looked like doors to an elevator shaft and a stairwell.

(*There have been a few more of those, but none in recent centuries,*) he admitted.

The scarlet-cream-and-gold-clad soldiers saluted their captain superior at their approach. One of them turned to summon the elevator. A shout echoed across the bay, the sound almost lost in the whining rumble of the next, normal-sized *Embassy* ship activating its thruster field so that, too, could glide sideways into a parking zone. Hearing it, Jackie peered back the way they had come. Someone was leaning out the airlock door, and a few moments later, one of the brown-clad Humans on the ground came running their way.

It was Corporal Gammoor. His white teeth gleamed in his face, displayed in a grin. Eager for good news, if curious, Jackie broke off from the others and trotted that way. That meant al-Fulan had to detour and follow her though Li'eth remained behind.

"Corporal, report?" she called out, raising her voice over the thrumming of the drifting, lowering *Embassy 2*.

"They've successfully transited Kepler 444, clear sailing all the way!" The engines of the *Embassy 2* shut off, leaving his last few words to echo among the nearest arches overhead. He slowed, since now they were within understanding range of each other. "Commander Graves says he just got the news that they've successfully scanned, *refueled*, and jumped past the Kepler 444 System. Two, three more good breaks like that, and we can start inserting new depots and shorten the jump-chain to V'Dan! At this rate, we can trim four, maybe even five days off the trip!"

"That *is* good news!" Jackie called back, grinning. "Go tell the commander to pass along some high praise to the ships mapping out the new route!"

"Yes, sir! Right away, sir!" He grinned and flicked her a salute as he did so, already turning to jog his way back to the ship.

Turning herself, Jackie hurried back to the others. Grand Captain Tes'rin eyed her approach, curiosity on his tan-and-cyan face. "May I ask what that was about, Grand High Ambassador?"

"As soon as we confirmed via the hyperrelays that *this* system was the one we were looking for, to return our V'Dan guests," Jackie explained, "we immediately started setting up modular supply depots and caches along the route that initially got us to your system. That route, determined by consulting a combination of our star charts and the memories of Leftenant Superior Ba'oul Des-n'yi, who was the pilot on board Captain Ma'an-uq'en's ship, originally aimed us toward what turned out to be Gatsugi space.

"From there, he was able to give us much more concise directions, but it still took some guesswork to get from system to system," she continued. Entering the lift—the personnel-sized lift, not the one for the great ships, which was already ascending again—she gestured up and over with her hand. "The path described by that route is vaguely a right-angle turn, like the two legs of a triangle. As soon as we knew that, Admiral Nayak took five ships off the task of setting up resupply points and instead put them on exploring the hypotenuse of the triangle.

"*That* means that—with luck and after a few months of putting the depots in place—any Terrans going home in the future won't have to spend fourteen days in space taking the long route. Kepler 444," she said, using the Terranglo words for the system, "lies just past the two-thirds point. It's what we call a cool red star, over 11 million years old, with several planets hugging it closely. Some of the systems we've encountered like that so far have had large debris fields, making it a bit scary to transit them for the first time. Apparently, this one isn't all that scary, which is great, but the *really* good news is that they found a source of water in the system suitable for refueling."

"That *is* good news," Li'eth agreed, familiar with the tedious process of capturing, processing, and refueling the Terran ships. The *Embassy 1* hadn't had to do it on their way to V'Dan, thanks to the ships that had gone ahead of them to stock those supply caches, but the *Aloha 9* had, on their initial trip back to Earth.

The lift, which had been moving during her explanation, came to a gentle stop. Grand Captain Tes'rin spoke as they stepped into a broad lobby-like area. It, too, had more Elite Guards standing watch, along with two Marines. "These elevators are attached to certain zones, according to which hangar floor is being used. This one goes specifically from Hangar 3, North 5 and 6, to the new Terran zone, formerly the K'Katta zone. This particular lift goes to only three of the floors within your zone, and only this level has free access; the upper two require biometric scans.

"This way to the security station," he directed, gesturing at the reception-like desk in the center of the lobby. "Your profile has been transferred from the *Dusk Army*'s quarantine medical records; you need only confirm your arrival by placing your hand on the scanner pad and stating your name for our records. Once you do that, Grand High Ambassador, you will have full and unrestricted access to every portion of your zone.

"All openings that have closable doors have biometric scans; doors that are already shut will not open for anyone with the wrong signatures. The scanner frames for the lifts and main entryways are also set to detect known explosives and chemical toxins, but those are a matter for the security teams on both sides of the zone to handle. The doors are a predominantly interior-security measure. As the head of your Embassy, naturally, no door will be locked to you within your own zone."

"Thank you," Jackie murmured. Her personal head of security spoke next.

"I have already reassured the Elite Guard that no one here would abuse such full and free access and have arranged to have the furniture we brought with us given deep scans down on the hangar-bay floors, since the density of some materials can interfere with their scanners. As can our ceristeel plating, but the only objects we will be bringing that have that kind of plating are our backup hydrogenerators and the portable relay station," al-Fulan stated. He gestured toward a stack of what looked like data tablets. "They have prepared explanation packets, complete with maps and emergency-procedure drills to study.

"All of our military personnel of the rank of sergeant and higher have been vetted for emergency access to all locations for security reasons, as will all medical personnel for their own reasons. Beyond that, the expectation is that you and Honorable McCrary will also have access as the two highest-ranked members of the civilian side . . . though technically as our on-site commanding officer, you would already have that level of access."

"For now, as not all of your own security personnel have arrived, we have stationed Elite at all access points, including the restricted upper floors where the residential suites are located," Tes'rin added. "If your troop numbers are lower than you like, our policy is to supplement public areas such as this lift lobby, the service lobby on the opposite side of that wall," Tes'rin stated, pointing behind the elevator they had emerged from, "and the three entrances of your zone that connect to the Guard Halls—you may have noticed the shape of the Winter Palace upon your approach; the wall-like buildings between the bulkier structures are the Guard Halls, which is where we house the majority of the Winter Palace defenses.

"The Guard Halls also provide a checkpoint for anyone wishing to approach your embassy, so that your people can double-check all arrivals and ensure that those who are supposed to arrive actually do. In this manner, you will be assisting us in protecting the Imperial Family," Tes'rin concluded, glancing at the prince standing behind her.

"As a good guest should," Jackie agreed mildly. At the direction of the female Elite manning the nearest side of the reception desk, she placed her hand on a scanner pad and stated her name, then accepted the pad offered to her. Its controls weren't too different from the ones they had seen up in quarantine, so she was able to turn it on, then off. Li'eth sent her a pulse of inquiry, but she lifted her chin at the broad, transparent monitors ringing the reception desk every few meters. "I'd like to see a map of the facilities."

"Of course, meioa," the guardswoman stated. Her hands glided over the controls, and the holding screen on the nearest one shifted, turning into a floor plan. "What would you like to see?"

"I've already seen the floor plans for all areas within this particular zone," Jackie explained, "but I'd like to see how everything relates to our fellow tenants, the Solaricans and the Tlassians."

"I cannot show you all of their zones for security reasons, but I can show you the general block of chambers reserved for them," the guard warned her. The map shifted to a three-dimensional display of a truncated, overgrown pyramid. "The blue territory is now the Terran zone. The pink territory is the Solarican zone, and the green area is the Tlassian zone. All beige areas are either buffer zones filled with shielding and emergency life-support equipment, or Elite-controlled areas.

"This corridor connects to the Guard Halls, where visitors from the Third and lesser Tiers will be checking in," the guardswoman continued, tapping a corridor that led to the relatively narrow "wall" that overlooked the great plaza they had seen. "This corridor connects to the section where Second and First . . . and Imperial Tiers," she amended, sneaking a peek at Li'eth, "would have access to your zone.

"This corridor over here is for all ambassadorial visits from the other races, including the Solaricans and Tlassians within the North Embassy Wing, and the other races from the South Embassy Wing. The Choya are this orange area here, the K'Katta have moved into this purple section, and the Gatsugi are this silver zone; pale gray is their preferred colormood for diplomacy, as it is completely neutral," she finished.

"You won't have as much face-to-face interaction with them as the other races, when it comes to diplomatic meetings," Tes'rin explained. "They prefer to use communications systems that blank out the actual colormood they are feeling. The Choya prefer to communicate more often by commscreen than in person, but for reasons of climate. They prefer the air to be hotter and wetter than most V'Dan find comfortable.

"The same for yet a third reason would be suggested for all

dealings with the K'Katta nation; we have been apprised of the possibility of any of your people reacting adversely to an unexpected encounter with members of the K'Katta race," Tes'rin said. "It has been suggested that, for the first few months, members of your delegation go nowhere without an Elite Guard escort to help smooth any accidental meetings, and that the majority of your initial contact take place via commscreens, which is psychologically more comforting to our kind."

Jackie smiled. "You speak 'diplomat' fluently, Grand Captain. We had already considered starting our initial discussions with their people remotely, but your reassurances are welcome. You have a very polite way of saying you'll be on hand to keep things calm should any of my people have a screaming fit of the *heebie-jeebies* if we physically bump into a K'Katta at some point."

"I don't know what a *heebeejeebeez* is, but I do know how to speak diplomatically, yes. I've been doing this for over sixteen years," Tes'rin allowed. He dipped his head, acknowledging the reality of the situation. "There are those V'Dan—including those who are cosmopolitan and worldly, not just the ones from aboriginal settlements—who are inclined to scream and have a fit out of fright. The K'Katta are very generous and gracious in the face of such things, but yes, it does help to have trained, diplomatic personnel on hand."

"Then I hope my people will not keep yours too busy," Jackie allowed. She turned to Li'eth and tipped her head at the screen, and switched languages to Terranglo. *"So where do you hang out?"*

Reaching around to the front side of the screen, Li'eth dragged everything downward and tapped a section of the next large, pyramidal block. *"Right about there. The center of the Imperial Wing has a gorgeous grotto-like garden with balconies for most of the suites of the Imperial Tier to overlook. I'll show it to you at some point, once everyone else trusts you."*

She smiled wryly at that. *"Let's hope they do."* Switching back to V'Dan, she stated, "I would like Imperial Prince Kah'raman Li'eth V'Daania to have access to the Terran embassy. In specific, to all general public areas, all Terran-only public areas, and to my designated personal quarters. Can you put that into the system?"

"That . . . is highly unusual, but if that is your wish, Grand High Ambassador, it can be done," the guardswoman stated, glancing at her commander. It took her a few minutes of tapping at the controls, then she had Li'eth press his hand to the scanner and state his full name. By the time that finished, the first group of Terrans had arrived from the *Embassy 1* and were piling their belongings to one side of the large, sparse lobby so that they could queue up for registering as well.

(*Okay, I'll bite,*) Jackie murmured as Li'eth moved out of their way. Tes'rin and al-Fulan both herded them into the lift, and al-Fulan pressed the button for the topmost floor listed.

(*We're in public; you had better not,*) he teased, catching and clasping her hand as they waited for the lift to rise. (*What did you want to ask?*)

(*I know that Li'eth means "Year of Joy," but I don't know about your other names.*)

(*Kah'raman means "King of Starshine." No giggling,*) he warned her, sensing her subthought. (*It's supposed to be quite serious. Li'eth, of course, is "Year of Joy," and Tal'u-ruq means "Charging with Spear." Ma'an-uq'en is a fairly common name, either for a personal name or a family name, and it means something similar to your "Mercy" but the full meaning is actually, "Withholding One's Full Power Out of Compassion."*)

(*Quite a mouthful,*) Jackie observed, following al-Fulan out of the elevator car. Li'eth followed her, and Tes'rin followed him.

(*Shush. Q'uru-hash means "Pricking with Pointed Wisdom." Both it and Ma'an-uq'en are old names, very honored . . . though Q'uru-hash had fallen out of favor until it was given to me. Just imagine all the poor children being called Q'uru out there . . . And of course, V'Daania means "of the Imperial bloodline." So what do all the parts of your full name mean?*) he asked her.

Tes'rin interrupted before she could reply, gesturing at the guards who were standing watch in the much smaller lobby on this level, four in gold and red, one in brown and black. "As you can see, more Elite have been stationed up here, with a *Teh'ran Mah-reen* as their overseer for this location."

(*We're going to have to work on your people's accent. And*

yes, I know half of my people don't pronounce V'Dan correctly half of the time.)

"The elevator to your specific quarters, Grand High Ambassador, lies behind two more security checkpoints. Since we are the same species, we have arranged for a minimum of useful furnishings for all rooms that were given a designated function, such as offices, exercise facilities, sitting rooms, washrooms, bedrooms, kitchen facilities, and so forth. A variety of V'Dan furnishing styles is also being made available for your people to select from a series of catalogs from vetted distributors.

"All furniture, both in the catalog and already present, has been thoroughly examined by Elite security teams to ensure that there are no hidden means by which anyone can directly or indirectly harm your people—this is a service we provide for all furniture throughout the Winter Palace complex," Tes'rin told her. "I understand that you have furnishings of your own that you wish to bring into the embassy."

They were passing another security checkpoint, again manned by Elites and a single Terran, this time a man clad in Navy blues, the gunner and copilot from the *Embassy 4*, al-Fulan's ship, apparently sitting watch at the checkpoint since his ship wasn't scheduled to fly anywhere.

Jackie spread her hands wryly, shrugging. "I actually have a specific preference in mattresses. Since I'll be stationed here for the foreseeable future, I arranged to have my preferred bed shipped all the way from Earth since there is no guarantee that you V'Dan have anything similar. I can make do on a variety of different types, and even sleep in zero gravity if need be, but I think someone of my rank can be allowed one little indulgence for a long-term posting, yes? That, and it does pack down quite small for its size."

Tes'rin smiled at her. "If *that* is your only indulgence, Ambassador, then you will be a rare flower in the garden of the Winter Palace's allies."

"Well, I *did* also arrange to bring three *papa he'enalu* . . . The best translation would be 'surf-board,'" Jackie added as that earned her a blank look.

Li'eth addressed the grand captain's confusion. "They have this sport that involves using a special, shaped board, as big as a person, to ride on the waves of the ocean surf as it rushes into shore. They call the sport *surfing*, and it takes great strength and skill."

"Not that much strength," Jackie dismissed. "It's for later, when I finally have free time. I brought two boards for myself, and one board for your people to examine, in case they should like to make a few more and try the sport. So just the two indulgences."

"Well, that is still a low number, Ambassador. The Solarican Grand High Ambassador, Trrrall, had around sixty items he wished brought into or changed in his quarters, and War Lord Krrrnang insisted on gutting and redoing all of the exercise chambers for his warriors within one week of his arrival. Speaking of which, I have offered to see if the War Lord would be willing to give your Captain Al'fulaan a demonstration of their fighting techniques. I have only been privileged to see two such demonstrations in my full career . . . so if they accept, I am hoping they will allow me to watch as well."

That stopped Jackie. The other three men stopped as well. She faced the Elite Guard officer. "Is that the truth, Grand Captain?"

"Is what the truth?" he asked, lifting his brows.

"That you have not observed the Solarican guards in practice? *Is* that the truth?" she asked him.

"Of course it is. We are forbidden from using visual and audio surveillance in the embassies of our allied guests. In fact, the only surveillance equipment we maintain in all guest zones are hazardous-situation sensors: fire, smoke, toxic-gas clouds, toxic-liquid spills, and structural integrity," he counted, ticking off the items on his cyan-splotched fingers. There were a few *jungen* marks on his face, but several more on his hands, making them look permanently marked with light, bright blue ink stains. "Those are the five things that can affect the safety and well-being of not only all our guests, but also the rest of the Palace structure and its inhabitants.

"Those are therefore the five things we monitor, and we monitor them with a mandatory round-the-day crew of at least three members of each embassy's own people in each zone's surveillance chamber, which is located in one of the nearby Guard Hall sections," he finished. "Will that be a problem?"

"So long as there is transparency in your actions and full, forewarned involvement by our own security teams . . . then no, there shouldn't be a problem," Jackie agreed. "I'm surprised that you don't want to watch how each embassy's security teams practice their combat capabilities."

That earned her a wry smile and a slight shake of the grand captain's head. "There is a large difference, Ambassador, between *wanting* to watch and being *allowed* to watch. We are not allowed, however much we might want to watch. Personally, I find the Solaricans very graceful. Their skill at combat is like seeing a silk ribbon dancing in the wind at the end of a tumbler's wand."

"Well, I'm not allowed to demonstrate my *own* combat capabilities in public," Jackie told him. She gestured for them to resume walking. "So you'll just have to settle for finding a compliant Solarican."

"The Space Force insisted upon that," al-Fulan asserted. "And I back their decision one hundred percent. We can be given all the reassurances on our safety on this world that you care to breathe, but there is always a chance that someone will want to attack Ambassador MacKenzie. The less they know about how prepared or not she is to defend herself, the better."

"I would say the same thing applies to me," Li'eth agreed, "save that the secrecy of my military identity, and thus my performance in the military, has been unveiled to some degree."

"The revelation of your true identity to my people has done more to ensure our trust than it could ever endanger you," Jackie told him. "At least, from us."

(*A cheap acknowledgment, considering your people are incredibly trusting,*) he reminded her.

(*Welcoming is not the same as trusting, Li'eth,*) she reminded him. (*We would have welcomed you warmly regardless. But my people trust you. I should like to strongly recommend to your mother that you be appointed liaison to the Terran embassy. You've gained a lot of friends over the last few weeks.*)

(*Even if I am lousy at your vocabulary-cube game?*) he quipped lightly.

(*Possibly even because of it,*) Jackie teased, smiling. (*There's the second checkpoint, and the elevator doors beyond. These corridors are all shades of white and neutral silver, and hints of United Planets blue. I'm wondering if they carried the theme into my personal quarters.)*

(*Probably,*) Li'eth admitted. (*From what I understand, it's been done in all the various embassies, using lots of white accented with each nation's colors. The Gatsugi aren't too thrilled by all the V'Dan Imperial scarlet we use, and gold is the literal color of greed for them, but they do allow our embassies to be decorated in our national hues.*) He paused, then added lightly, (*And if you ever get to visit their embassy, feel free to wear gray glasses . . . ah, your* sunglasses, *I think is the Terranglo word. They tend to overindulge in color.*)

(*I'll consider myself duly warned and scrounge up a pair for when I go visiting in person. But after umpteen days in quarantine gray, I think I'll be happy to be mugged by a visual rainbow,*) she teased back, entering the last lift with his fingers still twined with hers.

Li'eth had to bite his lip to keep from laughing. That was, until the grand captain eyed their joined hands. "Your Highness . . . from a security standpoint . . . is it necessary to hold hands with the Grand High Ambassador?"

"Very. We are holy-paired," Li'eth stated, lifting their hands.

"If he wasn't in a *Gestalt* with me, as my people call it, I would certainly never allow him or any other V'Dan full and free access to my quarters," Jackie added firmly. "Nor am I going to allow that access to anyone else, even among our own people, aside from a trusted few. Even the cleaning staff will have limited access."

"And there are the thorns on the flower. Which is good," Tes'rin told them, as the lift doors opened onto a tasteful white-and-pale-blue-decorated miniature lobby. "The more guarded you are, the more I will relax in regards to your personal safety, Ambassador. I will never relax fully, of course, but I am in charge of all security measures for the Terran zone. I worked for a while in the South Embassy Wing, and the Thumb of the Son of Cho insisted for the longest time that he didn't need to alert any security details whenever he wished to use the water gardens for swimming in, on the far south side of the building."

"That sounds like you have some interesting tales to tell,"

al-Fulan offered to his V'Dan counterpart. "Once we get some currency exchanges going, any chance I can buy you a meal, and we can exchange tales?"

"No alcohol, as I'm always in charge, even when I'm not on duty," Tes'rin demurred. He palmed open the double doors across from the lift and gestured them to enter a sitting room with yet more silver-and-blue furnishings, couches, chairs, end tables, and so forth. "But some food while we chat would be good."

"No alcohol, I agree," al-Fulan agreed, grinning. "I wouldn't drink it for religious reasons, anyway. But I wouldn't say no to a medium-rare steak. I'll buy the first meal after the bureaucrats have figured out a payment exchange system."

"I assure you, it's already on my list of things to do, gentlemen," Jackie confirmed, stepping between the two men as they each moved back to let her enter her new quarters. She tugged Li'eth in her wake as she spoke. "In fact, I think it's number five: set up a value exchange rate, service for service, facility for facility, so that each government doesn't have to keep paying for each other's expenses without any recompense. Sort of a preliminary economic exchange.

"Now, let's see what amenities you V'Dan have in store for me . . ."

CHAPTER 8

"Finally."

The single word dropped into the quiet of the inner salon. Empress Hana'ka Iu'tua Has-natell Q'una-hash Mi'idenei V'Daania set her cup of *caffen* on its gilded coaster on the equally gilded table next to her firmly padded, gilt-edged scarlet chair. Gray eyes, edged with faint lines he hadn't seen before, watched him approach to within three lengths and lower himself to one knee.

She left him there, waiting for permission to rise, while she studied him.

It gave him time to come to terms with his surroundings, at least. Li'eth had almost forgotten the ostentation of life in the Imperial Tier. That chair was very unlike Terran furniture, which tended more toward comfort than impressiveness. All of the furniture here in this private but still formal sitting room was meant to be impressive. Gold and silver, *nassen*-bone carvings and other ossified, opalescent stones, rubies and garnets and so forth, luxurious fabrics woven from rare, colorful fibers—with red and cream predominating, of course—and every bit of wood carved and accented by the finest artists.

When he had first left the Summer Palace for officer's training, there had been a number of decorations throughout the training facilities and dormitories, but everything had seemed inordinately plain compared to what he had known growing up. When he reached space and his first assignment, the austerity of an actual Imperial Fleet ship was downright ascetic, a shock of cultural blandness. Seeing all the strange artworks the Terrans put into their quarantine, the little touches here and there and everywhere in their tour of Terran locations, had been a bit of a reverse culture shock in turn. Not just because it existed but because it was so different.

The austere settings of V'Dan quarantine had drained away some of his tolerance for such things. He felt like the chamber was too busy even though it was virtually unchanged from all the years he had passed through it on a daily basis before his induction into the Army. However, his mother had changed more than this room, with its treasures stretching back for generations, centuries, even millennia for some of them.

It wasn't just the gold-and-scarlet War Queen regalia instead of the flowing dresses she had favored prior to his departure and the start of the war. It was those little lines at the corners of her eyes. The thin strands of silver threaded through her gold-and-burgundy hair. The frown line that pinched together between her brows. The doubt shadowing her aura, like thin gray veils that sucked the color out of anything they passed over.

Finally, she lifted and flicked her hand, curling her fingers inward in a sideways sweep that invited him not only to stand but to come to her. Li'eth immediately did so. Hana'ka rose to meet him, opening her arms. Relieved that he wasn't in full disgrace, Li'eth embraced her, clinging to his mother. A corner of his mind marveled at how short she felt compared to him, but then part of him insisted she was still his tall, strong, proud mother from when he was young. Back when he had been a mere boy who had to physically as well as emotionally look up to her.

He eased his grip when she pulled back, only to have her hand cup his striped cheek. Her gray eyes searched his for a long moment, the one that matched hers, and the one that had been colored by *jungen* fever.

"Did they hurt you?" she demanded softly.

Li'eth blinked, unsure what she had heard. "The Terrans? Of course not. They've been very—"

"—I meant the *Salik*," his mother corrected. Her thumb brushed his cheekbone, stroking the finger-wide stripe that reached down into the upper edge of his slowly growing stubble. "Did they find out who you were?"

"No. I had applied a fresh coat of plasflesh just that morning. My beard grew out, but enough of the stripe was concealed," he reassured her. A memory flashed through his head, of a hand, severed from its owner. "They tormented me, eating one of my bridge crew in front of me—a piece of her—but they didn't touch me."

Hana'ka gripped both of his cheeks. "I *will* kill them," she promised, mother to son, not just Empress to subject. "I put off your going into the military for the longest time because . . . because of the prophecies. When your ship was lost . . . ." She blinked, her eyes glimmering with unshed tears. Hardening her gaze, she looked at him sternly. "I cannot withdraw you from the military, but I *am* going to post you far from their reach—"

"—I cannot leave the Grand High Ambassador," Li'eth reminded her. He didn't mean to, but he *could* sense her underthoughts, transient images of some remote moon outpost at the farthest edge of V'Dan territory from Salik predations.

Her hands slipped from his face, dropping to grip his shoulders, and her worried determination slumped into disgruntlement. "Kah'raman, whatever you *think* this is . . ."

"It *is* a holy pairing," he asserted, dropping his hands and stepping back, forcing her to let go of him. "Does it not say in the *Book of Saints*, the Teachings of Saint Wa'cuna, that when the enemy of surf and sky rains fire upon the Eternal Home, the Holy Pair shall cast those fires aside? I am a *pyrokinetic*, Mother, with hands that now burn with holy fire. A fire that is finally under my *own* control. *Look*."

Lifting his hand palm up, he concentrated. Heat welled under his skin for a moment, then it leaped up a thumb's length, forming a bright spark that became for just two breaths an intense, golden-white flame. He extinguished it, since burning the very air was difficult.

"Since when has *any* holy fire-caller summoned and extinguished flame upon command?" Lifting his other hand, he frowned in concentration, and lit the air for another two seconds. Returning his gaze to her startled face, Li'eth said earnestly. "Not in seven hundred *years*, Empress. Not since the blighted reign of Emperor Kah'hiak, when his successor, Empress Na'tosha had Saint Gile'an on her side to help her overthrow her mad cousin . . . and even then, Saint Gile'an had to invoke *emotion* to evoke his gifts. I am perfectly calm, and I can still call fire.

"These Terrans have skills and training beyond anything anyone but the Immortal herself could imagine. They have machines that can *detect* holy energies, Empress," he added, invoking her title to remind her that he wasn't making these assertions for his own sake though his own happiness was at stake. "With those machines to monitor their efforts, they have developed training systems that *work*. I have only had a few months' worth of training—the presentation in two days' time, the Grand High Ambassador has trained in her abilities for *years*, and it will leave the entire Empire breathless.

"Together, *we* are that prophesied holy pairing. And that means I *must* stay by her side. Even if it weren't for the massive amount of data the Terrans have collected on why physically and psychologically it isn't a good reason to be parted, the prophecy says we will save V'Dan. Since we are at war, and we will need their help in winning it, you should appoint me as our military liaison to the Terrans," he told her. "For the good of the Empire and the good of the Alliance, we need them on our side, we need them to cooperate, and we need them to share their technologies."

His mother turned away from him. She stared unseeing at the stone mosaics on the wall framing the window overlooking the inner gardens, at the artworks of thousands of years carefully displayed and dusted by countless loyal servants. Perhaps even at the elegant porcelain ewer his sister Mah'nami had broken and been forced to learn how to repair, as punishment for her carelessness. Li'eth waited for her to answer his suggestion.

". . . You expect me to put my trust in an intangible prophecy that never once mentioned that these people, these Second Empire members, are *children*."

"They are *not* children, Empress. And maybe *that* is why it was never mentioned," Li'eth pointed out. Hana'ka turned to face her son, and he nodded. "Yes, Mother. It wasn't mentioned *because* their markless states do not matter. They are adults, they are mature, they are skilled in many ways, and they possess technology no one else in the known galaxy has. Advantages no one else can access, let alone duplicate . . . unless we become their allies.

"We need to become their *friends*," he coaxed her. "Their Ambassador and I are perfectly poised to build that understanding, that alliance, and that friendship, *because* of our holy pairing. We have every reason because of the bond between us to want to encourage cooperation between our two nations."

She eyed him a long moment before crossing her arms and turning slightly away. "I do not understand their data. This . . . *siy-kihk* science of theirs. Such things have *always* been the realm of saints and priests, of mysticism and prayers, and not the purview of women and men of science."

Li'eth was not used to seeing his mother being stubborn like this, save for certain moments, deep in the privacy of the innermost chambers of the Imperial Wing . . . when his father was right and his mother was wrong. Biting his lip to keep from laughing—she hated knowing she was in the wrong, and it wouldn't be proper to show any sense of triumph—Li'eth spread his hands. "They *have* made it into a science. They also have an interesting saying that applies to this moment, Mother."

"What?" she asked, skeptical.

"A sufficiently advanced science can look like magic to the uneducated . . . until they have learned the secrets of that advanced science," he told her.

"I am told they do not even have artificial gravity," she pointed out, freeing a hand to gesture upward, toward the stars. "How advanced could they be?"

"Neither did we when we met the K'Katta," he reminded her. "I have a question for you. Why is my sister Ah'nan the Imperial Grand High Ambassador to the Alliance, and my sister Mah'nami is not?"

"Because Imperial Princess Mah'nami is gifted at comprehending advanced mathematics, while Imperial Princess Ah'nan is gifted at comprehending cultures and languages." She didn't have to append an *of course* to her statement. It was implicit in her tone.

"Yet Ah'nan could learn through hard work and extra study to be better at math, and Mah'nami could learn through hard work and extra study to be better at alien languages. They are like the Terrans and the V'Dan in that respect," he said.

"Your analogy is imprecise . . . but it is not flawed," Hana'ka allowed. Not too grudgingly, either. Dragging in a deep breath, she relaxed her folded arms, letting them drop to her sides. "Do you really think they can be of any use in our war with the Salik?"

"I believe it. They are very different, and in those great and many differences, Empress," he informed her, "the Salik will *not* understand what they face until it is too late. That, and being able to communicate near instantly across the whole of the known galaxy will be unbelievably useful," Li'eth allowed. He tucked his hands behind his back and strolled over to see if he could spot the joint where the ewer had been repaired.

"They only occupy one star system, from what you've told me in your reports," she reminded him, trailing in his wake. "Their fleet appears to be remarkably small."

"They produced more than thirty new ships during the time we spent on Earth, and those are the ones I know about. A few of them were as big as the Ambassador's vessel, the rest the same size as the smaller ones."

"Oh, well, such a marvelous fleet of thirty tiny, ungravitied ships in just a handful of months. Praise V'Neh, V'Yah, and

U'Veh for watching over us all with their munificence!" Hana'ka caroled sarcastically, lifting her palms in mock-Trinitist prayer.

"We were on Earth for only a few *weeks*, Mother. They have seven-day weeks like we do, even if their days are a bit shorter," he added. "I am certain I was not informed of just how many ships they actually have in production. I am also told that because of their own prophecies—short-term as opposed to long-term, but still tangible—that they have been increasing their production capacity for months beforehand, of both ships and the probe-things that contain their communications gear. And they have been recruiting and training new soldiers."

"Which they will cram onto their tiny ships," his mother scoffed. "Or should we send some of our transit guards with pugil sticks to help pack them in properly?"

"Soldiers we should send our largest ships *to pick up*," Li'eth countered. "They are terribly overcrowded, Mother. They hold *lottery drawings* to see if a particular couple can have a third child. Promise them land and resources on a V'Dan colony-world in exchange for fighting for us on the ground, and they will cram in themselves. Quite eagerly, I think."

"It would do no good to pack Terrans onto our ships," she told him. "That'd just be more food for the Salik once they've disabled our vessels. They would have to train for months to grasp V'Dan technology."

"I meant, transport them and put them on the *ground*," Li'eth countered. "We just need to use our much larger ships to transport them. Once they're on the ground, they can fight without needing to know how to fly our ships. All they'll need is to know how to fight on that particular planet or moon, or on a space station to help defend it. That can be taught to them in transit."

"You may have a point. But I'm not sure we can spare that many ships for transporting all those troops," Hana'ka muttered grimly. She reached up to touch the spot where her daughter had broken the gem-studded flask, then lowered her hand. "Our fleet is scattered all over the place right now, trying to transport our own troops . . . and we cannot evacuate the colonies that are falling to the enemy's ground-based advance."

"Then let their ships serve in place of ours—they don't need to be large in a fight when they can be fast and maneuverable," he reminded her. "And their weapons don't have to be plentiful. Their military leader—the title is strange, they call him an 'Admiral-General' of all things—he informed me that they can use nonradioactive bombs capable of destroying entire cities—he said this *not* to threaten us," Li'eth added quickly as she turned to him, her cheeks flushing red and her eyes narrowing. "He said it was to inform me as a courtesy that their fleet may be literally small in both the size of each ship and their numbers, but that they can deliver very powerful blows to our enemies.

"He also stressed he would not recommend using these water-bombs of theirs anywhere other than in the depths of space, so as not to damage our living spaces."

"And you believe him?" the Empress asked her son.

"I have reason to believe that I have not been given lies. They have withheld information, as is their right, but they have not lied," Li'eth stated. "Certainly, I am better at reading auras now than I ever was, and his aura held no deception."

She eyed him up and down before moving away. "I wonder if you are somehow now contaminated by the beliefs of these people, that you advocate for them."

"I advocate for *our* people," Li'eth asserted, following her.

"Does your holy partner know that?" Hana'ka asked dryly.

"She does, and she approves of it. Just as she advocates for her people. She is *also* wise enough not to press when I tell her I cannot give her certain information. Just as I am courteous in kind about not prying further when told I cannot be told." For a moment, when she settled onto her chair again, he thought she would have him kneel. But his mother flicked her hand to the side, offering him one of the other, slightly less ornate, seats. "It is called diplomacy, Empress. I learned it well."

"Yes, your Nanny did a good job of raising you, didn't he?" she agreed. Bracing her chin on her fingertips, she tapped her jawline. "Why *would* they give the position of Grand High Ambassador to someone who is bound in a holy pairing? Particularly when they say it will only bind the two of you tighter together?"

"Maybe they really *do* want an alliance with us, and see this as a means to ensnare our cooperation," he offered.

"But if you two are a holy pairing, which they agree is like a holy marriage, you could sway *her* into coaxing her people into giving us far more concessions than we could give them," Hana'ka pointed out.

Li'eth smiled at that. Smiled, and shook his head. "No, she wouldn't. She has more iron in her than all the metal at the core of our world. She is honorable beyond all contestation, Eternity. Honorable, and honest. She put her career on the line, presenting that very possibility before her people's highest levels of government. They have faith she will represent them better than anyone else. It also may help that she has the former leader of their nation as her Assistant Ambassador."

"The what of the what?" Hana'ka asked her son, giving him her full, if confused, attention.

"You didn't read the report I sent on that?" Li'eth asked.

"I have a *lot* of reports to read. Mostly, I read the summaries," his mother confessed. Her fingertips tapped on the curled, carved armrest of her chair. "I barely have time to read those, either. Every time a new ship comes into the home space, blaring the latest in bad news, I have a thousand fires to extinguish and a thousand wounds to bandage on the morale of the Empire."

"Assistant Ambassador Rosa McCrary was, up until the start of their current year, the Premiere of the Terran United Planets Council. She was your equal for I think five years," Li'eth told her.

"For five years? Did someone depose her? Why isn't she in exile, or under lock and key?" Hana'ka asked.

"They *elected* her to serve a five-year term," he explained. "Their whole government is a . . . a cross between people rising to power based on education level—they all have to pass strenuous tests in understanding science and such—and their willingness to serve as a part of the bureaucracy—but with stiff penalties for bribery and corruption—and having the freely voted confidence of the people backing them. It's all very confusing, but at the same time sort of like what the Valley of the Artisans has for its government."

Hana'ka wrinkled her nose. "*Bah*. Giving people a say in their government doesn't always work out for the best. Particularly when they are not trained from birth for it."

"She does come from a bloodline with government officials in it. Her mother is the assistant governor for the region that she herself served as Councilor—their governors execute the laws, seeing that they are carried out, while their Councilors listen to the people and make or change the laws," Li'eth explained. "And her grandfather was a Councilor of a different region before he perished with many others in an attack by insurgents of some sort."

"So not everyone in their Empire thinks their government is perfect," the Empress mused, smirking a little.

"Neither are *we*," Li'eth reminded her. "The Imperial bloodline has remained in the hands of the descendants of War King Kah'el for five thousand years, yes, but sometimes it has been jostled to the right or the left by a few ranks of relationship."

His mother sighed, deflating a little. "So long as ours is not the *last* generation . . . I really do not want to see the Salik fighting on V'Dan itself, Kah'raman. So far, we have kept them away, but we cannot replace our great ships at the rate the Salik can destroy them. The only troop-transport-sized ships I have at this moment to send to this *Earth* place to pick up extraneous troops are the ships of the home fleet."

"So let the Terrans help. Ask them to prove themselves in the next attack," Li'eth suggested, leaning on the armrest closest to his mother.

"They brought a diplomatic embassy to V'Dan, not a war fleet," she countered.

"They brought *soldiers* ready to fly and fight. Their Admiral-General Kurtz assured me their ships are prepared to defend V'Dan. All except for two of them," he amended. At his mother's curious glance, he explained. "If our system is attacked, the *Embassy 2* will take off with Assistant Ambassador McCrary on board and retreat to a known but unoccupied system until they receive word that everything is safe, or are given the signal to retreat to Earth. Or are not contacted after a certain number of days. The *Embassy 1* will remain in the presence of the Grand High Ambassador at all times as her personal transport."

"That . . . is clever of them," the Empress acknowledged. "It ensures that they will hopefully keep safe at least one person with high authority who has the most accurate information on us, who is also familiar to us, should for some reason their chief ambassador perish."

"I would rather she *didn't* perish, as that would condemn me to a slow death," he muttered.

"Assuming you truly are a holy pairing. I've been reading the reports of complaints by the High Priests on that subject," she muttered back. "They do not like being upstaged."

"Speaking of which, my Empress . . . I think it would be best if *you* undertook some of their *psychic* mind exercises," Li'eth offered cautiously. "As well as the Imperial Consort, of course. He will benefit quite a lot, but you will benefit greatly as well, in your own way."

She frowned at him. "Did they hit you on the head? Either the Salik or the Terrans? I am *not* blessed with holy gifts, Kah'raman. I was not born with them. They have not manifested at puberty, nor at any point in the following five decades."

"Master Sonam Sherap was the man who taught me," Li'eth explained. "He is a *professional* teacher of gifted abilities, and he told me that *all* Humans have the ability to learn how to center their spirits, strengthen them by grounding them in a firm foundation once centered, and how to *shield* their minds against casual intrusion.

"Jackie and I *also* caught a certain holy priest among the Sh'nai trying to read *my* thoughts. Without my permission, which is a very serious offense in Terran eyes. She suggested that my entire family should be trained in such mental disciplines, to prevent our minds from being swayed by the Sh'nai priesthood. Particularly you, to ensure you are free from undue influences. Just as I am now free from undue influencing from the Sh'nai."

"Yes, they told me about that. Or rather, mentioned how you just *had* to be influenced unduly by their Ambassador, with all this supposed nonsense of the two of you being a holy pairing," his mother pointed out dryly.

Li'eth shook his head. "It is not nonsense, and they would never attempt to influence me mentally. Invading and changing another person's mind without their permission would be about as offensive to the Grand High Ambassador as it would be for you to urinate upon the Eternal Throne during full Court."

"Kah'raman!" Hana'ka exclaimed, scandalized by the suggestion.

"That *is* a nongratuitous, accurate description of how offensive it would be," he defended himself, braced against her scowl of disapproval. "They are a very honor-conscientious people, Mother."

"So you *say*."

"So I *know*."

She stared at him, studying his face. Breathing deep, Hana'ka let it out on a sigh. "*Fine*. So they're honorable and conscientious, and this training will supposedly keep everyone out of my head."

"It will protect you from *casual* intrusion," Li'eth corrected. "Master Sonam stated that once I attain the same Rank 15 as Jackie's ability to speak mind-to-mind, her *telepathy*, a trio of three Rank 8 *telepaths* could still breach my mental defenses if they deliberately worked together to do so. But they have very firm rules against that sort of behavior."

"Well, may the Saints bless us with *more* miracles," she muttered, rolling her eyes and flipping a hand.

A door opened, and she quickly straightened, the serene, somewhat stern mask of the War Queen dropping back into place. Li'eth found himself straightening as well, slipping back into the old habits of formal presentation and demeanor among others. He almost slumped again, seeing who it was, but something about his eldest sister's coolly composed expression had him warily maintaining proper posture.

"Welcome back, Imperial Prince Kah'raman," the Imperial Heir stated.

"Thank you, Vi'alla," he replied. "It's good to be home."

Her left eye ticked just the tiniest bit on the underside. Stopping three lengths from their mother, she lowered herself to one knee. Vi'alla was wearing a dark red civilian variation of Li'eth's uniform, not quite military in style but close enough to echo her mother's War Queen garments. The color had purplish undertones, making it go well with her fuchsia-crescent marks. She rested her hands on her bent knee and regarded him levelly, if briefly. "I see the military has taught you informal habits."

She turned her attention to their mother, but the damage was done. The hint of censure in her tone irked him. Li'eth reminded himself that it had been a while since she had served. "The ways of the military have nothing to do with my greeting, Vi'alla. You are my sister. I show my love and affection through the intimacy of informality."

"Then it is the influence of these Terrans that have soured your etiquette," she dismissed, giving him another brief look. "No matter. You are safely home, and seem to be healthy and well. That is what matters. Eternity, will His Imperial Highness be staying with us for a while before returning to his duties in the Fleet?"

Hana'ka gestured for her daughter to rise. "No. I am going to appoint him as military liaison to the Terran Grand High Ambassador."

Slowing a little as she rose, Vi'alla slanted her gray eyes at her brother. The movement wrinkled the crescent on her left temple and brow, giving it the curve of a bull's horn. *Or a devil's horn, given what I saw of Terran mythology,* Li'eth thought. Then castigated himself for the uncharitable thought.

A tap on his mind alerted him to Jackie's mental presence. (*Is something wrong?*)

(*My eldest sister is simply being my eldest sister.*)

(*Ah. Sorry. Good luck, and have a nice supper.*)

(*I'd say the same for you,*) he replied, (*but I know you're stuck with packet foods until your kitchen facilities can be set up properly.*)

(*Assuming we can find them while we're unpacking.*) She sent him a mental hug before ending contact. It reminded him of the warm welcome her family had given him and his surviving bridge officers, replete with real hugs and those flower-and-leaf garlands which they had called *na lei,* and the hugs many others had offered throughout the *lu'au* feast, particularly as that afternoon on the beach had worn on into evening. So very different from the formal interactions between his family members.

His mother and sister broke off their very polite, restrained debate over the wisdom of ". . . encouraging this nonsense of a holy pairing," according to his sister, when their father entered the chamber. Imperial Consort Te-los shared more looks with his eldest daughter than with his eldest son, though her hair was blond and his brown. On her head—as on Li'eth's and their mother's—her *jungen* marks could be seen in the streaks of burgundy and fuchsia that permanently tinted their locks. Te-los had brown curves for his marks, which blended into his chest-length brunette strands, leaving his hair looking rather plain even when looked at closely. Until his hair turned fully white with age or was shaved away, no one could easily see where his scalp had been marked.

Imperial Consort Te-los was also the only member of the family who did not have to drop to one knee before Her Eternity. He did bow formally, however, before crossing to his son. Li'eth rose to meet him, both embracing tightly. They shared more than just some of their looks; both men were holy ones.

(*I am so very glad you are alive, my son,*) his father sent. It was ragged and uneven compared to the smooth telepathy of the Terrans, but that was understandable given the differences in training. (*I have been praying to every Saint that could possibly hear that you* would *be the V'Daania destined to escape death by evil hunger and bring back allies that will win our war. I am both sad and glad that it came true.*)

(*I was praying for it, too, Father,*) Li'eth whispered back. He shoved away thoughts of his time in that Salik cage, focusing instead on images of Jackie. (*I can't wait for you to meet my holy partner—you will love her, I think, as much as I am coming to love her. She and the other holy ones have much to teach us about our gifts, too.*)

(*I look forward to learning all about her and her people's ways, my son,*) Te-los agreed. (*Though I think after several decades in the Imperial Court, I might be able to teach* them *a thing or two about reading auras, yes?*)

Li'eth smiled. (*Possibly. I should like to send one of our ships to bring the teacher who taught me much about such things. I think he* would *like to know all that you have learned through experimenting and observing over the years.*)

(*I shall look forward to meeting him, then . . . and I shall not monopolize your welcome home, Kah'raman.*)

They both hugged harder, then patted each other on the back and parted. Li'eth looked toward his eldest sister, but she had already taken her seat at the Empress' right. No hugs from that direction. He wasn't too surprised; Vi'alla believed firmly that the Imperial Blood should not show signs of affection in public.

"Kah'raman!" The half shout came from the same door his father and sister had used, which was a different one than he had entered through. Balei'in, youngest of the siblings, rushed across the floor to hug his brother, only to be checked by a very stern throat-clearing from his eldest sister.

Skidding to a stop, Balei'in started to go down on one knee, his indigo-marked face flushing on the paler spots with embarrassment over Vi'alla's chastising. Hana'ka flicked her hand, giving him permission to not even bother. With the dexterity of a twenty-five-year-old, he relaunched himself at Li'eth without even touching knee to ground. Laughing, Li'eth hugged his youngest sibling, his only brother. He even lifted the younger male off his booted feet for a moment before Vi'alla cleared her throat again.

Balei'in muttered something very uncomplimentary in Solarican under his breath. Li'eth only understood part of it, but it was enough that he coughed an affirmative in reply. The others were arriving, starting with Royal Consort Dei'eth, Vi'alla's husband. The eldest of her three children was still only sixteen years old, too young to appear in court. The same with Ah'nan's children; she was next in entering the room, second-born of the Imperial brood. Her wife, Royal Consort Na'ju-la came with her, as did their Consort Royal, Chor'ru, trailing behind. All three of them dropped to one knee in unison

As they did so, Li'eth realized that Vi'alla barely even looked at the Consort Nanny. His mother acknowledged the man, but her heir did not. *When did she get so rude? He's a Nanny, a professional of the Fourth Tier . . . no, wait, he's Third Tier, a professor of Early Childhood Development. I keep forgetting he gave up his career when Na'ju-la asked him to sire children with her and Ah'nan.*

He was sorely out of the political loop. Dealing with officers was a bit more straightforward than this. Mainly because, Li'eth acknowledged as he hugged his next-eldest sibling, her wife, and their consort, in a military situation the seniormost-ranking officer got to decide just how formal or informal things could be.

The rules and regulations of the Imperial Army were very clear on that point. It was very much like a clear-cut game of *ca-mei, co-mei*, Short Wall, Long Wall—the Terrans had a similar, simple ball-racket-and-wall game called *pilota*, he had learned. Compared to the straightforward and thus very clear "if it's in the lines, it's good; if it's on or outside the lines, it's bad" rules of *ca-mei, co-mei*, Imperial politics was like trying to play guanjiball and the complex Solarican tile-placement game of *kaskat* all while riding on those Terran surfboard things at high tide.

He was very much out of practice, but as he hugged his next sibling to arrive, Mah'nami, Li'eth found himself slipping more out of, well, *being* Li'eth, captain of the Imperial Fleet, and more into being Kah'raman, thirdborn Imperial Prince. When the servants arrived with predinner drinks, he braced himself for a long evening. Most of his family loved him and were pleased to have him home, but he knew he had a lot of careful studying ahead of him, to gauge how the various undercurrents of Imperial favor and power flowed and moved these days.

The sooner he got back into the habits of studying, weighing, and watching everything said around him, including his own words, the sooner he could use all that information to hopefully pave a smoother path to the Terrans becoming the Empire's new best friends.

CHAPTER 9

MAY 18, 2287 C.E.
JANVA 12, 9508 V.D.S.

The great Tier plazas were modular. Jackie discovered that when the Terrans emerged from a set of tunnels that ran underneath the flagstones. The outer edges had been raised in risers that towered like valley walls on either side, lined with throngs

of excited, cheering, curious V'Dan. Overhead, snow drifted
down out of an overcast sky. The flakes struck the nearly invisible force fields of the Winter Palace and were shunted to either
side with little sparks, tracing a nearly Gothic-arch outline far
overhead. If those sparks made a sound, the noise from the
crowd drowned it out.

The force-field towers rose up above the grandstands, with
giant projection screens hoisted between them, showing in detail various angles of the Terrans' appearance. Those walls
and the fields overhead also kept the air warmer than expected, particularly for a day in a seaside city that was cold
enough to snow. She was glad she had heeded the Elite Guard's
advice on what temperature to actually dress for. As it was,
her outfit was drawing some unusual stares. All of their clothing elicited stares.

Around the outside, forming a rectangular shield wall, the
Space Force Marines and Navy crew members who were not
guarding the embassy zone and their ships had donned full,
formal Dress Blacks. The Marines had their dress swords at
their sides; the Elite Guard had declared that the swords were
acceptable weaponry for an escort guard to bring into the
Empress' presence, though ranged weapons of any sort would
not be allowed. There were three flag bearers, one for the blue
flag of the Terran United Planets with its silvery-white oval
map of the surface of the Earth enclosed in a laurel wreath,
one with the flag of the TUPSF Marine Corps in brown and
gold, and one with the flag of the TUPSF Navy in blue and
gold, to differentiate it from the main flag.

The civilian members of the staff clustered in the center of
their honor guard wore a colorful array of formal clothes in
shades from pastel pinks and lavenders to indigo and forest
green. Jackie herself wore white. It wasn't her best color, or
even her favorite color, which would have been some shade of
orange or perhaps a bright, cheerful peach, but the white of
her pantsuit would be easiest for her to work with during her
formal greeting presentation.

The pants were a necessity; the top formed a petal-skirted
dress in layers of the finest, lightest-spun silk, some sort of chif-
fon, or perhaps organza. Whatever it was, it floated on the mild-
est of breezes in layers like a peacock's tail. Even her sleeves

had a similar effect. In front, the layers were knee length, mid-shin at most; in back, they trailed on the ground, guaranteeing no one could walk closely behind her. Jackie picked her dresses to look good, not because she knew what they were made out of, and this outfit was no exception.

Their approach to the Imperial Tier started at roughly the midpoint of the Fifth Tier Plaza, where the tunnel ramp emerged up into the center of the makeshift grandstands. It took them five minutes of walking to reach the start of the steps leading to the equally vast Fourth Tier Plaza, and a full minute to mount those steps. Staring down the long, artificial valley floor to the next set of stairs, at all the risers filled with yet more tens of thousands of people, Jackie began to feel a sinking sensation inside.

(*Overwhelmed?*) Li'eth asked. He was hovering deliberately in her mind, ready to step in with a quick explanation of how to fix any protocol they might have missed, or skipped, or fumbled during this event. (*I know it's a bit more than the biggest crowds you exposed us to.*)

(*No . . . well, yes,*) she allowed honestly. (*But I could deal with the crowds. I've spoken to the whole United Planets on several occasions, tens of billions at a time. It's my presentation to your people, not my speech, that has me worried. It's going to take us ten more minutes just to get to the Third Tier,*) she told him. (*And who knows how far across the Second, and the First . . .*)

(*They're shorter and smaller,*) he reassured her.

(*But my presentation is for everyone to see,*) she protested. (*This is a lot of everyone.*)

(*Our cameras will pick up and project everything.*)

(*It's . . . not quite the same thing . . . I think I may need a seat when I'm done.*)

(*I'll speak with my dear cousin about arranging for a seat for everyone as soon as your Premiere is introduced. That is the earliest we can arrange it—though it would go faster if your Premiere requested it,*) Li'eth pointed out.

(*I'll slip a little* Português *into my speech.*) The cheering of the Fourth Tier crowd was just as enthusiastic, if with somewhat less whistling. She realized the clothes of the last tier were predominantly shades of gray and green and brown.

These were more gray and blue and purple. (*Are the people of each Tier limited in the colors they can wear?*)

(*Of course not. No one can fake an Imperial Army uniform, of course, and red and gold together are discouraged—true gold, not brassy gold. I think those are simply the colors popular for winter coats in the price ranges for those Tiers in the last few years,*) he offered. (*Each Tier has popular clothing designers.*)

(*That . . . makes sense, actually. Certain colors do fall into and out of style as the years progress,*) she allowed. A mock sigh gusted from her mind to his. (*I certainly haven't seen a decent orange with hints of peach in three years . . . Ancestors, this is a long walk. My cheek muscles are going to be aching at the end of all this smiling.*)

(*You do have a lovely smile,*) he told her.

She could feel her face growing warm. (*Thank you. I like yours. I think I'm even getting used to the stripe on your cheek.*)

(*Oh! And after all I've done to view you as mature instead of stripeless,*) he teased. (*Is that how you repay me?*)

She laughed and lifted a hand to wave, parade-style. They were in a parade after all, so she did it on the other side, too, just as she had a few times while down on the Fifth Tier Plaza. (*I mean, when you smile just right, it kind of does this weird thing where half your face gains five years in age, from the way the color bisects your eyelid.*)

(*Then that would make me a year older than you . . . No, I think I shall remain a younger man to you. After all, the older someone is, the more firmly set in their career they tend to be,*) he said. (*That means you'll have a higher salary, and can keep me in a manner to which I'll become accustomed.*)

She almost snorted inelegantly. (*Nice to know some things translate across the cultural barrier. There's just one major flaw with that idea.*)

(*Oh?*)

(*This is your world,*) Jackie pointed out. (*You are the one in this pairing with access to actual money.*)

(*Ah, true. I shall endeavor to collect my pay, so that I can support you in your old age.*)

(*Oh! And after all I've done to encourage our bond, the romance is gone!*) she protested, laughing again.

(*You actually haven't done all that much,*) he pointed out wryly.

(*We have to let word get around of our bond, and let people get used to the idea. Little steps. One Tier Plaza at a time,*) she added. The stairs to the Third Tier still looked like they were a few more minutes of walking away, so she waved again to the throngs of people lining the valley of uplifted flagstones. (*How long did it take your people to build a plaza floor that could be turned into grandstand bleachers?*)

(*It was my . . . hmm. Mother, Grandfather, Great-grandfather . . .*) he countered. (*No, wait, there's an easier way to count. It was done by my ancestor two Emperors before we met up with the K'Katta. So pre–interstellar space exploration, about five hundred years ago, Emperor Mah'kien. He was sick of his Fourth Tier wife's relatives complaining to him that they couldn't see any of the special celebrations when everyone was all on the same level.*)

(*Wait, Fourth Tier wife?*) Jackie asked, waving and smiling some more. The stairs to the Third Tier were drawing closer. (*I always thought royals and nobles were too interested in keeping to their "own kind" to marry into the lower classes. That's the way it used to be, back on Earth.*)

(*That would be biological suicide,*) Li'eth told her. (*We caught on quickly in the first half of the first millennium, post–War King, how if you do that, you inbreed idiots onto the throne. That was the first major shift toward a collateral line that had outbred itself into the lower ranks. They were merely cousins to the throne, distanced by four generations of marrying fresh blood from the lower Tiers. Only they weren't Tiers at that time, more like informal castes . . .*)

(*It took a couple hundred years to refine the system, but the law is the law. We have to marry common, unrelated blood by the fifth generation, or the throne goes to a collateral line. Usually it's every three to four generations,*) he said.

(*Your father?*) she asked.

(*Noble-born, as was my paternal grandmother, but Great-grandmother was from the Third Tier. Father is Second Tier, though, not First Tier, so far less related than you'd think. He's the son of an ergrave . . . that's a rank above baron, but below a . . . viscount, I think is the appropriate level in*

*Terranglo. Baron and baroness, ergrave and ergress, viscount
and viscountess, count, countess, margrave, margress. That's
Second Tier nobility.*

*(Then you have First Tier, which starts at the bottom with
duke, duchess, high duke, high duchess, grand dukes and
grand duchesses . . . not counting any of the military ranks,
or the ambassadorial or bureaucratic peers, the uppermost
rank of the priesthoods—the lowest of which are Fourth Tier
for the apprentices and Third Tier for the common, parish-
level priests . . .)*

The conversation was interesting, and carried her attention
up through the Third Tier. Some of it even involved some of
the aliens she spotted in the crowd though most of the faces
were Human. Jackie had the impression that Li'eth and his
family were resting comfortably in chairs, awaiting for the
moment when they would be called outside, and envied him a
little bit for it.

There was a bit of a fumble with one of the two the Terran
robots carrying their own projection screens on the steps to
the Second Tier, but a quartet of Marines swept in, two from
either side, lifted it up before it could fall, and carried it double
time without missing a step to the next plaza level, where the
two technicians assigned to it were able to sort out its legs before Jackie, at the end of the processional with the last few
guards, caught up with them. It swiftly caught up with its
partner near the front, and the Marines went right back into
position, again without missing a beat.

There hadn't been much whistling on the Third Tier trip,
and by Second Tier, there was none to be heard in that plaza.
Plenty of applause, a bit of cheering, but the energy grew more
and more restrained the closer they came to the last two sets
of steps. The noises from the Fifth and Fourth Tiers were now
just a rush of sound, while the polite applause up ahead
swelled into sound. It came, she realized, from a slightly different style of clapping. Some of which was echoed on the
Second Tier, a sort of back-of-the-hand-to-the-palm smacking. It was effective at making noise without producing any
truly sharp sounds. Restrained, in other words.

The steps between the Tiers were fewer now, too. She could
almost see the flagstones of the First Tier from the Second.

There were still thousands around them, but not more than fifteen, maybe twenty thousand on the Second Tier, and only a few thousand on the First Tier. As they mounted the last few steps, the Marines spread out into a shallow rectangle, forming two lines with the Navy crew members, clad in black with brown stripes, black with blue stripes, even one or two with gray stripes. The civilians in between and the robot tenders moved to points a third of the way across the flat part of the plaza on either side.

Those robots shuffled their hexapod legs outward, then squatted and unfolded their projection towers several meters overhead. The three outermost poles unfurled with flexible, transparent membrane screens between them. For the moment, those screens remained blank, but studded all over the poles were Terran audio and visual pickups, which first blinked green, then flicked to pinpoints of red, showing that they were now streaming from the steps of the Winter Palace to the hyperrelay probe that had been delivered to a barren patch of the inner face of the tidally locked innermost moon, V'Neh.

At the same moment, the Imperial Family walked onto the Imperial Tier Plaza, flanked by Elite Guards in formal cream-and-gold suits embellished with red. That contrasted against the bright blood reds worn by the ruling family, save for the War Queen in a very fanciful version of the Elite's dress uniform. The highest of the plazas was only about thigh high to the First, and about the size of four grand-performance stages at most, so the Terrans had a good view of everyone once they were spread out.

Behind the Imperial Tier Plaza lay a very weathered, temple-like building with heavy columns, many of which had been replaced, but some of which looked weathered enough to be several thousand years old. Jackie had a brief glimpse of not just one huge doorway beyond the V'Daania clan, but of two more, and of a strange, sarcophagus-like block deep inside, bathed in a pool of light from overhead. That made her curious, but she didn't have time to ask Li'eth about it. The rituals of greeting were about to begin.

The master of ceremonies for this event was not Imperial First Lord Ksa'an but rather an elderly gentleman whose name Jackie did not know; he was literally named Master of

Ceremonies in V'Dan, giving up his name to his title the moment he had stepped into his position during the reign of the previous Emperor. The position was inheritable, and he had three daughters and a son working with him; after a period of study, she had been told, one would eventually be selected to succeed him when the white-haired, yellow-spotted, heavily tanned man was ready to retire.

His robes were cream and white with bits of yellow, orange, and red embroidered over it, forming either stylized tongues of flame or stylized flame-colored flowers, she wasn't sure which. He had a podium platform off to the side, halfway down the steps. Reaching the podium and its discreet pickups, he lifted his arms into the air, a move echoed all around them by the giant projection screens. Within bare heartbeats of his arms going up, the roar of the crowd vanished, leaving only a hushed silence punctuated by a faint sizzling sound overhead from the snowflakes zapping against the force field protecting them from the weather, or worse.

"Kneel now on bended limb," Master of Ceremonies intoned, each word delivered with crisp, slow, stately introduction. "For you exist within the benevolent, watchful protection of Her Eternal Majesty, Empress Hana'ka Iu'tua Has-natell Q'una-hash Mi'idenei V'Daania, Shield of the Twenty-One Worlds, Jeweled Sword of Heavenly Vengeance, War Queen of V'Dan, our One Hundred Sixty-First Sovereign of the Unbroken, Eternal Empire!"

His upturned palms flicked down, and everyone dropped to one knee in near-perfect unison. A discreet glance to either side as she lowered herself along with the Terrans showed that the nobles of the First Tier had risen from their seats so that they could drop to one knee themselves. Jackie saw most of them bowing their heads, but as per protocol instruction, she did not lower hers. Neither did the Grand High Ambassadors—she recognized the current Tlassian equivalent of their Grand High Ambassador, Warrior-Envoy S'ssull, who knelt with his head held level and his gaze steady—nor did any of the members of the Imperial Family who were direct descendants, she saw.

The Imperial Heir, Princess Vi'alla, was introduced next, then the Imperial Consort, a handsome older man named Te-los, followed by the other four Imperial offspring. Jackie smiled a little more warmly at Li'eth's introduction, though they used his first name, Kah'raman. The Imperial Matron came next, followed by the Royal Consorts, and a fellow with the title of Consort Royal—something to do with begetting heirs with Ah'nan and her wife.

Shi'ol had given the Terrans an explanation in Terran quarantine, but Jackie had only listened to it with half an ear at the time; the official explanation during their time in V'Dan quarantine hadn't exactly stuck, either, but then she'd been far more busy trying to work out the logistics of introductions and arranging how the embassy would function, and drafting initial proposals for all the meetings that would come. It had sounded vaguely sensible at the time, which was good enough for her.

For her own life, Jackie had Li'eth . . . once they got past all the cultural and protocol hurdles. There'd be no need for a consort heir-begetter at that point, since the two of them were the same species and initial genetics tests had shown the two factions should still be able to interbreed just fine. Once they got around to it, of course. If they wanted to have children; she and Li'eth had yet to discuss that possibility.

Finally, the signal was given for the people to rise and for most of them to resume their seats. Pushing to her feet, Jackie ignored her slightly throbbing knee. Long minutes of kneeling on hard, cold stone hadn't helped things. She longed to rub the spot, maybe warm it up, but had to stand there looking serene.

"Eternity, Sovereign of V'Dan, before you now stand new potential allies to the Eternal Empire and the Alliance. Will you grant them your permission to be known unto you, unto your people, and unto your allies?" Master of Ceremonies intoned.

"I will," Empress Hana'ka stated. Her voice echoed down through the layers of plazas, amplified and projected from the screens on either side. "Let the Blood be seated."

A gesture of her hand, and something emerged out of the stones behind the Imperial Family. A massive gold-and-ruby throne for her, with somewhat lesser but still heavily gilded chairs for her heir and her husband, and equally ornate, cushioned, backed benches for the rest. They sat arrayed in a curve like the shell of the temple wall and its semicircular ranks of golden granite columns behind them.

Jackie had another glimpse of that sarocophagus deep inside the temple, and realized where the light was coming from. It pooled down from a great, pale golden crystal for a capstone set on the peak of the roof. Yes, the clouds were still delivering snowflakes but those clouds were lightening up, growing paler and brighter as they shed their load while moving past the capital. She filed that away for later, though, only briefly wondering if she'd get a chance to look at that innermost room some other time. She had to concentrate, now.

"Eternity. V'Daania. U'V'Dan," Master of Ceremonies intoned, using the most formal name of their people, double-articled pronoun and all. "Standing before you now are the people of our eldest legends, the sons and daughters of the True Motherworld, descendants of the survivors of the Before Time who were left behind to guard our ancestral origins. These are the *Terrans*, the people of the Terran United Planets, our ancient, lost kin."

It was rather backwards to put it that way to Jackie's point of view, since "V'Dan" itself literally meant "The Lost," and her own people had never lost their homeworld in exchange for another place, but she wasn't going to quibble over tiny semantics.

"Standing before you are the guardians of these people, the Terran United Planets Space Force *Marines*. They stand before you in the Black of Space and the Brown of mud, where water meets land."

Oh thank goodness, he got it right. She had put Darian Johnston in charge of making text-and-audio pronunciation files for Master of Ceremonies, since he had the most blended and thus most easily understood accent of the five linguists in the embassy.

"They are the Elite Guard of the Terran Armed Forces, and are led by Captain Hamza, son of Tariq, son of Ioseph, of the family al-Fulan."

Captain al-Fulan took three steps forward and bowed crisply.

"At their side are their brothers and sisters in war, the Terran United Planets Space Force Navy, led by Commander Robert Graves, one of the brave rescuers of the survivors of the Imperial Warship *T'un Tunn G'Deth*."

Robert strode three steps forward as well, stopping equal with al-Fulan. He, too, bowed.

"They and the might of their military come before you with the wish to greet you now with a *haka*, a traditional war dance of one of the regions of the Motherworld formerly under the command of Colonel Jacaranda MacKenzie, chief rescuer of the survivors of the *T'un Tunn G'Deth*. Do they have your permission to perform this ceremony exhibiting their might and their bravery, Eternity?"

"They do."

Captain al-Fulan broke formation with a crisp right turn, took two steps forward, turned right again to face the Terrans, and hollered strongly, *"Taringa whackarongo! Taringa whackarongooo!"*

That was her cue. Closing her eyes, Jackie dropped to her knees visually. Her white dress shattered outward in a silent explosion of snowflakes. Fireworks whistled up overhead, exploded, and formed rippling banners of V'Dan lettering, evoking gasps from the crowd.

The lettering was a translation of his shout. *"Listen now with your ears! Listen now with your ears!"*

More explosions set off behind her, each Tier plaza getting its own set of translation banners while the camera views on the projection screens split briefly in chaos before following the captain, the lettering, and herself . . . standing now before everyone in formal Dress Blacks striped with Gray for the Special Forces, Blue for the Navy, and Brown for the Marines, all of whom had been put under her command in this system.

Thrusting up her hand, she let out a ferocious-sounding scream and grasped an archaic war-spear that materialized out of the air in a flash of light. It was a brutal-looking thing, fashioned from hard wood lined with shark's teeth and decorated with long leaves and bright feathers. The crowd gasped and called out in shock. Even the Empress raised her eyebrows, as did most of her family. Only Imperial Prince Kah'raman remained calm. Serene, even, with a little smile playing around his lips.

Jackie didn't exactly see it, though she could feel it through their link. She had her role to play, and did so with a strong shout.

"Kia rite!" Overhead, the lettering shifted, scrawling *Prepare yourselves!* The woman in Dress Blacks with three stripes

down the sleeves and trousers, medals clustered on the left side
of her chest, charged forward with a scream, moving to the
forefront of the two officers. She skidded to a stop and repeated
her yell, letting it echo off the temple walls, spear raised sideways to the Imperial Family since they weren't actively threatening anyone, just demonstrating their power and their will to
do so if necessary. *"Kiaaaa riteeeee!"*

Graves and al-Fulan yelled out the next two commands,
one after the other. *Hands on your hips! Bend your knees!*
With a group yell, the Marines and the Navy personnel immediately shifted so that they all faced outward, dropping into a
broad-footed stance, crouching with their hands fisted and
forearms parallel across their chests, one hovered over the
other. All of them made faces, teeth bared, eyes rolling, some
flicking out their tongues.

Needless to say, it startled the V'Dan. The contrast between the black-clad warriors and their colorfully clad, calmly
smiling civilian counterparts emphasized their fierce expressions. Words blossomed overhead when al-Fulan continued.
Slap your hands on your thighs, giving all mighty blows! It
was not an exact translation, but rather meant to get the full
context across. *Stomp your feet—stomp your foes—as hard as
you can!*

Hands raised and ankles raised, only to drop in hard, palm-
slapping, heel-smacking blows. Jackie shook and slashed her
spear while the others moved in unison. Rhythmically, the
two groups of soldiers chanted in three beats with a long-
drawn vowel, *As hard as we can! We take all we can!* Palms
slapped legs twice, then their chests, then lifted to the sky. *I
fight! I die! I live! We fight! We die! We live!* Fingers shifting
into fists, the uniformed men and women punched the air in
front of them. *This is the strongest of beings, who fought and
has fetched down the Sun, causing it to shine again!*

They dropped to one knee with a hiss, and Jackie called out
again in Maori, writing the translation large overhead. *We
capture the sun and the stars! We fight from the ground to the
sky!* The Marines repeated her words, pumping their fists
toward the flagstones and slapping their elbows with more
fierce looks, shouting *We fight from the ground!* The Navy
overlapped them halfway through, rising with their fists thrust

in the air. *We fight through the sky!* Jackie outlined the golden words with brown and with blue. Each group repeated their line a second time, then all of them resumed the half-crouched stance of before, slapping their forearms, their biceps, their chests, all while chanting and shuffling forward one broad step at a time. *One upward step! Overcoming obstacles! Another upward step! Overcoming all foes! Another step up— the Sun shines on us!*

It would have been dramatically perfect if the sky had cleared enough for a real ray of sunshine to beam down to them at that moment. They had to make do with Jackie spinning her spear and pointing up and off to the south, where a false ray of sun glowed upon their group like a broad spotlight, just as everyone shouted, *Dawn! (Survival! Victory!)*, and posed with yet more fierce glares and threatening gestures. A beat later, all of the crouching soldiers straightened back into upright stances. One, two, three, four steps backwards, some larger, some smaller, all in crisp military precision, and they returned to a crisp, rectangular line guarding the still-calm Terran civilians in their midst.

Black-booted toes touched the broad flagstones the moment everyone was in place; those who faced backwards or to the side spun to face forward. Jackie herself spun in a circle and dropped like a pile of sand, her black-uniformed body vanishing in a puffed ring of dark, quickly dissipating smoke. Her real body, on its knees all this time, pushed upward in a billow of white fog that curled up, floated out, and vanished into air, leaving her standing in her white civilian clothes. Making herself—her true body—invisible was not easy, but the white surfaces allowed her to bend light holokinetically around her body more effectively than black or any other shade could. Overhead, the last bolded word and its subtexts faded like golden fog.

Immense cheers and screams burst out from the lowest Tiers, rippling forward all the way to the First Tier Plaza.

(*That was* magnificent!) Li'eth praised her through the hubbub. Warm subthoughts wrapped around her psyche like a hug. (*The cameras picked up two at the rear who drew their swords and licked the blades. That was* truly *intimidating at that size on the screens—you couldn't have seen it from here,*

I think, but Grand Captain Tes'rin was biting his lip, trying not to grin at the display. The auras of the Elites are all very impressed! . . . Of course, they think you're crazy, but it's the kind of crazy the military can respect.)

(*Good,*) she returned. Her earpieces had shifted when she had dropped to her knees to conserve strength and allow herself to concentrate. She tucked them back into place as discreetly as she could; she needed them for later. (*Good. I wasn't expecting to have to project words so far away. I'm glad I get a little break before the next presentation. And you can tell the grand captain that this is the* short *version of a war-themed* haka. *The march-out version includes full description of battle weapons used— modern and archaic—plus threats of what will happen to the bodies and souls of our enemies, and how we will humiliate them with tricks that are "older than the Moon."*)

He chuckled. Yes, that was definitely a smile on his face. She could see it easily, now that her attention wasn't split over so many places.

Master of Ceremonies let the crowd roar for a bit, then held out his hands to either side, palms up for a few seconds . . . and turned them palms down. Quiet immediately fell, obedient to his gestured commands. It had been debated whether or not to introduce the two Platoon lieutenants, Lieutenant First Class Jasmine Buraq and Lieutenant Second Class Simon Paea, but that would have required introducing the various officers of the Navy . . . and since most of the Navy crew members *were* officers, protocol deemed it was more expedient to just introduce the two officers in charge of the two military branches that had been brought. So all that remained was for the presence of the Terran military to be accepted by the head of the V'Dan Empire.

"Warriors of the Terran Empire," Empress Hana'ka stated in the near silence that followed. Her words echoed down through the Plazas from the projection-screen speakers. "Your ritual display of courage, ferocity, and willingness for battle is impressive. We are honored by this cultural display, and we hope that your people will not have to display such things through true combat. I am informed, however, that we share a common saying despite our many differences. That saying is: 'Do not hold your breath.'"

A faint ripple of laughter could be heard from the various Tier sections.

She paused to let it die down, then continued. "We are at war with a foe who will not differentiate between your people and ours. Understand that if you choose to stay, your lives will be placed in the same peril as those of our Empire."

"The Space Force Marine Corps stand ready to fight, Empress," al-Fulan called back.

"The Space Force Navy stands ready to fight," Graves agreed soberly.

"The Army, the Special Forces, and the entire Terran Empire stands ready to fight if need be, both to save ourselves, and to save those around us who are our hosts, our allies, and our friends. Among our 195 people in this embassy, 156 of us are trained and willing to fight," Jackie stated from her place at the center of her delegation. Ksa'an had explained that they need not shout to be heard; the V'Dan had pinpoint-precise microphone pickups that would project their voices to the screens. The haka had required it, but now she need only speak normally to be heard. "It is hoped we will not have to, as we do prefer peace and cooperation with all . . . but as both our peoples say, we will not hold our breath for that."

"Your willingness to defend yourselves and those who stand with you is appreciated. The might of the Terran military is welcome in our Empire as our honored guests," Hana'ka told them.

The commander and the captain both bowed and stepped back to either side. At a gesture from each man, the Marines and Navy soldiers in the front line shifted to either side as well. Some moved to stand at the sides, while a handful of others spread out and dropped to one knee, visibly showing that they were still ready to defend their charges though they just as clearly did not consider the Imperial Family a big enough threat to remain standing. That brought the attention of the watching crowds to the patiently waiting civilians in their midst.

"The civilian contingent of the Terran embassy," Master of Ceremonies continued, "is composed of thirty-six scholars, historians, law-speakers, economic experts, and other assorted specialists of the Third Tier, five holy ones of great skill, the

Assistant High Ambassador, and the Grand High Ambassador. Eternity, will you receive these people into your Court?"

"I will."

(*He's just confused my sister Mah'nami, who specializes in mathematics. She's muttering that 156 plus 36 plus 5 plus 2 does not total 195,*) Li'eth whispered in her mind. (*She says it totals 199.*)

(*Well, there* is *some overlap. Three of us "holy ones" are in the military, but we're counted as embassy staff just like the other two psis, and I get counted an extra time because I'm the chief Ambassador.*) She fell silent, listening to the introductions of the four psis, since Clees, Darian, Min, and Aixa, as holy ones were all considered Second Tier in rank. That meant they were worthy of an introduction to the Empress.

Master of Ceremonies had to use approximate translations for their abilities, such as ". . . senses the emotions as well as the thoughts of animals and aliens alike . . ." for Aixa's xenopathy and xenoempathy. Of the four of them, only Min Wang-Kurakawa had an ability that could be displayed physically. Things like telepathy and aura-reading just could not be *seen* by anyone.

Min, however, was an electrokinetic as well as a powerful telepath. The lieutenant, clad in her Dress Blacks, removed her cap from her short black hair and handed them to a fellow soldier, then removed her jacket and handed that over as well. Doing that revealed how her gray shirtsleeves had been rolled up to the tops of her biceps. Planting her feet, raising her hands high, and dropping her head back, the young but well-trained lieutenant summoned electrons to her body. A thin line of brilliant blue-white light arced from one bicep to the other. It crackled and pulsed, writhing in place for a moment before traveling upward like the crawling spark of a living Jacob's ladder. Another one rose, and another as well.

The crowd went wild over that. So did her hair, her chin-length, feathered cut fluffing out and up, higher and higher. A full dozen high-voltage traveling arcs crawled up to her wrists before parting and snapping up and off her spread fingers, magnified on the viewing screens so that every little flash and twist pulsed across every Tier. Min ended the effect with a slash downward of her hands and a *crack* of lightning that drooped her static-raised strands of black hair. It also sent a puff of ozone scent wafting slowly across the plaza, inadvertently making three fellow Terrans sneeze. Grounded and safe to touch once again, she folded her bare arms across her chest.

(. . . *I think I just saw all four High Priests expel in their undergarments,*) Li'eth quipped in her mind.

(*Shhh. Behave, or I'll make you transfer energy to me for the presentation.*)

(*I should probably do that anyway. We've progressed to the point where I don't* have *to touch you to be useful, right?*) he asked.

(*It's not nearly as efficient, but yes. That would be helpful,*) she agreed. (*I should get a little more energy back than it'll cost me to concentrate. Unless . . . do you think I could get away with calling you down here to assist me?*)

(*Well, you could always ask. If Mother says yes, it'll put a small wrinkle in the Master's timetable, but not a huge one,*) he added. (*He's quite capable of handling the occasional deviation, such as Mother's little jest. He wouldn't be Master of Ceremonies, otherwise.*)

"Presenting unto the Empire the extraordinary, honorable Assistant High Ambassador, Rosa M'Crary," Master of Ceremonies announced. The glottal was a little more pronounced than it should have been, but he managed to get it a little more Terran-sounding than V'Dan, at least. "Former Councilor of Western Australia Province for five years. Former Councilor of Melbourne Prefecture for ten years. Former Councilor of Victoria State Prefecture for fifteen years, having served with an unprecedented 93 percent approval rating from her entire constituency for ten years running."

The V'Dan had no idea what that meant, but they did applaud. They also didn't know that the ten years of serving the megapolis of Melbourne, Australia, had come after serving the state prefecture. Rosa, gracious to the last, merely smiled and stood there, looking elegant in a light aquamarine gown spangled with diamante that glimmered in snowflake patterns all over her gown every time she moved.

"Most recently, Assistant High Ambassador McCrary has held the position of Premiere of the Terran United Planets for four years, succeeded by her assistant, the former Secondaire Augustus Callan, stepping down in accordance with Terran prophecy so that this great stateswoman could be here to greet the peoples of the Alliance and grace them with her knowledge and understanding of decades of service in Terran politics."

A smattering of applause, confused but polite, met his words. Jackie knew the V'Dan didn't understand. One of her staff members, however, took exception. The man called out an impromptu, "—All hail the Honorable McCrary!"

Every member of the Terran delegation turned in ragged unison and bowed to her. Even Jackie bowed her head though not her body. (*Dammit. Now if they don't also bow to me at the very least, I'm going to lose face.*)

(*Sorry,*) Li'eth sympathized.

(*This is why we* practiced *this stuff in the hangar bay on the* Dusk Army, *so protocol accidents would not happen.*) She sighed mentally though she kept her serene public smile firmly in place, watching Rosa nod in acknowledgment. The older woman stepped aside and turned to face Jackie, deliberately calling attention to the younger, brunette woman. It was now her turn, the last Terran on the planet scheduled to be introduced. (*Oh well, here we go . . .*)

"And now, Eternal Empress, the most important member of the Terran delegation comes before you. She is a holy one of high skill among her people, many-gifted by the saints of her culture, a remote-seer of the seventh rank, sound-maker of the seventh rank, far-seer of the ninth rank, light-shaper of the eleventh rank, world-mover of the twelfth rank, and mind-speaker of the fifteenth rank, also blessed with the ability to touch and learn from animal and alien minds! A trueborn descendant of Councilors, Governors, and the Holy Jessie James Man-Killer, She Who Walked Barefoot on Their Moon, this meioa has served with an 89 percent approval rating in just one term as Councilor of the many great archipelagos of *Oceania*, covering one-quarter of the Terran homeworld!"

(*Aaaand that sounds* far *more impressive than it really is. Oceania is slightly less than half of one percent of the entire population of the Terran United Planets,*) Jackie quipped dryly, still smiling serenely. (*Even after we lost several islands permanently over the centuries to global warming, though we did get a few back once we corrected the overheating problem . . .*)

(*That's good to know the truth, but don't you represent the entire Terran United Planets now?*) he reminded her.

(*Where anything to do with exo-Terran interests are concerned, yes,*) she added, just as Master of Ceremonies stated the same.

". . . Now having been granted the full authority of overseeing all non-Terran interactions for the entire Terran United Planets, the Terran embassy presents Grand High Ambassador Jacaranda Leilani MacKenzie!"

Thankfully, Rosa herself solved the problem of patching the protocol hole. She immediately lowered herself to one knee, resting her hands on her thigh. In rippling waves, the others quickly dropped as well, and remained on one knee, as if they were still giving honor to the Imperial Family.

Hoping she looked regal, Jackie paced slowly forward until she stood a few meters in front of the captain and the commander. The fine gauze petals of her sleeves and her skirts wafted around her, their hemless edges fading and blending, some still trailing on the ground while others were kicked up by the air turbulence of her own movements. It almost could have been a wedding gown back home, but the white was for holokinetic reasons, not cultural ones.

"*Aloha*, Eternal Empress Hana'ka Iu'tua Has-natell Q'unahash Mi'idenei V'Daania," Jackie stated smoothly. Or rather, properly, with each glottal stop precisely placed. She knew she got it right from the surge of pride the woman's eldest son sent to her on a subthought. "I greet you in the name of the Terran Empire.

"*Aloha.* I greet you with this word that is the core of the spirit and the culture of the people of my mother's mother, the people of the Hawai'ian Islands. I greet you in the spirit of *Aloha*, which has many meanings, from Hello to Good-bye, Affection to Peace, Compassion and Mercy and Love. *Aloha* is said with the spirit of coming together, with the idea of sharing with each other the essence of life and all of its prosperity. It has become the word of greeting and the word of parting for our entire nation, and the name of our capital city, to remember always to come together in the spirit of its meanings.

"So I give unto you, as one duly appointed representative of a great nation to another of equal and wonderful esteem, this greeting of peace and caring, sent from all of our people to all of yours. *Aloha. Aloha kākou.* Greetings of love and peace to everyone, for it is good, and beyond good, to finally meet you, our long-lost cousins. *Aloha kākou.*"

"*Aloha*, Grand High Ambassador," Empress Hana'ka returned. "We are pleased to meet our long-lost cousins as well, and doubly pleased that it is a meeting filled with peace, friendship, and cooperation." She paused, then said something that was not scripted. ". . . I personally greet you, Ja'ki Maq'en-zi, and your assisting crew, with my gratitude as a parent for the safe return of her son. I greet you in the names of those families who had their own kin returned safely to them. Thank you."

"I will hope that we will not have to do that again," Jackie admitted. "But as your people are regrettably at war, none of us should hold our breath."

Hana'ka nodded slightly, then returned to the introduction scripted carefully by the protocol officers on both sides. "I understand you have a presentation to give, before introducing us to your communications technology, and through it, an introduction to the leader of your people."

"Yes, Eternity," Jackie agreed.

"You may do so," Hana'ka instructed her.

It was her turn to deviate from the script. Drawing in a breath, Jackie offered a wry smile for the cameras. "I would gladly do so, Empress . . . but I must first confess that I am . . . overwhelmed by the size of this venue, the great Plazas of the Winter Palace, and the sheer numbers of our audience. If I were to roughly estimate the number of people here . . . the Fifth Plaza alone has at least two hundred fifty thousand people. A quarter million, at a Plaza that is around fifteen *mi-nahs* of walking from right here."

"The risers of the Fifth alone can seat three hundred thousand V'Dan citizens," Hana'ka informed her. "With all seats claimed in all Plazas, and counting the Elite and staff who are ensuring the crowd and your greeting are managed smoothly . . . there are approximately nine hundred thousand of my people in attendance."

"As I said, Eternity, I am a little overwhelmed by the venue—your transportation system alone has my deep admiration. There is no shame in admitting I am made breathless by the willingness and the eagerness of so many of your people to greet mine in person in this fantastic public display," Jackie stated, gesturing to each side of the First Tier stands. "But I must confess I underestimated just how far my presentation would need to cover. As it is a projection of my holy abilities, my personal energies, and as I would not wish to deny *any* of those who have patiently gathered here their chance to witness this presentation in person . . . I must respectfully request assistance in that performance."

Hana'ka quirked her brow just a little. "How may the Eternal Empire assist in this . . . Terran matter?"

"I request the presence and assistance of Imperial Prince Kah'raman. In accordance with your people's prophecies, he and I have been joined in what you call a holy pairing from our first meeting aboard the Salik warship. Together, we can do what one of us alone cannot. Together, we can give my presentation to everyone gathered here, as is the intent of my people. May I have his assistance, Empress, so that your people can see firsthand what we can accomplish when we work together?"

Behind and to her left, she heard Robert whisper in Mandarin, *"She did* not *just say 'In accordance with prophecy' . . . Please* tell me she did *not* just say that—that one's older than space travel!"

On the other side, she heard al-Fulan hiss back in the same tongue, *"Shhh! Do* not *make me laugh on camera!"*

It was now painfully hard for her to keep a straight face, too. Subtly fisting one hand, Jackie dug her thumbnail into the side of her middle finger, giving herself some pain to distract away the urge to laugh. She hadn't even considered that archaic, clichéd joke, but there it was. *At least I didn't* end *my request with ". . . in accordance with prophecy." That would've been the actual punch line.*

". . . Imperial Prince Kah'raman, are you willing to assist?" Hana'ka asked after several seconds of considering it.

"Yes, Eternity," he confirmed. "I am both willing and ready to assist."

". . . You may assist the Grand High Ambassador," the Empress allowed, gesturing toward the waiting Terran.

Rising, he bowed to his mother, then descended the steps. Jackie was glad there was no nonsense about turning one's back on the sovereign being a deadly insult. Descending steps backward would have been an invitation to a broken neck.

(*More like one of my ancestresses deciding she'd rather have the extra second or so of warning from someone having to turn around to ensure an accurate ranged assassination strike. She'd seen her father killed by a traitor who had a very fast draw. Because he was backing up, he got off his shot before the Elite knew he intended to fire. He was killed in turn by those guards, but not before slaying the Emperor. Needless to say, it left an impression on his daughter,*) Li'eth stated. (*You haven't forgotten the rest of your introduction to this, have you?*)

(*No, I have not.*) Out loud, she addressed him as he approached. "Your Highness, please stand at my side and run through your grounding and centering exercises, as you have been instructed. I should be ready for your assistance by the time you are ready to give it."

"As you wish, Grand High Ambassador."

(*I will be heartily glad when all this formality is over. That title is three words too many for casual speech,*) Jackie muttered mentally. Lifting her gaze, she found a discreetly hovering V'Dan camera and looked at it, making her gaze seem to look out from the projection screens to every person watching around them. "As was noted in my introduction, I am a daughter of the Mankiller line of *psychics.* My ancestress was able to walk on the airless, sun-scorched surface of our moon, Luna, without needing a pressure suit, or even a pair of boots.

"Like her, I am capable of creating fields of force to lift, block, and hold things, via what we Terrans call *telekinesis,*" she informed the crowd. Suiting action to words, she lifted off the ground, hands stretched out, skirt panels shifting subtly as they caught the slight air currents around them. That caused a gasp from everyone, one that echoed down from the First Tier to the Fifth in the distance. "The word *kinesis* means 'movement in response to a stimulus.' *Tele* means to affect something at a distance.

"*Telekinesis* therefore means being able to move something at a distance, without touching it directly." Gently, Jackie lowered herself back to her feet, still speaking. "My ancestress was also known for her *pyrokinesis*. *Pyro* is a word that means 'fire' . . . so, like His Highness, she could 'move' fire. Together, the two abilities allowed Jesse James Mankiller to wrap herself in a bubble of air and remove the thermal energy of the dust and rock of our moon's surface so that she could literally walk barefoot upon its surface without burning her feet, and without having her breath and her blood boil into the vacuum of space.

"But what my ancestress was widely know for was *holokinesis*. The word originally meant 'whole' or 'complete' but which has also come to mean 'visual' and 'light.' His Highness and I have the ability to share what we call kinetic *inergy*, a word which in Terranglo means 'inner energy.' With his assistance, he will be like an amplifier to my communications broadcast, giving me the energy to increase the scale of my presentation so that all of you may see it and enjoy."

(*Ready,*) Li'eth whispered in her mind. He felt calm and centered to her. Jackie gave him a mental nod in return though she kept her gaze steadily on the camera broadcasting her face.

"The music that has been selected to accompany this visual display of light will be projected by my *sonokinesis*, which means the 'movement of sound,' which in turn is tied to my *holokinesis*. Like my ancestress, I am able to paint images of sound and light for all to see . . . entirely with the power of my mind." She shifted her gaze to the Empress seated at the center of the Imperial Tier. "This music was selected by my people to honor our location, Eternal Empress.

"It was written by one of our great composers from our classical era roughly six centuries ago, a holy man by the name of Antonio Vivaldi. He composed many kinds of music. One of these was a symphony titled *The Four Seasons*. The fourth section, or *concerto*, is named 'Winter.' It has three movements to its composition. I will perform all three movements for you today."

Discreetly reaching into the left pocket of her trousers, she fingered the controls on the device tucked inside. At the same time, she offered her right hand to Li'eth. He accepted it, turning to face her as she turned to face him.

(*Deep breath . . . remember Sonam's lessons on energy transferrence. You are the grounding pillar, but instead of flowing energy down into the earth of this world, you will be pulling it up out of the ground—only out of the ground—and streaming it into me.*)

(*Should we kneel?*) Li'eth asked her. (*You knelt for the previous projection, and your fellow Terrans are still kneeling right now.*)

She nodded, bringing her left hand forward as well, control wand carefully caught between her palm and her thumb. Li'eth cupped her hand in his, helping to support the small device. Together, they both lowered to one knee, then the other, almost touching each other. A swell of whispers and murmurs rose at the projected images of prince and diplomat kneeling on the stones of the Plaza, then silence descended again.

CHAPTER 10

Silence . . . and nightfall. A twilight that spread from the First Tier Plaza to the Imperial Tier, to the Second, Third, Fourth, and finally to the Fifth Tier a full kilometer away. That alone caused another swelling rush of sound, for it was still technically midday. The moment the noise of the crowd died down again, Jackie hit the PLAY button, and focused hard on projecting not only the soft but rising, staccato violin and harpsichord notes in her ears, but the twinkling of stars written high in the darkness overhead, a darkness that blended with the occasional skittering of sparks from force-field-zapped snowflakes.

As the music gained in volume, layers of instruments adding in every few measures, she brought in a distant view of the

Sun, at first a pinprick, then a larger, brilliant dot in the darkness. It soared from where it swooped into view of the First Tier, down and down and down, to the Fifth Tier before vanishing into the streets and buildings of the Winter City. As the music grew louder, *The Earth, Our Motherworld* appeared. It grew larger and larger; *The Moon, Luna* came briefly into view as the stars shifted, spinning so that the white-gray clouds and snowfields, blue oceans, and green-beige continents could be seen.

When the opening violin solo spilled across the Tiers, the view of the planet grew huge, swelling to hover directly over everyone's heads. The planet spun past, its oceans and continents and subcontinents labeled, forming a rotating reference map for everyone to study for a few bars of music, before it vanished and recoalesced by the Imperial Tier. Only the world itself shifted, enlarging and sliding seamlessly from hanging overhead to hovering beneath everyone in a great half-circle shift.

The smooth image blurred and zoomed, dipping below the clouds of a half-sunny day, to one of a set of islands lost in that vast expanse of blue. The southern half was thick with green vegetation and carefully blended buildings, the northern half was desert-dry and red-soiled, and in a rounded crater, a cluster of iridescent, green-glazed, and spherical-petaled buildings sat. Two sets of text floated past, Terranglo lettering and V'Dan words and phonetic equivalents, spelling out: *Aloha City, Island of Kaho'olawe, Hawai'ian Islands, Pacific Ocean, Earth, Capital of the Terran United Planets.*

The image whirled and swept down to the shoreline, where locals in *na lei* danced and played with fire on reddish-gold beaches to entertain their honored guests. The soaring images slowed as people looked up, looked at everyone there, and smiled and waved. Faces young and old, light-skinned and dark, hair that was short and long, curly and straight, white and black, blond and brown and red. The visitors on that shore, the dancers, everyone smiled and waved to the camera that was Jackie's memories, mostly real, partially constructed to be strung together into a cohesive holokinetic display.

The view of those illusionary people did not linger long—barely two seconds; none of these images lasted longer than that at most—before soaring down into the water past the men and women gliding along the leading slopes of the waves on colorful boards, exchanging the view of the air-filled land, for a water-filled view of the sands and the seaweed beds, the bright varieties of corals and the colorful swarms of fish. Whales breached and turtles swam, dolphins leaped, birds soared. They did not stay underwater long but leaped with those dolphins up among those birds, then arced up higher, faster, briefly retreating the vastness of the world to a slowly twisting curve. It wasn't long before the view dove metaphorically down toward the axial center of that end of the world, albeit with a brief slowdown over a set of rugged valleys.

There wasn't much in the landscape to see—some briefly glimpsed penguins waddling along a mostly barren shoreline—but the view soared slowly, almost majestically along the rocky terrain. The words *Antarctic Dry Valleys, Driest Spot on Earth* floated past, along with *Average Yearly Precipitation: None*, and *It Has Been 60,718 Days Since the Last Measurable Snowfall*. Those letters and the rock-and-gravel valley drifted at a quick, steady pace down through the Tiers.

Artistically, Jackie added a single snowflake, which swirled and wobbled through the air of the valleys but never quite touched the ground before swirling back upward as it bobbled along. That provoked a laugh of amusement from the V'Dan, before they gasped as the images gained speed and swept up over the ridges, onto the vast glacier plains of the remote continent.

Bright sunlight glared up from the snow as they approached a cluster of buildings. Humans emerged from the structures, about three hundred or so, all of them wearing brightly colored cold-weather clothes and waving their heavily gloved hands, smiling in welcome. More golden lettering accompanied them, reading *Amundsen-Scott Research Station, South Pole, Antarctica, Earth, Population: Varies*, before the brief stop turned into another swift journey away from that place.

A flash of sunlight rippled down the length of the Tiers while the holokinetic projections swept westward toward the Fifth Plaza. Those up by the Imperial Tier were the first to see the scene leaping up and outward, soaring past all the snow, over the rugged, increasingly narrow, hooked peninsula and the strait separating it from South America, and down to the grazing fields and narrow but steep mountains of the Andes.

Those grassy fields filled with suntanned *gauchos*, cowboys and ranch hands in layered outfits tending herds of various domestic animals, gave way to high, snow-strewn mountains where locals tended herds of alpacas and showed visitors how to twist grass into ropes outside ancient ruins of their ancestors' mighty preindustrial empires, some of them rising among sprawling neighborhoods of ancient, archaic, and advanced buildings. Those in turn became the leafy jungles of the *Amazon River.*

Up along the isthmus to a system of locks and canals, supplemented by great rectangular screens that swept past, showing grainy, black-and-white images of those canals being dug, alongside full-color images of time-elapsed transits through the rising and lowering waters of those canals. Up north again, from mountainous jungles to cactus-covered deserts, to sprawling urban cities where the dark-haired, tanned, smiling faces of *Mexico City—Population 19,543,250+* slowed and smiled and waved, grandfathers with grandchildren in their arms, grandmothers showing grandchildren how to make favorite foods, mothers and fathers teaching and working, walking and playing, cheering the kicking and headbutting of a white-and-black ball in a *Football Game* while hundreds of thousands of screaming, flag-waving sports fans cheered on their favorite teams.

From there, the view continued northward, curving east past farmlands and wilds, towns and cities, to meet and learn the names of the vast expanse of the Mississippi River, the snow-dusted Appalachian Mountains, on to the white-marble monuments of a quiet city, *Washington, District of Columbia, Former Capital of the United States of America*, and its columns and domes and monolithic structures, its many solemn-faced statues. Every time the images slid farther down the Tiers, heads turned, still reading the lettering attached to each brief image.

From there, the view slowed briefly along the sobering, white-dotted fields of *Arlington Military Cemetery*, before moving on to the towering megastructures of *New York City, Population 26,708,350+* with its streets and skybridges thronging with people clad in layers to ward off the rain falling onto the roadways. Some of the residents stopped to smile at the projected viewpoint, while others just continued on their way, busy with their many lives.

A leap upward and out allowed everyone to orient themselves to see themselves soaring over the Atlantic Ocean once more. The viewpoint reached a cluster of islands filled with green, rolling hills. At one particular cluster near the tip, the view slowed to see a carefully preserved, stone-constructed village built into grass-topped sand dunes, *Stone Age Village of Skara Brae, Mainland, Orkney Isles, Scotland, Preserved in the Sand by a Storm Approximately 5,000 Years Ago.*

The view soared southward past cities and villages and yet more smiling, waving people, many of them paler of face and hair than before. They came to *London, England, Population 31,498,600+*, which was a mix of heavily carved stone structures, modern architecture, and a wide variety of people.

On and on it went, never, ever lingering long. Down through Europe, past a collage of images plucked from here and there, medieval castles and modern cities, vineyards and orchards, mountains and meadows. Rectangles slid past of charcoal and iron-ochre drawings of ancient Humans—listed as the *Chauvet Cave Paintings from Approximately 30,000 Years Ago, France*—while the surrounding images turned into a drier region and a carefully excavated city from antiquity, *Pompeii, Roman Empire, Buried and Perfectly Preserved by Volcanic Tephra Ejected from Mount Vesuvius 2208 Years Ago.*

The plaster casts of the eruption's victims sobered and quieted the murmurs and gasps of appreciation and awe from the watching crowd. But like everything else, that scene didn't last long; Pompeii whirled away, replaced by a parabolic arc over the Mediterranean Sea to the *Relics of the Ancient Egyptian Empire, Pyramids of Giza, Sphinx*, and the ruins of ancient temples along *The Nile, Longest River on Earth.*

Those gave way to the great *Sahara Desert* and its rolling dunes, before edging into the farmlands of *Central Africa*, the smiling, sun-darkened faces of city dwellers. As the first movement came to an end, the images took a side trip to *Olduvai Gorge, Tanzania Province, Site of the Oldest Paleoanthropological Records of Mankind's Ancestors.* The arrival of their whirlwind tour to this spot was timed just as the music came to a close.

Having practiced this in private in a slightly different way, Jackie quickly hit the pause button on her remote control. She had to do so because she had to set up five versions of the exact same thing. Applause broke out, but she didn't drop the illusion so much as change it.

The holokinetic images stopped moving, but the landscape itself expanded, enlarging and focusing on a gentleman with almost blue-black skin and light beige clothes digging painstakingly carefully in roped-off sections of desert rock. He looked up from his pit, smiled, waved, and spoke in lightly accented Terranglo, with a translation in V'Dan floating over his head, along with his name, *Professor Massey Mdee, Director of the Department of Paleoanthropological Studies, University of Dar es Salaam Prefecture, Tanzania Province.*

This could have been done by flatpic screens—Terran 3-D screens required the viewers be seated within a much closer range than most everyone in the stands around the Plazas, though that would have given some of the attending aliens a headache—but even with three-dimensional holography, it just wasn't as immediate, as *real*-feeling as holokinesis in the hands of a high-ranked psi. The man, his surroundings, and the translation of his words were as big as five duplicate houses, carefully replicated from the First—and Imperial— Plazas to the Fifth. Yet despite the oversized image, everything from the folds and weaving of his clothes to the wrinkles at the corners of his eyes, each individual, tightly curled strand of his hair, the realistic way he smiled patiently as he worked, spoke of the soul of the moment.

Energized by Li'eth, who was still patiently feeding her energy drawn up from the stones beneath them, Jackie discreetly hit the PLAY button again, and broadcast sonokinetically what she heard through her headset earbuds, resuming the visual displays.

"*Aloha, people of V'Dan. I suppose you want to know about our shared Human origins, yes? The paleological records of our evolutionary ancestors stretch back 65 million years to the first vaguely primate-like species,* Plesiadapsis, *and they were everywhere, on every continent that could sustain life at that time."* A skeleton model of an animal with a tail clinging to a tree trunk floated blithely over his head. *"Over the eons, the offspring of those precursors eventually evolved into various species, splitting into three branches. The first became the monkeys."*

Again, an image of several different tail-bearing creatures floated past, their paws possessing primitive thumbs that clung to tree branches and rocks. The director paused, smiled, and continued his lecture.

"The second branch became the great apes." Another pause, and this time larger, more-powerful-looking creatures, tailless, furless, and with somewhat humanoid faces and larger, more humanoid hands, came into view, lolling among tall grass and trees, some picking at fruits. *"And of course, the third branch, that one became the ancestors of the ancient Humans, starting with the arrival of a species we call* Sahelanthropus tchadensis, *and evolving toward* Australopithecus afarensis . . . *and the very famous partial skeleton named 'Lucy,' who is over 3.2 million years old."*

The skeleton that floated unnoticed over his head was indeed partial at best, but it came with an image approximating what the creature might have looked like when alive, along with the words *Artist's extrapolation* appended. Dr. Mdee pointed at the soil next to him, and the bones exposed by his painstaking work.

"I am currently working on excavating the skeleton of a species named Homo habilis," he stated. Above floated a brief explanation, *Homo = Man; Habilis = Skilled.* *"There is still some contention after several centuries of discovery and examination as to what should be grouped where, but these beings are believed to be our earliest Human-like ancestors.* Homo habilis *are among the first definitive developers and users of stone tools. From them, our people evolved through a few other variations and side cousins into* Homo erectus, *which means 'Upright Man.'*

"It is believed that by shifting to a two-footed gait, our ancestors freed their hands for greater tool use, which stimulated greater capacity for intelligent thought." He grinned and dipped his head. *"Of course, it could have been the enlarging brain that caused a greater need to walk and carry*

tools. We will never know, of course, but we can always try to test our theories based on the evidence at hand. From Homo erectus *came a few more species, until we reach the final split in the family tree of tool-users. That split went from the species* Homo heidelbergensis *into the now-extinct* Homo neanderthalensis, *our long-lost cousins who died out over thirty thousand years ago, and the branch known as* Homo sapiens, *the scientific name for our modern Human species, approximately two hundred thousand years ago."*

Overhead the words *Sapiens = Wise* floated by. Oblivious to it, Dr. Mdee continued speaking.

"The progress of Human evolution was slow; it is only in the last few breaths in the timeline of the universe itself that we as a species have begun to evolve our technologies and our understandings. And of course, we are still searching for the meanings of life, the universe, and everything in between," Dr. Mdee continued. *"But we do know a few things.*

"Our mutual ancestors' earliest artworks, cave paintings and stone carvings, stem from over forty thousand years ago. Farming on a wide scale began just over ten to eleven thousand years ago—before your people somehow left our world," he added, making it clear this recorded projection was meant for the V'Dan people to see and understand. *"Copper tools were crafted seven thousand years ago, astronomy was being studied six thousand years ago, bronze alloys were smelted four and a half thousand years ago, and iron was in use three thousand years ago.*

"I do not know the history or progression of your people and their civilizations, but ours only reached into space 330 years ago with our first artificial satellite, Sputnik,*"* Mdee stated, bracing his forearm on his upraised knee, his posture and his expression that of a teacher confiding to a favorite student. *"318 years ago, we landed the first Human on our moon, and 179 years ago, the first strong, fully recognized psychic walked* barefoot *on that same moon.*

"Which, I admit, is a very long way from the footprints that were left by this fellow here," he added, turning just enough to tip his head at the skeleton he had partially excavated. *"We haven't* found *his or her exact footprints, of course, just some footprints of others like him. Such things lie at the mercy and*

the whims of fate, the right preserving circumstances, and luck. You can always take the time to view them on our data archives. Or perhaps even visit in person someday.

"Most certainly, I have not covered all of the paleoarchaeological evidence of our joint species' evolution on this world . . . but then you are not listening to this as students enrolled in one of my classes right now. Perhaps you might be one of my students some year. I think I will look forward to that." He smiled and dipped his dark head. *"As it is, I shall simply end this lecture here with a smile, with my thanks for your attention, and with a good-bye from Olduvai Gorge, in the Province of Tanzania, on the continent of Africa, in the oldest known birthplace of the Human race on the planet Earth, our Motherworld. I must get back to work, now.* Aloha."

With that, the dark-skinned, beige-clad man turned back to his meticulous pick-and-brush work, gently excising the softer stone from the mineral-hardened bones in the ground. This time, Jackie didn't have to pause the prepared audio she was projecting. She simply let the image shrink and fade into savannah. As the second movement of Vivaldi's "Winter" began, she swept their view over the wild herds that were the fame of the continent, over the great gray bulks of elephants and long-necked giraffes, massive herds of grazing wildebeests and more.

That view included the visually stunning zebras, which elicited started exclamations of appreciation above and beyond what Jackie had expected. She firmed her concentration, spooling past the savannahs to glimpses of the ancient stone terraces, plazas, and courtyards of the great Eastern African civilizations, interspersed with modern towns and cities. From there, it was a leap to the great island of *Madagascar* and some of its unusual, razor-sharp karst formations, then up over the *Indian Ocean* to the southern jungles of *India*, with its rich histories, giant cities, and colorful markets.

Mumbai, Indian Subcontinent, Population 48,905,800+, Earth's Most Heavily Populated City was the most important of those. From there, they rose up into the snow-choked Himalayas—*Mount Everest, Also Called Sagarmatha and Chomolungma, Highest Mountain Measured from Sea Level, Elevation 8,848 Meters*—and its elevation in approximate V'Dan units.

That image retreated westward locally, heading down the ever-broadening Tiers, but the view actually soared *to* the west Earth-wise, heading in a great loop over the drier regions of the 'Stans, provinces that still occasionally gave the Terran United Planets fits of religious conflicts. From there, they went to *Istanbul, Formerly Constantinople, Seat of the (Eastern) Roman Empire, Which Lasted for 1,480 Years and Ended 834 Years Ago*—on up to Moscow—*Population 24,567,150+*—past farmlands and taiga forests, all the way to the *Arctic Ocean* and its wintery cap of ice.

Everywhere the images went, they paused now and then for a second or two to see people smiling and waving, sometimes shyly, sometimes enthusiastically. Every last Terran Human visible utterly lacked V'Dan jungen marks; skin tones ranged from pale creamy white to ruddy peach, olive tan to chocolate brown and the intense melanin of Dr. Mdee. In some places, the skin colors were mixed; in others, one shade or another predominated, and a few had freckles, or moles, but no unnaturally colorful marks, no unnatural shapes or patterns. Just Humans.

As the second movement came to an end, they settled briefly in a village on the edge of the Arctic Ocean, ice-blocked and lit only by streetlights. The inhabitants were willing to smile, though; pale-skinned, dark-haired, round-faced, the people of that village had braved the blowing snow and arctic breezes that were as much felt by *telekinesis* as seen, though the air that was stirred was warm, not icy-cold. They came outside and waved at the incipient Ambassador, giving her a view of their world. The winds slowed, and the snow switched from streaming past to swirling down out of the sky, dusting everything lightly.

The music started up again in the third movement. Leaving behind that winter-locked fishing village, the images arched once more up into the troposphere and back down again, down to the meandering barrier of the *Great Wall of China*. Terraced rice paddies beyond its edges turned into karst mountains, and from there became jungle-cloaked mountains that turned into flatter terrain with waterways and ancient temples labeled as *Angkor Wat, Cambodia*. From there, the landscape turned to islands aplenty before reaching the continent of *Australia*, its animals, people.

They swept around it and came back up through the islands, and from the coastlines of *Vietnam* and *Korea* to the great city of *Beijing, China, Asian Continent, Population 46,722,550+* and its sprawling mix of buildings ancient and new. From there, they traveled up past glimpses of the herders of *Mongolia* into skies above the remote mountainous reaches of the *Kamchatka Peninsula* and the *Bering Strait*. Down over the upper reaches of *Alaska* and the start of the *Rocky Mountains* in the western Canadian provinces, to snowcapped peaks, evergreen trees, bright-spangled cities, vineyards, and fertile valleys, to sun-drenched beaches that turned into a leap across the Pacific once again.

Once more, the viewpoint drew near the *Hawai'ian Islands*, only this time to see the world briefly turn into an illustration. With the ocean stripped away, the label on the Big Isle became *Mauna Kea, Tallest Mountain on Earth from Base to Peak, 9,966 Meters (4,200 Above Sea Level)* with the number translated into V'Dan measurements.

Swerving up through the island chains to an island a bit north of the capital, the viewpoint glided down to one of a set of buildings amidst a sprawling city. *Music Department, Honolulu University, Oahu, Hawai'ian Islands*. Tucked into the building, through grand doors that opened up into a lobby, and into an indoor auditorium filled with red-cushioned seats facing a stage, the watching V'Dan got to *see* the actual musicians clad in black-and-white clothes. They performed sweetly on their violins, violas, cellos, bass violins, and, of course, the harpsichord.

The moment those soft, sweet chords exploded abruptly into passionate, rapid nodes from the soloist, the ceiling vanished, and the world fell away. The view rose up through the sky, faster and faster, until the Earth itself fell away within just a few heartbeats; by the time the orchestra joined the soloist, the planet was nothing more than a marble, while the surface of the Moon zoomed in fast and close, eliciting startled gasps across the crowd. The surface spun rapidly, then slowed, showing primitive equipment abandoned alongside pristine-looking, barred bootprints in the gritty, barren, gray-white soil of a fenced-off area near a dome-sheltered colony.

A voice-over—the only one during the music—came on

the moment the dome and fence appeared. Since it was in English, the V'Dan version accompanied the location name. The words *Apollo 11 Landing Site, Tranquility Base, Sea of Tranquility, Luna (Moon)* were accompanied by beeping noises and a voice saying, *"That's one small step for Man . . . one giant leap for Mankind."* At that same moment, five screens popped up at each Plaza, showing the grainy, overblown, heavily shadowed image of the very first of the original visiting astronauts slowly and cautiously hopping down the short reach from the bottom of their lander to the lunar surface.

Then all of that spun away, too, zooming over the terrain to another location with another dome, and another fenced-off area. This time, though, the footprints in the lunar soil were a mix of shoes with a much more complex imprint than bars, patently bare-foot marks replete with individual toes . . . and a lunar-soil version of a snow angel. There was no voice-over, but there was another billboard display, a close-up of the last line of a large, square, bronze-cast plaque near that grit-swept angel that read, *". . . Let the Men of Earth Never Underestimate the Power of a Woman Again."*

The Moon leaped away, vanishing along with the Earth into the starry night, lit only by the local star, which expanded back into normal, natural, V'Dan-style daylight as the last few notes of music played. Overhead, the clouds glowed gray-white, and only a few stray flakes could be seen wiggling their way downward. The great projection screens abruptly reordered themselves, switching from various wild angles aimed upward to zeroing in and focusing on the two Humans kneeling facing each other at the front of the lines of equally kneeling Terrans.

For one single heartbeat, silence reigned supreme, broken only by tiny little zaps from overhead. Then a massive surge of sound crashed over them. Even the restrained First Tier attendees cheered and clapped palm to palm, and whistles could be heard from the Second Tier on back. Wave after wave of enthusiastic sound that pressed in all around.

It was a good thing her performance didn't have to move on to anything else right away. Master of Ceremonies didn't even bother to raise and stretch out his hands for a full minute or more, and that gave Jackie and Li'eth time to replenish the energy she had used. Indeed, more was coming in all around them, a psychic storm of kinetic inergy being shed by living beings who were thrilled beyond decorum by what they had just seen. Even Jackie could see the aurastorm of enthusiasm, delight, awe, passion, curiosity, and more.

Both of them had to shut their eyes and just breathe while they stabilized themselves. As the noise gradually died—very gradually—Li'eth managed to push to his feet and helped lift Jackie to hers. It took them both another half-minute to untangle their minds, but that was fine, since the crowd was still applauding with fervor.

(*I think my knees may threaten to give out when we stop touching,*) he murmured in her mind. His gray-and-burgundy eyes were very bright. A little dazed, even. (*That felt . . . riding along with your mind, giving you the energy to do all of that . . . That was very much like lovemaking . . . but without any sex whatsoever. I don't . . . I'm not sure how to recover from that . . .*)

(*I haven't . . . I was told a Gestalt was intense,*) she agreed. (*I've been in multimind efforts, as many as twenty—no, twenty-four, that one time—but never a Gestalt. We were one for almost all of it. And now I have to face your mother with the knowledge that we have been as intimate as two minds can be without bodily acts . . . and I am trying* very *hard not to blush right now.*)

(*. . . Do you think this will have affected the progression of our bond?*) he asked hesitantly.

Oddly enough, the question cleared her mind with the urge to make a tart retort. (*Do you think?*)

Li'eth thought about it a moment, then bowed over their joined hands. (*Good. I am growing tired of constantly having to retire from your presence. I'll "encourage" Mother to assign me as swiftly as possible.*)

(*Good.*) The applause was finally dying down. She dipped him a curtsy though that was a Terran gesture, not a V'Dan one. (*We do have to face her right now, though.*)

He snuck a peek at his mother. (*Her aura is still almost as astounded and amazed as everyone else's, though she has mastered her external expressions—I do think I saw her gaping by the time it all ended. Certainly, she* was *on her feet within seconds, applauding with the rest . . . Now that she is reseated, she'll go back to being Empress again.*)

"Ambassador, we have pingback from Earth," a voice murmured in her left ear. It was one of the technicians assigned to the robotic projection towers. "*Three-second delay, going live in three . . . two . . . one . . .*"

"I am afraid that, after a performance like *that*, my own appearance may seem a bit anticlimactic," a new, male voice stated in V'Dan.

Imperfect V'Dan, with a lingering bit of Terran accent, but it was intelligible. The words were projected from the twin towers the Terrans had brought, accompanying an image of a face, unmarked and only mildly age-lined, on each of those rectangular, tri-part screens.

"Nonetheless, I am Augustus Callan, Premiere of the Terran United Planets, leader of the many peoples of Earth, Mars, and beyond," he stated, introducing himself. "Commander-in-Chief of the Terran United Planets Joint Armed Forces of the civilian Peacekeepers and the military Space Force, former Councilor of the Prefecture of Porto, descendant of the ancient kings and queens of Portugal and Europe . . . and I greet you, Eternal Empress Hanaaka of the V'Dan Empire, you and your people, in the name of the Terran United Planets, and with spirit of *aloha*."

Jackie winced internally. The longer-emphasized European *aa* was not the same thing as the emphasized-with-glottal-stop *a'* of Imperial High V'Dan. She had given Premiere Callan their language herself, but mental knowledge of pronunciation—however accurate—did not always translate into exact physical replication.

(*It's okay; the Solaricans and Tlassians have some trouble with our glottals,*) Li'eth reassured her. (*The Gatsugi, Choya, and K'Katta like them, however. It is still the easiest language for everyone to pronounce though I suspect Terranglo may soon supplant that.*)

(*Easier in pronunciation, perhaps, but it is at times an insane language, requiring a great deal of memorization,*) she warned him. Around them, the visual pickups on the cameras, both hovering and stationary, had shifted to project Premiere Callan's image in greater detail. The giant screens also alternated with images of Empress Hana'ka, who was address-ing the Premiere.

"I greet you in kind, Premiere Callan. *Aloha*, as you say. It is incredible to think we are conversing with someone on a world hundreds of light-years away," she added, before falling silent.

Six seconds passed, just long enough for people to begin getting restless. In the last three of those, Callan nodded, nod-ded again, then spoke. "Yes, almost as incredible as finding long-lost cousins hundreds of light-years from home just as we have begun to explore our nearest stars." He smiled. "And found you living on a world with a very similar year-length, at that. Now, allow me the pleasure of introducing the rest of our government to your people . . ."

This was the boring part for Jackie. She knew who many of the other Councilors were—she had worked alongside them for the last five years—and so she was free to let her mind wander while Callan introduced his Secondaire. Except it only wandered to the burgundy-striped man at her side. (*Do you think you should return to your seat now?*)

Her reluctance made him squeeze the hand he was still holding. (*I think I'd rather stand here while I can. The more our people see the two of us together, the more natural it will seem. Let's not push the thought of separating us into any-one's mind until they think of it. Or rather, the Empress thinks of it. She did, after all, loan me to you for an indefinite length of time.*)

Jackie quirked her brow briefly, glancing at him, then reviewed his mother's words. (*. . . Yes, she did, didn't she? No specifying that it was just for this moment only. I think I shall have to find a subtle way to thank her.*)

(*It was as much your own wording as hers,*) Li'eth pointed out. (*Now, I understand that some of the embassy members will be going on a tour of V'Dan and the insystem settlements, much as the others and I did of your Sol System. But Rosa told me she will be going on that tour, not you.*)

(*That is correct,*) Jackie agreed. (*I'll be eyebrow deep in second-stage preliminary agreements, prioritizing a few more things, smoothing out the roughest edges, sending informa-tion packets back and forth, consulting with our economists*

*and yours to establish value rates for basic necessities . . .
and trying to figure out how to not only pay back the Empress
for her generous hospitality but how to start pulling our
weight financially. I don't suppose your people know what a
souvenir is?*)

He blinked twice and gave her a sidelong look. (*You and
your people are planning on selling* souvenirs *to the Empire?*)

(*Why not? A little something from the Motherworld—
something that can be sterilized, of course, and nothing that
could cause harm to either ecology, but something that says,
"I have a little something from the Motherworld." A touch-
stone, an anchor, a connection to long-lost history—I can tell
you for sure that my people are anticipating yours will produce things that are similar.*)

(*We are familiar with the concept of souvenirs, woman,*)
Li'eth stated wryly. (*I was just thinking . . . well . . . the long-
lost Motherworld would end up being a lot more mystical and
hallowed, and not so . . . so . . .*)

(*Normal, for a planet infested with Humans?*) she quipped,
and got a mental dirty look.

(*Yes, if you want to put it that way. I am sorry you won't be
able to go on that tour with the others,*) he added, returning to
the original topic. (*But selfishly glad you'll be nearby.*)

(*Oh, I'll go on a tour of V'Dan. It'll just be one held at a
later date.*)

(*Considering you forgot to list coordinating the insertion
of Terran military assistance into the war and all that your
technology might be able to do, "a later date" might be a* very
long way off,) he reminded her.

(*So we'll do it on our honeymoon. You V'Dan do have a
concept similar to that one, right?*) she asked, sending him
suggestive images.

(*We also share the habit of spanking those who are
naughty until they learn better,*) Li'eth retorted. A faint hint of
a blush crept across his cheeks even as he said that. (*No teasing me during something that'll be all over the info-matrices
for the next ten thousand years. Some of my reactions will be
more visible than yours.*)

(*Fine. Let's think about the reception coming next. You've had two days to start assessing Imperial Court politics. Any advice?*) Jackie asked.

(*I'm still behind on* all *the gossip, but you'll want to be extra-polite to the following people.*) Li'eth murmured their names in her mind, attaching faces and even spotting them in the crowd for her, subtly drawing her attention with little glances right and left. Most were V'Dan, but some were true aliens.

The introductions and explanations came to an end, with Premiere Callan saying, ". . . Now that your people understand a little more about ours, and how very different we are, I am told our broadcast technicians are ready to pass along the presentations your people have prepared for our embassy staff. Part parade, and part performance art, yes?"

"That is correct," Hana'ka stated. She rose from her seat and lifted her hands. "Let the very stones of our world welcome our honored guests, providing them with comfort as we provide them with our entertainments."

With the faintest of rasps and a hint of a hum, two rows of flagstones rose on either side of the First Tier Plaza, just in front of the ones serving as risers for the patiently watching nobles, officers, and bureaucrats of the highest ranks. They rotated as well, spinning a quarter turn backwards to reveal low-backed sofa-like structures, cushioned surfaces that would be easier to sit on for any length of time than an actual hunk of stone would be.

"Grand High Ambassador Maq'en-zi, Assistant High Ambassador M'Crari, we welcome you to the Imperial Tier for the length of this celebration in your people's honor, as direct representatives of your people and your leader, Premiere Callan," the Empress stated. She gestured to the chairs that had been discreetly brought up to either side of her throne, placed between it and the chairs of her husband and eldest daughter.

While her fellow Terrans rose and split to either side, Jackie carefully shielded her mind and offered her left hand to Rosa; her right hand still clasped Li'eth's left. The older woman accepted graciously, and the three of them walked toward the steps of the Imperial Tier. Even with her shields clamped tight, Jackie could sense some of Rosa's thoughts. They weren't disruptive, though; the older stateswoman radiated satisfaction with how things were going, and a touch impressed by the sheer scope of Jackie's projections.

Empress Hana'ka was already on her feet, but as the trio approached, the Imperial Consort rose as well. Rose, and met his son's gaze. Te-los stepped to the side, gesturing at his vacated chair, then turned and bowed to his mate, backed up a step, and settled in his son's empty seat.

(*That's . . . an interesting choice,*) Li'eth murmured. (*And an encouraging one.*)

All three of them bowed before the Empress. Hana'ka pulled her gaze from her husband and flicked her hands. Obediently, Jackie and Rosa parted company, with the older woman moving to the Empress' right, Jackie and Li'eth to his mother's left. They had to part hands as well, just so they could turn to face the ever-broadening courtyards stretching into the distance.

A second subtle gesture, and the four of them seated themselves. The chairs were close enough that it was easy to give in to instinct and drape her left elbow on the armrest, while Li'eth draped his right, allowing their hands to clasp and twine. A couple of the projection screens picked up the image of the Grand High Ambassador and Imperial Prince holding hands, but not for long; those images were quickly supplanted by Master of Ceremonies. He stepped back up onto his podium, lifted his hands, and commanded, "Let the festivities begin!"

From out of side tunnels between rows of stone risers, the performers emerged, starting with marching bands playing various instruments. Some were familiar—there were only so many different ways to make a drum after all, along with flutes and pan pipes, and of course horn-style instruments were as old as conch shells, plus plucked string instruments—but others were downright strange. The way the notes were arranged were also a bit strange, somewhere between the pentatonic and the octave. They were matched in harmonic frequencies, and lovely in their exoticness, but they weren't the widespread scales and keys of common Terran tunes, either.

(*Father wants you to know something,*) Li'eth stated as she tried to focus on the music.

(*I heard him,*) Jackie demurred. (*He didn't mean to project, and I didn't mean to overhear, but his shields and focus are, well . . . V'Dan. Please inform him I thank him deeply for the courtesy of allowing us to sit together and that I appreciate his faith in our holy bond.*)

Nodding slightly, he passed along her comment. The musicians marched and danced, then swung around to the right side, heading down toward Second Tier, while those from the Second Tier Plaza closed ranks and moved up along the left. (*. . . He's willing to make an appointment for lessons.*)

(*Please apologize to your father. I cannot in good conscience allow such lessons—from myself or anyone else in our delegation—until I have the Empress' permission. He's too close to her, and I will have no accusations of undue influence over someone in such a close position of trust.*)

(*. . . Father says he hoped you'd say that, but he still wishes to learn, once you both have permission.*)

It was her turn to nod subtly. She was somewhat distracted by the next incoming performance; the stones of the stairs had been realigned, turned into more gradually sloped ramps, and the group following the musicians were literally rolling up the ramp. (*It's on my to-do list . . . Ooh, ring dancers! And synchronized at that! I've only seen them a couple times back home, but these ones—wow!—they are* vastly *better than ours.*)

(*It's an ancient art form,*) Li'eth explained, filling her in on the background. (*Just under eight thousand years ago, the first giant bronze hoops were forged. Originally crafted for wine barrels, they were incorporated into performance art by the peoples of the region of Cas-Remath when . . .*)

CHAPTER 11

MAY 19, 2287 C.E.
JANVA 13, 9508 V.D.S.

It was a good thing Grand Captain Tes'rin came early to escort Jackie and a few of her fellow Terrans to their first official meeting the next day. Everyone was exhausted from the reception, still a bit groggy, and trying to orient themselves on the maps of the Winter Palace over breakfast. Even with an extra hour and a half for sleep, it had been a long day. Jackie certainly was thinking of asserting a midday mandatory siesta policy so that people could nap and relax halfway through the longer V'Dan day rather than attempt to stay up an extra hour before trying to sleep it off in just half an hour's extra rest. At the very least, *she* might end up needing a siesta.

Local supplies still had to be arranged, furniture selected, and hundreds of little meetings set up in order to get familiar with various V'Dan departments to determine which were similar to Terran ones and which were a bit too different to categorize easily. Tes'rin patiently explained how to get from point A to point B, point A to point D, from C to G and W while Jackie hurried through the last of her breakfast and scurried off to change into her waiting uniform.

The very first meeting, out of necessity, was going to be a military one. The V'Dan didn't fully grasp the capabilities and incapabilities of the Terran *Embassy* fleet, or even the fact that it *was* a military fleet as well as a diplomatic one. The Terrans did not want to, as the ancient phrase went, cut in on anybody's dance without asking, in case that turned it into a charlie foxtrot. But they were both occupying the same system, and had a common foe, and that meant they would have to coordinate defense efforts from the start.

As Admiral-General Kurtz had lectured Jackie before leaving Earth, they were not *officially* at war with the Salik, but it was highly probable that the Salik *would* consider Terrans and V'Dan to be one and the same thing—tasty targets— and somewhat likely the aliens would come looking for the Terrans in specific, thanks to her choices and actions on board that enemy warship. Only somewhat, because only the Terrans had interstellar communications, which meant word of what she had done would spread relatively slowly through the Salik fleet. Nor were they officially allied with the V'Dan and the Alliance, though that, too, was merely a matter of time.

So when Tes'rin guided her and her clutch of combined military and embassy personnel down to the service tunnels under the Winter Palace grounds and into a tram that sped them north toward the government wings, she went in her Dress Blacks, her medals pinned to her chest and her silver eagles to her lapels, shoulder boards, and the center of her cap.

With her were Captain al-Fulan, Lieutenant Second Class Paea, the leader of the Second Platoon—Lieutenant Buraq had been left behind to remain in charge of the ground troops at the Embassy—Commander Graves, Lieutenant First Class Colvers—she didn't get along with him personally, but he was well versed in orbital and insystem combat—and her two Space Force translators, Lieutenant First Class Darian Johnston and Lieutenant Junior Grade Min Wang-Kurakawa, plus the historian, Adelle Mariposa, who was there to record the meeting for translating and sending back to Earth. Mariposa did not have a military uniform, of course, but by either conscious or unconscious choice, she had selected a black pantsuit to wear, and so blended in with the small, soberly dressed crowd.

The chamber they were escorted to was not far from the tram system. The actual structure, barrel-vaulted with elegant Gothic ribs and lined with monitor screens, looked not too dissimilar from a Terran tactical-command chamber. The central table also looked somewhat like the Terran version for such things; its surface held a giant workstation screen, with some areas dark and others lit with lists, schedules, spreadsheets, star charts, and other graphics. The lettering was different, the layout of the home system certainly not the same, and the uniforms on the bodies already in the room were brightly different from the sober colors worn by the Terrans, but beyond that, it wasn't too alien.

Empress Hana'ka was already there. Since the protocols for this sort of situation—military and somewhat urgent—had already been discussed, Jackie and company merely bowed when they were about halfway to the table before finishing their approach. As she straightened, Jackie spotted not only Li'eth near one end of the table, but a familiar dark-blond-and-hot-pink figure as well, Leftenant Superior V'kol Kos'q.

"You're here on time. Good. Thank you, Grand Captain Tes'rin; that will be all for now. Take your seats, everyone," the Empress directed, while the embassy liaison thumped his fist to his chest and departed. Her outfit today was comparatively austere in its decorations and frills to yesterday's public appearance, but her military-cut coat was still cloth of gold. She smoothed it as she sat down. The Terrans eyed each other, eyed the seats settled along the broad, oval table, and seated themselves, with Jackie taking the seat directly across from the Empress, al-Fulan to her left and Paea to her right, with the others sorting themselves out.

Settling into the surprisingly comfortable padding of her rolling chair, Jackie set down her portfolio case and extracted several stacks of clipped-together papers and a datapad. She did so hoping this meeting would go better—or at least more respectfully—than last night's reception, postparade. It had been limited to just the Imperial Family and the members of the First Tier who had cared to attend. At first, everyone had been polite and welcoming, but as the afternoon had rolled into local evening, the attitudes of the *jungen*-marked members of the reception toward the markless Terrans had started surfacing in subtle ways.

None of it had been blatant. The most overt of the remarks were ones about the ignorance of the Terrans, but mentioned in a sort of condescending way. Other, slightly less obvious comments were somewhat arrogant "gentle corrections" of what the Terrans knew versus what their V'Dan hosts knew . . . or thought they knew.

There had also been the irksome habit of gravitating toward Dr. Du, asking her opinion more often than anyone else, and glancing her way subtly and not so subtly to see if she was going to confirm what other Terrans were saying. Jackie had taken pity on her, dismissing the pathologist back to the embassy when Li'eth noticed Jai's aura flaring like a facial tic, for all the woman had done her best externally to seem calm and unbothered.

Li'eth and his crew had long since sketched out the insignia for the various rankings in the V'Dan military A check of the metal shapes pinned on the red-and-gold uniforms of the men and women seating themselves around the table showed that most were generals and admirals of various ranks. Officers of the First Tier, in other words, with only Li'eth and V'kol for Second Tier officers who had leave to sit with them.

Or rather, the pair held the right merely to stand behind two of those brown swivel chairs, until the Empress stated, "At this time, I elevate Imperial Prince Kah'raman V'Daania, Captain of the Imperial Army, to the rank of Grand Captain. I do so in order to make him a peer in rank to *Cur-nel* Ja'qi Maq'en-zi."

One of the generals slid a box down the table. V'kol intercepted it neatly. Opening the lid, he set that on the table and started removing Li'eth's solid steel triangles from his uniform for him. Hana'ka continued while V'kol replaced those triangles with large, solid brass squares.

"I hereby appoint Grand Captain Kah'raman V'Daania as our military liaison to the Terran embassy. Leftenant Superior V'kol Kos'q is here as his attaché. They are both given leave to be seated at this table in that role," Hana'ka stated. A gesture of her hand allowed her newly elevated son and his companion to take their seats. "Having gifted you Terrans with this liaison and attaché, I *request* that your military leadership seek their counsel and heed their advice while guests within any V'Dan- or Alliance-held system," she continued. Her gray-eyed gaze met Jackie's. "Will you comply?"

"Whenever there is the time and grace to consult with Grand Captain V'Daania, that will be the preferential action of my people, yes. But we shall not hold our breath that such will always be the case," Jackie stated formally, using yesterday's catchphrase. "However, with good, flexible planning, we should be able to set up a system of cooperative checklists and preemptive orders today that will ensure cooperative compliance across a wide variety of situations—and before any of you might say, 'the two of you can share intel and orders as quick as a thought' because of our holy pairing *Gestalt*, please understand that it depends on both of us being aware of a situation that may be happening beyond our actual knowledge. Such as if I am occupied by something else and am not available to handle it, or if Grand Captain V'Daania has not been informed of a particular piece of information."

"That is a remarkably prudent viewpoint, Grand High Ambassador," one of the other women at the table observed. She had an X-shaped set of insignia, but only in outline. That made her a high general, or perhaps a high admiral, depending whether she was with the ground troops of the Army or the starships of the Fleet. "I'll admit that last night I didn't think you'd have much in the way of military genius among your—"

"—Okay, *that*?" Jackie interrupted firmly, pointing at the woman. "That right there? Stow it, web it, lock it, and *ignore* it, High General."

"High Admiral," Li'eth clarified when she paused for breath. "The knotwork is different on the coat plastron braiding. I apologize for not having clarified that, earlier."

"Thank you, Liaison," Jackie allowed smoothly. "I shall endeavor to study and memorize the difference. High Admirals and Generals, Grand Admirals and Generals, please take this *warning* to heart at this time. *We are not V'Dan.* We are most definitely, especially, certifiably *not* juveniles. And we are *not*, as a group, inexperienced in military matters.

"There is only one person at this table among the Terran delegation who has *not* faced combat, and that is our historian, Meioa Mariposa, who is here to personally record this meeting. She will then hand-carry that data to our hyperrelay systems for direct uploading to the Terran United Planets Space Force without running the risk of a lightwave broadcast between here and the relays on our ships being picked up by the enemy in space, to ensure strict security protocols are maintained at all times.

"Even Lieutenant Junior Grade Wang-Kurakawa, the juniormost member of our military forces seated at this table, and who graduated from her Special Forces Academy just over five months ago, has faced off against an enemy so technologically advanced, you would *shova v'shakk* yourself at the thought of having to face them. And by the grace of Terran holy gifts, which is our only weapon against them, she scared *them* off, preventing them from kidnapping and experimenting upon Terran subjects," Jackie continued sternly while the majority of the V'Dan around them looked offended at her vulgar words. "Carve this message on your brains. *We. Are not. Children.* We are *not* inexperienced soldiers.

"So kindly get that arrogance and condescension out of your tone, your vocabulary, your approach to my people, and apply a Winter Palace–sized load of *respect* to the Terrans at this and all future meetings. Those assumptions of your supposed chronological superiority are not only *wrong*, they will do the *opposite* of what this meeting is about. Which is to secure not only our cooperation with your preferred military procedures, but our *interest* in helping save your hides.

"Condescension and arrogant attitudes do *not* build friendships, meioas," she told the red-and-gold-clad officers around her. "They most *certainly* do not belong at a meeting of potential allies. Is that *clear*?"

The high admiral, just as taken aback as the rest of her peers, blinked, opened and shut her mouth a few times while Jackie lectured her, then finally shifted her gaze to her liege in the silence that followed. She stared in a way that silently asked if the Empress of V'Dan was going to allow such bold chastising to go unpunished, or at the very least unanswered.

"High Admiral Z'bennif, I believe you owe the Grand High Ambassador an answer," Empress Hana'ka stated calmly. "I suggest you start with an apology."

"Eternity—"

"—Maq'en-zi is correct," Hana'ka stated. She didn't have to raise her voice or emphasize any words to hold her officers' attentions. "We are the same species, and have the same general tonal emphases and expressions for things like arrogance, condescencion, and contempt. These Terrans are our potential allies . . . and by prophecy, we will act to keep them as our allies. It is expected that they in turn shall be equally polite, attentive, and respectful toward us."

Catching sight of the Marine captain glancing her way, Jackie gave him a subtle nod, allowing him to speak in her place.

"One of our people, Eternity, a gentleman by the name of Ziad Abdelnour a few centuries back, gave us a now-famous quote," Captain al-Fulan stated. "He said, 'Trust is earned, respect is given, and loyalty is demonstrated. Betrayal of any one of those is to lose all three.' We will give you the respect you are due, but you must give it in return to earn our trust, as we shall earn yours. With a double foundation of those two things between our people, there will be ample opportunity on both sides for loyalty to be demonstrated in the war that lies ahead.

"For myself, I would say that we should take great care here and now to place our weapons on embankments of solid stone rather than shifting sand, lest we find the dune toppling our cannons to the valley floor, and our munitions *accidentally* striking at friendly targets instead. That requires a solid foundation of trust and respect," he finished.

Hana'ka looked around at her officers, few of whom were looking either at her or at the Terrans. "Does anyone else wish to say something on the subject of treating these Terrans as our equals, versus as children?"

"I have a question, Eternity," one of the generals near Li'eth stated, a grand general from the look of his solid gold X insignia. At her gesture, he eyed Jackie. "You said that every military member at this table has had combat experience, yet the only enemy you have mentioned are some sort of vastly superior beings who can only be harmed by holy abilities . . . and you have only introduced three of you as being holy ones. If there are only three of you who have faced this enemy successfully, I would like to ask—with respect and curiosity— where have the combat experiences been attained for the rest of your officers?"

Jackie winced a little—more internal than external. He just had to ask that question. Drawing in a deep breath, she explained, "We have a region, called the 'Middle East,' which lies at the confluence of three or four continents and subcontinents, depending upon how you look at them. It is also a vast region of the confluence of several religions, some of which are close to each other in all the key elements and historical background, but which differ vastly in the details and the cultural implementations. Based on all the archaeological records we have been able to uncover . . . that area has been in conflict for at *least* as long as your people have been separate from ours, even if the origins of most of those religions officially started only slightly farther back than your War King's lineage began."

"Every once in a while," al-Fulan stated, contributing to the explanation, "my kinsmen in those regions get a bit too zealous, and what we have come to call the Bush Wars flare up again. They supposedly started with a legend of a burning bush declaring moral and religious superiority for one group over all others—which obviously caused a lot of warfare, though war was not unknown in the region before then—and they have since then been triggered by all manner of bushes. Conqueror bushes, greedy bushes, spice-trade bushes, religious bushes, resource bushes, idiot bushes, ideological bushes, vengeance bushes . . . you name it, and it'll go up in flames like a fat-soaked bush in the area."

"We may be a united government for the vast majority of our people, even on the regional level," Lieutenant Paea added from al-Fulan's other side, "but not everyone agrees with the idea. There are other regions that have experienced turmoil as well. Most recently, the eruption of al-Tair, a volcano along the southeast edge of that confluence of continents, caused a region to be cut off from immediate assistance in evacuation. Ideological fanatics decided to seize control of the region, and the civilian Peacekeepers were unable to stop them. Our company, under Captain al-Fulan's command, was the closest force to respond at the time. We do have fresh combat experience under difficult circumstances, I assure you."

"As for the Space Force Navy, we may not be able to dent the hulls of Grey ships," Commander Graves stated, "but we are trained to fly close enough to get a psi within countering range. That means being able to evade and outmaneuver ship-capturing equipment. We also train extensively for enemy combat in case any of those ideological fanatics get their hands on a starship . . . and we train for enemy vessels with all manner of capacities and weapons cargos, from slow-moving atmospheric craft to ships that can teleport across a battlefield. Instantaneously.

"About the only *good* news concerning Grey tech is that whatever permits them to pop around instantaneously is too large to put on any ships smaller than your space station, *Dusk Army*," Robert confessed dryly. "That, and it doesn't seem to like targeting small, fast, dodging vessels; nor does it seem to be usable near large gravity wells, such as getting too close to moons or planets. As for their *reasons* for trying to kidnap Humans, we're still not sure. The only good news in that is how they don't seem inclined to kill us, just experiment on us. Since we believe heartily in the concept of bodily autonomy for all, we have gotten exceptionally good at strike-and-run sorties and other forms of tumultuous skirmishing."

His words garnered a few confused frowns. Colvers stepped in for him. "I was informed in one of my conversations with the Countess S'Arrocan that your people have what is known as the 'coin-and-cup' game. We call it the 'shell' game, where you hide a pebble or a coin or such under one of three or more containers of some kind, all of them identical. You mix them up rapidly enough, the enemy will not be able to get a clear shot at the cup containing the coin . . . in this case, someone with the mind tricks to thwart the enemy and chase them away."

"Mixing them up fast enough to confuse them as to which ship has the 'coin' might also work, if we weren't dead certain they can lock onto that ship, once identified," Robert said. "So we mix them up beforehand so they don't know which is the important ship until it's already whipped past and stung them into leaving. Not everyone in the Special Forces Psi Division is as strong as MacKenzie, so some of those ships have to get very close."

"Our ships are therefore constructed to be fast and highly maneuverable," Brad stated. "Some of that comes from being small, reducing the energy requirements to move their mass. The rest of it comes from engineering design and piloting skill. I've been going over the public files on your artificial-gravity designs; if we can implement them into the next batch of our ships, we can increase our maneuverability by 500 percent. The training to get over the new flight capacity learning curves will take a few weeks, but couple that with our hyper-space engines, and we can increase the efficacy of our usual in-and-out tactics, which is strafing our lasers from the edges of combat and firing drone missiles for further targeting obfuscation and hopeful impact."

"By 'hopeful' impact," Robert clarified for his copilot and gunner, "he means we still have yet to do any training runs against derelict Alliance vessels so we can test our weapons against your hulls and know exactly what we have to trade and what we need to upgrade."

"Which brings us to the purpose of this meeting, meioas," Jackie stated, picking up that thread. She reached for the top-most stack of clipped papers. "Since our communications and computational systems are still mostly incompatible, the SF-SF—that's an acronym for Space Force Special Forces—has pulled together a list of general specifications on what we can do with the *Embassy* fleet itself and collated them into a printout summary.

"Please pardon the font we used for your language; our coders didn't have a lot of time to make it look pretty," she added, unclipping the stack, selecting a sheet for herself, and handing the stack to al-Fulan, who took one and passed it to his left as well. "On the bright side, there should be enough copies for all. Naturally, there are a few things *not* listed in this summary. We may be generous and openhanded by preference, but we are neither innocent nor stupid. You can, however, trust us when we say we prefer peace over war and friendship over enmity.

"Or as the Afaso martial arts system, which holds the tenets of practical pacifism close to its heart, likes to say . . . we may not care to *start* any fights, but we sure as hell will finish them."

"Grand Captain Maq'en-zi, you are *not* leading this meeting," one of the other grand generals stated—no, he was a grand admiral, Jackie realized. His knotwork had the same loops to it that the woman, the high admiral, had, and which some of the others—presumably the generals high and grand alike—did not have on the golden front panels of their coats.

"No, I am not," Jackie agreed smoothly. "Your Empress is leading this meeting. However, given that she has not interrupted me, she has for the moment ceded the floor to me. For which, she has my thanks, as I'd like to dispense with unnecessary delays."

"She has what the what?" someone asked, a man seated next to the high admiral who had condescended but who was carefully being silent now. "That is a very strange phrase."

Li'eth quickly stepped in, reaching out to Jackie's mind for a better explanation. "The term comes from their parliamentary government. The person doing all the talking may not be the leader, but usually they talk while standing in the central floor space between or before the risers holding the other members attending that meeting. That floor space, where the speaker stands, is normally under the control of the highest-ranked person at the meeting . . . or, alternately, under the control of the person arbitrating the meeting, or even the person who assembled the meeting. To 'cede the floor' means to hand over that right to speak—but not the control of the overall meeting—to the next or current speaker."

"*Cur-nel* Maq'en-zi is correct," Hana'ka said. "I am allowing her to speak. That *is* why she is here, gentlemeioas. I, too, would like to dispense with unnecessary delays. Your comment about who is leading this meeting, Grand General Ma'touk, is a double-edged sword. I appreciate your defending my authority. However, the way you expressed it was dismissive of the Grand High Ambassador's right to discuss her people's military expertise." She accepted the diminished stack of printouts being handed to her, took one, and passed the stack to her left, then fixed the general in question with a pointed look. "I believe you owe our incipient ally a brief apology."

". . . My apologies, Grand High Ambassador *Cur-nel*," he stated, dipping his head.

Wrinkling her nose on the title-stacking, Jackie eyed either end of the table, then addressed the Empress. "Eternity, I would like to suggest that we dispense with ranks and titles for this meeting. Our Terran ranks are immaterial to this discussion; you are not in our chain of command. We are here because we are the experts who have been assigned to *be* here. And since we are not in *your* chain of command, your own ranks—I should say, *their* own ranks," she amended, "are equally meaningless to us though we acknowledge they are important to you.

"Until we are cooperating together—and we have not even set up a system for that just yet—such things are mouthfuls that are getting in the way. Particularly if I keep having to switch hats, so to speak, from being military advisor to being civilian representative and back, over and over."

"We *do* have an idiom about switching hats when switching points of authority," Li'eth stated dryly when she finished and looked around.

"Thank you, Liaison. If this were one of my civilian side meetings, I would have a small rebellion on hand from all the nobles who would protest that protocol is everything," Hana'ka stated, her gaze holding steady with Jackie's. "But as this is a military meeting, and the War Queen expects her military to be efficient . . . we will dispense with titles for the moment. We rarely use them as it is when we are alone," she added, giving her officers a pointed look. "In the interest of expediency, we will afford our Terran guests the same familiarity and courteously assume them to be our equals."

Another of the women at the table not quite snorted in reply. She gestured with a medium-purple-striped hand, aiming a vaguely dismissive sweep toward the Terrans. "Eternity, they are *hardly* our equals when not even—"

"—Our. Equals," Hana'ka asserted, cutting off the high general seated near her son's attaché. "Or did you suddenly gain an overwhelming amount of extremely detailed information on Terran military might in the last nanosecond? No? Did you miraculously morph *into* a Terran military advisor, an expert in all things related to their combat skills and technology? No? *Leftenant Superior* Kos'q knows more about Terran military capabilities than *you* do, High General, and he lies near the bottom of the Second Tier in rank. However, he has my respect for that knowledge, and for his willingness to share it with us both in his debriefings earlier and in this particular meeting."

(*Well,* that's *a good sign,*) Li'eth whispered in Jackie's mind.

(*What is?*) she returned, curious.

"As it stands, Generals, Admirals, the only people in this chamber who know the most about the Terrans *are* the Terrans. I will give them the full and thorough respect that superior knowledge deserves, and hope that, by it, we as a nation will earn their trust. I suggest you start giving them a high level of respect and trust as well, in the hopes that we will attain their loyalty to our most pressing cause."

(*She's firmly on your side at the moment. Of course, you should give her an overt show of your trust and respect in return.*)

(*Already on it. Also, I like your mom. Or rather, your Empress,*) Jackie clarified. (*I haven't "met" your mother, yet.*)

(*Eventually, you will,*) he allowed.

"The Eternal Empress has our respect for striving to remember that we are not V'Dan," Jackie said quietly. "She remembers that we are not to be judged as V'Dan, by being careful not to judge us as markless V'Dan juveniles. She in turn knows that we are striving not to judge you as Terrans . . .

which means we are striving not to be offended by each and
every condescending, dismissive remark. I do admit, however,
that it will be easier if you kind meioas would help hold up
your own end of that task by *refraining* from doing so.

"We came here believing that you are experts in V'Dan
military capabilities. We also came here with the expectation
that you would understand and grasp that we in turn are
experts in Terran military capabilities. Shall we get back to
discussing those capabilities in mutually respectful ways?"
Jackie asked. "Or do any of you have another inappropriate
observation to make?"

The high general blinked and stared a few moments, then
looked at her liege. "Are you going to chastise them for talking to us that way, Eternity?"

"Apparently, you *did* have another inappropriate observation to make," Hana'ka stated wryly. "I find it disturbing
that these Terrans merely *look* like children. Yet even more
disturbing is how those of my highest-ranking officers who
are here, and presumably have been listening to everything
they have had to say . . . are *not* acting like adults."

"Eternity, I would—" the purple-striped woman tried to
protest. A swiftly raised hand cut off her words.

Hana'ka stared at each of her officers in turn, ending with
her son. Very few of them—Li'eth included—met her gaze
steadily. "You are soldiers of the Empire, sworn to defend our
people and our planets to your very last breaths. I should not
need to remind you of these things, but it seems I must. At *any*
moment, the Salik fleet could come *here*. They have the exact
same ships, weapons, and capabilities that we have, with the
added advantage that *they* know exactly when and where they
plan to strike.

"*We* do not have the Terrans' interstellar communications
capability, which at the very least could alert us of enemy
ships headed along a particular path and thus triangulate on
their next probable system full of victims. We also do not have
their ability to transit light-years in mere seconds," the Empress added sternly. "So *we* cannot follow them on their vector,
leap ahead, and coordinate with the locals to set up swift
ambushes along possible flight vectors.

"We can do that with their communication devices, but

only if those devices are already in a system . . . and they won't be placing the first one outside this system until later today. They are here to offer us these things, yes, but we will not have their loyalty if we do not give them our respect. I trust I am making myself clear in this matter."

(*Definitely on your side. For the moment,*) Li'eth cautioned his Gestalt partner while the other officers tried not to look too uncomfortable at the dressing-down they were receiving. (*In truth, the Empress is always on the side of the Empire. If you ever pose a hazard to the Empire, she will act accordingly.*)

(*Duly noted, and already understood.*) Out loud, Jackie said, "Thank you for defending our right to be respected, Eternity. And thank you again for your willingness to see us as the adults we already are, in spite of the cultural differences between us. Now, if everyone understands these things, may we please return the subject to something a bit more time-sensitive and useful, such as establishing some field-test demonstrations of Terran starship capability? Everyone has a copy of the first printout, yes? I believe Commander Graves and Lieutenant Colvers were about to suggest looking into that. With your permission, Empress, shall we get to it?"

"Yes. We shall. U'Veh, our farthest moon, has salvage-processing yards for the remnants of starships too badly damaged to be repaired in this system," Hana'ka stated. "It also is home to an Imperial Fleet gunnery academy, which uses some of those spare parts for target practice. It shouldn't be any trouble to give your people some chunks to test."

"Commander?" Jackie said, looking at Robert. He nodded and picked up that subject.

"We've brought some spare munitions for just that chance, and some scraps of our own hull plating for testing with your weapons, too, if we can borrow some of your better academy students to test it. Plus cameras and other sensor arrays to start crunching numbers."

"Crunching . . . ?" an admiral asked.

Li'eth replied even as Jackie dredged up an answer. "It's an archaic term for computing or calculating. I believe it came from the sound of manual computational devices having their barrels cranked, which is similar to our own version, cranking the numbers."

"Then I don't see why it can't be called cranking," the general muttered. "No offense is meant, but that word makes more sense to us."

"None taken. Vocabulary differences are the least of our concerns right now," Jackie smoothed over.

"Right . . . well, we do want to *crank* the numbers," Robert allowed, altering his vocabulary slightly. He lifted up the sheet in front of him. "Now, we ran some passive scans of your hulls. The underlying tensile strength of your bulkheads is impressive, but the actual skins are made of more of the same metal. We haven't seen any signs yet of the actual thermal coefficiency of our *ceristeel* exterior ablation plating . . ."

"Negative, *Embassy 11*," Jackie asserted via the commlink between her location on V'Dan and the system, nine light-years away, where *Embassy 11* had found itself gliding toward a starfight between the local defense fleet and far too many Salik ships. That system contained the world of Hom-Do, or Second Home in the local tongue, the first outsystem world colonized by the Empire. "Do *not* engage. You do *not* have permission to engage. Is that understood, *Embassy 11*?"

(*What . . . ?*)

"Understood, sir. We will follow that order . . . but we don't have to like it, sir," the comm tech on board the *11* replied.

(*Dammit, can't a man use the washing room without . . . !*)

"I don't like it either, Lieutenant Commander, but your cargo is more important than the impact one tiny ship could have—wait, someone get me a system chart!" Jackie ordered, looking up from the commscreen. The aides around her were mostly civilians, but the abrupt discovery of a Salik attack in the next inhabited system had sent some of those aides running for military personnel. "Where are there other colonies in that system, right now, right at this moment in space-time?"

One of the aides had already turned to her workstation and was punching up the data. ". . . I have it," she asserted after just handful of seconds. "It's twelve minutes away, but that's in V'Dan measurements."

"We installed converters on our ships. Stream the exact coordinates on the same channel," Jackie directed. "Give them physical marks to calibrate—planets, moons, asteroids. *Embassy 11*, I know twelve minutes is a little close, but if you can, short-jump to nearspace of . . . uhh . . ."

A second aide came over with a datapad in his hands. Jackie quickly studied the system schematic while the screen she had been using filled with coordinates and distance measurements, and nodded.

"The planet Chan-Do, it's marked here as a refueling station, so it's bound to have ships on hand. Put yourself on a parabolic course around it, aim for the processing station at the gas giant Lyzir-Do. At Chan-Do, broadcast in lightwave V'Dan that Hom-Do is under attack, and at Lyzir, tell them to stand guard against anything headed their way—can one of you officers get me an authorization code?" she asked the trio of uniformed officers who hurried into the room. "Some sort of call sign so my people can tell yours in the ships around Chan-Do that this warning is legitimate?"

There was a solid-steel triangle like Li'eth had originally worn, a brass-square outline, and a silver four-point star outline. The one with the star outline led the way, fixing on Jackie as the center of everyone's focus. "What's the situation?"

Jackie swept her hand over the system display. "We were about to drop off the first communications array at Hom-Do. *Embassy 11* is still about seven minutes away in transit, less than half a minute lightspeed lag, when they saw Hom-Do coming under attack less than two minutes ago; our ship is not at liberty to engage, but they can get to Cham-Do in . . ."

"Two minutes thirty-five seconds to jump, sir," the lieutenant commander on the other end stated, hearing her words. "We're feeding the coordinates and changing vector now. We might overshoot a little; ten minutes is the shortest the hyperarray can safely transit, but we'll be within thirty seconds lightspeed lag at the farthest."

(*Done and on my way,*) Li'eth told her.

(*Washed your hands?*) she teased dryly while the general— she double-checked the knotwork, yes, general—gave the crew of the *Embassy 11* a set of code words to use.

(*Of course. Almost there.*)

The fueling stations of Chan-Do and the processing station at Lyzir-Do had low population numbers but heavy clusters of ships. That meant they were heavily defended for a low-yield prize. Hom-Do, however, was a borderline M-class world with a temperate-zone-style climate at the equator, rather large ice caps, and a lot of geothermal springs. She and the others in the Terran delegation had learned about it and other V'Dan colonyworlds during their time in quarantine. It had a very bad ratio of ships per capita.

All the Salik had to do was get enough ships past the blockade to land and start doing damage on the planet. Like taking captives. Or rather, food. She and the others had been warned that Salik warriors would fight all the fiercer to take live sentient prey because if enough were taken, then everyone could get a bite before their victims bled to death. Not just the officers.

". . . And if you take a parabolic toward Treskan-Do and 'jump' to it," the nameless general was saying, "you can warn them as well. They won't be able to get any ships there in time to help with the battle, unlike Chan-Do, but even if they just send three, that'll be three more than Hom-Do will have for patrolling its skies and picking up debris while the colonists are unpacking the sweeper ships."

"Understood. Ambassador, permission to follow the outlined flight plan?" the lieutenant commander on the other end of the screen asked. Beyond the workstation, Li'eth entered the room, a little flushed in the face from hurrying, but only a little.

Jackie looked over the amended drawing on the aide's tablet and nodded. "Permission granted. Take your time coming back to Hom-Do and park yourselves five light-minutes out. Do *not* approach until the enemy has completely left the system *and* the locals are aware of who you are. At the very least, wait until after the ships from Chan-Do have had time to explain how they got there so fast."

"Understood. Sirs, one thing," the lieutenant stated. "This many jumps, no matter how short . . . we're going to be around 45 percent fuel by the time we get back. We will not be able to continue to the next system without refueling."

"Li'eth, do you know if the ships with the vaccines have made it to that system yet?" she asked him.

"I . . . don't think they have. We've only just finished distribution in this system," he told her. "Inoculations *are* being given to all outbound V'Dan crews. I know that for a fact. But I don't think we've shipped anything to the other colonies for direct distribution just yet. I can check, but it's better to be cautious than pandemic."

"You heard the man, Lieutenant Commander. As soon as you have safely deployed the hyperrelay, report back to V'Dan for refueling."

"Aye, sir . . . and our two minutes are up. We'll speak with you after we've jumped to Lyzir-Do, when we have a long parabolic to get us to the next location. *Embassy 11* out."

"V'Dan base out," Jackie agreed. She straightened and nodded at the aide. "Thank you, meioa, for that system chart."

He smiled. "Thank *you*, meioa. I have cousins living on Hom-Do. They might come to the party late, but the ships at Cham-Do will get there before that fight is over, and they'll do it a full eight minutes faster than the Salik will expect." He winced a little, but still smiled. "I don't know if my cousins will be in any of the areas that are being attacked . . . but I have more hope that they'll survive."

"We'll do what we can, but the fleet's primary mission is to give *your* people communications abilities," Jackie told him. "We're still not yet ready to engage directly in this war if we don't have to . . . and we don't have to, just yet. For myself, I'll wait to hear how the battle goes, then count my successes. But at least we won't have to wait hours and hours," she acknowledged.

"A wise outlook, Ambassador," Li'eth agreed. "It will be a few minutes before they can contact us again, yes? Would you like something to drink while we wait?"

"I'll try that *caffen* stuff. It's not very stimulating like *coffee*, but it tastes a lot better," Jackie admitted. "Actually, if we could blend the caffeine of the Terran version with the gentler taste of the V'Dan, horticulturalists and plantation owners would make millions."

(Anything *that would make your coffee taste better is a bonus, in my mind*,) Li'eth muttered. (*No offense, my love, but that drink is* disgustingly *bitter. Even if it does wake me up slightly within the first four sips, it's not worth a fifth*.)

(*Whereas I could have five cups of yours and barely feel an energy buzz. No offense taken, and none given*,) she agreed. (*I think I'll sink some personal money into hybrid research*.)

(*Oh? Are you wealthy?*) he asked, moving toward the *caffen* dispenser in the nook just off the main communications rooms here in the government wing.

(*Not by as much as you'd think. I could retire for a good ten years, and be able to travel, or retire for fifteen if I were frugal, but I'd eventually have to go back to work either way. A livable wage was mandated by law back at the foundation of the United Planets, and I make good money as a translator, but I only received my highest salary while I was an actual Counselor. That ended when I stepped down. My Ambassador's salary is a little bit less, but it was explained to me that part of my funding was tied up in the embassy—food, housing, that sort of thing. Like being in the military, only said food and housing are a lot better in quality.*)

(*I cannot imagine you'd get to keep a trio of surfboards mounted on your walls as an officer of the Space Force,*) he admitted.

(*You have a vividly accurate imagination. If I were just an officer again, I'd be on system patrols. I am deeply grateful your people are located far from the region the Grey Ones occupy. No room for a 'board on board,*) she concluded—in Terranglo, so he'd get the pun.

She got a mental chuckle in return.

MAY 22, 2287 C.E.
JANVA 16, 9508 V.D.S.

The twenty or so priests and priestesses, she expected. Li'eth, she expected, too. This was, after all, a session scheduled and arranged to explain, demonstrate, and teach the absolute basics of Terran-style holy-gift wrangling. But when she entered the medium-sized reception room set aside for such classes, Jackie had not expected to see Li'eth's father.

Both men were clad formally, Li'eth in his uniform, his father in that uniform-like style that most V'Dan wore, though his outfit was some sort of fabric with a slight, satiny sheen to it that had been dyed in shades of light and dark brown. The color contrasted richly with the pale pastel layers worn by the priesthood standing and sitting in clusters around the room, and, of course, proved a definite contrast to the simpler lines the Terrans were wearing, such as her own peach-and-rose pantsuit.

A quick glance around the room showed they were missing only two Terrans, Aixa and Clees. Swerving toward the prince and his father, she moved to greet them first as the highest-ranking people present. "Imperial Consort Te-los, we are honored by your presence, and particularly by your interest in learning Terran mental disciplines. You have my personal reassurances that we will do all that we can to honor and respect your trust in us."

"I have had the opportunity to question my son and learn of the training you gave him, Grand High Ambassador," Te-los said. "I can sense how much more powerful he has grown with just a few months of that training. His mind is now closed to me whenever we touch. I should like to gain that ability for myself."

"You will gain it if you pay attention and practice the techniques we will teach . . . but please, when the moment is not formal, call me Jackie," she offered.

He smiled and bowed slightly. "I would be honored."

"Good. And good morning to you, Li'eth," she added, turning to his son. She reached up a hand to touch his face, since that was the most skin showing. He returned the gesture, stepping close and lowering his forehead to hers.

(*Good morning.*) He sighed, the sound more sleepy and content than he physically looked. At her subthought inquiry, he explained, (*More nightmares about the Salik pens. I didn't sleep well.*)

(*Well, greet me out loud so we're not being rude to the untrained and the nontelepaths in the room, and we'll get going soon. Hopefully, you can sort out and smooth out the unsettled feelings during the grounding and centering exercises.*)

(*Yes, meioa.*) He smiled and pulled his head back, though he still cupped her cheek. "Good morning, Jackie. Are we ready to begin?"

"We're still waiting for Aixa and Heracles. It's a full morning session with a lot of people, so we'll need all five telepaths on hand. And I should go greet the highest-ranked priests, now," she added. Reluctantly removing her hand, she moved away from the two men.

(*We're going to follow you, to ensure you have a subtle show of Imperial Blood approval at your back,*) Li'eth warned her. He still sounded sleepy, but also content and amused. Like a big cat getting ready to purr. (*Father truly is impressed by the changes in my abilities, but then he knows the most about how they used to be.*)

(*Understood.*) Approaching one of the most familiar robed figures in the room, a dark-skinned woman with pink spots that trailed down the edges of her hairline and vanished into the collars of her layered clothes, Jackie smiled at her. "High Priestess Tar'eth Truthspeaker. It is good to see you again. It is even better to see you without having to be in quarantine at the time. I am glad you are here, willing to learn Terran techniques."

The older woman lifted her head, looking down at Jackie. Not because she was taller—she was actually about the same height as Jackie, 165 centimeters at most—but as a sort of affectation. Finally, she lowered her chin. "You speak the truth. I am glad to see that."

Drawing in a slow, deep breath, Jackie smiled, and merely said, "If you keep an open mind and a willingness to learn, then in time, you will come to understand us better. For instance, we do not lie about such things. It would be counterproductive."

The other person she meant to greet drifted their way. "Grand High Ambassador."

"Superior Priest De'arth of the Open Mind," Jackie greeted formally. "Welcome to the Terran embassy. I hope you, too, will find great value in our teachings today."

"That remains to be seen," he stated skeptically. Then blinked and flushed, looking past her shoulder. "Imperial Consort Te-los . . . Imperial Prince Kah'raman. Good morning, Your Highnesses."

Jackie stiffened, feeling the priest reaching toward Li'eth's father with mental fingers. Throwing up a shield between the two men, she narrowed her eyes. "High Priest, what you are doing is *extremely* rude."

The tendrils splayed out to either side, trying to find a way past her interference. Quirking one of his brown eyebrows, the brown-squiggled, pale-skinned priest asked, "What do you mean?"

"Everything and everyone within this embassy zone is to be considered under Terran law, by command of Empress Hana'ka V'Daania . . . and we have laws about *psychic* conduct, High Priest," she informed him. "Among those are rules about *not* probing anyone else's mind without their permission. I can see with my inner eye how your gifts are reaching out from you toward the Imperial Consort. He is here under *my* protection, and while he is here, *no one* will touch his mind without his clearly and freely expressed consent, given in advance."

"I still don't know what—*ah!*" he gasped, as Darian joined them.

The expression on the young, dark-skinned man's face was stern, bordering on cold. "*I* can see it, too—and I am the one who smacked your probes this time. You *will* learn appropriate behavior."

"You two remember meeting before, yes? If not, meioas, this is Darian Johnston, an officer in our military and a strong *psi*, a holy one in your terminology," she stated, gesturing toward the newcomer. He was a stark contrast to everyone else in the room but Min, as both of them were clad in camouflage grays, button-up shirts tucked into trousers, both sets newly issued for this mission. "Darian, I believe you remember Superior Priest De'arth of the Winter Temple, and High Priestess Tar'eth of the Spring Temple."

"I remember. I also remember you had to have your mental fingers smacked at our original meeting, for reaching when you had no permission to do so," Darian added, eyeing the older man. "I trust you are willing to learn, and use, proper mental discipline through our classes?"

De'arth straightened his shoulders and looked down at the slightly shorter man. "I am a high-ranking priest of the Winter Temple!"

"You have the self-control of an infant," Darian stated bluntly. "Close your mouth and open your ears, and you will finally learn a few things. Your religion means nothing to me, and your rank means nothing to me. The only way you will impress me is by how carefully and thoroughly you do learn, today."

"You will find, Superior Priest, that all of us hold that

general sort of opinion," Jackie said before De'arth could speak. She raised her voice by tightening her gut, projecting to the rest of the room without actually shouting. "Your training is inadequate by our standards. We are not impressed by your rank, and we are not going to be swayed by any mysticism. We are here to teach. If you are not here to learn, and learn with the respect due to your teachers, then you should leave.

"We will have no students in this class who are not here of their own free will," she added. Aixa entered the room, slowed to look around, then shrugged and moved to join the two psis while Jackie spoke. "But do understand that we will also *not* permit anyone to violate the right to mental privacy all sentient beings possess. Not in our presence. We will stop you, and warn your target of your attempts, unless and until we hear you request and receive permission to continue from your target in our presence. We will also continue to monitor you to ensure that, in your imperfectly trained attempts, you do not injure any such willing targets."

Min joined them, adding to the conversation. "Our rules are very strict on proper psychic behavior. If you stay, you will learn them. If you leave . . . you will still be subject to them in our presence." She let that sink in a moment, then softened her expression into a modest, wry smile. "We have only a few classroom rules. While a subject is being taught, the only teacher in the room *is* the teacher; all others are students, or assistants appointed by the teacher."

"We will be strict but reasonably fair," Darian added. "If you need help, ask and we will assist you. If you think you know how to do something . . . *ask us* before you do it because we want to help you learn how to do it in the best and most efficient, useful ways. That means watching what you do. You might know a good technique, or you might not. It might even be something we have not considered, though the chances of that are admittedly rare."

"Above all," Aixa stated, "we *do* want to help your people learn these things." She fixed her gaze on the Winter priest. "We guarantee that if you pay attention, follow our instructions, and practice carefully, you will see significant, palpable increases in your abilities . . . which will become a great benefit to your nation when wielded wisely."

"With that said, everyone please move over there," Jackie ordered, pointing to her left to a clear spot near the door. "Please take your belongings with you, too. I am going to re-arrange the furniture while we await the arrival of Heracles, our official instructor in these abilities."

"You are not the teacher?" Tar'eth asked, raising her brows.

"I am the strongest psi in the embassy, but that does not make me the best teacher. I will be helping him, as will Aixa, Darian, and Min, but Heracles Panaklion is a fully trained, licensed, and experienced instructor in psychic abilities. Please move to that space by the door, now."

Tar'eth nodded, gave her a slight bow . . . and planted her dark hand on De'arth's pastel-covered shoulder to get him to move when he lingered. When the others were out of her way, Jackie looked over the waiting furniture. It had been arranged in conversational clusters, which was fine for a reception or a party but not as useful for a group lecture. Thinking for a few moments, she finally held up her palm and lifted most of the furniture, one piece after the other, until they were all floating. As she did so, the conversations of the others died out.

The V'Dan equivalents of end tables and coffee tables moved out of the way, stacking at the far end of the room. In near silence, Jackie worked patiently, carefully, not wanting to damage the furnishings. While the couches moved back against the far wall, all but five chairs arranged themselves in nested semicircles. Those five chairs, she sent up high and left them hovering in silence. As soon as the other chairs and sofas touched down, a few small tables returned to rest between some of the seats, but most stayed along the back wall.

Once they were down, throw pillows floated off the sofas under her silent command. More came soaring slowly out from a stack in the near corner. Those, too, arranged themselves in neat curves with spaces in between. Jackie cleared her throat, dragging her gawking audience's attention back to her. "Please find a seat, whether it's on a chair or down on the floor, which-ever you prefer, and make yourselves comfortable."

CHAPTER 12

"What about those hovering chairs?" Te-los asked warily, pointing up toward the floating furniture.

"I'll be bringing them down where everyone is standing as soon as everyone moves," she explained. "Those are for the instructors to use—you need not fear an injury, Highness. So long as no one tries to attack me, my control is absolute. If someone did try, I might throw one at them in self-defense, but I doubt anyone is going to do that. Everyone, please take a seat and make yourselves comfortable."

Min stepped forward as the others moved toward the indicated areas. "Don't forget to loosen your clothing. If you are warm, feel free to take off an outer layer if you like. This is not a formal feast or a presentation before your Empress. This is a classroom. In the act of concentrating, some of you may find your body temperature rising, so please be ready to reduce layers if need be. In fact, the more comfortable you get yourselves now, the fewer distractions you will have plaguing you.

"We will be getting more comfortable, too." She demonstrated by unbuttoning her own shirt; pulling it out of her trousers, she showed the plain gray tank top underneath. Muscles flexed in her arms as the young Asian woman neatly folded and rolled her camouflage shirt. "So long as you are covered from shoulders to thighs, you will be perfectly decent by Terran standards for this exercise."

There were now enough people out of Jackie's way. She brought the five chairs over everyone's head, ignoring those who startled and ducked out of the way; the ceilings were more than four meters high on this level, which meant plenty of room for telekinetic furniture arranging. She even brought over a couple of end tables to settle between the chairs. Just as she brought the last chair down into place, a purple-toned pink affair with rounded armrests and a sort of leatherlike covering, Clees entered the room.

He did so juggling a briefcase, two pads, and trailing four hovercameras. Two of the hovering machines belonged to the Terran control pad in his left hand, which he thrust at Darian. The other two belonged to the V'Dan version, which he held out to Jackie. Finished with her task of furniture shuffling, she accepted it.

"Put those somewhere where they have an excellent view of the room and can pick up the sound fairly well, please?" he requested both of them. He set down his briefcase as soon as they had the pads, and turned to the others. "We are all here to learn Terran-style holy-gift control, yes? Good! In fact, it is *good* to see so many people here for today's introductory class to Terran-style lessons in *psychic* abilities."

(*I was thinking about setting one of each type on each side—those two tall lamp things look like they have flat surfaces for their support struts,*) Darian suggested to Jackie. She nodded in return, and they each positioned a hovercam there. She had to turn both lamps a little so that they had unobstructed views, but the split-screen projections on each pad showed an excellent broad swath of the chamber and its occupants.

Gesturing at himself, clad in an off-white suit with a dark gray shirt and matching shoes, their instructor introduced himself. "I am Heracles Panaklion of the Psi League—you may call me Clees if you like—and I come from the land of Greece, which was the birthplace of several important concepts that have shaped our modern life—everything from common citizens being able to vote on laws, to attempts at defining life, the universe, and everything in between . . . to the very important task of applying a scientific, logical, empirical-evidence-based approach to how we try to grasp and understand the events and ways of everything around us."

Done with positioning the cameras, Jackie set her pad down on the nearest table. As the older man continued, she unbuttoned her rose-hued jacket. Peeling it off, she draped it over the back of one of the chairs, revealing her sleeveless peach top, dusky, tanned arms, and the tattoo marks over and around her right shoulder and arm.

"This science-based approach may seem shocking to those of you who come from a system of training that has been deeply rooted in mysticism for thousands of years," Clees continued, pacing a little with a finger raised. "But I assure you, it has been tested and proved to be quite effective. Today's class will be four and a half hours long, and will focus on terminology and the absolute, most basic lessons that all *psis*—short for *psychic* or 'holy one'—all of us have to learn.

"There will be lectures, discussion sections with question-and-answer periods, some questionnaires so that we can get an idea of what you can do, what you know about doing it, how you go about doing it, and how you feel about doing it. Plus water breaks, washroom breaks, and, of course, the all-important *practical* lessons in the three most basic arts of psychic-ability management, something we like to call grounding, centering, and shielding. This will be followed by a buffet-style luncheon provided by the embassy's culinary staff.

"So, you will all have a chance to sample a variety of foods prepared the Terran way, as a reward for your good behavior and attentiveness. A good reward, yes?" he asked, grinning and spreading his hands. He received a few nods, and sighed, placing his hand over his heart. "No, no, my new friends, you must have *enthusiasm* for these lessons. You are all too stiff and formal—six of you are still standing, the rest of you are all seated in chairs . . . no, we shall challenge this!

"In order to learn, you must be comfortable. Not just physically, but mentally and emotionally. We are all here for the common cause of learning, yes? Then we all have something in common. This makes us all allies, for this learning is not a competition to tear each other down. Rather, you gain more when you help build each other up. So! While my assistant Aixa hands out some sheets with terminology printed on them for you to study and take with you," Clees stated, opening his briefcase and handing a stack of papers to the older woman, "we shall begin by introducing each of your five teachers, starting with me, then moving on to the rest of you. We shall each mention at least two of our abilities, *and* we shall each of us mention something that we like, something we enjoy doing, or something we enjoy seeing each day.

"I am Cleese, I am a Rank 13 telepath—a speaker of

minds—and a Rank 7 clairvoyant and clairaudiant—that means I can see and hear things in places I send my mind, even when I do not send my body—and my favorite thing to do outside of my work with the psychically gifted is being an amateur videographer. As you can see, I have already arranged for two sets of cameras to record this session. The ones recorded with the Terran equipment will be used for our own purposes, primarily as a means of keeping track of all the things we have taught you, so that in future sessions, we can fill in any gaps before moving on to additional material.

"The ones recorded by the V'Dan equipment will be processed by kindness of the Elite Guard during our meal. They will then give you recordings to take with you as you leave. We are still in the process of translating the audio languages as well as supplying translation texts for them, but we do hope to have official Psi League training guides translated and made available within a few more months." He turned and looked at Jackie. "Will you introduce yourself next, your name, some of your abilities—you don't have to name all of them—and something about yourself?"

"Of course." Nodding as he turned and seated himself, Jackie stood. "Hello, everyone. I am Jackie, and I am a Rank 15 telepath, a Rank 14 xenopath—I can communicate with alien minds, and read the thoughts of animals with higher intelligence capabilities—and as you have just seen, I am also a telekinetic, Rank 12, someone who can move objects without physically touching them.

"As for my hobbies and interests, I enjoy the watersport of surfing, which was developed by my ancient ancestors among the tropical islands of Hawai'i, which is where our capital is located. It involves using a lightweight, waterproof board of a specific shape to slide along the slopes of incoming ocean waves," she explained. "I'm told your tides are a bit complicated because you have three smaller moons instead of one big one, but I am looking forward to riding the local waves someday."

A young man in pale green robes edged with autumn leaves raised his hand, palm toward himself, V'Dan-style. Clees lifted his chin. "You have a question?"

"Yes. I understand you are all unmarked, which is strange to think of that as being natural, but you, Grand High

Ambassador, have been inked with tattoos. Why have you not marked your face and your hands to show you are an adult?" the priest asked. "Why only your shoulder, and with such strange marks?"

(*He means well,*) Li'eth quickly offered, while Jackie struggled to keep herself from rolling her eyes. (*He's just ignorant.*)

(*Yes, I know.*) Out loud, she stated, "That is because they are *not jungen*-style tattoo marks." Turning sideways to the group, she pulled back the sleeve opening of her shirt, displaying as much as she could. "The line drawing in the center, of the eye shape with eight 'rays' splitting the center, is called the Radiant Eye. It is the symbol of the Psi League, the main nonreligious training and service organization for those with psychic abilities. I got the tattoo of it because I have been a member for several decades. It is inked in black because that is the official color and style, black on a plain background.

"The sprays of blue flowers draped around it are actual drawings of *jacaranda* flowers, which is where my first, or given, name comes from. The black pointy triangles surrounding those things are not triangles. They are the teeth of a shark, which is a fierce predator in the waters around the Hawai'ian Islands, the land of my mother's mother's people. In the custom of my mother's people, a shark is seen as a powerful creature, and its teeth in a plain black tattoo means 'protection.'

"There are three rings of shark's teeth around the Radiant Eye and the jacaranda flowers because three times now I have faced off and sent fleeing the greatest enemy of my people, protecting our home system from their attacks. The center of my protective strength lies in my mental abilities, as represented by the Radiant Eye, yet I am also free to be as delicate and beautiful as a subtropical flower.

"These tattoos are filled with rich cultural and personal meaning. They are not meant to be color slathered on my skin in order to help others discern my physical age. I already have adult secondary sexual characteristics for that." At his blank look, she clarified bluntly, "I have *breasts* for that. I don't need a tattoo to show my age."

He blushed and looked away.

Darian stripped off his outer shirt, rolled up the short sleeve of his tee shirt, and twisted in his seat, displaying his own bicep. "My skin is a bit dark to see it easily, but if you look carefully, you can see that I, too, have a tattoo of the Radiant Eye."

"Why don't you introduce yourself?" Clees urged him.

"Right. I am *Lieutenant* First Class Darian Johnston—the equivalent of a Leftenant Superior—and I am a telepath, Rank 9, a xenopath of Rank 8, and I have a mix of talents that allow me to sense the history of an object and write down what its users were thinking about, if they ever thought about anything strongly. I can do this even in languages I myself do not know, and give a sense of what the symbols mean, if not an exact translation. I enjoy working with the military and plan to keep with it for as long as I am physically fit and mentally able. I guess you could call it my hobby as well as my career, because I love what I do."

A nod from Clees, and Min introduced herself next. "I am Lieutenant Junior Grade Min Wang-Kurakawa. My rank is a fancy version of 'ensign fresh out of the Academy,' since before we left Earth, I had not yet served six months and am thus not eligible for any promotions just yet—Terran regulations state that you have to serve six months in a particular type of duty post before advancements can be considered, and this post is very different from the last one.

"I am also a Rank 9 telepath, though I cannot communicate with aliens. I can, however, communicate with and understand machines," she added, flicking her almond-brown eyes over to her dark-skinned colleague. "Darian and I have been attempting to arrange for access to any chunks of Salik machinery that might contain important information. At the very least, I can link minds with him, and he can then draw diagrams of what I myself can sense, but not articulate or explain. I am hoping to learn the language of the Salik with the help of one of my xenopathic colleagues, either Darian, Aixa, or Jackie, so that I can more directly translate what I'll be sensing. But that requires capturing and interrogating one," she finished.

"And a hobby or an interest?" Clees prompted her.

Min blushed a little. "Right. I like dogs. They're descendants of four-legged, domesticated, pack-minded predators known as wolves. They're very kind and sweet and can be quite clever when well trained. If I were a xenopath, I'd have gone into the military's animal-handling corps, what we call *K-9*. The letter-and-number combination is a homophone—sounds similar to—the word *canine*, which is a fancy scientific name for the dog family."

"We have dogs on V'Dan," Te-los reassured her, smiling. "I prefer the company of hunting *gats*, myself, but we do have dogs here at the Winter Palace."

"I, ah, I suppose that makes sense, if you only left ten thousand years ago, and our joint ancestors domesticated wolves into dogs around twenty to twenty-five thousand years ago," Min allowed, blushing a little more. She cleared her throat and regained her composure, once more an officer and not an awkward young lady. "I hope I'll have the chance to see some of your dogs, Highness."

"Next?" Clees prompted.

"Ja, ja," Aixa dismissed. "I am Aixa Winkler, and I do not eat meat from animals smarter than a dumb fish because I am a powerful xenopath, Rank 11, as well as a xeno*empath*, Rank 7—which means I sense the emotions as well as the thoughts of many land animals and even some birds—and I have a degree in biology. I also have the ability to sense changes in the weather. We have been here only for a few days, but I can tell that we will most likely have heavy snowfall by tonight. So you had better travel carefully if you are going anywhere tonight.

"Unfortunately, I am only a *metrosentient*, meaning I can sense and determine the weather. I am not a *metrokinetic*, which is someone who can actually *do* something about the weather. Which is a pity because I am getting old enough that my joints will soon be aching with every little change in temperature, air pressure, and humidity," she added dryly. "As for hobbies, I both knit and crochet, which is where you take some yarn and either a pair of stiff long rods or a hooked tool, and you use them to hook together loops . . . yes, you have hands raised?" she observed as over half a dozen did just that. "So you know what crocheting is? Good. We shall have to exchange patterns at some point—yes, Darian?"

He lowered the hand he had raised. "I crochet sometimes, too. Mostly little hats for prenatal infants. One of the sergeants on the first ship I served on showed us all how to do it, and taught us how to do it for a good cause."

"That's good to know," Clees praised him. He turned to a priestess who had hesitantly taken a seat on two cushions she had stacked together on the floor. "And you? Tell us about yourself."

"I am Junior Priestess Mel-thanth of the Spring Temple . . . and I am affected by the emotions of others," she said. "Which is why I chose to sit on the floor, away from the others. It . . . isn't personal."

"We will be able to help you with that," Clees reassured her gently.

That seemed to cheer up the somewhat shy young woman. "I, ah, also can sometimes see glimpses of the future in my dreams. I keep a journal by my bed, and write in it every morning. My teachers in the Spring Temple tell me that all the best of the foreseer Saints did that, in case they dreamed of something that would someday come true."

"We can help with that as well," Aixa told her. "Writing down one's visions and dreams in a journal is indeed the first step. Eventually, we will be able to show you how to dream lucidly, remember everything, and even guide your dreams a little . . . though it is a delicate balance between remembering vividly as you navigate a *precognitive* dream, and guiding yourself right out of the dream and into waking up enough that your own thoughts and preferences don't start interfering with those delicate, foreordained visions . . . but we can teach you."

"Precognition, or visions of the future, foreseeing events before they happen, is the single most difficult psychic ability to master," Clees agreed. "That is not because it is difficult to remember the visions with enough clarity to write down the details accurately . . . though that is a part of it. No, the hardest part of precognition is that the future is mutable. It shifts with each of the actions we undertake. Some things can be changed, other things will happen anyway. It is not always clear to see what is happening right now and determine if it will help or harm something that might or might not happen tomorrow."

"Do you have any interests or hobbies, Mel-thanth?" Jackie asked, curious.

"I collect sand from places I've never been. I suppose that seems strange to you, but I have my friends and family collect sand from the beaches and lakes and rivers they visit," the young woman amended. "I have little jars of sand from five different worlds, a jar from each of our three moons—I'm Sh'nai, not a Trinitist, but I still wanted some from the moons—and from several places around V'Dan, including from the Necropolis of Dawn. I'm hoping . . . that is . . ."

Jackie smiled. "I'll see if we can have some sand shipped from Earth—the Motherworld of our species—and perhaps some from Mars, and from our own moon. I cannot guarantee any, but I will put in a request for it. And I don't think that's strange at all. You must be very busy with your holy work here in the capital if you cannot travel yourself, so it makes sense that you ask your friends and family to gather it for you."

She nodded shyly.

"Next?" Clees prompted, before the young priestess could gush over the generous offer. Checking herself, Mel-thanth politely turned to the next V'Dan psi to be introduced, as did everyone else.

MAY 24, 2287 C.E.
JANVA 17, 9508 V.D.S.

The felinoid on the other end of the screen, Count Daachen, flicked his whiskers forward, a positive sign from what Jackie had been told, but his silver-and-gray-mottled ears still flicked forward and back in uncertainty. "This call is coming frrrom the V'Dan homeworrrld?"

"Yes, Your Excellency," Jackie confirmed. This communication link suffered from a five-second lag, meaning a ten-second turnaround.

Once again, she was in the main communications room of the government wing, the chamber that had the most important messages processed from around the planet, from the local moons, and eventually from each colony and station within the system if it wasn't delivered by insystem mail couriers. The technicians were eager to integrate Terran hyperrelay communications into their systems as swiftly as possible, but they were also capable of discretion, which meant keeping to their own work, aside from an occasional glance toward the Terran in their midst. The Terran and the Solarican, technically.

The Solarican at her side, War Lord Krrrnang, flicked his own cream-and-ginger ears. *"Rrrzach mauwfren yaah krrihl vzhnoken trraah."*

The count—or at least the V'Dan equivalent; it was some sort of system-lord who oversaw the colony *Embassy 8* had reached a little while ago—flicked his shades-of-gray ears sharply forward at whatever the War Lord had said, golden eyes widening. *"Sharrrull?"*

Krrrnang nodded solemnly.

Count Daachen flicked his ears back and switched back to V'Dan. "It is good to knnow these things. Where shall we put this . . . device?"

"The V'Dan military suggests a stationary location, rather than a circling orbit. Things in orbit tend to get noticed and shot down by the Salik," Li'eth stated. "Particularly when they move."

"It must, however, be an airless location. The communication device requires vacuum to function properly," Jackie clarified. "My people will place it if you can give us V'Dan-Standard coordinates for your system."

"You have put juvenniles in charrrge of this new technology, Imperrrial Prrrinnce?" Daachen asked politely.

Almost politely. Jackie bared her teeth. She knew that was an impolite thing to do in Solarican terms, but his comment was equally impolite. "We are a different group from the V'Dan, Excellency. Separate, with our own culture and our own government as well as our own technology. This technology is *ours*. It does not belong to the V'Dan. Nor will it belong to you. The device must *not* be tampered with to learn its secrets, or it will explode."

"You should nnnot put the conntrol of explosives inn the hands of chilldrren, Highness," the count stated, ears flicking back and staying back.

"You insult our allies, Count Daachen," Li'eth replied coldly. "I told you they are not V'Dan. You insult them as if they were. You will apologize to the Grand High Ambassador."

One ear twitched, but the count didn't speak immediately. Jackie narrowed her eyes. "The fact that we are even having this conversation is proof of the value of an alliance with my *non*-V'Dan nation. It is its own proof that you should treat us as what we are: adults who should be respected for our willingness to share our non-V'Dan technology. But if you dislike the idea of nearly instantaneous conversation with other star systems, and all the military advantages it brings, my people will be happy to remove our communications array from your system and leave you to your fate."

"I do nnnnot deal with chillldren. I willl speak with the one who has authorrrity overr you."

"Krraach vann garrach llarr!" the War Lord ordered. Immediately, the two Solaricans got into a shouting, hissing, snarling match that actually made them sound like cats.

Seeing the male at her side bristling—literally, his fur was starting to stand out on his snarling face and his tensing arms—Jackie reached over and touched him. *"Enough.* Calm yourself, War Lord. Calm yourself, Count. There is an easy way to handle this matter."

Considering that what the alien had said was exactly what he had said to Captain Li on board the *Embassy 8,* Jackie checked the console of the workstation and pressed the button that opened the audio link to the ship.

"Captain Li, you are instructed to rebroadcast the conversation we have just had with Count Daachen on all local communication wavelengths, all the way through these orders to you. You will then remove the communications probe from System Nephrit 113 and continue to the next inhabited system, where you will offer that probe to them instead. You will also explain to them that, due to the insults given by Count Daachen of the Solarican nation to our sovereign Terran nation, the Nephrit System has been denied access to our communications technology for the foreseeable future."

"You cannnnot do that!" Daachen asserted. As he started ranting again, Li'eth reached over and turned down the volume on his channel.

"To the people of the Nephrit System, as the Grand High Ambassador of the Terran nation, I can only state that this is the consequence of your local leader's decision to repeatedly insult a potential ally, and his refusal to apologize when directed to do so by a high-ranking officer of the Solarican nation. Please understand that this was not the wish or the intention of the Terran nation. We came in peace to offer you

an immense advantage over the Salik, our mutual enemies. We expected to receive a reasonable amount of respect for our generosity. We will not, however, tolerate disrespect.

"You may bring your concerns to the Terran embassy, which is located at the Winter Palace on V'Dan, but please understand that the V'Dan government has no authority over the Terran government. The Solarican government has no authority over the Terran government or our technology, either. You will respect us as a separate nation, you will respect us as adults, and you will need to find a legal way to either get Count Daachen to show us a great deal of respect on top of several apologies for his repeated insults, or you will need to find a legal way to remove Count Daachen from power and place someone into his position who has far more intelligence, forethought, and compassion for your people. I hope, in the meantime, that the Salik do not choose to target your system. As the V'Dan say, I will not hold my breath.

"I am Jacaranda MacKenzie, Grand High Ambassador of the Terran nation, and I accept the consequences to the Terran nation of my decisions in this matter. I expect nothing less for Count Daachen on the consequences of his decisions to the Solarican nation. These are your orders, Captain Li. Please carry them out," she finished.

"Acknowledged, Ambassador. Embassy 8 *out."*

Reaching for the controls again, Jackie ended the communications link with the main colony settlement in the Nephrit System.

"You have teeth annd clllaws, Grand High Ambassador," Krrrnang stated quietly. Jackie quickly checked his face; his ears were back, but his whiskers forward. There were several things about the Solaricans that were uncatlike—their limbs, their faces, their ability to speak—but ear, whisker, and tail postures were oddly not among them. Then again, they did quirk their brows like a Human, narrow their eyes when angry . . . purse their lips when they smiled, as not everything was alike.

"They're called fingernails, and they're not so magnificent as your own . . . but yes, I can wield them hard enough to scratch and draw blood," she said. "When provoked."

"You may ennnd up scrrratching yourrself," he warned her.

"I am employing something called the prisoner's dilemma.

One variation of it goes like this: If one person offers a bargain and the other cooperates in honesty, both profit by it. If one person offers a bargain and lies to the other, then the liar gains, and the target suffers a loss. If that one person offers an honest bargain and the other lies, then the offerer loses, and the liar gains. If both lie, both lose. In some versions, both know the rules, but neither can communicate with each other. In other variations, they know the rules and can communicate both before and after any exchange."

"It is a commonnn thrread in most Allliance species that cooperrationn brrrings greaterr rewarrds," Krrrnang agreed.

"True. But life involves more than just two players, and the way to get ahead in the game lies in playing multiple rounds with multiple people," Jackie told him. "The rule to succeed in most instances is to *always* open negotiations honestly and fairly. If they cooperate with you with equal honor, then you both profit by it. If they are dishonest or cheat, you punish them on the second round. If they correct their behavior and turn honest in their dealings, you immediately are honest and honorable with them as their reward. If they continue to lie and cheat, you cut them off and move on to the next person.

"The trick is to make sure that everyone else understands the consequences of cheating you, so that when you approach them, they know that you will deal honestly with those who are honorable and that you will not deal with those who are dishonorable," she told the War Lord. Her gaze flicked to Li'eth and back to the Solarican. "So far, the V'Dan are mostly treating us with honor and respect. There are a few rough spots, but the benefits outweigh the irritations and the insults.

"We are also kindly and generously making allowances for the fact that their culture—not yours, but theirs—has a certain primitive attitude toward skin color being the sole determination of a person's knowledge and maturity levels. It is something my people fought long and hard to give up over the centuries. We finally did so just before the AI War just under one hundred years ago," Jackie added. "It was hoped that, given how they've been out among the stars longer than we have, and that they've had genetic throwbacks to nonmarked versions of their *jungen* virus, that they would have lost such attitudes long ago as well."

"But we have not," Li'eth admitted. "I am sorry so many of my people are unable to look at you and see you for who you are, not who they expect you to be."

"Your remorse is admirable, Your Highness," Jackie allowed. "It remains to be seen if our repeated requests to be treated as Terran adults instead of V'Dan children will be heeded over time."

Krrrnang eyed each of them in turn, his ears flicking back a little. "I am tollld the two of you arrre twinnnned seers. Yet you speak as if you arrre onn opposite sides."

"The Terrans have faith that their Ambassador can keep her work and her private life separate," Li'eth explained, turning his attention to the alien. "After having seen her in action as a diplomat and a stateswoman, I have that same faith as well."

"A strrrrange statement," the War Lord pointed out. "What if her worrrk and her prrrivate llife come into connfllict?"

"We will deal with it, if it ever does," Jackie told him.

The Solarican eyed each of them, then pursed his lips. "I should lllike to be a *perrsnit* underr the nearest table whenn it does."

Jackie gave him a blank look for a moment, then comprehension dawned. She smiled—carefully without showing her teeth—and replied, "We say 'a fly on the wall.' But yes, I'd imagine that would be an interesting moment. One I wish to avoid."

Krrrnang flicked a look at the Imperial Prince and back. "This is a warrrning to all the memberrs of the Alliance, then—allll of them—that you will nnot tolerrrate dishonorable dealings."

"Yes. If the Count apologizes properly, we will reward his system with a hyperrelay system," Jackie agreed.

"And by 'properly' . . . ?" the War Lord fished delicately.

"He has to acknowledge in actual words what his error was, pledge he will not repeat it, treat all members of the Terran delegation with the respect we are due as adults, and apologize not only to my people, but to his own people for . . ." She trailed off, realizing that there was an incoming message on the V'Dan bandwidth the *Embassy 8* was using. Tapping the controls, she activated the audio link. "Embassy 8, *this is Ambassador MacKenzie, go.*"

"Count Daachen has just threatened to destroy us if we do not leave the hyperrelay in place, sir," Captain Li stated. *"How shall we respond?"*

"Correction," Jackie muttered, disappointed and bordering on disgusted. "That is what he *could* have done to salvage this situation . . ."

"Ambassador, could you please clarify that statement, sir?" Captain Li asked through the open link.

"I was speaking to someone here, Captain. Could you please connect me to Count Daachen?" Jackie requested. *"Video, so he sees who he is talking to once again."*

"Of course, sir."

A moment later, the screen blinked on, and the gray-striped Solarican bared his teeth. "I thought that woullld get your attennntion."

"Count Draachen. I am stating this in the presence of War Lord Krrrnang, military advisor of the Solarican embassy to the V'Dan Empire, so that you know just how seriously the Terran United Planets takes you. The crew of the *Embassy 8* has stated you have threatened to attack their vessel if they do not leave a hyperrelay unit in your star system," Jackie stated, making sure she pronounced the V'Dan words carefully. "If any vessel, armament, or even a pressure-suited person of the Solarican nation attacks a Terran citizen or a Terran vessel, it will be considered a declaration of war.

"This means that *all* Solarican-controlled systems with Terran communications technology will have that technology immediately destroyed, and all future systems will be denied access to that technology until such time as the war ends and all war criminals are handed over to Terran authorities for trial and punishment . . . and I will remind the Solarican nation that not only do your people *not* know where mine come from, *we* can coordinate both attacks *and* defense across planetary orbits and different star systems alike.

"War Lord Krrrnang," she added, deliberately turning down the incoming volume on the channel with the wide-eyed, ear-back count as he started cursing, though not the outgoing feed. "I will have to revise my earlier statement on what it will take to get my people to deposit a hyperrelay in the Nephrit System."

"What will it take, Grand High Ambassador?" the alien asked softly. Politely, though his ears had flicked low and his tail was now lashing, flinging the ginger, cream, and brown strands this way and that.

"Someone with actual common sense and courtesy in charge of that system," she told him flatly. "You are, of course, free to leave Count Daachen in place, but the Terran government will not deal with him. We will not deal with anyone who, upon delivering an insult and then refusing a request to apologize for it, chooses instead to threaten the lives of our sovereign citizens. *Captain Li, continue your assigned task of removing the hyperrelay probe from the system. You may close the link to the Count, but keep an open channel from your ship to the* Embassy 1 *at all times. I want to know to the lag-time second what happens to your ship while you remain within the heliopause of Nephrit 113.*"

"*Understood, Ambassador. We will keep this channel open and clear. Closing the link to the count.*"

"I should lllike to speak with him firrrst, beforre the connectionn clloses," Krrrnang requested.

"War Lord, he threatened one of my ships," Jackie stated flatly. "If you wish to speak with him, you are going to have to get into one of your own ships, travel there the normal, pre-Terran way, and speak to him in person—he might be in the mood to travel *here* to lodge his complaint, as I instructed, so make sure someone here can handle him if he does so while you're on your way there. Either way, I suspect that *I* would like to be one of your *perrsnit* creatures under the nearest table for *that* conversation. This is known as the punishment phase of the prisoner's dilemma. If he wants our advantages, he is going to have to learn that his bad choices have consequences."

". . . You have an excelllent earrr for accennts, Ambassadorr," the War Lord stated politely. His ears were up again though they twitched as though they wanted to flatten, and his tail was still snapping from side to side. His whiskers were trembling, twitching somewhere between forward and back. "I must forrrmally protest this actionn."

"I know. I will be delivering a protest to Grand High Ambassador Trrrall shortly," she added. "After I have made sure the *Embassy 8* leaves the Nephrit System safely. If it does not,

I will have to deliver notice that we deem that to be a declaration of war." Lifting a finger, she pointed at the War Lord. "I don't care what your people do to Count Daachen. That is your business as a sovereign nation. However, he is a thoughtless idiot, and my nation will not interact with him."

Li'eth winced. "Grand High Ambassador, that is *not* a diplomatic thing to say."

"No," Jackie agreed. "But it is an accurate description. Every diplomat, bureaucrat, and statesperson in *my* government is expected to be both educated and capable of reasoning through the long-term consequences as well as the short-term consequences for the majority of our decisions. Nobody is perfect, but we are expected to try to think of several possible consequences in advance. This is because we are held responsible for those decisions.

"War Lord Krrrnang, I give your people the courtesy of presuming that all of your own government officials are equally educated and thoughtful until each individually proves otherwise. We acknowledge that no sentient being is perfect, so we can even be flexible and forgiving at times. Up to a point." She looked him in the eye. "That particular set of decisions, insulting myself and my people, refusing to bow to the dictates of courtesy by apologizing, and then on top of that, *threatening* my people . . . was idiocy piled upon shortsighted idiocy."

War Lord Krrrnang flicked his ears. "I am . . . unnable to rrremark upon the inndividuall in questionn at this time."

"I understand, and I sympathize." She started to say more, but the commlink to the *Embassy 8* interrupted.

"Ambassador, the cargo is secure, and we are getting under way for our next destination. No sign of pursuit."

"Acknowledged, Embassy 8. *Good luck, and keep the channel open until thirty seconds to departure,"* she ordered.

"Acknowledged."

"Grrand High Ambassador . . . if the lllink is going to remain openn for a llittle while longerr . . ." Krrrnang suggested, glancing at the console.

"This is the part where, in the prisoner's dilemma, everyone *else* gets to see the punishment in action," Jackie told the furred alien. "We will not deal with those who think threats of destruction and slaughter are an appropriate choice when given the chance to make a new friend."

"If yourrr ship rremains in the system a little llongerr," the War Lord stated, "I can rrrequest our Grrrannd High Ambassador make a decisionn on rrreplacing him."

She wanted to help him, but Jackie shook her head slowly. "I'm sorry, War Lord. His actions have consequences. Your *inconvenience* at not being able to use our other-than-light communications capacity is less important than driving home the lesson—"

"—Clawing out the lesson," Li'eth interjected, giving her a better phrase. He sent her an undercurrent of attached examples of how it should be used in different situations, according to the Solarican mind-set.

"Thank you, Liaison. Your inconvenience, War Lord, is less important than *clawing* out the lesson that no one can threaten the Terran United Planets without bleeding from their self-inflicted wounds," Jackie stated, picking one of those subthought examples to use on the Solarican. "We have no intention of starting a fight with your people, but please be aware that we are prepared to fight all the same. Like the prisoner's dilemma, played over and over, our action is to begin negotiations politely. Our *reaction* will depend upon how we are treated.

"The point, War Lord, is to make this moment unpleasant enough that your people will work harder to avoid it than they otherwise would have strived," she said.

"The innsult was givenn by Count Daachen," Krrrnang pointed out. "Not by me."

"The insult was given by a government official," she countered flatly. Softening her tone, she said, "Think of it this way: I now have an example to hold up to anyone else as to why it would be inappropriate to continue insulting me."

"But the peoplle of that system—" he pressed.

"—Are no worse off than they were before." She shook her head again. "They are undergoing the exact same risk of unwarned invasion as before. They have to endure the same hours-long transit of your faster-than-light starships in order to get any news or orders from anyone. The only difference is now you and they know there is another, better way . . . and that the leader in that system assumed too much authority, and has made some potentially, but only potentially, costly mistakes."

His ears flicked back, and his whiskers twitched down. His tail flicked once, then he spoke. "You, MacKennnzie, act lllike a plant-eaterr . . . and pllot like a nnight-hunterr."

"I will take that as a compliment, from one warrior to another," she allowed. "The next system on the *Embassy 8's* flight plan is also Solarican. As per standing orders, the *8* will attempt to enter around a light-hour away from the main settlement and slow its speed in order to observe for traffic patterns before making its final approach. If you wish to go visit Grand High Ambassador Trrrall, you'll have about an hour and a half before anything happens, maybe two."

"That, I shalll do," Krrrnang agreed. He bowed and headed for one of the doors.

Jackie waited until the fur-trimmed military advisor was out of sight before turning and slumping back against the edge of the workstation counter. (*That . . . was not pleasant. I hated disappointing him.*)

(*You're playing a potentially dangerous game.*)

At that quip, Jackie shot Li'eth a sharp look. Arching one brow, she asked, (*Is that what you think? That I am playing a game far more dangerous than threatening lives?*)

He held up his hand close to his chest, palm inward in V'Dan style, and tipped his head. (*Not in immediacy, but in scope, yes.*)

(*Prisoner's dilemma,*) Jackie returned. She folded her arms across her chest. (*I have to establish that the Terran United Planets does have a line, that it will be drawn, and that anyone who steps over it will face the consequences of overstepping proper behavior.*)

(*That is an odd set of metaphors,*) he murmured. It was a mental aside, not an invitation to discuss etymology. (*You cannot hold the whole of the Solarican Empire hostage for the actions of an individual.*)

(*I can if that individual was appointed by their government. But you're making it sound more dire than it truly is,*) she told him. (*I would be happy to deal with a flunky, an assistant, a somebody-who-isn't-that-idiot. Or that idiotic. How these Solaricans react to my statement that we will not deal*

*with Count Daachen anymore will illuminate the true state of
their politics. Is he there because of nepotism? Did he bribe
his way to that post? Does he have enough money or black-
mail secrets or whatever to keep that post? Is he honestly just
that arrogant? Will he sit on his county throne and sulk, or
will he charge here to your homeworld to lodge more of his
insults in person? Or will he realize the error of his attitude
and come here in person to apologize?*

(*Does the Grand High Ambassador of the Solaricans to
the V'Dan Empire have the authority to step on him and his
tail until he behaves, or the authority to make him step down
and have someone else step up into the count's role? Will
Trrrall even feel like he should bother or not? Will the War
Lord send a ship to the Nephrit System? I did not choose to
stir the pot,*) Jackie told her partner. (*But I am going to take
advantage of the swirls to see what sinks to the bottom or rises
to the top.*)

He blinked at her. (*I keep forgetting you are a lot more
devious than you seem.*)

She smiled slightly; his sending had undercurrents of wari-
ness, yes, but more swirls and eddies of admiration and respect threaded throughout than that sense of uncertain caution.
She took it as an edged compliment, the kind where Jackie
knew she didn't dare let herself get a swelled head. It would
not do to fall into the trap of believing her actions were always
going to be for the best, after all. Staving that off meant ana-
lyzing her motives each and every time.

(*Be glad I use my powers for good, then, I guess,*) she told
him. (*I really would rather get along with him, and I would far,
far rather get along with the Solarican Empire, and all the
rest. But your communications isolation leaves each system's
foremost leader in a precarious position. They end up so
immersed in protecting their own system and their own interests, due to how long it takes to communicate with everyone
else, they forget that their decisions can have very far-reaching
consequences for other systems as well as their own.*

(*I can understand the reason behind his actions even as I
must stand against them. An understandable reason is not the
same as a license to act as though theirs is the only source of
authority.*)

(*You have a remarkably sophisticated culture, Bright Stone,*) Li'eth observed dryly.

(*We've had a hundred thousand years of evolution, and a hundred thousand variations to explore, learning how to make it so,*) she agreed. (*But then so have you, in your own ways.*)

(*Thank you.*) There was a pause, then both of them shifted awkwardly. Li'eth blinked and frowned slightly. (*I'm feeling restless again. How long has it been since we held hands?*)

Jackie twisted and checked the chronometer on the workstation monitor. (*Not quite one hour. The spans are definitely getting shorter.*)

(*We will have to be more intimate than just holding each other, soon,*) he warned. (*I can distract myself with work, as can you, but in these lull moments . . .*)

She felt her cheeks growing a bit warm. (*I know. I'm trying to figure out how to break the news to your mother that her precious baby boy, for his own sanity's sake, has to sleep with a foreigner who looks like a child.*)

(*That would be my job, not yours,*) Li'eth stated. He shifted just enough so that their matching poses of folded arms and backsides leaning on the counter behind them allowed their upper arms to touch. Both were wearing sleeved outfits, so it wasn't nearly as effective as skin-on-skin, but it did soothe some of the need to be close. (*Speaking of some of us being in close proximity to you Terrans . . . while I requested V'kol be reassigned to my side, Ba'oul and Dai'a were given leave to go home for a little bit before being reassigned—they nearly died a very ugly death, and I don't begrudge them wanting to go home. However . . . Leftenant Superior Nanu'oc has finagled her way into sticking around the Winter Palace through her Second Tier connections, even though her county lies a lot closer to the Summer Palace than here.*)

(*Oh?*) Jackie asked. (*And this is important because . . . ?*)

(*Rumor has it she's been seen in the company of one Lieutenant Brad Colvers. On several occasions,*) he told her.

(*That . . . is not exactly a pairing I would have picked,*) Jackie admitted slowly. (*I mean, I know they started getting to know each other a little more because of her punishment assignments, but I wouldn't have picked either of them as interested in getting to know the other side.*)

(*Neither would have I,*) he told her. (*But there you have it . . . Should I do something to send her off on an assignment, so you don't have to accidentally encounter her again?*)

Tempting as that thought was, Jackie shook her head. (*No. They do have a right to see each other, if that is what they wish. And if I can't blame you for wanting your best friend to stick around, I can hardly blame her from using her own influence to stick around for him. If that's why she's sticking around. She might still be trying to find a way to get back at me somehow, though you'd at least think she'd realize I'm too firmly ensconced in my much higher rank, by now.*)

CHAPTER 13

MAY 27, 2287 C.E.
JANVA 20, 9508 V.D.S.

In person, Count Daachen was a bit more canine than felinoid to Jackie's eyes. She wasn't sure why, possibly something about the jaw and nose, but that was the impression she had. It also occurred to her, as he entered her formal office with his ears turned back, whiskers down, and nostrils flaring a little with each angry breath, that the noses of the Solarican race were more Human-like than truly catlike.

"I do nnnot apprrreciate being kept *waitinnng*," he growled, glaring at her. His garments were shades of gray, layered so that they echoed his tabby-striped appearance. The hemlines of his sleeveless thigh-length vest and knee-length robe fluttered to a stop a second after he did. Jackie thought he looked rather good.

A pity he's a modofrodo in his attitude. She wouldn't dare say the epithet aloud, choosing instead to speak politely. "Greetings, Count Daachen. You look well groomed today. That outfit is very flattering."

"I did nnnot come here to discuss ffffashion!" he hissed, tail lashing.

"That's rather odd," Jackie replied lightly. "Because what you're upset about is nothing more than fashion. Even more strange, your people are born so that some have marks, and some are markless, yet you do not get upset at how they stay that way for the whole span of their lives . . . unless they get deliberately modified, of course. But here you are, upset that *my* people are born markless, and stay markless, for the entire span of *our* lives. And all because the V'Dan—an entirely separate nation—are born markless but develop spots and stripes and swirls and whatever at some point during puberty.

"It's all rather shallow compared to truer maturity. After all, maturity is something that looks beyond mere surface appearance to gauge the quality of the *person*, not their mere appearance," she added dryly, staring at Daachen but addressing her words to the other person in her office. "Would you agree, Grand High Ambassador?"

"I woullld," Grand High Ambassador Trrrall purred, his tone languid yet amused.

The count whipped around, grunting faintly when that caused his tail to hit Jackie's desk. *"Meerr shnalll gu Trrrall?"*

Seated in one of the padded but lumbar-free chairs in Jackie's office, the Grand High Ambassador of the Solaricans gestured with a black-spotted, white-furred arm toward the younger male. He, too, addressed his counterpart, not the count, and he did so in V'Dan.

"I am a bit concernned, Grrrand High Ambassadorr, that the esteemed Count Daachen did not see fffit to visit me ffirst. It is the task of *alll* Solaricanns to visit with theirrr *own* embassy firrst, befforre lodging a compllaint with a fforeign nationn," Trrrall added. He held the gaze of the startled count. "This is how we avoid diplomatic innncidents. Sinnnce you have not donne this, it is good that I am alllrready here."

"Count Daachen, do you have something to say at this time?" Jackie asked politely.

He looked between her and his people's ambassador to the V'Dan, and pointed at her. "This V'Dann rrrefuses to sharre their communnnications technology with our system!"

"This beinng is *nnot* V'Dan," Ambassador Trrrall stated

bluntly. "You arre attempting to judge herr people as if they arre *Vedoychrr* when they arrre actually *Sillgrenn*."

"They arrrre V'Dann. We are all *Alliannce*," Daachen insisted. "We are not near the *Vedoychrr*, let alone the others!"

Vedoychrr, Jackie realized, was most likely the name of a pocket of Solarican settlements. Or rather, a set of allies near a different pocket of settlement. "Trrrall is talking about a metaphor, Count. My people have a saying that also applies. 'When in Rome, do as the Romans do.' It means that when you are dealing with people of a specific culture, you should deal with them on their own terms, not on any other nation's terms. After all, surely you would not apply the courtesies and protocols required of the V'Dan Empire to someone from the K'Katta nation . . . would you?"

His ears went down and back at that, and the count's tail flicked as well. Trrrall rose from the chair, graceful despite his age. "Count Daachen, you have serrved our Queen well enough . . . but you have grrrown too arrrroogannt for yourrr position. You will rrretire—this is withinn my authorrrity," he added, pointing a claw-tipped digit when the younger male started to speak in Solarican. "I speak in V'Dann so that the beinng you insullted unnderstannds. By yourrr choices, you have caused a dipllomatic incidennt that has caused innnjurry to yourr citizenns.

"War Lord Krrrnang has already rrreached Nnephrrit 113 by nnow. He is infforming your system of yourrr demotionn and is instrructing your househholld to pack everrything. They will come herre, and your ffamily willll be rrreassigned elsewherre. You will rrremain here in our embassy untill the nnnext ship home is rrready to depart, orr a suitable rrelocation colony is picked."

"Grand High Ambassador," Jackie stated carefully, puzzled by the punishment. "I do not wish to challenge your authority in this matter, but isn't relocating his entire family a bit harsh? Could he not just be given some other job in the Nephrit System?"

"The severrrity of his insullt could have rrrepercussions throughout all Solarican ennclaves," Trrrall told her. "If therre is a way to get yourrr communications system to reach our homeworrrld ffrom here, then it could rrreach the Queen's

Empire anywherre in the galaxy. Thrrreatening your vessell with violennce is *beyonnd* unacceptable behaviorr. Our Queennn does nnnot apprrrove of extorrrtion. It does nnot rrreflect well upon our nnation to be the *first* with a diplllo-matic incident."

He pinned the gray-striped count with a hard look and his whiskers forward, his ears down. Daachen shrank back subtly . . . then lifted his chin and tilted his head to the side. His ears were flat, whiskers down, tail close to his legs, with only the tip twitch-ing. She realized after a moment that he was exposing their spe-cies' equivalent to a jugular vein. A posture of surrender.

She took pity on the count. "Actually, the V'Dan have already had the dubious honor of creating the first diplomatic incident. But he did not mean to cause the problem, he apolo-gized promptly, and he took steps to ensure it would never happen again. Not only within Terran jurisdiction, but within V'Dan as well. We have forgiven him for it."

"I apolllogize forr insultinng you . . . and yourr people. Grrrand High Ambassadorr," Count Daachen stated.

Quickly holding up her hand V'Dan-style, palm toward herself, Jackie shook her head. "My people have a saying. 'Too little, too late.' Your attempt at an apology comes a little too late to do any good. I am not angry at you, Count, but I am disappointed in you. For the sake of your family, who are blameless, I shall see if I can influence your Grand High Am-bassador to be lenient and allow your family to stay within visiting range of the people they may have come to know and love in the Nephrit System.

"After all, it would take at least a few more Solarican colony leaders being rude to my people and me before I'd ban the use of our communications arrays from all Solarican sys-tems just from verbal abuse," she admitted to Trrrall.

"Then I shalll be more gennerous with his rrelocationn," Trrrall returned. He flattened his ears and whiskers a little. "I do apollogize in advannce, Ambassadorr MacKennzie. I also have been tempted to view you as youngerrr than you rreally are. I shall strrruggle to make surre it does not affect our ffu-ture interractions."

"Your honesty is respectable, your regret is honorable, and both are deserving of leniency," she replied.

The count looked between the two of them, then asked cautiously, ". . . Will my system . . . forrrmer system . . . be given access to your communications?"

"In time," Jackie told him. She shook her head when he flicked ears and tail. "That unit was reassigned elsewhere. Your system will have to wait until Nephrit 113 can be worked into a new delivery route. We have limited ships available, limited refueling resources, a finite production rate, and we are reserving spare relays for capital systems. Such as this one, which has seven major population hubs scattered throughout the system, and the home system of the Gatsugi, which has six."

"Come, Count Daachen," Trrrall ordered. "We shall leave the Grrrand High Ambassadorr to her work. You annd I have rrreporrts to write. Ambassador, we shall connntinue ourr discussion laterr."

"Of course," Jackie replied smoothly.

Neatening his robes, the elder statesman shooed the younger out of Jackie's spacious office with a flick of his clawed fingers. The gesture was a bit Human-ish, but their tails told the real story. Trrrall's was curved up; Daachen's drooped down.

Very Human-like, and very feline, and very something else, she decided. Daachen's arrival had been delayed so that Trrrall could arrive swiftly—War Lord Krrrnang had explained to her people about the proper protocol of reporting to their own embassy first, in case Daachen came all this way and failed to follow that protocol. The two of them had exchanged a few pleasantries and comments about their impressions of the V'Dan Winter Palace before Daachen had entered the room. It wasn't much of a conversation to continue, but Jackie did look forward to it.

Now if only she could view a discussion with, oh, say, the K'Katta Grand High Ambassador with equal equanimity and poise.

MAY 30, 2287 C.E.
JANVA 23, 9508 V.D.S.

Pacing, unable to sit still, Li'eth moved restlessly back and forth while he waited for the Terrans to reach the Imperial

Wing's formal *mo'klah* suite. He didn't see the gilded furnishings, the friezes on the walls of famous scholars and other geniuses, the uniformed staff waiting for the signal to bring in the first of several light courses. Nor did he really see the snow swirling beyond the windows. Not that it mattered; the entire Winter Palace was designed so that no one had to go outside if they did not want. Indeed, the *mo'klah* suite held two real fires in the fireplaces on opposite walls, keeping the chamber comfortably warm.

Some of the Terrans, Li'eth knew, had a midafternoon snack called "high tea." In specific, it had been an experience he and his surviving officers had experienced while chatting with the Governor of London on their tour of Earth. The experience had involved a specific beverage, little flavorful sandwiches and blended pastes spread on crackers, biscuits savory and sweet, fresh fruit, and sauces for dipping and smearing.

Oddly enough, there was a V'Dan version practiced by the higher Tiers, too, only it was called *moh'klah*, after the main drink served at such meetings, a mix of *klahsa* and *caffen*. There were tea bushes on V'Dan, genetically very similar to their Terran cousins, more so than coffee versus *caffen*, but tea was drunk in both nations by those who liked its astringent qualities more than the slightly bitter *caffen* . . . or their very bitter coffee.

There was also a treat on Earth very similar to *klahsa*: chocolate. Terrans had focused on developing the ratio of *klahsa* paste or powder to *klahsa* butter, creating dark, milk, and light chocolates. V'Dan had some of that, but his people had also focused on using processed cane sugar into *cho'klah*, raw cane sugar into *meh'klah*, and honey into *sah'klah* for the sweeteners used, and powdered inner bark from the *cimmon* tree, which was a genetic cousin to the Terran *cinnamon* spice, forming the piquant *ri'klah* version of *klahsa*. Those were just the base flavors, too, without adding fruits and other ingredients.

Tea-leaf blends came in a bewildering number of varieties; their high tea with the city governor had included an interesting taste-testing presentation on several different types, with a display of hundreds of more varieties. *Mo'klah* came in its own set of varieties, ranging from dark to light *klahsa*, to which the percolations of *caffen* beans had been added, and whether they'd been roasted or not, and for how long.

Thinking about *caffen* and coffee, tea and *klahsa* was better than fretting over how much he was missing her physical presence.

Being quizzed on what he thought the Grand High Ambassador and the Assistant High Ambassador might want was a bit awkward. He knew what he liked; Li'eth's personal favorite for breakfast was a spicy-sweet white *ri'klah* blended with green—unroasted—*caffen* beans. Later in the day, he tended to prefer darker, richer flavors, dark *klahsa* blended with roasted-bean *caffen* served with a hint of *ushen*, juice concentrate made from tart berries. But that was something one could only get reliably planetside. Being stuck in space for years, he had learned to take his *caffen* plain, since sugar and especially *klahsa* was usually rationed for kitchen use, not personal.

He did have the advantage of knowing a little bit about Jackie's tastes. She liked her coffee with sweetener and cream-rich milk, though if she had the option, she would pick an iced tea, unsweetened, with a bit of lemon or lime. And he knew she liked chocolate. Rosa McCrary, however, was a stab in the dark. Li'eth had tried to ask subtle questions, but . . . telepathy didn't allow for subtlety. Subthought, yes; subtlety, not really. Jackie had finally asked him directly what he wanted to know and why.

Her reply to his statement that the chefs wanted to know for a formal *mo'klah* service had been refreshingly blunt. (*Li'eth, we are both used to being offered strange local delicacies wherever we travel in the United Planets back home. I personally have eaten bugs, spiders, eels, sea slugs, land slugs, snails, snakes drowned in wine, bird's nests made out of bird spit, and worse. I am quite certain that whatever your chefs deem suitable for your mother, the Empress, to safely eat will be fine with the two of us.*)

Her comment about eating spiders had pricked him with astonishment, so she had mentally muttered that she hadn't looked while they were being prepped, the meat had been pulled out of the carapace, impaled on some sticks, and marinated before being grilled, and would he please stop thinking about it and move on to a much less phobia-inducing subject, thank you very much. Naturally, he had complied, but it had left him with ambivalent feelings.

On the one hand, she was far braver than he was. On the other, he didn't want to ever have to explain to the K'Katta that a small number of her people were accustomed to eating something which was the equivalent of a K'Katta eating a small monkey. The K'Katta might or might not be bothered by such a concept.

Hands clasping and unclasping, he paced. All these formal meetings, formal attire, formal manners . . . it was getting harder to control the urge to just rip off his coat and his shirt, pull off any sleeves she wore, too, and hold her against his bared chest. *Don't think about* her *bared chest, though,* he ordered himself sternly. *Respect at all times . . .*

(*Almost there . . . I think,*) Jackie murmured in his mind, just as someone entered the room. He turned, but knew it wasn't her. It was his father, accompanying the Empress. His mother. Li'eth dropped to one knee out of respect and received a gesture to rise. Fingers and feet moved again, the one set interlacing and clenching, the other set moving and shifting.

"Kah'raman," he heard his mother say. He turned to eye her, and caught a hint of puzzlement in her aura though her tone was level and calm. "Is there a reason for your pacing?"

The doors on the other side of the room opened, accompanied by an announcement from the Elite Guard at the forefront of the small group on the other side. "Presenting the Grand High Ambassador Ja'ki Maq'en-zi and Assistant High Ambassador Roza M'crari of the Terran Empire."

Li'eth knew it should properly be Terran United Planets, but *Empire* was something his own people understood. An empire was a strong thing. An empire had an existence spanning nearly ten thousand years. An empire had culture and tradition and respect. But a set of united planets led one to thoughts of unions, and unions were things found among the skilled laborers of the Fourth Tier, a lower caste than the Third Tier all foreigners were supposed to be deemed.

(*Your mental shields are very tight,*) Jackie murmured, praising him. (*I can barely follow your thoughts.*)

(*Master Sonam would be proud of me. I've been practicing,*)

Li'eth replied, easing the tight cloak he had wrapped around his mind.

(*That, and he would probably call us idiots for barricading ourselves from each other,*) she added. She and Rosa both dropped to one knee in respect for his mother, exchanging polite greetings. (*The tighter we shield each other out, the more our suffering grows. We spent half an hour cuddling yesterday, yet I have my hands clasped together to keep them from fidgeting today.*)

(*Same here,*) he agreed. He caught the eye of one of the servers and made a discreet gesture. Bowing, the man herded the others quietly out of the room, giving them some temporary privacy.

The two women were now exchanging polite greetings with his father. Both looked lovely; Rosa wore a dress that floated with layers of aquamarine and white. Jackie wore her black dress with the oversized, vividly colored flowers along the fluted sleeves and hem. They looked very different from the military-style clothes he and his parents wore. There were days when he wished he could get out of his uniform, but he was an officer of the Empire until the war was won, or the war killed him.

Li'eth stepped forward and bowed to Rosa. "Honorable McCrary," he stated, getting her name out the Terran way rather than the V'Dan version. "I hope you will enjoy the delights of the Imperial kitchens. One of your staff members said he thought you enjoyed dark chocolate. I hope our dark *klahsa* version will please you."

"I'm looking forward to it," Rosa said, smiling. She let her gaze drop a little down the front of his uniform to his clenched hands, then returned to his eyes. Switching to Terranglo, she asked, *"Are you experiencing separation anxiety? How bad has it grown since I left for our tour of the system?"*

He had a choice. Her polite question no doubt had been phrased in Terranglo to allow him to save face since the only other person who could understand it at the moment was his holy partner. Li'eth chose to answer in V'Dan, however. "I thank you for the kindness of your inquiry. The separation anxiety Jackie and I feel has been growing quite strong. If you have noticed it after only ten days of absence, then it will soon grow noticeable to those who have been here all along, and thus would not notice more gradual changes."

"Separation anxiety?" Hana'ka asked, her tone half-mother, half-Empress.

"Allow me to explain," Rosa offered to Li'eth and Jackie. "You have your Gestalt partner to greet. Eternity, Highness, when a holy pairing such as the one your son and our Ambassador have is deliberately restricted and restrained from progressing, both sides often start displaying some of the following stress-related symptoms . . ."

Li'eth didn't bother to listen to the rest of it. He didn't even greet Jackie verbally. He just stepped up to her, wrapped his uniformed arms around her black-and-flower-clad body, and pressed his cheek to her temple. It wasn't quite enough, even though she stood as close as she could, arms wrapped around his waist.

They stood like that, bodies as close as they could get, absorbing each other's warmth. It was not enough, but it was all they had for the moment. He heard his mother attempt to get his attention, her tone an impending chastisement, only to have her cut off politely by the ex-Premiere.

"To be blunt, Empress, the *only* way to get these two comfortable enough in their Gestalt is to *let* them be intimate," Rosa stated. "If they spend their nights together, it would recharge the batteries, so to speak, and do so strongly enough that they could get through each day. *We* have no problem with this concept, we Terrans," she added. "We understand the phenomenon. We know it is as necessary as drinking clean water and breathing clean air."

Jackie held him closer, not wanting to let him go. Li'eth rubbed his cheek against hers, feeling her breath against his ear.

"The only thing stopping them from doing so is a lack of *support* from your government. Open, accepting support. Give your son and our representative your support, let everyone know that you believe them when they say they are a holy pair, that they are bound in a Gestalt, and they will be free to be remarkably calm and happy all day long.

"And yes, I know it's your precious, grown-up baby boy

cuddling with a strange woman who has no *jungen* marks. I realize you have conflicting opinions on this matter," Rosa added, not unkindly. "But there isn't anything we can do to change what they are to each other, other than accept it and give them our support. If you love your son, it will be easier to support him if you remind yourself that you love him."

Li'eth could not let that one go. "It is not considered proper for an Emperor or an Empress to show love in public."

"It has had a bad habit of turning the recipient into a target, in the past," Te-los added.

"Well, you don't have to *say* how much you love your son in giving his relationship your seal of approval," Rosa returned with a hint of tartness before softening her tone. "You could even claim it is a purely political move, in the hopes of influencing the Terran Grand High Ambassador to look upon you and your people all the more favorably, giving you an advantage in negotiations with us. Your other offspring, Imperial Princess Ah'nan, is almost to our home system, but the reports we've been getting whenever they slow to sublight to do a navigation check say she's been using our hyperrelay via the escort shuttle almost nonstop, making a lot of arrangements in advance of her arrival. Apparently, she has been quite polite and charming while doing so, and is doing a good job representing your interests to our people . . . but that's not quite the same thing as swaying our representative *here* to like you even more."

"And would it?" Te-los asked, curious.

"Not really, as I am quite careful to separate my feelings for His Highness from my opinions of V'Dan . . . but that wouldn't stop any of us from presenting it as such," Jackie stated. She had to adjust her head so that her lips weren't pressed into the curve of Li'eth's neck in order to speak. "I do understand how the actions, words, and deeds of one man do not represent an entire people, but that is not the important point to consider. What it will do instead is convince *your* people to take *our* bond seriously, and thus our other assertions by extension, increasing cooperation as well as understanding through your acceptance of our claims."

"I would take this conversation more seriously if you stopped embracing my son and faced me," Hana'ka told them.

"Mother, I do appreciate your concern," Li'eth replied, holding on to Jackie. "But while I am younger than the Grand High Ambassador, I am a fully grown man, and she is a fully grown woman. We are both long past our impetuous youth. We embrace because it is *calming*. If you would rather have us remain agitated . . ."

"She does have a point, though," Jackie told him. Aloud, for the benefit of the other three in the room. Easing back, she looked up at him. "We do have a *mo'klah* to attend, before the careful effort and timing of the chefs are ruined."

He cupped her face before she could fully step back. Li'eth felt the subtle pressure from her cheek when she leaned into his palm. (*I don't want to wait anymore. I will come to you tonight . . . if that is acceptable?*)

Her cheek warmed, turning a little pink under her natural tan. (*We* should *wait . . . but I don't want to, either. I am tired of waiting.*)

Looking into her brown eyes, Li'eth felt his own face grow hot at the thought of finally . . . A delicate throat-clearing dragged his attention back to the others in the room. Rosa was looking up at the frescoes painted on the ceiling off to one side. His father had a brow arched, and his mother had hers drawn down a little in a thoughtful frown. Releasing his partner's cheek, he turned to face the older trio, his near hand instinctively seeking Jackie's.

"We have just now decided that we have waited long enough," Li'eth stated.

"But we will be discreet," Jackie promised.

"I will visit her at the embassy, where her people will not be upset by such things," he continued.

"Which they will not," Jackie confirmed. She tipped her head slightly. "Technically, there will be some upset bettors in the Gestalt pool as to the exact timing of it, but they will not be upset that we have chosen to progress our bond."

"You will not do so," Hana'ka stated, her frown deepening.

Jackie arched her brow. "With respect, Empress, unless *you* are one of the people participating, you have no right to say anything about what two fully grown adults choose to do in mutually consensual privacy."

Faint pink spots appeared on the Empress' cheeks. "I did not mean *that*. I meant being *responsible*."

". . . If you are referring to avoiding reproduction, all members of the Terran military are required to undergo birth-control shots. My last set of *beecees* were just before leaving Earth," Jackie stated.

"And I requested the male version," Li'eth told his mother. "We did think about that in advance. We are not thoughtless children."

His mother glared at him. It was subtle, but it was a glare. She flicked her gaze to her husband, who was standing there with a faint, calm smile on his peach-and-brown-marked face. The picture of serenity. "Why are you happy about this?"

"Actually, I was thinking we should banish Superior Priest De'arth from the area," Te-los stated out of the blue. His wife blinked at him, confused. So did Li'eth, and both Rosa and Jackie looked equally confused. He raised his hand, palm toward himself. "Nothing overly blatant, of course. Just give him an assignment that will take him away from the Court and the Terrans for a good . . . two, three years?"

"Why would you want to do that?" Rosa asked, voicing Li'eth's own concern. From the way his mother nodded, it was Hana'ka's as well.

"Because the more I learn the Terran ways of holy gifts, the more he complains about its being unnatural, how I shouldn't allow these foreigners to influence me . . . and yet how *diligently* he seems to be studying their techniques," Te-los stated.

"How is that related to the conversation about our son and the Ambassador?" his wife asked.

"All of us who have been attending Master Clees' classes in mastering our abilities *have* been mastering them. We have a long way to go, still," he allowed, dipping his head toward Jackie, "but our improvements are quite tangible. Because of that expertise, I have been able to *see* him attempting to probe my thoughts in those few times he has been nearby while the Terrans were not around to slap his mental hands . . . and I have been able to keep him *out* of my head.

"My topic is related to their topic," he asserted calmly. "They are experts in all matters of our holy gifts. They *understand* how holy gifts work. If they can wrest such changes in not only our son, but in me and those others they have offered to teach, then it is quite possible De'arth will grow strong enough in these new techniques to resume reading my mind. The Terrans have stopped him from doing so when in his presence, and at the same time, they have very carefully not done so themselves.

"So I recommend to you, Empress, to have the Superior Priest relocated elsewhere and denied access to these lessons. I do not think he has the Imperial Family's best interests at heart, and as a result, I can no longer trust him in my presence," Te-los told them. He glanced at his wife again. "Nor can I trust him in yours. At the same time, I *do* trust Ja'ki and her fellow holy ones to be honorable and ethical. I trust her to know what she is doing with our son. I recommend that you believe in their bond and allow it to proceed at a pace which is comfortable for them—a pace their own experts in such things would recommend, according to Assistant Ambassador M'crari—rather than at a speed more convenient for us.

"As the Grand High Ambassador has rightfully pointed out, *we* are not going to be in that bed with them," he finished lightly, if bluntly.

(*I like your father,*) Jackie quipped lightly.

Li'eth squeezed her fingers, pleased she was happy with the thought of his father's being on their side, but waited for his mother to make up her mind. She eyed the Terran at his side a long moment, then asked, "Do *you* think Superior Priest De'arth is acting unethically around the Imperial Family?"

"Te-los . . . has he attempted to read your mind *after* receiving instruction in Terran techniques, including our strict ethics versus expediency guidelines?" Jackie asked the older male.

"He has. Two days ago, in fact," the Imperial Consort added.

"Then by Terran law, he is doing so deliberately and needs to be contained and corrected," Jackie told her.

"However, he is a *V'Dan* citizen, and our laws have no authority outside the bounds of our embassy zone," Rosa added. The spotless blonde shrugged. "We are, by our own ethical code, unable to do anything to him outside of that zone. Aside from blocking him from reaching toward other's minds without clearly expressed permission."

"That, we can do," Jackie agreed. "*If* we can catch it when it actually happens around us."

"What about the other priests?" Hana'ka asked, frowning softly.

"As far as we have been able to tell, they are sticking to Terran guidelines . . . but we don't mingle with them very much outside those classes," Jackie cautioned her.

"I've not caught any of them reaching toward our minds other than De'ath," Li'eth stated. "The rest seem to be enthralled enough by what they are learning to follow the spirit as well as the letter of their teachings. We have no laws, no rules or guidelines, on how the holy ones should behave, other than an expectation that they will behave in a Saintly manner."

"And that—" Te-los started to say.

"That's hardly—sorry," Rosa apologized.

"You first," he offered politely.

She nodded and restated what she had been about to say. "Saintly behavior is hardly a concrete set of rules, since from what little I've studied of your many different saints, they themselves behaved in a wide variety of ways. Some of them seemed less than perfectly ethical beings."

"Which is more or less what I would say," Te-los agreed.

"Then I shall find a way to exile him without offending the Winter Temple. In the season of their power," she added wryly, almost sardonically. "In a way where he will not try to pervert his holy gifts by reaching into my head to alter my thoughts, either to make me change my mind or merely to make me forget why I summoned him."

"That's odd," Rosa observed. "Why would you have to have him in front of you, within mind-reading reach? Why not just send him an order?"

"Because the law is that high-ranking priests, particularly from the current ruling Temple, cannot be dismissed from the Imperial Court without a chance to petition the . . . yes. I see how long and deep this goes," Te-los stated grimly. "This will not be an easy task."

"If you like, I could loan you the use of a telepath. All of us are strong enough to sense and block any attempt he might make," Jackie offered. "Clees and I may be busy, and Aixa is helping him with the lessons since she has the most experience in teaching next to him. But aside from language transfers, Darian and Min are at a loose end until we can get her some Salik computer equipment to investigate in a link with him so that he can decode and write out whatever she finds."

"We already know what their technology can do," Hana'ka said, eyeing Jackie askance. "It is the exact same as ours."

"She means the two of them have a way to extract *coded* information," Li'eth clarified. "I think this is a conversation that would taste better when spoken over a cup of hot *mo'klah* at this point."

Hana'ka considered his point, and gestured at the table. "Then be seated. We will have the first course served, then continue this conversation. At least it will not be one revolving around military needs or economic equivalents."

Jackie moved toward the indicated table, set with delicate dishes and four lesser chairs arranged around the table, along with a fifth fanciful enough that it was clear who would be seated there. Li'eth let her go, facing his mother. "And the subject of her and I pursuing our comfort and health over your convenience?"

For a moment, he received the mask of the Empress in reply, a bland, slightly stern look that had made many hesitate through the years on whether or not to press further for an answer. Li'eth merely raised an eyebrow, the one bisected by his *jungen* mark. His mother stared back, then sighed.

"Be. Discreet. Do not stay all night," Hana'ka ordered. "And I do not want to hear a hint of gossip about it. Not because I don't want to hear such things—which I do not—but because I will have to juggle the Temples into a more favorable alignment for revealing such things. Exiling the Superior Priest will not simplify that task."

"We will be very discreet," he pledged, following her to the table.

CHAPTER 14

Halfway to the last elevator that led to her quarters, Jackie and Li'eth were startled by an insistent, rapid, patterned beeping. Rattled, it took her a few seconds to identify the source, the thick, ornamental-looking bracelet circling her left wrist. Stopping, she stared at it while her mind caught up with the meaning behind the patterns of rhythm and tone.

Li'eth, holding hands with her, felt her shock resonate through their fingers. Without a contrary thought, he turned and bolted along with her, matching her stride for running stride. He hit the stairwell door—the lift would be too slow—and let her hop over the railing, twisting to land with a touch of telekinetic cushioning. His own skill was weaker, less well trained; he jumped only a few steps, falling behind a bit.

The running didn't sit too well on a full stomach, not when both were full of tasty Terran food from their late-evening meal. After their *mo'klah* get-to-know-you meal with his parents and Rosa, Jackie and Li'eth had sat through hours of comm conferences with the Choya about how the placement of the new hyperrelay units were going. There wasn't supposed to be anything scheduled.

That particular alert had not only the two of them charging down the stairwells, but others as well, most of them Marines. At least two of the Humans on the stairs were members of the crew for the *Embassy 2*. Emerging on the main floor in a stream of bodies, they were joined by Rosa McCrary, who was being hustled toward the lifts to the hangar bays.

An aide came hurrying up. "McCrary! Here's the data dump!"

"Thank you, Jules." Rosa accepted the block from the man with a nod. She eyed Jackie, who was approaching from the other side, headed in the direction the aide had turned and fled. "I'm on my way outsystem, Jackie. We're going to take the first jump of the new shortcut route—I'll see you when I see you."

"Take care," Jackie agreed, having to speak over her shoulder as the two women swept past each other. "I'll send you the all clear as soon as we know they're out of the system!"

(*Data dump?*) Li'eth asked. They couldn't run now; there were too many bodies scrambling either toward the communications room or toward their guard posts. The beeping from her wrist unit was a warning that the Salik were invading the V'Dan home system. *Where* was still unknown, but as their backup Ambassador, McCrary had to flee to safety. That much he knew.

(*Everything that this embassy has recorded, up to the second the alarm goes out to evacuate Rosa, gets dumped into portable storage. It serves as a black box of information up to that point. Including our comm call with the Choya Grand High Ambassador,*) she added. There were now fewer people in the halls though the communications hub was now a bit crowded. (*Everything from this point on gets sent live to Earth. They're still too far away to help directly, but they'll know what's going on . . . and if nothing else, they'll have a record of all negotiations for the next Ambassador to study.*)

(*That's a rather grim thought. I'd rather you did not die,*) he warned her. Brown- and blue-clad bodies made room for them at the central workstation table. Two were clad in the gold and scarlet of the Imperial Fleet.

"Report," Jackie ordered, rather than responding to his sending.

"Fourteen Salik warships came out of the black at V'Durun, Colonel," Robert reported. He was the seniormost officer on hand until her arrival and pointed at the star-system map covering most of the surface.

"That's the eighth planet in our system, an ice world about four light-hours away," Grand Captain Tes'rin told her.

"I know," Jackie reassured him. "Robert convinced me to establish a hyperrelay there in exchange for free hydrofuel since water is a 'waste' product once the methane and such has been siphoned off for processing into your version of fuel. What's the tactical situation? How many V'Dan ships are there? Do we have any of ours in the vicinity?"

"*Embassy 3* is inbound, low on fuel but fully insystem," someone said from a workstation beyond the main table. "They have enough for maneuvers and some lasers, but only enough juice for two short jumps at best. They're fourteen light-minutes away, but they're the closest ship we've got."

"*Embassy 14* is inbound, but they're still in the . . . NHK-4148 System, one jump away," another aide added. "They got the alarm while still at one-third Cee. They're ramping up to half Cee so they can jump, but are holding course and awaiting orders, sir."

"*Embassy 8* isn't due back for another three hours; they're still processing lunar ice around that new Gatsugi colony, Brown-Valley-Green," a third told her. "Their captain says they can jump short on fuel with just a little more, but it'll still take half an hour to get into space and up to speed."

"*Embassies 10* through *13* are being readied for takeoff. *Embassy 2* . . . has McCrary in sight and will be launched in two," a fourth reported. "All others are too far away to help, sir."

"From the looks of things, V'Durun has twenty-eight combat-capable ships at the moment, but they're outgunned by the warships," Tes'rin stated. "Launch your ships and get them to here, and here," he added, touching the map so that it zoomed in on the nearspace around the eighth planet, cold and white with blue striations.

V'Durun had a large moon—almost large enough to be a binary planet partner, though it still circled its partner far more than the other way around—and the Salik ships were a bright red scattering of triangles near the space station orbiting the far side of that moon from the planet. He tapped the map as he continued.

"You bring them in there, harass them, and the other ships can attack from here, above *here*, and from down here, forcing them away from the planet and its satellite," he told them, touching the display. The Terrans blinked at him. He looked up, lifted his brows, and said, "Well? Launch your ships! You are the only ones who can lend your help to the people out there!"

"Stand down, Grand Captain," Jackie told him. Her heart ached—she knew Li'eth could feel how awkward she felt, having to do so—but she said it anyway.

He bristled, straightening. "These are V'Dan lives at stake! You have to go help them!" He looked at the others, then at Robert. "Launch those ships. *Now.*"

Commander Robert Graves eyed the Imperial Elite Guardsman and shook his head. "Sorry, meioa, you are not in our chain of command. None of us are gonna take orders from you."

"Grand Captain Tes'rin, your expertise on the ground is appreciated. Please confine your directives to that and only that," Jackie reminded him. "Now, be quiet, and remind yourself that your job is to help ensure the safety of *this* embassy zone. You are not trained to command a fleet of foreign warships . . . and you have *no* clue what our ships can and *cannot* do. Be silent, and be respectful."

"I thought you were supposed to be adults, full of responsibility and compassion for others, not children only playing at being ones," he countered.

Every Terran stiffened, but it was Li'eth who found his voice first. In an icy tone, he demanded, "One of the jobs of the Elite, when assigned to an embassy, is to be *courteous and respectful at all times.* You owe these Terrans an *apology,* Grand Captain. You are *not* aware of the strategic needs of the Terran fleet in this war, and you have no say in their tactical choices. Apologize."

". . . I apologize, Grand High Ambassador. I apologize to your people as well. I . . . spoke out of turn, when I spoke out of concern for my fellow V'Dan. I hope you will find a way to save them, and find it fast," Tes'rin added.

As apologies went, it wasn't the best. Barely adequate, in fact, and a bit accusatory. Jackie didn't have time to chastise him about it, though. "If those fourteen warships are the size of the one that captured the *Aloha 9*, then our handful of ships aren't going to make more than a dent in the Salik attack. Adding in our forces will not stop their attack, and it will only put Terran technology and Terran personnel in grave danger."

One of the workers beyond the ring of soldiers at the table spoke up. "Ambassador, the *Embassy 2* has taken off."

"Sir!" another aide called out. "*Embassy 15* just got to the Choya home system. It looks like they're under attack as well."

"Have the *15* pull a broad parabolic," Jackie decided. This was similar to a scenario she, Graves, al-Fulan, and Admiral Nayak back home had discussed over the hyperrelays. "They are to scan, but not engage; at the first sign of pursuit, they are to leave the system and not go back for six hours. Tell the *14* to continue on course but not jump just yet. Order the *3* to release one-quarter of their missiles and have them random-walk into striking range so that the Salik won't be able to trace them back to their point of origin all that quickly."

"Launch the *10* through *13* and have them short-jump out to V'Durun," Robert stated, catching on to which scenario she was using. "They are permitted to launch one-quarter of their own missiles, and let the *13* take up a position on the insystem side of V'Durun, so it can coordinate the launched missiles carefully with the *Embassy 3*. Use them when it looks like the Salik are going to be at their most vulnerable—remain at least ten light-seconds away, and do your best guessing on when to throw a missile their way. Instruct the *10*, *11*, and *12* to spread out in a triangle around the planet and its moon, and fly a parabolic at about twenty light-seconds out."

Jackie nodded and laid down the law, her eyes flicking briefly to Tes'rin's face. "All personnel. *None* of our ships are to get within engagement distance. I repeat, *none* of them are to engage the enemy directly. The *3* and the *10* through *13* are to *watch* the Salik carefully, and only target their missiles if they have a good shot at damaging the enemy without harming the locals," she added, glancing at Robert. "Their foremost job is to watch and plot every possible escape vector used by the Salik warships.

"Coordinate their findings with V'Dan astronavigation in the Imperial Fleet. We want to know *where* they are headed next. It might be a system with a hyperrelay, or it might not be. We've been prioritizing stringing the lines of communication to the various Alliance capital worlds, not necessarily to our nearest occupied neighbors. But I repeat, we will *not* engage the enemy directly. That would be suicide."

"The tests we performed," Robert told the others, "showed that our *ceristeel* hull plating is vastly superior at reflecting and dissipating heat from energy weapons, and they can take a hit from a projectile, but our infrastructure materials are inferior to what your ships are made out of; the bulkheads will buckle and break twice as fast as anything the Salik have. The *Embassy* fleet cannot take on a single Salik warship and survive without heavy backup at this time, but it *can* watch to see which way they go," he explained, looking over at Tes'rin, "and in doing so, figure out if they have a specific target they are going to hit up next, whether that's insystem or not."

"*That* is something we can do, and do well with our ships, Grand Captain," Jackie told him. "*Without* slaughtering our people or destroying our ships needlessly. To do otherwise would be like trying to throw pebbles at a horse in the hopes of slaying it—and I know you V'Dan have horses among your *d'aspra* animals. We carefully considered this sort of scenario both before leaving Earth and reconsidered it just days ago after the data from the firing tests were done being analyzed. This is the compromise which the best Navy personnel here and the Command Staff back home could come up with, given our limited resources, limited combat capacity, and even more limited refueling abilities. We are bringing in heavier armaments, but they are not here right now."

"It is a sound choice," Li'eth reassured her and her fellow Terrans. "It isn't all that far off from what I heard at the Fleet's discussion a few days back, while you were doing your morning exercises. We might not be able to get spare ships to V'Durun in time, but we *can* instruct the Imperial Fleet to get ready to take off and head outsystem on a moment's notice. If it looks like they're going to scatter, we can have rescue vessels there in just a few hours. If it looks like the Salik are headed in the same direction to a second target, we will be ready to go after them."

"Colonel, I recommend advising the *Embassy 14* to come straight in to home base here on V'Dan," Robert told Jackie. "I know they were supposed to swing out toward the Tlassian sector once they refueled at V'Durun, but we might need them here in case this is a feint, and the Salik switch course to hit the capital."

"Do it," she ordered. (*Li'eth . . . I won't be able to leave until I can give the all clear and bring Rosa back. I'm sorry. Duty has to come first when lives are on the line. Even if we*

*can't save every life out there. Not even if all fifteen ships went
to fight.*)

(*I know,*) he reassured her. His hand found hers and clasped
it with a little squeeze. (*This is war. People are going to die,
no matter what we do. We'll have a better chance at getting
the Salik this way later—and if nothing else, Master Sonam
said that what we really need is just sleeping together, skin to
skin. I'd be very happy with that alone.*)

(*Your mother said nothing overnight,*) she reminded him.

(*My mother didn't say anything about the Salik interrupting
us, either. Besides, I'm your military liaison, as well as cultural
facilitator,*) he reminded her. (*I cannot leave until this particular fight is all over, either . . . and it could take all night.*)

Sighing, she raised her voice. "Okay, people, we have a
long night ahead of us. This battle won't be resolved in a few
minutes. If you're not actually needed at this point, stand
down and get some rest . . . and if one of you could kindly get
His Highness and I some coff . . . er, some V'Dan *caffen*, that
would be great."

(*Thank you for remembering I cannot stand your version,*)
he half teased.

(*I admit yours tastes better. We just need to increase the
caffeine content to make it actually useful for us Terrans, is
all,*) she half teased back.

JANVA 24, 9508 V.D.S.

Three hours later, just a little past midnight local, it was all
over. Between some well-placed missiles—not all of them, but
some had struck their targets to very good effect—and the
unexpected arrival of three V'Dan warships, the mining settlements on and around V'Durun were battered and bleeding,
literally and figuratively. But they were still mostly inhabitable
and mostly intact.

More than that, the Salik fleet had retreated and jumped
along two similar vectors . . . and the *Embassy 12* and *Embassy 13* had been ordered to jump to the two systems in that
direction that were possible targets. They carried the news to
the main inhabited planet of that system, as well as intended

to visit the outlying space stations. Neither system had relays, yet. That was another reason to send the ships; it would take four jumps and a refueling for the turnaround, but they would have communications abilities . . . which played havoc with the schedule of systems that *should* have gotten those two units, but that was the potluck of war.

It would take the Salik over two full days to reach either of those locations, but that was fine; V'Dan warships were in pursuit. They had been alerted almost instantaneously via the fledgling network of Terran hyperrelay communications linked to V'Dan lightwave channels the moment the watching Terran crews had realized the Salik vessels had started to flee in a specific direction. The whole thing had been vastly superior to finding out about the battle over four hours later via slow-moving lightwave broadcasts.

Despite the very real and unpleasant loss of lives, the battle of V'Durun was being viewed as a success. As much as the V'Dan strategic analysts wanted to go over this cobbled-together dry-run version of what the Terran ships *should* do, because they could do it best with the least loss of lives . . . it was late, almost everyone was tired, and it could all be analyzed in the morning, when lightwave telemetry was matched to what the Terrans had broadcast of the battle.

Li'eth kept expecting another ambush or emergency of some sort, but they made it to Jackie's quarters unbothered. Like her office, most of the furnishings were V'Dan though there were distinct touches from Earth. Her office had one of her surfboards mounted on the wall, bearing a vibrant, intricate image of Aloha City and the island's south shore in a long, panoramic shot taken from some boat a little way from land. He recognized the Tower, the Lotus, and the buildings that served as temporary dwellings for the constantly rotating guests of the Fellowship, though the angle was lower than he had seen, gliding into the capital in a private shuttle.

From the gossip in the Winter Palace, visitors to the Grand High Ambassador of the Terrans thought it was merely some sort of odd Terran combination of painting and sculpture, and not an actual, usable object. The second board, decorated in abstract lines of red, cream, and gold, had been donated to the Empire along with V'Dan-subtexted videos demonstrating how they were built and how they were used. His people were still trying to figure out the why of that latter part, according to rumor.

The third board, hung on the wall of her parlor across from the entrance, he had not seen since Jackie had packed it away. It bore giant blooms of flowers, all of them bearing five petals in a swirl. Some were blush pink or rich red with darker centers, others were yellow with hints of red at the bases. Many were peach in hue, and one particularly beautiful flower, deep red striated and edged with darker purple, sat at the back of the board, above the fin on the opposite side. Bits of greenery poked out here and there from under the blooms painted on the board, making the elongated oval a vivid, welcoming splash of color on the whitewashed walls.

"I miss surfing," Jackie murmured, palming the door shut behind him. "Even during the busiest of weeks back home, I could always get away for an hour or two. I was rarely away from a tropical beach and a surfing shop where I could rent a board for a little while."

"I'd like you to have that free time. I just keep telling myself, 'when the war ends,' then try to find a way to make it end." He turned and pulled her into a hug, but only for a few moments. Long enough to yawn behind a quickly raised hand . . . which she echoed. Resolutely, Li'eth stepped back from her. "We need to go to bed. Both of us are tired, and we need to be sleeping horizontally, not leaning against each other until our knees give out, and we fall down."

"Agreed." Taking his hand, she led the way, gesturing vaguely. "Private kitchen and dining area, private study, front washroom, spare bedroom, spare bedroom, master bedroom with its own washroom . . . but you've already had a tour."

He grinned, then yawned again. Once he was done covering his mouth—a courtesy concept both V'Dan and Terrans shared, which was good because the Choya, Tlassians, and Solaricans didn't like seeing bared teeth without actual provocation—he started unbuttoning his jacket. The drawback to sleeping here instead of in the Imperial Wing was a distinct lack of fresh uniforms to change into. "We'll need to set the alarm to go off at sixth hour."

"I thought you got up at seventh?" Jackie asked. Her voice was muffled by her dress being pulled over her head.

"I do, but I . . . huhh . . ." He lost his train of thought. Her undergarments were rather unlike a swimming garment.

Jackie blushed. She started to bundle up her dress, then changed her mind. Snapping it at him, she whapped his arm with the hem. "Snap out of it. The Terran military is unisex integrated. Now, you were saying you wanted to get up at sixth hour?"

"Uhh . . . yes." He dragged his attention away, mind conflicted between those curves and the fact they were markless. Returning his attention to his own clothes, he draped his uniform jacket over the back of a chair and sat down to remove his boots. "Sixth hour, because I'll need to return, wash, and change clothes, and meet with V'kol to discuss my schedule. He's been doing a lot of the behind-the-scenes work, so mornings are the only time I really get to see him. The rest of it is through the comms."

"I'll set it." Moving to the bedside clock, she bent over and fiddled with the buttons.

One boot off and the other pulled halfway free, Li'eth looked up, and gaped. (*Don't do that!*)

Jerking upright, she looked over her shoulder at him, one brow quirked. (*What? Don't do what?*)

(*You . . . rump!*) he accused. He draped his socks over his boots, then tucked the boots under the chair. (*We're supposed to be going to sleep.*)

(*Well, it wasn't deliberate,*) she pointed out. Turning back, she stooped again. (*And I still have to set the clock. It's just easier to read the controls at the back like this.*)

(*Saints, you are going to be the death of me.*) Standing up, Li'eth closed his eyes and unbuttoned his pants, then his shirt.

(*Just a "little death,"*) she quipped back, and sent him a subthought explanation.

Li'eth blushed and cursed under his breath. He kept his eyes tightly shut until he was turned around, facing the chair instead of her. (*I'll risk a diplomatic incident and spank you for that.*)

(*Only if you want it returned, swat for swat . . . and yes, I'll stop teasing you.*)

He heard what sounded like the opening of a lid, followed by a rustling of cloth. (*Please tell me that's sleepwear.*)

(*Nope. That was my clothes hitting the hamper. I am all the way naked, now. It'll be more stabilizing—for both of us. Off with your underpants, Highness,*) Jackie ordered. (*I . . . ohhh . . . you have a gorgeous back.*)

(*Is that retaliation for my admiration of your rump?*) he asked, neatly laying out his shirt and trousers on the chair.

(*No, back, not backside. Muscles,*) Jackie clarified, her underthoughts rich with appreciation. (*I do admire physically fit men. And you have some interesting stripes—does that one on the back of your thigh start on your rump? It's been months since I saw you naked . . . and I was trying to be polite and not examine in any real detail. Even if you have a spectacular set of gluteal muscles.*)

(*Visit the washroom first,*) he directed her, refusing to answer the question. (*I'm going to keep my back turned so I don't . . . I am tired, and I do not need to be stimulated right now, because I need sleep more than I need sex. Neither do you, so no staring at my buttocks. I'd appreciate some help in keeping things calm for now.*)

(*I'm going, I'm going,*) she promised. A moment later, he heard the door slide shut, and let out the breath he'd been almost holding. (*I know, Li'eth, it's not fair. Women take longer to get stimulated than men do. Usually. And by the time I'd be ready, you'd be ready to sleep.*)

(Exactly,) Li'eth agreed. (*I'm glad you know the timing of the hormones. I really am exhausted . . . and I really don't want to disappoint you. But we're not hormonal teenagers just past the first flush of jungen fever. So to speak. We can discuss this in the morning, alright?*)

(*In the morning,*) she agreed. (*Though if you snore in your sleep, I reserve the right to poke you until you stop.*)

(*I'll share that right,*) he sent. Padding to the bed, he pulled the covers down. (*Do you have a preference on which side?*)

(*No, pick one.*)

(*Nearest to the washroom door for me,*) he decided. (*Since I'll use it after you.*)

Turning on one of the bedside lights to low, he turned down the overhead ones, leaving the room in a soft gloom. That made the trio of *na lei* she had hung on the wall cast some odd shadows. Li'eth took a moment to peer at them, studying how they could look so fresh. Actually, they had been made from some sort of resilient fabric, stiffened, shaped, and colored to look like flowers and leaves, he discovered. *Problematic when it comes to dusting and cleaning, unless they're washable . . .* The central one had what looked like jacaranda flowers woven into it, while the outer two on either side had peach-hued flowers. Nothing else decorated the chamber yet, but he suspected it was only a matter of time. Everything she had chosen so far called for bright, cheerful colors.

The sparseness and modern furnishings contrasted with the sturdy antiques he had grown up knowing. Admittedly, the Terrans hadn't been able to bring a lot of their own furniture because of space constraints, but their versions had been refreshingly different in design and delightful in comfort. Very few things in the Imperial Wing had been designed for that. They weren't uncomfortable, exactly, but it hadn't been the main priority in their construction.

With the covers pulled back, he eased down onto her bed. It had some give to it, and an odd sort of movement he couldn't quite identify. Lying back and stretching out, he discovered what it was: an air bladder of some sort, beneath some sort of softening surface that accepted his curves and angles. Within seconds, he could feel his tension draining away . . . which warred with the need to use the washroom.

Thankfully, the door opened after only a couple minutes, spilling enough bright light to make him wince and wake up out of his light doze. Grimacing, he blocked the glare with a hand, then blinked at the colors swirling around Jackie's lower half. That . . . (*That's not an aura, is it? Is that some sort of gown?*)

(*It's a projection of a type of robe or dress called a* caftan. *It's not easy matching an illusion to the real movements of a body, even my own. I'm only putting in a half boot's worth of effort. Your turn at the bathroom,*) she added, crawling onto her half of the bed.

Li'eth sat up with a grunt and headed for the bright light. (*I do need it, yes.*)

(*I put out a new toothbrush in a wrapper for you,*) she added politely.

(*Thank you.*) Using the facilities, he scrubbed his face with a washcloth and realized his stubble would need trimming in

the morning after he returned to his quarters. Even if she had
a Terran-style *razor* thing, he preferred the V'Dan version.
Scrubbing his teeth, he rinsed his mouth, unbraided and
brushed out his hair, then rebraided it to keep it tidy while he
slept. It, too, would need a wash soon.

Smothering a yawn, he turned off the main lights to the
washing room. Leaving the night-light lit, he padded into the
bedroom. Jackie had the covers drawn up almost to her shoulders, both bared and one covered in her black- and blue-shaded
tattoos. She pointed at him. (*Off with the skivvies, soldier.*)

Face a little hot, he turned his back and removed them,
awkwardly flinging the garment at the chair. It barely made it.
Sitting down, he tried to get into bed decorously, but Jackie
leaned over, her shoulder and cheek pressed against his ribs.
Her hand stopped his from drawing the covers over his lap for
a moment, then she reached for him, gently lifting and turning
his flesh. He held himself carefully still for her examination,
trying not to let her touch arouse him.

A moment later, she finished. Her withdrawal was coupled
with a soft laugh, a low, richly amused chuckle. He knew it
wasn't aimed at him in any way, but he still had to query, (. . . ?)

Her reply was a mental singsong of smugness. (*I know
what millions of ladies and gentlemen across* both *of our
empires are dying to know: Is His Imperial Highness striped
or unstriped down there? . . . And now I* also *know what you
look like when aroused.*)

(*Ah. And . . . what do you think of what you have discovered?*) he asked, slipping the rest of the way onto the bed
and lying back. The bed jolted after a moment, hissing and
humming. (*What? What is it doing?*)

(*Relax; it's just the mattress boxes—the airbag cushions,
each one no bigger than a child's head or so. There are dozens of them under the main padding, which is a layer of what
we call memory foam. The boxes are hooked up to thin tubes
and a series of quiet pumps with monitors. They will adjust to
your pressure points every time you move,*) Jackie soothed
him. (*Mostly around the hips, which are the biggest indenta-
tion point, but there are sensors to detect other points of
weight distribution as well.*

(*It's all automated, and it's set to medium-firm at the*

moment, which is what I like, but adding a second person spikes the pressure a tiny bit because of the unified cushion and cover on top, even if most of the bladders beneath are individual compartments. We'll see if that's the right firmness for you in the morning—it doesn't detect any difference if just one person lies down, but if it's a second person, it's going to attempt to automatically calibrate for the weight,) she added.

The adjustments finished . . . and Li'eth found himself remarkably well supported. Blinking, he muttered aloud, "I see why you wanted to import this thing."

"It does pack up easier than an archaic mattress," she agreed. "And it was my other point of indulgence. I'm still waiting for a day I can try surfing, but eventually I'll find a day that's not busy, the weather is good, and there's a decent beach within traveling distance."

He lay there a few moments, enjoying the comfort, but it wasn't enough. She was right next to him, just a handspan away. Rolling onto his side, Li'eth hesitated, then rolled against her, wrapping his arm around her ribs and sliding his right knee over her right thigh. *(Much better . . . Now, you were chuckling over something?)*

(Mmm . . . one moment, I'm enjoying this feeling . . .) She scooted a little closer, nuzzled his cheek with her own, then sighed. *(I really liked what I saw, Li'eth. But . . . tired. Sleep, now. Yes?)*

The bed adjusted under them. Li'eth nodded, nuzzling her back. *(And I liked what I saw, but . . . sleep, yes . . . Saints, Jackie, I feel . . . I feel like I'm in Heaven, pressed body to body with you. I don't . . . Words,)* his sleepy mind asserted, as if that alone explained everything. Sighing, he snuggled close and relaxed. *(Such joy . . .)*

(A whole year's worth,) she agreed, more serious than the pun on his name would imply.

He would have agreed, save that between one breath and the next, he dropped into exhausted sleep. But not alone. Jackie dropped with him, body and mind melded with his.

———

Li'eth didn't know when dreams turned into reality. And he didn't care. He didn't care quite a lot, right up to the point

where everything ended in heavily panting bliss. Right up to
the point where he felt someone rapping on his mental walls—
on both their minds—with a rather pointed, insistent pattern
meant to get their attention.

(. . . *Yes?*) Jackie asked cautiously, reaching out to see who
it was. Li'eth, his thoughts still entwined with hers just like
their bodies were entwined, recognized the other woman just
as swiftly. Aixa, the eldest of the other four Terran telepaths.

(If *the two of you are done,*) the German stated briskly, (*it
would be* good *if the two of you learned how to* shield *those
sorts of thoughts.*)

(*I wasn't . . . thinking,*) Li'eth mumbled, face suddenly hotter than any other part of his sweat-soaked body.

(*Precisely. You were both lucky you don't know how to
project empathically, or it would've bothered more than just
those of us who can read thoughts. Darian and I have been
shielding you for the last half hour . . . but for the first half
hour, you were causing a ruckus while we were still trying to
figure it out.*)

(*Our deepest apologies, Aixa. We . . . didn't have time to
practice on Earth, where we could've gotten lessons in how
to, ah, be intimate in a Gestalt without leaking over onto
everything. It's my fault,*) Jackie added. (*I forgot that that
might happen.*)

(*Well, I'm happy for both of you. Now, don't do it again!*—
I mean, you can do it, but *shielded, fraulein!*)

(*I got it, I'm shielding, I promise,*) Jackie pledged. Aixa
retreated . . . and the slight sense of pressure in the air faded
as well. She quickly put up a bubble of her own kinetic inergy
around the two of them. (*Ancestors, that's embarrassing . . .*)

Li'eth started to agree . . . then broke down in snickers,
which he tried to smother into her inked shoulder. They
quickly became chuckles, then turned into helpless laughter.
He felt her trying to query as to why, but he simply could not
explain it, other than just . . . joy. All-encompassing, thoroughly pervading joy. That, and the best night's sleep he'd
ever had, and full, saturation-level pleasure, like a sponge
tossed into the ocean and allowed to sink to the depths, over-
flowing with liquid satisfaction.

He kissed her shoulder, feeling aroused once more. Jackie

groaned, however. (*We can't, Li'eth. It's already half past six. Neither of us heard the alarm go off . . . which is an absolute first, for me. I've never been so deeply involved in lovemaking before that I . . . that I, uh . . .*)

She broke off with a giggle. Another escaped her in a sort of *snerk* sound, then the rest of them pealed free, echoing off the walls of her bedchamber. Her joy hit him then, purified joy, straight through the link bonding them together. It went straight to his head, too. Before they knew it, they were—

(Verdammt, fraulein! *I told the two of you to* shield it*!*) Aixa snapped.

Both of them stopped moving, freezing in place. Sheepishly, Jackie replied, (*Sorry, Aixa . . . but it is* our first time together. *Add the effects of a Gestalt on top of that, and, well . . .*)

(*Yes, yes, I know. But I am* trying *to eat breakfast, and such things are not appropriate at the* verdammt *dining table. Thankfully, most of the embassy is mind-blind to such things, or we'd have soldiers and staff members rutting on every available surface.*)

(*Okay, okay, you don't have to draw me a picture of a boot to get the message!*) Jackie retorted. (*We'll stop . . . particularly since you're ruining the mood.*)

(*Fair's fair, you ruined my* blintzes. *You'll need to approach lovemaking like any other lesson in psychic abilities,*) the older woman lectured them both. (*That means calm, clearheaded,* planned *practice sessions—and focus on the practicing of the* shielding *as the most important thing.*)

(*Yes, we do understand. Enjoy your breakfast, Aixa.*) Sighing, Jackie stared at the ceiling. The curtains were drawn against the glow of the lights illuminating the Winter Palace grounds, but there was light coming in from the washroom. (*We do need to get up. And shower. It may be my favorite scent right now, but this isn't the sort of perfume that smells of professional behavior.*)

Li'eth chuckled at that. Kissing her shoulder, he moved away. (*I'll go first, and get the shower started. You'll want to hurry, or you'll miss the soaping cycle.*)

(*Oh no, we are* not *sharing a shower. We'll be even later if we do that, and get another lecture from Aixa,*) she told him. (*I'll shower first. You will shower after I am through.*)

(*Yes,* meioa,) he quipped, teasing her for her autocratic decision. She was right, but he had to tease her for it.

Self-discipline was not easy. She was . . . breathtaking. Expressive. Warm and sensual and caring, and . . . it was a good thing the temperature of the water in the shower was adjustable; he needed to shiver like that by the time he got out. Combing his hair didn't take long, but when he started to braid it, his now fully dressed partner shooed his hands away from his head. With just a bit of thought and a minute of work, tugging this way and that on his scalp, she had it plaited and tied off before he knew it.

Except it wasn't a standard, simple plait. Li'eth frowned at the mirror, twisting this way and that. He pulled the tail forward. "What . . . ?"

"We call that style a fishtail braid with a twist down each side, a fancy variation. It'll match your uniform a bit better than that simple one you usually wear," Jackie added. Her hair had been pulled up into a braid that wrapped all the way around her head, with no end in sight. Almost like a reddish-black crown, albeit one with hints of kinks from her natural curls.

Her outfit was military as well, if in mottled shades of camouflage gray rather than anything formal. Then again, he knew she wore her "fatigues"—what an odd thing to call them—when she had her self-defense exercises scheduled in the mornings. Usually at the same time as his, though sometimes his were taken over by meetings. As were hers, sometimes.

He tossed his plait back over his shoulder. "It does look good. Thank you. I should go . . . I need to get breakfast."

"Have some here," she offered. "That'll save you time even if it's just buffet food. That, and I can feel how hungry you are, the same as I am. One thing, first."

Curious, he leaned closer at her beckoning . . . and received a kiss for his troubles. A brief one. It ended in a smile as Jackie pulled back. He wanted more on a primal level, but . . . the kiss itself was satisfying enough, in its own way.

"How do you feel? In your level of restlessness, I mean," she added in clarification.

Li'eth considered her question, evaluating himself internally. "Remarkably calm and centered. You?"

"The same." Jackie smiled, her dark eyes glowing with satisfaction. "Ready to take on the mountain of paperwork ahead of me, in fact."

He nodded and followed her out of the washroom. "As much as I want to come back tonight, I should probably stay away. I'll stay tomorrow night," he added quickly, feeling a pulse of disappointment. "Not that we could keep my presence here overnight a secret."

(*Aixa implied that our, ah, "leakage" didn't spill over any farther than the nearest sets of rooms, where the nontelepathic are concerned,*) she told him, reading his subthoughts. They passed from the hallway to the parlor, heading for the front door. (*Anyone sleeping in this sector is both smart and trustworthy enough to be discreet . . . and the other telepaths* won't *tell anyone else. They'll yell at us in private for any indiscretion, but they'll otherwise be discreet about it.*)

She touched the door controls and started to step out, only to quickly step back. Li'eth almost ran into her, hastily moving back. Spotting the reason why, he made room for Lieutenant Jasmine Buraq as well. The tall, brown-skinned woman had a datapad in her hand and had been only a few lengths away when the door opened. She stepped inside as soon as she had room and lifted the pad the moment Jackie shut the door again.

"Colonel, I have some new regulations from the Command Staff, sir," the platoon lieutenant told her. "Lieutenant Paea took the call personally, but since he's still on watch for another few minutes, I said I'd run it to you. You're going to have to tell everyone. Orders like these . . . have to come from the chain of command." Pressing the tablet into Jackie's hands, she apologized. "Sorry, sir, but the buck stops here."

Visibly confused in both her expression and her aura, Jackie flicked past the cover letter, which bore the official military-themed seal of the Premiere of the Terran United Planets, Commander-in-Chief of the Space Force. All four Branches of it.

Li'eth politely turned his back in case it was sensitive information, only to hear her suck in a sharp breath. ". . . What's wrong?"

She pulsed a subthought that said it was okay to turn back

and look, and waved the pad when he did so. "It's . . . they've done it. They've gone and implemented Peacekeeper-style corporal punishment in the military. Caning," Jackie added. "Blows from an antiseptic-soaked stick upon the buttocks, and/or the upper back, depending on the severity of the crime. The cover letter . . ."

"*Caning?* Even in the Empire, that's . . ." He had no words for it, but from the subthoughts swirling through her mind, he could tell this was for a lot more than attempted harm of a member of the Imperial Tier.

"Remember how I pressed for colonization rights for anyone who wanted them, if they chose to fight in this war of yours?" she asked Li'eth. He nodded. He had sat in on several of those conversations since their arrival. "Well, the moment the ink was figuratively scrawled on that deal, and I told the Premiere, Callan announced it to the United Planets as a whole . . . and enrollment in the military jumped 850 percent overnight. It's been growing since then. Demands for recruitment have gone past 1,000 percent since this point last year—since the start of *this* year, before I was even roped back into my commission as an officer. They are overwhelmed by raw recruits."

"Saints . . ." he breathed.

Jackie nodded. "They've pulled in every single person they can spare *just* for the training camps, several of which are new, and several more are being cobbled together. 'In order to instill the proper level of discipline in numbers of troops that will outmass the commissioned and noncommissioned officers, it is the regretful decision of the Command Staff and the Council of the Terran United Planets to implement the harsh discipline of caning for the following list of capital crimes against military law and military discipline . . .'

"The list looks like there are at least forty things on here, maybe even fifty," she added, flicking through the pages on the datapad. ". . . Here it is. We'll be receiving a cross-commissioned Peacekeeper force within the next ten days, as all such crimes from this moment forth are to be considered punishable under the new system, though . . . anyone causing problems before the moment this is announced to everyone under my jurisdiction . . . will be tried under the old system. And I am ordered to report it immediately to everyone."

"Like I said, Colonel," Buraq told her. "The buck stops here. Sorry, sir."

"Not your fault." Jackie sighed.

"I've sent word for everyone—civilians included, since they also need to know all of this—to gather in the assembly room," Jasmine told her. "I took the liberty of citing an emergency announcement for Terran personnel only, and used it to request the Elite Guard fill in at all our external checkpoints. One of Tes'rin's night-watch officers is filling in the roster. Everyone should be assembled and ready or at least be at a private listening post within half an hour. That goes for all the ships on patrol. They'll all be drifting insystem wherever they are, hyperarrays on and waiting for your speech."

"Good call," Jackie praised. She shook her head "This is . . . This is Mauna Kea waiting to explode—I'm sorry, Li'eth, I'm going to have to focus on this. You can still have breakfast here, if you want, though I know you have a schedule to keep."

"Eh, get it to go," Buraq told Li'eth. "It's Southwest style; you could get a breakfast burrito, and eat it on your walk back to the Imperial Wing. Cheese, eggs, salsa, bacon crumbles, onions, you name it. Even fresh-picked, Terran-style spinach if you want it, since it's finally big enough to harvest."

"That . . . actually sounds good. I like your 'salsa' stuff," he agreed. He glanced at Jackie, who was now deep into reading the tablet in her hands. ". . . Make sure she eats, will you?"

The lieutenant smiled. "Of course. Can you find your way out? I need to badger the colonel into her formal Dress Blacks. This isn't something you reveal to the troops in casual clothes."

Nodding, Li'eth opened the door and stepped out. (*I'd kiss you good-bye, but I want to be discreet,*) he told Jackie, striding for the elevator. (*I'll see you later.*)

(*You bet your sweet, striped rump, you will,*) she returned, not so deep in thought that she didn't hear him. (*I'd kiss you anyway, but I don't have a lot of time to read all of this. I have to be ready to answer any and all questions about it.*)

(*Good luck, then,*) he wished her, and shielded his thoughts so that she could have the mental space to concentrate fully on the task ahead. Given what he knew of Terran politics and the Terran military, it seemed odd that they would choose such a thing. On the other hand, if recruitment *was* up tenfold from what it normally was ... *Then again, everywhere I went, people were under orders to have only two children, one for themselves and one for their partner to be each person's designated heir ... and any such thing as a third child was granted by a* lottery *process ...*

So yes, I can see why they'd be so enthusiastic about the possibility of literally fighting to win a plot of land on some colonyworld where—presumably—there won't be any such family planning restrictions.

He hesitated a moment, then reached out to Jackie. When she gave him a wordless reply, letting him know she was paying attention, he asked, (*Should I tell my mother about this? Or keep it a secret?*)

(*Tell her, but ask her to be discreet until she can figure out how to* guarantee *those plots of land. I don't want a backlash getting back to the United Planets from the Empire if the locals protest having a bunch of Terrans dropped in their backyard. Especially since most of these will be ground troops because it'll be hard to get enough people trained in time as pilots—the facilities for training* that *are considerably more limited than for training infantry divisions.*)

(*But they'll be far more effective in ground-based assaults, freeing up the V'Dan Army to join the Fleet. At least the Army has a baseline familiarity with our ships and how they function ... oh Saints, we have to divert ships to Earth to pick up all those soldiers. How soon will they be done training?*) he asked her, stepping into the lift when it arrived. (*Does it say?*)

(*Standard training time is three months. Some types of training require extra classes, but ... ah, here it is. The first wave of troops were recruited back last year. Most went into either pilot training, and they're just getting out of that, noncom officer training and the same, or ... specialist training. Munitions, sabotage, and preliminary training in survival techniques for space stations, dome colonies, and potentially hostile terrain. They'll all need crash courses in local flora and fauna and V'Dan life-support tech ...*

(*The second and consecutive waves are mostly infantry, with specialists being pulled out for intensive training once they've shown aptitude. Officers ... that takes a bit more training. We still won't have enough officers for another four, five months, and they'll be spread thin. Ah! Here it is . . . Shakk. Tell your mother to send each wave of ships headed to Earth filled with tanks of whatever fuel you need. We'll store them in orbit for refueling because you're going to have about three hundred thousand ground forces ready to go in one month's time, inoculated, provisioned,* jungen-*dosed, and waiting.*)

(*More like* explosive *shit, but yes, that's . . . as you Terrans say,* wow. *I'll tell her right away,*) he decided. (*I'll have to tell the Elite to let V'kol into my quarters while I change; otherwise, I'll never get his report heard at this rate. I will rejoin you later, my love.*) The endearment slipped out of his thoughts and into hers without any hesitation or censorship. After last night, there was no doubt in his mind that they were meant to be together. Not the lovemaking, though that was fine, but the *togetherness* of the two of them, free at last to spend hours just . . . being . . . together.

(*And I, you,* ke aloha,) she replied, warming him with the Hawai'ian words for *beloved.* Li'eth knew she used the language for all the things she held personally dear. For those moments when she felt Terranglo—or V'Dan, or any other language—just was not enough.

(*You'll have to teach me to speak your grandmother's language someday,*) he told her. (*Your words of love and whenever you're talking passionately about something, they are very musical-sounding.*)

(*I'll make some time later this week, then. Oh! Ask your parents if Te-los can have that language transfer he wanted, and ask them which one of us should do it. For several reasons, I'd suggest myself,*) she added, (*since I'm doubly trained for discretion in politics as well as psychic situations, but it's entirely up to them.*)

(*I will. Go study,*) he ordered, nodding to the Terran guards at the checkpoint for the innermost lifts. No Elite Guards would be posted here, but they would be found at the three entry points to the Terran zone of the North Embassy Wing. Their brown uniforms reminded him of something, though. (*Jackie, you said that there would be a Peacekeeper contingent sent from Earth for this . . . caning thing. Why Peacekeepers? Aren't your Marines handling internal policing matters?*)

(*Oh! Right, that's an easy one to answer. The Peacekeepers have been using caning as a disciplinary measure for years. There was a huge problem with corruption among the various police forces until they borrowed the tradition from a couple of the nations in Southeast Asia and applied it strictly to the Peacekeeper groups—civilians get other punishments, but the Peacekeepers are supposed to be* examples *of proper legal behavior. When a Peacekeeper goes off the rails, they* have *to be punished for it; the world won't put up with another Vladistad and its cultist regime ending with millions dead or dying, or the earlier troubles, with thousands of people outright murdered by law enforcement officials just because of their skin color—we are* never *going back to skin-based prejudices again.*

(*Anyway, they already have a whole list of rules and regulations for how it is carried out; only female corrections officers may strike female prisoners, and males with males— physiological or posthormone replacement therapy, on the grounds that the strength being gauged and used will be what the body can take. Blows are to be made in very specific locations only, starting from a very specific height, everything is to be monitored by medical professionals . . .*

(*Since we're basically on our own, days of travel from Earth, they'll be sending a specialist group to work with us in case we have any infractions big enough to warrant a caning. I only glanced through, but it looks like there's a mandatory viewing session for all personnel within range of witnessing a caning— public shaming on top of a graphic reminder not to break the laws; this is actually brilliant from a slightly twisted pointed view.*

(*Until the military can get its own corps of trained individuals up and running—and this includes mandatory psychological testing and telepathic screening to ensure no sociopaths or psychopaths get into that kind of power and position—we have to rely upon the civilian side. Most likely, they'll be former military officers who are having their own commissions reinstated, like mine was . . .*

(*Anyway, I'm done changing, and headed to my office to do a lot of reading in a very short time. I'm sending Jasmine to pick up a burrito for me. I'll see you later, my love.*)

Stepping into the next elevator, Li'eth nodded and smiled to himself, grateful the lift was empty. (*And I, you. Ke aloha.*)

He felt her smiling back through the link. (*Very good pro-nunciation, Your Highness. We'll make you a proper* kane, *a Hawai'ian man, eventually. That, and we'll need to get you a proper surfer's tan.*)

CHAPTER 15

JUNE 4, 2287 C.E.
JANVA 28, 9508 V.D.S.

"Groceries?" Her Eternal Empress, Hana'ka V'Daania, re-peated dubiously.

She paused her cup of *mo'klah* halfway to her mouth in order to frown at Jackie. The two were enjoying the *caffen*-flavored hot chocolate in private, no husband or Gestalt partner or anyone else. It was supposed to be a moment of privacy so that the most sensitive of topics could be broached between the two governments.

"You want to talk about groceries? The selection and pur-chasing of food?" Her Eternity repeated.

"Yes," Jackie confirmed.

"Two scheduled hours of being alone with me to talk about anything you found important yet sensitive . . . and instead of talking about integrating Terran troops into the V'Dan mili-tary's needs . . . you want to talk about shopping for *food*?"

"Yes."

Those gray eyes stared at her, so very like her son's left eye, though she at least didn't have any *jungen* marks coloring the right one like he did. Hana'ka blinked, digesting the unusual topic, and finally took a sip of her drink. When she had swal-lowed, she spoke. "Very well. Let us discuss shopping. Is this a Terran cultural thing?"

"It's a V'Dan cultural thing, Hana'ka," Jackie stated. They had given each other leave to use their first names during this early-afternoon meeting. Reaching for the display pad she had brought in earlier, she activated it, selected what she wanted to display, then propped it up on its built-in stand so that the Empress could see it. Jackie didn't need to see it; she had *been* on a couple of these trips. "These are shopping expeditions undertaken by the Terran embassy quartermaster and her staff, using the expense accounts your government has generously loaned to us.

"Most of it has been for food, some of it for clothing, some of it for supplies. But mostly food. The most basic, frequently made purchase required to sustain life. Among those items purchased were attempts to garner samples of the local versions of alcohol—a vice both our cultures share. Despite having V'Dan government-issued identification paperwork, despite sending people with *graying hair* to these establishments . . . the reactions of the liquor sales staff have been distressingly consistent."

Peering over the device, she found and pressed the PLAY button. The tableau that had been recorded scrolled to life. It wasn't very long, and the sound was a little tinny, but it was distinctly a V'Dan male clerk eyeing a large set of boxes that had been brought to the sales counter. *"Do your parents know you're spending this much money?"*

"Liquor *is* a semicontrolled substance," Hana'ka stated. "No one under the age of twenty-two may purchase it. Without *jungen* marks . . ."

"That video shows the purchase of Terran-analogous and V'Dan native fruits that have been packed in crates," Jackie countered. "Ripe, unprocessed fruit, not fermented. The next video shows an attempt to purchase clothes."

On cue, just seconds after she fell silent, they both heard the next clerk say, *"These clothes are a little bit too mature for you, don't you think?"* The one after that, the employee shook his head—Jackie could see the motion of it even at her steep viewing angle—and said, *"I'm sorry, but I can't in good conscience sell any of this to you. How do I know you're actually going to take all this meat to your parents to cook? You could be a Rite of Spring cultist, for all I know."*

"We're not sure what the Rite of Spring cult is," Jackie said quietly, "but we can infer it isn't something polite people do in public. The next one is the typical liquor-sales reaction."

"I'm sorry, but you cannot be in this facility. You are all underage, and I'm going to have to ask you to leave."

"But we are *of age. We're Terrans—see our ident cards?"*

"Identities can be faked. Get out now, or I'll call the city guard to arrest you."

Another break, another scene. *"Sorry, but I can't sell that to you. The Empress would pull my liquor license herself if she knew. And don't think you can come back here with fake tattoos, either. You'll have to bring actual authorization letters of the courts permitting you to be tattooed as legal adults. Now get out of here!"*

And another. *"You really should be buying looser clothes than those, meioa-o. You put on something that tight and revealing, you'll be mistaken for a Maruto."*

Jackie reached over and paused the recordings. "Your son, when he took grave offense at Countess Shi'ol Nanu'oc calling me a Charuta—to the point of nearly causing a diplomatic incident by using his holy gifts to attack her in his outrage—explained that the story of the underaged Charuta included her enlisting her younger brother, Maruto, in their attempts to seduce and ruin the adults around them with their pederastic efforts. This was *not* a compliment, Hana'ka."

"Well, a few shops with unworldly staff members . . ." Hana'ka tried to point out. Jackie shook her head, cutting off the older woman.

"This has been a consistent reaction for over two hundred shop visits, Hana'ka," she told her hostess. "Including five shopping expeditions I myself joined to ascertain the truth in person. The rate for those who treat us as *customers*, not children, is around 17 percent. That means roughly 83 percent of all such visits result in being called children, up to and including the use of culturally serious insults like this one. In all of the liquor shops, my people have been turned down. Every single one. *Even* when they presented their imperially certified identification papers proving we Terrans are to be accounted full legal adults in the eyes of the law.

"So yes, I do need to discuss the problem my people have had in buying food. And clothes. And anything else," Jackie asserted. "We have been lucky so far, in that your people have been supplying the vehicles *and* drivers we need to get around, but eventually we *will* need to take the appropriate classes and get our own driving certificates. And there are *three hundred thousand* soldiers, men and women, all of them legal adults by both our age standards, who are going to come to fight for your people in the next few months . . . and they will run into *this* cultural attitude problem, over and over again."

Hana'ka stared at the display screen a long moment, shaking her head slowly. She finally flipped her hand at it while Jackie was taking a sip of the rich mocha-like drink. "Why bring this to me? I may be the Empress, but this is just the way my culture is. This is the way our culture has been for ninety-five hundred years!"

"And this is not the way *Earth's* entire culture has been for over one hundred thousand years . . . with the exception of an idiotic period of skin-based prejudice that ran for about five hundred years or so," she allowed. "More than that, an entire culture *can* change within a single generation. Entire clusters of cultures can *be* changed, with hard work and full official support. So please don't play the 'this is the way my culture has always been' game. It won't work with me."

Jackie knew she was hedging a very fine line with that statement. Various tribes and factions and nations on Earth had gone to war in various locations over differences in ethnicities, religious beliefs, cultural clashes, and so forth—including skin color—but never as a problem for the entire world. Until, of course, the period between the Age of Colonization and the Age of Insystem Travel.

Hana'ka studied the image on the tablet, and sighed. "Over 80 percent, you say?"

"It's a very widespread problem," Jackie said. "Even someone I thought had been *trained* to avoid making that sort of mistake—as in their job would be on the line if I told you who it was—made the mistake of reacting to my people as if we were children at one point recently."

Hana'ka narrowed her eyes. "One of the Elite assigned to your embassy zone?"

"Your Highness is perceptive, but I will not mention who, as they apologized quickly enough when I chastised them for it . . . and they have not made that mistake since," she added. "I will not have anyone punished for making a mistake if they

are willing to admit to it when called out and are willing to
apologize and put some effort into not making that same mistake again. I do not ask for perfection, but I do ask for your
understanding of just how deep this problem is."

"What do you want me to do about it?" Hana'ka asked.
"Make a public announcement? Make it a *law* that all Terrans
who claim to be adults should be treated as adults?"

"I do not think such a law would catch on—that is to say,
be seen as enforceable, even participated in—unless and until
you can put some real feeling into why it is *necessary* to treat
Terrans differently," Jackie told her. "I had an idea, watching
your son shave this morning."

That made his mother roll her eyes. Her cheeks turned
slightly pink. "I thought we were not going to discuss that."

"I'm not discussing *that*," Jackie confirmed. She leaned
forward, setting her cup down and bracing her forearms on the
table, her hands lacing together. "I was looking at the patch of
jungen-burgundy stubble on his cheek, at the base of the stripe
that covers his right eye. When we found them, none of the
three men had been able to shave for the entire length of their
incarceration by the Salik."

"Are you going to have the Terran males stop shaving?"
Hana'ka asked her. "Beards *might* convince a few shopkeep-
ers, since most males don't grow proper beards until their
twentieth year, but it won't do anything for the female adults."

Jackie shook her head. "No. Watching him shave reminded
me that he *also* had most of that cheek stripe covered up. From
just below his lower eyelid down into his stubble line, by some
sort of flesh-adhering face paint that could only be removed
by high-content alcohol."

"Plasflesh, yes," his mother confirmed. "The Imperial
Family has been using it to disguise our facial markings since
about a hundred years or so past the point we developed widespread distribution of photography, when every member of the
Family became easily recognizable to the masses in the ranks.
Before that point, we used face paints that had to be applied
every day."

"Well, I'm not going to ask you to use the old-fashioned
paints," Jackie told her. "Or maybe I will, depending on what
you have available. No, I challenge you, Hana'ka, to try some-

thing. For just *one full day*, I want you to cover up every single mark you have. Even your hair. Put on a markless blond wig, use blond paint on the burgundy strands, whatever it takes. *Hide your* jungen *for one day*," she stressed while her hostess blushed and frowned, shaking her head. "Live *one day* as a Terran in appearance on this world. I think you will find it *very* enlightening.

"Oh, and feel free to tell your people in advance that you are doing this. I wouldn't want you thrown out of the Winter Palace from an accusation of being an impostor," she added, picking up her cup of *mo'klah* again. "I don't have to take the reverse test to know that I would be treated *very* differently if I painted my skin in V'Dan stripes with your plasflesh stuff. My point is that your culture should not have to demand that *my billions of citizens* coat themselves in the stuff just to be treated with common courtesy and respect.

"I don't think you can see it, just yet. I don't think you can really *grasp* that problem until you have *lived* it. So I am challenging you. Remove all traces of your *jungen* from your appearance for twenty-four V'Dan Standard hours."

Hana'ka studied Jackie for a long moment. She picked up her own cup, sipped at the slowly cooling beverage, and mulled it over. Finally, she asked, "What do I get if I go through with it?"

"Well, considering it's a personal bet between you and me, I could be flippant and say 'surfing lessons' . . . but how about enough ceristeel plating to coat your personal transport here on V'Dan? Hovercar, aircar, ground car, whichever one you like, custom fitted. Your garage mechanics can get us the exact dimensions for replacing all panels and the undercarriage, and we'll get you hull plating that's far more laserproof than anything you currently have," she offered. "That's worth quite a lot of money, economically . . . and quite a lot of peace of mind."

"Enough of your hull plating for every vehicle in the Winter Palace," Hana'ka bartered.

That made Jackie wince. "I can't authorize *that* much, meioa. In fact, I don't think the entire Space Force has that much ceristeel to spare—I've *seen* how many hovercars fly into and out of all the hangars around this place, so no way. Nothing for anyone else's use. Just for your personal use, or your immediate family's use. But how about . . . five cars, all with identical silhouettes?"

". . . Twenty."

"Deal." Jackie offered her hand.

Hana'ka narrowed her eyes. "You accepted that deal too easily."

"A deal is a deal. Twenty identical sets of ceristeel body paneling made to exact V'Dan specifications for twenty identical planetbound personal transport vehicles, either aircars or ground cars, but not both." She wiggled her fingers a little.

Sighing, Hana'ka extended her arm as well, clasping Jackie's forearm to forearm. "How soon must I do this?"

"Well, tomorrow is a holy day for the Winter Temple, right? The extra day of the month that only happens nine times a year?" Jackie asked. The Empress nodded. "Then within one or two days after that. How about Fevra Second? Make a public announcement on the First, or as close to the revelation time as possible, and do not try to rearrange your schedule in any way. Go through a regular day's work looking like a Terran. Military meetings, budget meetings, diplomatic meetings, all of it."

"And how soon will I get my plating?" she asked.

"I'll put in the order right now, if you like. All I need is a chance to speak with the right engineers here on V'Dan, get the exact specifications for vehicle armor, then send the requisition forms to Admiral Nayak. He'll get the ceristeel industry working on the problem within a day, as soon as we know the exact dimensions. After that . . . it depends on how quickly they can program the manufacturing process to those specifications, but I'd say twenty panels would be ready to ship within two weeks, maybe a month at most."

"Yet you want me to do this in three days?" the older stateswoman challenged her.

Jackie tipped her head. "Well, it is a *reward* for doing it . . . so you have to prove that you actually *do* it."

"Then why put in the order right now?" Hana'ka asked, puzzled.

That earned her a quick, mischievous smile. "Because *eventually* you'll want that plating anyway . . . and we'll have it ready and waiting for the right incentive to *sell* it to you. At the regular economic-valued price."

Hearing that, Hana'ka winced. Jackie gave her a small, sympathetic look, but only a small one; she knew the other woman knew exactly how much ceristeel cost. Those had been among the many trade factors hashed through in their economics-integration sessions. More to the point, Hana'ka knew that Jackie knew that she knew.

"I feel like I'm being extorted into this . . . An Empress should not be extorted," Hana'ka asserted.

"It's hardly that, Eternity," the Terran Ambassador told her. Jackie sipped at her *mo'klah*, swallowed, and added, "If anything, my side is the one that could be considered under extortion since price for price, we're paying the most out of pocket. A little plasflesh paint, a little hair coloring, and all you have to do is walk through your daily routine like you normally would. I have to convince an admiral of the second-highest rank to *pay* for all that ceristeel, when the Navy is busy building as many ships as it can, and needs all the hull plating it can get."

"True, but you *are* asking me to do something no Emperor or Empress has ever tried," Hana'ka countered.

"I presume you mean since the time of War King Kah'el," Jackie said, leveling the other woman a look. "I may not know more than a fraction of V'Dan's history, but I do know that the Immortal High One ruled for five hundred years longer than your bloodline has sat on that very same Eternal Throne . . . and I personally know she has no *jungen* marks."

Hana'ka narrowed her eyes a little. They narrowed more, accompanied by a frown. A sip, and she continued to cogitate. Abruptly, her eyes snapped wide open, wide enough that Jackie could see the whites all the way around those pewter-gray irises. Jackie quickly flung up her hand, sensing the name that the Empress was thinking so loud, anyone above a Rank 6 in telepathy who could have been in the room with them would have heard it.

(*Stop,*) she ordered telepathically. The sending startled the older woman enough that her cup jostled in her hand. Hana'ka quickly set it down. Jackie sent again. (*Do not say her name aloud. You and I both know this is being recorded by your security staff. Even I, a Terran, could guess that revealing her identity would cause all sorts of problems. I apologize for sending my thoughts to you, but rest assured, I am not reading yours directly. Except for the fact you were thinking that name so loudly, I could hear it through my shielding.*)

Looking a little pale, Hana'ka set down her cup. ". . . I would like to discuss a certain topic of my own, now."

Drawing in a deep breath, since she had expected something like this the moment she used her telepathy, Jackie nodded. "What would you like to discuss?"

Hana'ka looked away for a moment, gathering herself for something. She looked at the younger woman and lifted her chin the tiniest bit. "I want lessons in how to shield my mind. And I want the trade language of your people transferred to me. Not just to my husband, but to *me*. I am told that this is an *intimate* process, that I will learn things about you in the teaching method, but I still want it done."

"A few things, though not many," Jackie admitted. This was not what she had expected; rather the opposite, in fact. "The first one is always 'the worst' as my people say. I learned a *great* deal about Li'eth—Kah'raman," she corrected herself.

His mother held up her hand, palm toward herself. "Call him what you like. If the two of you are a holy partnership, I can hardly stop it. And that is what multiple names are for, to give a child a choice of what they preferred to be called by their closest family and friends."

"Thank you. A question. What made you decide this would be an acceptable thing to do?" Jackie asked, curious. "You are technically placing your mind—the last bastion of privacy you have—in my hands. What prompted you to trust me in this matter?"

"I am told you did this thing, giving our language, to your own highest-ranked leader, your Premiere A'goo-stus Callan."

Jackie had to bite her tongue for a moment against the pronunciation attempt. Very carefully not mentioning it, she said, "Yes. I did so personally at his request."

"If your own leader trusts you . . . and given the honor and honesty you have displayed to my people so far," Hana'ka allowed, "then I shall choose to trust you."

"Well, at this point, I am familiar enough with Imperial High V'Dan, I can transfer it without learning excessive amounts of your personal life. *Some* things will come across," she warned her hostess, pouring more *mo'klah* into both their cups, since both were low, "but that is only to ensure that I am attaching the correct pieces of vocabulary to the requisite bits of memory. And I certainly will not use any of that information against you."

"I have been Empress for twenty-seven years and grew up watching my father rule for decades before that. Tell it to the other ear," Hana'ka stated dryly. "I *know* you will use some of it against me. I am willing to take that risk."

Jackie met her scoffing gaze levelly. "That is not our way, Eternity. That is not the way of our politicians these days, and that is definitely not the way of our psychically gifted. In fact, of any group of people, any section of society, you will find that it is the mind-speakers of my people, the telepaths, who are the *least* enamored of the idea of reading someone else's thoughts. Mental privacy is our highest goal in life—if you have ever been in a location where the walls are so thin that you can constantly hear people in the next room talking and talking and talking, you would have a glimpse as to why. Your people can *think* of mine as markless children inside the privacy of their own skulls. The only thing we *require* of them is that we be *treated* as full adults."

"Yet you want me to undergo this test," Hana'ka pointed out.

"You don't have to, of course," Jackie allowed. "But it will help you understand just how important it is to address this cultural rift between our people. If you want our business, you have to treat us with respect. If you want our troops to defend your worlds, freeing up your own to man your ships and space stations, your people have to understand, with all the conviction you as their leader can muster, that mine must be treated with respect. If they are to settle on your colonyworlds and contribute to the local businesses, economies, and social interactions, they *have* to be respected as they are.

"My people do not care if yours are brown-spotted or blue-striped, or carry no marks at all. We find such things to be silly, shallow, and a concept we left behind over a hundred years ago. It wasn't easy, but we left it behind. We are able to accept you as you are and treat you with the respect of a fellow adult. Your son and his fellow officers were treated with respect by my people well over 83 percent of the time during their stay on Earth."

"And you want my people to accept yours. I may be the Empress, but I am just one person," Hana'ka reminded her.

"You are the Eternal Empress. Your people look up to you with great respect and consider your word to be law. If you say we must be respected—and keep saying it, and enforce it—then we will eventually be treated with respect."

Again, the Eternal Empress mulled it over. Finally, she said, "I will do it . . . in exchange for language and mind-shielding lessons. For myself and my husband, and anyone else in the immediate Imperial Family who wishes them—all the ones who were on the Imperial Tier, plus our children and grandchildren who were not there."

"I cannot make any such transfers with children, I'm sorry," Jackie apologized. "The mind of a child is too under-developed, and the vocabulary too inadequate. You really should take the ceristeel plating; the cost is considerably higher for that than for a couple dozen language transfers . . . which we would give you for free anyway, in the interests of smoothing diplomacy."

"For free?" At Jackie's nod, Hana'ka shrugged. "Very well, then. Let it remain unsaid that I tried to cheat you with a costly set of armor in exchange for a little face and hair paint, for I have offered otherwise."

Jackie wrinkled her nose. "I suspect you'll think you were *short-sheeted* instead, after your day is up . . . Ah . . . how do I explain *that* euphemism in V'Dan terms, since there's no direct analog . . ."

Hana'ka picked up her cup and gestured for Jackie to go on.

JUNE 8, 2287 C.E.
FEVRA 2, 9508 V.D.S.

Jackie finished reading the last subparagraph and sat back, nodding slowly to herself. "This is good. This is *really* good. Rosa, Surat," she told her Assistant Ambassador and the historian assigned to help her in her research, "this is a *solid* document. Li'eth explained to us what goes into an Alliance

Charter, and I've read over the V'Dan and the Solarican ones in my spare time . . . and I think this is comparable to both. I think we can take these to the Alliance Assembly . . . whenever they can get around to having one, what with the war and all. Have you run this past the Council?"

Rosa shook her head. "No. I was going to do that after running it past you. I should do it in person, though."

"I can run it to the Council," Surat Juntasa told her.

"While 'politician' may no longer be a dirty word, young man," Rosa told the slightly younger male, "I do still have some fame and clout on my side. It'll get onto the discussion docket faster, and be taken more seriously, if I, as a former Premiere, present it to the Council as a good idea. You're intelligent and articulate, but you haven't been a Counselor yourself. You don't have to recite the Oath every single workday for umpteen years."

"Tell me about it," Jackie muttered. "I almost forgot to do that, the day the news about the new corporal punishment regulations came out."

A noise outside their conference room interrupted whatever Surat meant to say. All three of them paused, frowning at the door. It slid open, letting a furious-looking ash-blond woman with fuchsia-pink crescents marking her face stride inside. Hurrying in her wake was her blond, burgundy-striped brother.

"Vi'alla, this is *not* appropriate behavior!" Li'eth snapped at his sister. "You do *not* barge into a private—"

"—*Quiet!*" Her Imperial Highness snapped, glaring down at Jackie. "*You* did this! *You* suggested this . . . this *humiliation* of the Empire!"

Jackie blinked at the finger being pointed at her face, then looked over to Rosa. "I believe the Crown Princess was not aware of her mother's announcement yesterday."

"She didn't make it yesterday as planned; she made it today," Li'eth interjected. "*After* appearing in Imperial Court without them."

"Without what?" Surat asked.

"*Without her holy* jungen*!*" Vi'alla snapped. She jabbed her finger again at the Grand High Ambassador. "I will have you dismissed for this . . . this *disgrace!*"

Jackie inhaled, prepared to defend herself. Rosa beat her to it. She stood up and looked down her nose at the princess even as she addressed the younger woman's accusation. "I suspect *your own mother* did not think of it as a disgrace or a source of humiliation when she agreed to do it of her own free will. Which was her choice entirely. The *only* shame being implied in any of this matter is in *your* head, Your Highness. *You* are the one thinking shameful, disgrace-filled thoughts about your own mother. Not any of us.

"But then, that *is* the point, isn't it?" Rosa asked, her tone level, if dry and just a little bit pointed at certain words. "To us, your mother, Eternal Empress Hana'ka V'Daania, has not lost *anything*. To us, she is still the powerful ruler of the vast V'Dan Empire. To us, she is still the War Queen defending her people with all of her might and all of her brilliance. To *us*, she is still a woman to be respected and obeyed by her people.

"She could paint herself purple from head to toe, dye her hair pink, and she would *still* have our respect. You *should* be asking yourself why *you* think she has lost all of that, just because she has temporarily hidden her *jungen* marks. Then, perhaps, you will understand the troubles that lie between our people and yours. Maybe, just maybe," Rosa added as Vi'alla bristled, "you will understand why we are increasingly *reluctant* to help a nation that is so consistently disrespectful to *us* . . . particularly if even your Eternal Empress can be considered a shameful disgrace by her own child just because of a little face paint and hair dye for a day.

"You have barged in here like a petulant, spoiled child who thinks she has the right to go everywhere, even into a house that is not her own," Rosa added. "This is not your house. This is the Terran embassy zone. Our rules apply here. Our culture applies here. And *we* judge people by the maturity of their *actions*, not the color or lack thereof on their faces. Have the courtesy to leave even if you haven't shown us any maturity. *Now*."

Jackie realized what Rosa was doing. What only Rosa *could* do . . . because if Jackie had done it, that would have ruined diplomatic relations far into the future.

"One moment, Your Highness," she stated calmly. "Rosa McCrary, you owe the Crown Princess an apology for your rudeness. Your comments may have been true, but their delivery was tactless and not diplomatic. The Terran United Planets expects better of its representatives, and you will apologize for it."

As she suspected, Rosa didn't hesitate more than half a second. Bowing, she said, "I apologize for my rudeness and tactless phrasing, Highness. Please accept that I am sorry for hurting your feelings. I shall try to be more tactful and diplomatic in the future."

"Thank you, McCrary. You may be seated. Imperial Highness . . . it would be best if you left now. You have had your say, and McCrary has had hers." Jackie looked at the still-somewhat-red-faced, slightly scowling princess. "She spoke the truth when she said we judge each other on our actions, not our appearance. And she spoke the truth when she said we still respect your mother as much today as we did yesterday, and as much as we shall tomorrow.

"She was not diplomatic about it, but I hope you will consider her point on how you view your mother right now, when she is markless for a day. I hope you consider carefully how your people have been viewing my people in this exact same way. I hope you think carefully about how rude and tactless that viewpoint makes your people act toward mine. And I hope you will also consider carefully how insulting and denigrating a people whose help you need is not the best possible course of action for securing that help, both now and well into the future.

"Have a good day, Highness. I hope you can continue to view your mother with all the deep respect she is due as your Eternal Empress, and as your beloved mother . . . and that you will give her the public support she deserves and needs as your undoubted Empress, marked or markless."

Vi'alla did not reply. She stood there for a few seconds, then whirled and strode out. Li'eth dithered a moment, then left to follow her out. A moment later, Grand Captain Tes'rin poked his head inside.

"Ah . . . Grand High Ambassador, I have come to apologize for that," he offered, slipping into the conference room.

Jackie arched a brow at him. "I was reassured, Grand Captain, that the Terran embassy zone would be considered sacrosanct. That no one could move about our halls without our specific permission, save only for emergency crews. I was reassured these things by you, yourself.

"Now, I realize my own people would be reluctant to cause a diplomatic incident by *shooting* her to stop her from approaching. But tell me, how did the Imperial Heir get all the way into this zone without being stopped by *your* people? At the very least, she should have been halted at the entry point by your fellow Elite Guards, working in conjunction with our Marines. A message should have been sent to see if I was free and available to see her. Which I was not. Neither informed in advance nor free and available."

He flushed a little. "The Elite . . . are under orders *not* to stop either the current sovereign or the current heir. They have the right to go anywhere in the Winter Palace. That is the law." Tes'rin started to say more, but something beeped. He pulled a device out of his pocket and looked at it. "Ahh . . . Her Eternity wishes to ask a question of you. She wants me to ask you, 'The whole day?'"

Jackie didn't pretend not to know what Hana'ka meant by that. "A full twenty-four hours V'Dan Standard. Every hour she shortens from that amount, she loses one full set of panels. Please also inform your Empress that we wish War Queen Hana'ka a *very* long and happy life . . . as we are less than impressed with her choice of heir, today. And that we are not so pleased with the Elite Guard's inability to protect the sanctity and protocols of the Terran embassy zone, when her heir rudely interrupted a private meeting in said zone, today."

That made the grand captain pale a little. ". . . As you wish. Please forgive the intrusion."

A bow, and he left. Surat cleared his throat and scooped up one of the tablets with the draft of the Terran United Planets Charter on it. "I'll just leave the two of you to discuss . . . things. On your own."

"Your tact and discretion are appreciated, Surat," Jackie told him. "Feel free to write it down in the long-term chronicles. The ones that won't be unlocked for fifty years."

"Yes, ma'am," the historian murmured, making his escape.

As soon as the door closed behind him, Jackie groaned softly and slumped forward, elbows on the table and brow in her palms. "Stars . . . Thank you for doing what I could not,

Rosa. And thank you for apologizing promptly when I commanded it."

"Thank you for making me apologize to her," the ex-Premiere acknowledged in turn. "One of the skills of a seasoned *junior* diplomat is the art of throwing oneself willingly on the sword of 'how dare you say that to me' just so your superiors do not have to do it themselves. I believe your own grandfather mentioned it a time or two in his political career."

"Yes, I remember him mentioning it to *me*, when I was young, and he was still alive," Jackie agreed. "He said a junior statesman could always be chastised publicly for stepping out of line, and thus make amends by satisfying the ego of the person insulted through their punishment, but a senior statesman must never step out of line, for they cannot be punished without damaging the reputation of all the power and responsibility they represent.

"So. What can I do for you, to make up for the gaping diplomatic wound you just made in your so very brave guts?" she quipped lightly.

"Arrange to have a true arachnophile come out and start handling the K'Katta negotiations," Rosa told her. "I can handle them for the most part, particularly via the communications system they helped set up for us . . . but every once in a while, I get the *wobblies* from the way they look and move. We now have enough information on each of the various governments, we should be able to start assigning ambassadors to each faction."

"I was thinking of that," Jackie admitted. "I was thinking we should pick someone with a background in art, interior design, or something along those lines, to help handle the Gatsugi. Someone hyperaware of the presence and use of colors, so they can pick up on what would be good colormood hues to wield around them."

"I was thinking of that as well," Rosa praised.

Somewhere out there, Eternal Empress Hana'ka V'Daania was getting a taste of just how awful it was to be a Terran in the V'Dan culture. As much as Jackie felt sorry for her, she had her own problems to manage today. She certainly wasn't about to take on the responsibility of somehow making Imperial Heir Vi'alla V'Daania look at her mother in the *right* way, instead of the "insulted" way.

CHAPTER 16

JUNE 9, 2287 C.E.
FEVRA 3, 9508 V.D.S.

"Hold on, sir," Lieutenant Colvers murmured. He moved closer than his usual preference. "You have some stray hairs on your uniform. It wouldn't look professional for anyone to see them when the cameras start hovering."

Jackie blinked but held herself still. *Brad Colvers, volunteering to help me look good? Has he finally gotten over his stupid prejudices against psis?* She felt him plucking a couple of times at the jacket of her Dress Blacks. She'd been in a meeting with the V'Dan version of a command staff, with no time between that meeting and this one to change clothes.

At the Eternal Empress' request, they had gathered in the Inner Court, which was a set of much smaller indoor plazas on the far side of that temple structure from the vast, outdoor Tier Plazas they had first seen. Hana'ka was going to end her twenty-four hours of life as a markless Terran in a public broadcast.

"Thank you," she managed in a polite murmur when he finished. Checking her shoulders, Jackie gave her jacket a subtle tug to straighten it and was glad Colvers helped her to look good. No more worries for her about straining the jacket buttons, these days; two hours of martial arts, general physical training, and psychic self-defense practice every single day toned her body to the point where she might even have to ask for a new, smaller uniform in a couple more weeks. She still would rather be surfing, but . . .

(*Here we come,*) Li'eth warned her.

"Time to stand up," Jackie ordered quietly. Five seconds after she and her fellow Terrans did so—just long enough to garner several bemused looks from the others in the First Tier section—Master of Ceremonies announced the approach of the Eternal Empress.

Unlike the outdoor plazas on the west side of the central hall, the Inner Court had permanent seating: cushioned, backed benches for the V'Dan and the Terrans, double-armrest chairs for the Gatsugi, chairs without lumbar backing for the tailed Tlassians and Solaricans, and perching stools for their K'Katta guests. They were angled slightly to either side of the main aisle and a bit more steeply beyond that, all of them facing the great pearlescent throne at the top of the last set of steps.

That throne was incredible. It seemed to have been carved from a giant pearl, or perhaps stuck into a megafauna of an oyster—there was no telling what on V'Dan had created it, but Jackie was dead certain it had not been anything back on Earth. Tall enough to tower over the head of a standing Human, it cupped the Empress like a personal amplification shell, iridescent rose-pink with the smoothest lines she had yet to see in Imperial furniture since everything else was carved and gilded beyond words. Then again, the Eternal Throne needed no gilding, just the polishing of millennia, and some golden cushions scattered among the scarlet lining its seat. A seat big enough for two, if they squished in together.

The pearlescent throne sat in front of a great, richly hued red curtain; spatially, if she had to guess their exact location, Jackie would have placed it at or close to the temple-like area with the sarcophagus or altar or whatever inside; she still had yet to ask if it was alright to view it up close. The stairs between each Tier were short and shallow, carpeted in more crimson, and there were a strictly limited number of seats available in each section, though only the First Tier was completely packed.

Oddly enough, most of the Fifth and Fourth Tiers were filled with teenaged children and a scattering of chaperones; no doubt they were school groups brought here to observe their governance lessons in action. The Third Tier looked to be filled with reporters and scholarly types, and possibly some guild masters or something. Second Tier and First Tier were, of course, nobles, with the addition of diplomatic delegates in the section closest to the Imperial Tier.

Only five members per embassy were allowed in the Inner Court at any one time. Since she had been coming from a military meeting, Jackie had brought Colvers to represent the TUPSF Navy—Robert was too busy overseeing the results of that meeting, which had included redistributing a few Terran ships to try to follow a string of Salik raids—and al-Fulan for the TUPSF Marines. Clees and Rosa had joined them for the Empress' announcement, and the older male was busy setting up the perfect viewing height on the one hovercam he was allowed.

Elite Guard regulations stated that it had to remain directly over the body of the operator at all times. Since the Terrans were seated off to the left end of the far right front row, that meant he could only adjust the view up or down. Not too far down, though; there were other recording devices floating quietly in the air.

Empress Hana'ka had brought a minimum entourage with her as well. Vi'alla, of course, as the Imperial Heir, and Li'eth, who was going to be appointed as a cultural liaison between the Terrans and the Empire, as well as their military liaison. Naturally, Imperial Princess Ah'nan was not present. Originally, she had been slated to go back to the heartworld of the local branch of the Solarican Empire after traveling to V'Dan with her wife, their consort, and their children specifically to greet the Terrans.

During the couple of weeks that followed that initial greeting, Imperial Princess Ah'nan, an experienced diplomat, had offered to go to Earth as the V'Dan Ambassador to the Second Empire. The Terrans had considered her credentials carefully, and after promising to inoculate the entire V'Dan warship meant to carry them to Earth, had given their blessing to let her go. That was where the original navigator for Jackie's crew, Ayinda Mbani, had gone, traveling aboard the same ship to help guide the crew to the Motherworld of their joint species.

Imperial Consort Te-los was not on hand, either. Nor were any of their younger children, Mah'nami or Balei'in, nor Vi'alla's husband. Just the three of them plus the Elite Guard stood on the highest level.

The Empress looked a little odd to Jackie. Her hair was pure blond, her skin flawlessly golden-tan. Her uniform, as always, was that of the War Queen, with the War Crown circling her brow in crimson and gold. There was not a hair out of place, but the face still . . . *Oh. Stupid,* she castigated herself behind her strongest shields, blushing. *She's covered up her short burgundy stripes.* That's *why she looks a little odd . . . and from the muttering of the natives in the audience, she looks beyond merely "odd" to her fellow V'Dan.*

Master of Ceremonies finished speaking, and those mutterings died down to a faint, rustling sea of hissed whispers. The Empress allowed the quiet to stretch for several seconds until even the faintest whispers faded, her expression a cool, almost stern mask. Finally, she spoke.

"I did not understand." That statement earned her several confused looks and a resumption of whispers. She paused a moment to let those die down, stirred up because the Eternal Sovereign no doubt rarely admitted to a flaw. "I was told, and yet I did not understand, nor did I *care* to understand, until these last twenty-four hours. Even my own husband of forty-one years felt awkward in my presence at night. Forty. One. Years, as wife and husband. I did not understand . . . but now I do."

She held out her hand to her left without looking. Imperial Prince Kah'raman V'Daania pulled a remarkably familiar hip flask from his uniform, and a kerchief. Jackie had to bite her lip and jam her thumbnails into the sides of her forefingers to keep herself from grinning openly. As she watched, Li'eth used the very same flask, the one Jackie had given *him* back home to reveal his *jungen*-marked identity, to dampen the kerchief. As soon as it was soaked, he handed it to his mother. She scrubbed it slowly, carefully over the backs of her hands, smearing off the tanned plasflesh makeup to reveal the short, almost symmetrical stripes on her hands and her wrists.

"The Terrans have complained to us that they are being treated as children because they do not bear the *jungen* marks of our kind. We in turn have treated those complaints as if they were the whinings of children complaining about a strict bedtime."

She handed the kerchief to her son, who carefully refolded it so that a fresh, clean side faced outward. Hana'ka gently lifted the War Crown from her head and passed it to her daughter, who held it carefully sideways, exactly as her mother had proffered it. No doubt there was some significance to that, say if she'd been handed it with the front of the crown on the far side from herself, she could've been free to wear it. Jackie didn't know, yet. She had been busy studying enough protocols and rituals to get through her own side of things; a course in the full rites, rituals, etiquettes, and histories of the Imperial Court still had to wait until all her many other responsibilities and tasks had been handled.

"We have acted in arrogance, believing that if they wish to deal with us, they need to *look* like us. To *be* us. We have willfully overlooked ten thousand years of cultural differences. Of history, of actions and beliefs, land and landscape, actions and interactions shaping our cultures in two very distinct, very *different* directions. Shame lies upon this Empire in forgetting those differences, just because they *look* almost like us."

Removing the pins hidden in her hair, she peeled off the loosely braided wig that hid her natural blond-and-burgundy-striped tresses. They had been carefully plaited so that the whole mass could be coiled under the wig without getting too messy or looking too rumpled once it was removed. With the pins reattached to the wig, she handed that to her daughter in exchange for the crown . . . then passed the crown to her son in exchange for the alcohol-soaked cloth.

From the faint frown pinching her daughter's brow, Jackie guessed that Vi'alla had not expected that maneuver. Yet it was necessary. Hana'ka used the cloth now on her throat and the edges of her face, scrubbing away yet more plasflesh to reveal the natural, dark red stripes that crossed her hairline onto her neck, forehead, and cheeks.

"The key word," the Eternal Empress stressed, "is *almost*. They *almost* look like us. And in our arrogant belief in our own customs and habits, we treat them based on what we *see*, and not on what they *are*."

A last swipe of her brow, and she handed the cloth to her son, who traded it for the crown. His mother did not put it on, however. "What these Terrans *are* is not open for debate. They *are* adults. They *are* honorable. They *are* mature. They *are* worthy and deserving of the same respect you would give *me*."

From the way both Li'eth and Vi'alla blinked at that statement, Jackie guessed that the Emperor or Empress never considered anyone their equal unless they *were* an Emperor, Empress, or other top-of-the-food-chain equivalent.

"It was *wise* of Grand High Ambassador Jackie Maq'en-zi to request that I hide my *jungen* stripes," Hana'ka continued. "I have discovered in these last twenty-four hours how *diminished* that respect became simply because of a change in the color of my skin. How *odd* is it that we no more object to a Solarican whose fur is one color, nor a K'Katta, nor a Choya.

"We do not look down upon the Tlassians, and we don't even disparage the Salik for being 'juveniles' because *their* skin does not change with puberty—we despise them for other, far more important reasons," the Empress stated, lifting the War Crown over her head. "But we do not treat their adults as juveniles. Yet we do mistreat our own species . . . and when we make ourselves look like them, we look down upon ourselves as well as them . . . for I found myself hating how 'childish' I looked."

She hesitated a moment, then brought that crown, with its stylized swords and rubies wrapped in a crimson-padded circlet, down onto her head.

"*I* did not change, over these last twenty-four hours," the ruler of V'Dan stated, lowering her arms to her sides. "I still have every bit of the wit and the compassion, the wisdom and the intelligence I had before beginning this experiment. I had all of those things and more all throughout it. *I did not change.* But your view of me did . . . and I *understand* now the massive struggle these Terrans face.

"Even when doing something as simple as attempting to buy *groceries*, they have faced prejudice based on something their own people do not have, have never had, and do not *need* to have in order to retain every bit of wit, compassion, wisdom, intelligence, technology, power, and *sovereignty* that they possess, all of it based upon their *own* culture . . . and all of it still completely valid within our own, once we strip away our spots and our stripes.

"They look upon each other and see the mature, responsible adults that they are. We look upon them . . . and we see nothing but the monochromatic hues of their skin. They should not have to be burdened by *our* rather shallow and thus childish view of what is and what is not mature. No one in *my*

Empire, citizen or guest, should have to struggle against skin-colored prejudice just to buy *food*."

Hana'ka let those contempt-filled words echo through the layers of the hall, amplified and projected subtly by whatever sound system the V'Dan had installed who knows how long ago. Jackie just knew that the Empress' words left dead silence in her wake, a silence broken only by the faint hum of a dozen or so cameras hovering midair.

"These Terrans among us *are adults*. Our own citizens turn into legal adults at the age of eighteen years. *Their* people are legally adults from the moment they turn eighteen . . . and as their years are a near match in length for our own, they shall be considered as legitimate as our own. To that end," Hana'ka stated, "I am revising Tattooing Compliance Law 112.

"Once a citizen of V'Dan—or any other *Human*—turns the age of eighteen years, by V'Dan Standard measurement *or* Terran—they do *not* need a court certificate granting them the legal right to gain tattoo-based *jungen* marks . . . or any other tattoos. All those *under* the age of eighteen years must still obey the law, but those of eighteen and older need only present a valid ident proving their age. They must also still sign the consent form of Tattooing Compliance Law 114, which prevents anyone from being *forced* to get a tattooed set of *jungen* marks.

"As has been pointed out to me," Hana'ka added dryly, "some Terrans may want to tattoo themselves to look like us out of an enthusiasm for meeting and supporting the ways of their long-lost kin. Some of our own citizens, who have suffered for far too long under these prejudices and bigotries against the unmarked—a condition based entirely upon the combination of the strain of *jungen* virus that infects them and their personal genetics, neither of which is under anyone's control—may wish *not* to mark their skin as a sign of their own enthusiasm for meeting and supporting the ways of our own long-lost kin.

"In accordance with, and in correlation to, these changes . . . I am enacting Sovereign Law 834,712. *Any* being of legal adult age for a given circumstance shall be considered an adult solely upon their legal age and the maturity of their behavior, and not by any prejudice or bigotry against the color of their skin. Any and all laws requiring *jungen* marks as a

basis for legal maturity are hereby modified so that such
requirements are no longer necessary. This ruling does not
and shall not invalidate any other requirements of those laws.

"I suggest my citizens struggle with learning quickly how
to treat *everyone* well, without regard to their marks or lack
thereof . . . or the law courts will find themselves inundated
with misdemeanor civil suits against bigoted behavior. I suggest you strive particularly hard to treat our Terran guests and
neighbors with far more respect from now on, for they *do* have
the right to buy food without prejudice. They have the right to
buy liquor without prejudice. They have the right to buy and
wear whatever clothing they prefer without prejudice.

"And they *will* be treated as our honored allies. *Without
prejudice.* So says the Eternal Throne." Her hands flicked out
to either side, and she and her son and daughter all seated
themselves on the huge throne and the two slightly smaller
chairs flanking it. Staff members discreetly moved up on either
side to accept the dirtied kerchief and the neatly braided wig,
while Master of Ceremonies smoothly launched into the next
piece of the day's business, which was some matter the K'Katta
Grand High Ambassador needed to have the Empress address.

(*Well. That was interesting,*) Jackie mentally whispered to
Li'eth. She kept her gaze firmly on his face, striving hard to
ignore the *creepycreepycreepy* view of the K'Katta delegation
moving up to the base of the steps leading to the Imperial Tier
as they made their formalized request.

(*Only interesting?*) he asked, his outward expression calm,
but his inner one holding the equivalent of an arched eyebrow.
Not over her arachnophobia, but over her mild reaction to his
mother's announcements.

(*I'm glad she learned what I hoped she would learn. She
only covered some of what I hoped she would,*) Jackie added,
(*but I can see why she hasn't tried to cover all of it all at once.
People are going to balk at this anyway . . . and if the way
your sister's aura is still swirling with anger aimed toward us
is any indication, it's going to be a long, hard, uphill climb to
get people like her to pay attention. To admit that treating us
as equals IS necessary, and to actually do so.*)

(*Fair enough. You aren't upset that our business isn't the
first on the docket, are you?*) he added, meaning his

civilian-side appointment. They both knew it was a mere formality since he was already acting as a cultural liaison as well as a military one, but protocols still had to be observed. Giving him the official title would give him an official level of authority to go with it.

(*Nope. I was actually hoping she wouldn't touch our part of her court business first because while her announcement about markless equality* is *important enough to be addressed first, the liaison business is not,*) Jackie told him. (*That means by putting our business in the middle of things, we are not being singled out in any other way nor given any overt favoritism . . . which makes her commands for equality all the* more *important, not all the less.*)

(*Mother put it in a similar way while we were waiting for Court to start, if not quite in those exact words,*) he agreed. (*I'm scheduled to work out right after Court, though it'll be an abbreviated session. You?*)

(*The same, though I'll be able to escape as soon as my piece of business is through,*) she told him. They had not had the chance to sleep together last night and hadn't discussed their business for today in any detail. (*Will you be joining us for lunch?*)

(*I'll be free to depart with you, actually—if I can borrow a set of exercise clothes from someone, would it be okay if I did my workout in the Terran zone? That'd save time. I can get a quick shower to wash off the sweat in your suite, if you're willing,*) he suggested. (*And I've already stashed clean uniforms in your suite.*)

She smiled up at him. (*Of course you can join us. You have the admiration of just about everyone in our embassy, you know.*)

He couldn't smile back openly, but he did give her a warm mental hug. (*Thank you.*)

JUNE 14, 2287 C.E.
FEVRA 8, 9508 V.D.S.

Li'eth looked up as the door to his mother's personal parlor opened unexpectedly. This was not the semiformal one that members of the Imperial Family gathered in before going to some group activity, whether that was Court or a meal. Only a handful of highly trusted servants would come and go in this particular room, and right now, none would have entered without permission. The person who entered, however, was not a servant.

"Vi'alla, I don't know why you are here, but this is not a good time to interrupt," he stated quietly. His eldest sister ignored him, however. Her gray gaze had fastened upon their mother and the Terran Grand High Ambassador. In specific, on the way they were seated, knees to knees, hands clasped, heads bowed in concentration. Almost like they were about they were praying.

Or rather, exactly like they were about halfway through the language-transfer process, if all went well.

"What is *she* doing with her?" Vi'alla demanded. She moved forward, frowning "Eternity, whatever this foreigner may be attempting—"

Rising quickly from his seat to one side, Li'eth got in her way. He got in his sister's way, and sidestepped when she tried to go around him, continuing to block her. "I *said*, this is *not* a good time to interrupt, Vi'alla."

"Interrupt what? That foreigner planting *thoughts* in our Empress' head?" Vi'alla snapped. "I know the pose a holy one takes when they communicate mind-to-mind! It was bad enough she has touched the mind of the Imperial Consort, but now our Sovereign?"

She shoved him to the side. Staggering, Li'eth turned and stopped her, reacting with his mind instead of his muscles. Reacting as he had been *taught*, and not just by instinct. Lifted off her feet unexpectedly, Vi'alla gasped in fright. So did he, albeit softer and out of startlement, not fear. Vi'alla dropped the instant his concentration wavered, stumbling and grunting in pain as she landed awkwardly on her feet.

Quickly firming his will, Li'eth concentrated again, scooping her up off her feet. It was hard—she was half-again as heavy as anything he had practiced with before now—but he managed it. Levitating her slowly back, away from their mother and his mate, he carefully held her still while he took a moment to step between her and them.

I see now why Jackie prefers not *moving while concentrating on things like this. Unless she is levitating herself, of course . . . and I'm not that good, yet.* Sweat beaded on his brow. He wasn't perfect at holding her properly vertical, particularly when she struggled. Lifting his hand, he gestured, righting her a little more.

"My instructor in these abilities, Master Sonam Sherap, stressed that it is *vital* not to interrupt a language transfer in action," Li'eth told his sister, holding her gaze as firmly as he held her body a handspan off the floor. "Their minds are moving as fast as the swiftest of thoughts. *Both* of their memory centers, their kinesthetic cortexes, their senses of sight, sound, touch, taste, smell, *all* of it, is being stimulated at maximum speed. Interrupt them for a second, *touch* them for a moment, and *your* mental energies will be like throwing a log in front of a speeding ground car.

"That vehicle may merely bump over the log with a painful jolt, or it could bound into the air and flip, crashing and tumbling, damaging everything inside and out. *You will not interfere in what you do not understand,*" he asserted, pinning his sister with his gaze as well as his mind. Li'eth ignored the trickle of sweat tickling its way down into his burgundy-striped eyebrow. "This is our mother's choice. *Not* yours, sister.

"I pledged our Empress I would defend her from *all* sources of interference while she endures this language transfer," he added formally. "And I will protect her even from her own Heir if need be."

Lifting his left hand, he focused, pouring heat into the air over his palm. It shimmered for a moment, then burst into bright flame more than a broad handspan in height. Carefully setting her on her feet, he released her telekinetically and pointed at the door she had used.

"Leave, and wait to be summoned. Whatever your news is, it can either be handled by you within the bounds of your authority as Heir, it can be handled by the Grand Generals and the Grand Admirals if it is a matter of the war . . . or it can *wait* for the authority of the Empress to handle it. I will let Her Eternity know that you had news you needed to discuss. When the transference is *over.*"

Free to move, Vi'alla narrowed her eyes at him. "I shall not forget this insolence, Kah'raman."

"This is *authority*, not insolence, Crown Princess. I have been appointed Guardian to the Empress during these hours. My authority to defend her sanctity and her choices outranks your freedoms and rights as Heir," he countered, giving her a hard, implacable stare. He had to end the projection of fire even as he spoke, but he kept his finger aimed at the door and even jabbed it a little. "Go."

"You and your little Terran cannot hide forever behind trumped-up protocols. If I find any evidence the two of you are colluding against the Empire—" she threatened.

"There is none. Now, *go*," Li'eth ordered. And gave her a telekinetic shove to force her toward the door.

Giving him one last, hard glare, his eldest sister stalked back out of the private parlor attached to their parents' suite. Only after the panel shut did Li'eth feel free to wipe at the sweat on his face. His hand shook as he did so, and the amount of liquid made him pull out a kerchief to mop it up. A glance at the two women, seated with their hands clasped and their eyes closed, breathing calmly, reminded him that facing down the Imperial Heir was worth it.

Returning to his seat nearby, Li'eth lowered himself into it and contemplated the grim knowledge that his eldest sister did *not* like the Terrans. She did not like them, she refused to understand them, and when Vi'alla took up the Eternal Crown—may that day be long and far away—she would *not* make a good ally for the Second Empire because of her arrogant belief in her vast superiority over the Terrans.

That was one conversation with his mother that he was not looking forward to having.

Vi'alla had been selected, trained, and groomed for the position of Heir for decades. Most of the Empire favored her eventual succession to some extent—informal polls placed her above 60 percent. That, he knew, was high enough to have made her a legitimate candidate for being a Terran Counselor, ironically. If she could pass the various tests in Terran sciences, law, and so forth, that was.

No, his eldest sibling was no true friend of the Terrans. Not much of a potential mere ally, either. She might tolerate them, and she had expressed admiration for their communications arrays and their swift-traveling ships, but that was it; Li'eth feared that if she could get her hands on *how* their technology worked, Imperial Crown Princess Vi'alla would steal their technology without a second thought.

All her eldest brother could do was sit in the provided chair off to one side, wait for his Gestalt partner and his Empress to come out of their transference trance, and pray to the Saints that his mother would live a very, very long time. Long enough for one of Vi'alla's children to grow old enough and wise enough to be appointed Heir instead.

It had happened in the past, after all. Heirs could even be nephews or nieces, or younger sons or daughters, or the children of those offspring—Ah'nan would make a better Heir, actually, particularly if one of Vi'alla's three children was not ready for the position. She wasn't *here*, but Ah'nan would make a much better Heir. Her latest reports from Earth—what a boring name for a planet, compared to the Salik's Sallha, which translated as "Fountain," or the Gatsugi's Beautiful-Blue—were already showing how her efforts at managing that side of the negotiations were turning out to be quite helpful. It wasn't treason to discuss her for the possibility of being a better Heir, under that context.

There were certainly plenty of precedents in the bloodline's forty-five hundred years. And technically, it was not a betrayal to consider his second-eldest sister as the better candidate for the Eternal Throne. But it *felt* a tiny bit like treason, since his eldest sister had been the Heir for longer than Li'eth had been striped.

JUNE 22, 2287 C.E.
FEVRA 15, 9508 V.D.S.

The increasing presence of Shi'ol Nanu'oc, Countess S'Arrocan, in the halls of the Terran embassy annoyed Jackie. For whatever insane reason the two of them had, it appeared that the countess and Lieutenant First Grade Brad Colvers were now officially dating. An unlikely duo in Jackie's opinion, but there it was.

An odd couple, since Shi'ol still acted superior around anyone who was markless, and Brad was about as markless as a Terran could get. He didn't even have any visible moles or freckles beyond one or two tiny spots on each of his arms whenever he wore short sleeves. But Shi'ol did behave herself, mostly. She might stare for a moment at Jackie and Li'eth, but she always averted her eyes after that moment and studiously ignored the two of them.

Jackie could tolerate being ignored. She now had so much on her plate, it was hard to find the time for herself other than late at night or early in the morning. A fresh influx of guards and staff had arrived, along with fifteen new ships for the *Embassy* fleet.

Embassies 16 through *30* came with experienced bureaucrats, scientists, historians, and several soldiers—Army, Special Forces, Marines, and Navy personnel, as well as Admiral Nayak, who had been reassigned to serve under Jackie, who had had her commission retired so that she was no longer forced to play double duty as an officer as well as the Terran Ambassador. It also came with the promised Peacekeepers, a cluster of ten sober, police-trained personnel and a corrections facility doctor who specialized in overseeing cases of corporal discipline.

The doubled fleet also came with a contingent of psychics sent from both the Psi League and the Witan Order. Some of them would go with Rosa when she traveled to each of the other races' capital worlds, in a mix of original and new staff and guards, to help her meet, greet, and present the Terran Charter to the member nations of the Alliance. It was the will of the Terran United Planets Council that the former Premiere should be the Grand High Ambassador to the Alliance at large, while Jackie remained Grand High Ambassador to the V'Dan in particular. Aixa Winkler had volunteered to go along as well, citing how well she and her "peer in age" got along. She was strong enough to serve as Rosa's staff xenopath, which made her an excellent choice in Jackie's opinion.

The current influx of psis numbered nearly twenty—a very large number in proportion to the others who had arrived—but that was because the Sh'nai Temples had finally bowed to the reality of Terran psychic-gift training. They had declared it superior . . . and someone from a department called the D'aspra Archives had scrounged up some vaguely worded prophecies that confirmed the "Second Empire"—the Terrans—would ". . . teach new ways of enlightenment and power, admonishing it be ever and only used for good, as coded in their writ and in their way."

Even with over twenty psis, most of whom were qualified to teach, and with the ability now to cover the explanation, demonstration, and teaching methods of nearly every form of psychic ability currently known to the Terrans . . . they still required Jackie's presence to help with some of it. To reassure the V'Dan priests and priestesses, and even now some Gatsugi psis and Solarican Seers, and a contingent of Tlassians of the priest caste, the Grand High Ambassador had to be on hand for these first new teaching sessions. To answer questions and give reassurances.

Even more were scheduled to arrive as time went on, in an influx timed to arrive every ten days or so. They now had a currency exchange going. New forms of Alliance technology were being integrated into existing Terran technologies, and some of their own—hydrogenerator tech, if not the recipe for making the catalyst itself—was being sold to the V'Dan. Things were starting to look up for everyone. Emerging from her private quarters in a good, hopeful mood, Jackie therefore found she had to ask an abruptly important question on a topic utterly unrelated to the influx of new personnel weighing on her mind.

"What is *she* doing on this floor?" she demanded bluntly, eyeing the green-spotted blonde, whom she had only seen in the lower levels before now. Shi'ol and Brad were just at that moment stepping out of the lift.

Colvers twitched a little at the demand but faced her politely. Somewhat politely, since his reply was as blunt-voiced as hers. "I *live* on this floor, remember? Just because Admiral Nayak is now in charge of all four Branches out here does not move me out of the suite I was granted as Robert's right hand. And I am *free* to bring whomever I like to my personal, private quarters, provided they have passed a security background check.

"Which Shi'ol has," Brad added tersely. "Or are you going to hold her past mistakes against her?"

The lift doors slid shut behind them. That meant she would have to wait for it to return to that floor if anyone else had summoned it on a different floor. Jackie met Shi'ol's gaze for a long moment before pulling it away from the rosette-spotted woman. She eyed Brad instead. "So long as she *keeps* her mistakes in the past, I will. And not one word out of *either* of you about my personal life or how it supposedly influences or adversely affects my duties and my loyalties. Is that clear?"

"Crystal, ma'am," Brad told her. Now that she was a retired colonel, he didn't have to call her "sir." She was still in his chain of command, but only because she was the official representative of the Secondaire and Premiere in all matters. He eyed her in her civilian clothes, a softly clinging pantsuit in deep orange scattered with peach and white flowers. "Is that what you'd call formal attire?"

"I'm going to a meditation class being held for Imperial Prince Balei'in, the youngest child of the Empress, and several members of the Solarican Seers' Guild and the Tlassian priest caste. He's a psychometric, like Li'eth, with the ability to read the history of the objects he touches. Since it's an ability I myself am starting to develop through the Gestalt, I'm going to be meditating with them, learning how to tap into those abilities consciously and under full control. In order to do so successfully, I have elected to wear comfortable, nondistracting clothes. Now, if you'll excuse me?"

She started to step around them. Brad turned to follow her. "One moment . . ."

Stopping, Jackie twisted to face him. "Yes?"

He frowned and moved around her. "Hold *still*, Ambassador. You're still our Grand High Ambassador . . . and you really need to start brushing your hair *before* you change your clothes."

She felt him pluck twice at the back of her right shoulder, then again at the left. Twisting to eye him, she watched as he shook his fingers, letting the hairs fall to the floor. Beyond him, Shi'ol smirked slightly, but only slightly, and said nothing. ". . . Thank you. I'll keep that in mind."

Striding up to the door, she pushed the call button. Thankfully, no one else had summoned the car. Stepping into the lift, she pressed the floor she wanted. Her last sight as the doors slid shut were of Brad wrapping his arms around an almost giddy-looking Shi'ol. The thought of the two of them together, doing . . . things . . . churned her stomach.

In that much, I guess I'm no better than Crown Princess Vi'alla, she thought, and sighed. Her Imperial Highness still did not like the Terrans, and in particular did not like Jackie. She was civil and courteous, but it was a cold courtesy at best. Fortunately, Jackie did not have to deal with Shi'ol. The woman had no voice in Jackie's level of politics or military interactions. Unfortunately, she still had to deal with Her Imperiousness, Imperial Heir Vi'alla.

Let it go, Jackie, she ordered herself. Breathing deep, she emerged on the right floor and strode past the security desk. *Let go of your irritation and get your mind focused on the class that lies ahead. You have very little free time right now to waste, and you need these lessons in psychometry. Just let the thought of the two of them float away and crumble into nothingness. You are calm, you are safe, you are in your own little bubble of protective safety . . .*

CHAPTER 17

AUGUST 4, 2287 C.E.
MARS 27, 9508 V.D.S.

Jackie nodded slowly, listening to the indigo-striped woman on the other end of the hyperrelay connection. With a greatly shortened and cache-provisioned route picked out between Earth and V'Dan, there were only a few seconds of delay between the two places. ". . . That's excellent news. I'm glad the first test runs of artificial gravity are progressing ahead of schedule, Ambassador."

"Please, I told you, call me Ah'nan," Li'eth's secondborn sister urged, smiling. "We are equals in our chosen careers, after all."

Jackie smiled. "I know, Ah'nan, and I appreciate the courtesy and friendship of it. It just isn't always easy to remember it. I was raised to always be polite and respectful in diplomatic circles. Mind you, there are days around here when I want to scream at the locals that I am *not* a child, and to stop treating my people like unmarked juveniles . . . I know your mother is trying, but your people just aren't getting it. Still, for the most part, I personally prefer to be polite, if not necessarily formal."

"Yet you are still formal. For myself, I find it amusing that a *Terran* is more formal than an Imperial Princess," Ah'nan stated, broadening her smile into a grin. It faltered in the next moment. "Are they really still having trouble remembering to treat your people like adults? I'll admit it took me a couple weeks to get used to the way everyone looks on this world, but most everyone I've met has been mature and kind, and now I cannot see your people as anything else. Surely the ones back home have also adapted by now?"

That made Jackie shake her head. "No, Ah'nan, they have not. Well, for a handful of days after your mother's experiment back at the start of Fevra, yes, but most of them have slid back into their habits of taking us for children and taking our generosity with our technologies for granted. I know we're getting more substantial items out of them than mere respect, but . . ."

Ah'nan nodded as soon as Jackie's words reached her over the two-and-four seconds of delay between them. "There is no such thing as 'mere' respect. Not having respect is frustrating, insulting, and unworthy of my people. Particularly when I get to join some of the meetings hosted by your Command Staff. They have some very clever ideas. Very different tactics. Very much into covert use of whatever cover lies around, staying out of immediate combat range, skirmishing instead of standing nose to nose with the enemy, taking the blows . . . Maybe you should use those sort of tactics on my people?"

"I think I have been, but I think it's just too subtle for your culture. Maybe I should just haul back and punch them one on the nose," Jackie half quipped. "I certainly feel like it, of late, and I am not a naturally violent-minded woman."

"Well, your ongoing restraint is appreciated by *me*, at least. And probably by my brother," Ah'nan added. She said something else, but a claxon blared abruptly and loudly in the hall outside Jackie's office at that same moment. Jackie jumped and twisted, trying to place the noise. It took her a few moments to recognize the patterns as a combination of *intruder alert* and *evacuate now.*

"—What is that noise?" she heard Ah'nan say. The Imperial Ambassador had raised her voice to be heard over the clamor, now that their communications lag had caught up to her side of things and bounced its way back. "Jackie? What's happening?"

"I don't know . . . That's the evacuation signal on top of an intruder alert. I'll have to call you back later," Jackie stated, and cut the connection.

Even as she pushed her chair back and rose, her office door slid open and Captain al-Fulan beckoned sharply. He had two more Marines with him, armed and watching the corridor. "Move it! You have to get out of here!"

What the . . . Her training didn't lag behind her confused mind. Jackie let her legs move her quickly out of her office and down the corridor. There were more Marines waiting at every junction, as well as in the stairwell leading down two floors. They flowed around her and the captain, some moving from rear guard to point, others holding position as they hustled the Grand High Ambassador in their midst toward the restricted-access doorway into the top floor of the nearest Guard Hall, the one that stood between the North Embassy Wing and the Imperial Wing.

"Hamza, what's going on?" she asked her chief of security.

"Someone smuggled a damned *army* of little robots into your quarters and tore everything to pieces," he told her. "We don't know how, and we don't know who, yet. Dozens of them, maybe hundreds. Damned V'Dan use too many robots," he added in a mutter, his hand on her elbow and his eyes flicking everywhere, trying to watch all angles at once. "When the automated security system finally went off and summoned the guards, they scattered into the vents."

"Their own version of an AI war was over two and a half centuries ago," Jackie pointed out. She hurried a little faster, her black-and-flower-printed dress swirling its fluted hems around her forearms and knees. "They literally don't have anybody still alive who remembers those days, unlike our people."

"Well, we only have a handful who are still alive who

remember," he allowed. They reached the checkpoint, where several Elite Guard in armored suits stood guard. "A Squad Alpha, Beta, Gamma teams, go with the Ambassador and keep her safe—you, Elites; split yourselves up," al-Fulan ordered, lifting his chin at the half dozen armored V'Dan. "I want four of you guarding this door, and two of you on the Ambassador, providing escort with my Marines. Delta, stay here to help guard it. Epsilon, you're with me."

It was a testament to their calling that the V'Dan did not argue even though they were not in the Terran chain of command. The lead figure just flicked her machinery-augmented arm, picking out the nearest three along with herself to stand guard, and pointing for the rearmost two to provide that escort. As she did so, she called out, *"Eyah?"*

"Eyah!" the two at the rear agreed.

"Hoo-rah," one of the Marines ahead of Jackie muttered. He took point for their brown-clad group, gun drawn and skating his boots quietly over the floor, ignoring the thudding of those armored V'Dan boots. Poking his head through the heavy, airlock-style pair of doors on this level, he pulled it back, nodding. "All clear. Move out!"

Hustling through the doorway, they moved rapidly from the connecting spur into the main corridor. On this level, there were few people passing back and forth. Few guards, for that matter, but then access up here was restricted. They didn't go far down the Guard Hall, just far enough to get away from the cross-corridor, to control how many directions an enemy could come at them.

"This is far enough. Elites, I want one of you on each side, facing outward. You've got scanners on those things, and we don't, so put them to use. Marines, I want you back-to-back; Gamma, face the walls. There are ventilation shafts up there, and for all we know, they can also chew through the walls or something. Ambassador, you'll need this," the lead male added, addressing Jackie.

He held out a spare pistol toward her, butt first, muzzle up, since they were on the top floor of the Guard Halls and there was no telling how solid the floors were when it came to projectile fire.

"It's got twenty-three in the magazine and a fourth in the

chamber, sir. I've got three more," he added when she hesitated. "Plus knives and batons and other things. You won't be depriving me of a weapon, honest."

Eyeing the gun, Jackie shook her head. She was an adequate shot at best; she had passed the Psi Division's requirements for the firing range just fine, but these Marines would be far superior. "If it's something mechanical, I'm better armed than all of you are. Bullets might stop a living being, but they won't necessarily stop a robot."

"Halt! Identify yourself!" one of the V'Dan Elite ordered, interrupting her before she could point out that as a telekinetic, her only real fears were laser- and stunner-based weapons.

Jackie turned quickly—and yelped, jumping back a little. There were four more Elite Guards, ones not in armored uniforms. They had emerged from the cross-corridor that led into the Imperial Wing, and were accompanying two K'Katta. Nerves already pulled taut by the alarms and the evacuation and the unknown danger of unknown rogue robots on the loose . . . the presence of two giant arachnid-like aliens just meters away had her heart pounding in her chest.

"I . . . sorry, meioas," she offered in apology. "I apologize for shrieking like that."

The pair were vaguely familiar; K'Katta fur patterns were nearly impossible for Human eyes to pick out with their limited types of color-sensitive cones, and both were very similar-looking females, save for a modest difference in size. Yet there was still something familiar about each of them.

Given where they had come from, Jackie guessed one of them had to be, ". . . Grand High Ambassador K'kuttl'cha? And, ah . . . Commander-of-Hundreds Guardian Twee-chuk-chrrr?"

The slightly bigger alien chittered, and the small box strapped to the top of that furred, tan, arthropodic head translated. She curled up a leg toward her abdomen as she spoke. "I am pleased to be remembered, Grand High Ambassador. I have been advising our Ambassador on the successes your Terran spy ships have been giving our forces and urging the V'Dan to give your people more support and leeway in the war."

Creepycreepycreepy . . . stars and my ancestors, I don't think I will ever get over this reaction to the poor things. It's not their fault, Jackie allowed, suppressing a shudder. *But creepycreepy . . .*

"Let them pass," the head of A Alpha ordered. "I suggest you hurry, meioas. We have robotic intruders in the North Embassy Wing. Get them back to their zone safely, Elites."

"Eyah?" the lead female of the four challenged him. She planted her hands on her gold-clad hips. "Are you ordering us around, Terran?"

"Hoo-rah," the Marine agreed. "I have my charge to protect, and you're in the way. Go on. Get your own charges out of the kill zone."

The other female chittered. Her native tongue seemed to hiss off the walls around them. "That is an unpleasant piece of vocabulary, meioa. I will forgive you for it, as you are clearly a Guardian. However, please consider being more cheerful and pleasant. Sweet sap pleases the guest far more than anything bitter."

"Ma'am," he stated, as the hissing grew louder, alarming Jackie, "I would be *happy* to discuss courtesy protocols at any time *other* th—"

"Look out!" the woman on Gamma shouted, jerking her gun up and shooting. The loud *blam blam blam* of her gun echoed down the wall as dozens of silvery *things* poured out of an air vent even as the grille covering it was still tumbling to the floor meters below.

Jackie didn't have time to throw up a shield; the Marine in charge flung himself on top of her, bearing her to the ground with a sharp, *"—Get down!"*

Hitting the floor hard enough to have the wind knocked out of her, Jackie lost control of the telekinetic shield she had been in the midst of throwing around herself. Skittering sounds fought with the blood pounding in her ears, the ragged rasp of air as she finally sucked it in—only to scream in agony as ice-hot fire lashed through her legs, her feet, her scalp, attacking her in lightning slashes right around the Marine desperately trying to shield her body with his own.

Panic flared her gifts outward in a burst of force that knocked everyone over, and knocked the swarming army of odd robots back. Even as she tried to get to her feet, the machines recovered with unnerving agility and leaped on top of her again, tearing at her clothes, her skin, her hair—Jackie pulsed again, and a third time, this time *holding* the sphere even as she levitated herself up off the floor.

The machines, looking like two silvery spider-things stacked one atop the other, unnerved her in their relentlessness. They leaped at her, most able to get themselves two, two and a half meters up before they bounced off the invisible sphere of her telekinetic shield. Her wounds throbbed and bled, forcing her to put on a second layer of shielding, a pressure layer to force her injuries shut.

The guards shot at the machines, but they were hampered by the way they were evenly spaced around the battle zone. The leader—his name came back to her like a tiny island of clarity amidst the chaotic sea of her dazed, aching panic, Corporal Okonjo—barked orders for everyone to get on one side, and for her to rise higher.

Pamf! "Jackie? *Jackie!* I—"

Li'eth flinched back as the sea of robots turned toward him. He flung up his arms, and a shield slapped up between him and them just in time to stop the nearest handful from tearing into his sweat-damp exercising clothes. Jackie quickly wrapped one of her own around him as well before the others could scuttle around behind. Lifting him up off the ground, she got both of them higher—and the damned things charged up the walls on either side, punching their claw-feet into the plaster-like material so they could try to drop down on the pair from above.

Except that the K'Katta, both of them, were already up there. With incredible fearlessness, both tan-furred females scurried into the mass. All ten limbs worked frantically fast, either clinging to decorative ribs on the arched ceiling, or grappling, twisting, and snapping the semidelicate joints of the metal beasts.

Seeing them handling the ones from above, and wrapped in the protection afforded by his hard-concentrating partner, Li'eth focused his fire on the ones directly beneath the two of them. Literal fire burst from the processors at the heart of each multilimbed bot, multiple *pop pop pops* that sounded wimpy compared to the harder *bangs* of the Terran weapons, or the sizzle of laserfire from the Elites' mechanized armor.

More guards came running up, mostly Elite, some Terran, but there was nothing they could do. Within another minute, nothing was left but dissipating smoke and an occasionally twitching limb . . . and that was when Jackie lost strength and collapsed. She managed to cushion her fall to the floor at the last moment, but Li'eth was on his own, thumping down—thankfully on his feet—a few meters away. What felt like every wound on her body broke open when her telekinesis failed, and she cried out.

"Jackie! No! No no no," Li'eth breathed, scrambling to her side. He placed his hands on her, hot and bright to her inner eye—visible only because her outer ones had closed. "No, you cannot die!"

"Sir! Sir, I'm a KIman!" one of the Marines asserted. "Sir—you can take my energy!"

Jackie dragged her eyelids open, but it was too much effort. (*Like with Sonam,*) she managed. His biokinesis was working on her wounds, trying to close them, but not fast enough. (*Here . . .*)

"Give it to her!" Li'eth snapped. "Both of us!" he corrected.

(*S' a case of taking . . . there. Like that,*) she sighed, feeling that soldier's hot but not psychic hand gingerly touching the cheek that wasn't bleeding. Latching onto his freely given energies, she *pulled*, feeding it into herself, feeding it into Li'eth, who shaped and soldered her flesh, superspeeding her body's natural urge to knit itself back together. Another Marine joined them, and a third.

The meld—a major Gestalt of the two of them, and a minor one of the three volunteers—ended in time for Jackie to feel nothing more than lingering aches, a bit of dizziness, and a strong thirst. ". . . Water," she managed out loud. "Water . . . and something to eat. Please."

Li'eth eased her upward, cradling her in a half-sitting position. "Anyone have some water?"

"Here, in my canteen," the female Marine stated. She unclipped it from her belt and unscrewed the cap, handing it over.

"Thank you," Li'eth told her. He helped Jackie lift it to her lips, letting her drink it all down to replace the blood she had lost.

A chittering to her left forced Jackie's eyes open. One of the two K'Katta had moved close, and was holding something small, glossy, and brightly colored in her forehand claws. "Here," the distinct translator-box voice of the Grand High Ambassador stated. "This is a honey-nut bar. Very popular among my people, and a big export from V'Dan."

"Thank you," Jackie managed. She let Li'eth take the half-emptied canteen in exchange for the packet, which the K'Katta quickly ripped open before letting her take the bar inside. It was sticky, sweet, and spiced with something almost like cinnamon, or maybe nutmeg. Nutmeg and a touch of mint. She chewed on the sticky mass, grateful it wasn't too thick or crunchy in texture.

"I have sent the Commander-of-Hundreds to look for something for you to wear," Ambassador K'kuttl'cha stated. "I will withdraw now so you will not continue to be frightened."

That made Jackie reach out. She touched one of those very spider-like limbs, discovering the "fur" was a mixture of stiff yet sleek fibers. "Ambassador . . . *thank you*," she stated as clearly as she could. "Thank you for fighting for me. I am in your debt. Yours and Twee-chuk-chrrr's."

Delicate claws lifted and curled around her sticky fingers. "There are no debts among friends, Ambassador." She let Jackie's hand go and backed up a little, chittering something that made the translator box emit a soft chuckle. "Besides, we realized quickly that they were only attacking *you*. The rest of us were in very little danger, save those that had touched you."

That made her smile weakly. To Jackie, those words meant no one else had been as badly cut up as she had, even if the Marine who had tried to shelter her had surely suffered a couple of wounds. "Still, it was very brave. Thank you."

"We may not prefer to *start* any fights," K'kuttle'cha stated, "but we do know how to *finish* them."

Jackie chuckled briefly. "*That*, meioa, sounds like the philosophy of the Afaso Order."

"Is it so?"

"They are monks who practice a form of mixed martial arts," Li'eth explained. More guards were arriving. "The Ambassador has learned some of their art. I have also fielded requests by them, passing them along to various training schools. They wish to integrate V'Dan forms into their Terran styles . . . and have even expressed curiosity toward the alien ones."

"I think at least a few of our Guardian-teachers would be happy to share their knowledge," the K'Kattan Ambassador allowed, her translator programmed to say the words in a kindly voice.

She said something more, but Jackie was more interested in the various reports between the Elite Guards and the Terran Marines. Something about a few having been caught, and trying to track their point of origin through the small ventilation shafts scattered throughout the embassy zone.

A new exclamation forced her eyes open. "Dayamn, meioa! What did you do, steal a curtain from the Imperial Wing or something?"

Turning her head toward the voice, she tried to see what was going on. All she could do was hear the chitter-translated reply, as there were too many bodies in the way. "That is precisely what I did. It will provide the Grand High Ambassador with body-decency, as per your social-taboo requirements."

Shakk, *that's right,* she realized. Some of the energy from the bar was finally hitting her depleted bloodstream. *I'm practically naked. I don't think even my underpants survived most of that, and my bra is half-off . . .*

(*What about your holokinesis?*) Li'eth asked her.

(*Gone,*) she sent back. (*I poured all my reserves into healing all those wounds. I'm feeling better. Help me stand up, and we can check my backside to see if we missed healing anything.*)

He hugged her gently but pushed to his feet. He grunted a little in doing so but managed to get upright with the help of a few others. Then her feet were on the ground, and while everything ached, letting her know her hide was a mess, nothing burned with the ice-hot pain of a knife wound. Or rather, the wounds caused by hundreds of razor-tipped metal claws.

"Here, the K'Katta brought you a curtain, sir," one of the Marines said. "I've a knife on me; you just tell me where to cut it."

He offered her the corner of a long, colorfully brocaded swath of . . . yes, Jackie recognized the fabric. It was an actual

curtain from within the Imperial Wing, something torn down
from one of their meters-high windows. She shook her head—
which hurt—and accepted the corner from him. "No, thank
you. I'll take it as it is. It should be long enough."

"Long enough for what?" Li'eth asked her.

Jackie wrapped the first part of the long edge around her
naked, bloodied waist and knotted it. Gathering more of it into
pleats, she tucked that into the makeshift waistband from one
hip to the other across the front of her belly, then unpleated
across her back, before finally throwing the last two meters up
over her breasts and down her back. With a little more effort,
she adjusted the part over her shoulder into yet more pleats,
which wrapped around her upper curves modestly enough.

The fabric was heavy and somewhat stiff, and felt like it
would stay pleated for as long as she needed it, so long as she
didn't move too suddenly or let the bundled brocade slip off
her shoulder; the weight of the *pallu* section hanging down her
back would hold the top of the makeshift *sari* in place. With
her half-healed injuries, there was no risk of her moving anywhere fast, however. Unless another attack came.

Holding on to Li'eth, she looked around for someone in
charge. Between the blood, the mangled machines, the bits of
her chopped hair that had fallen free, the guards milling
everywhere . . . "Someone get me a report," she ordered. "Are
there any more of those things? Who else is injured? Organize
yourselves, people!"

"I've got this!" a familiar voice asserted. "Make a hole!"

Wading through the others, the muscular frame of Lieutenant Second Class Simon Paea reached her side. He nodded
briskly and made his report. Jackie leaned on Li'eth for
strength while he did so.

"Captain al-Fulan is working with the Elite Guard, doing
a sector-by-sector sweep of the vents, rooms, and corridors in
the embassy zone. Grand Captain Tes'rin has ordered reviews
of all security scans from the moment the K'Katta cleared out
of there for us, though he's dead certain everything was clean
before we moved into the zone.

"Admiral Nayak was in the city having lunch with a couple
of the V'Dan Grand Admirals and is on his way back. The only
personnel injured were yourself and Corporal Okonjo. His

wounds are mostly superficial, but the robots destroyed the front part of his clothes, wherever he touched you. I cut off a length of the curtain before it got to you and made him a *lava-lava* for decency's sake. Medical personnel are on their way, but the Elite are insisting they cannot move either of you until al-Fulan and the Elite teams working with our people have finished that sector-by-sector search, including these halls. They don't want any stray 'bots following you to the infirmary."

"Did you get them all?" she asked him.

"As far as we *know*, they all zeroed in on you somehow and tried to get to you," Paea told her. "We suspect your DNA may have been used, since it went after your clothes, your bed, anything you used as a seat in your quarters, the carpeting . . . and, of course, you." He squared his shoulders a little, his deeply tanned cheeks darkening a bit more with a flush. "I apologize for not being able to stop them in time, sir. You're my Counselor. I should have protected you."

"It's alright, Simon," Jackie reassured him. "When Corporal Okonjo is healed, please *gently* remind him that I am a telekinetic, and that jumping on top of me like that startled me out of forming a telekinetic shield. Both of us would have been far safer if he'd only *told* me to get down without trying to physically ensure it."

"I will let him know that, sir," Paea agreed.

"Gently," Jackie repeated. "His actions were completely in the right place for most people in that sort of situation. We don't want to ruin that reflex for the others' safety."

". . . Yes, sir."

"Doctors coming!" someone called out. The brief, narrow corridor the others had made for the Marine lieutenant widened, allowing several medical staff to drive their cart-sized hovercraft right up to both Jackie and Okonjo.

The triage was made quickly; Okonjo was rushed off first since he was still bleeding. Li'eth had focused on healing *her*, not him. Her wounds while far, far greater in number, were half-healed, and that meant scabbed pink and very tender. While her mind was still worrying over the corporal's condition, one of the medics looking over Jackie muttered something that made her do a double take.

"Excuse me—what did you say? Just now?" she added.

The male, ash-blond and spotted in dark orange bilateral symmetry, shrugged. "I just said it probably didn't help that you're dressed like this."

"I *wasn't* dressed like this," Jackie asserted. She pointed at the mangled snippets of her clothes that were still strewn around the floor, some of them lying in puddles and smears of her own blood. "I was clothed in pants and a blouse and what used to be my shoes. I am wearing this curtain as a *sari* because it was the quickest way I could retain my dignity."

"Oh, I've seen you wearing your *clothes*," the young medic mocked back. "You dress far too provocatively. *I* heard these robot things went after your wardrobe, first. They probably thought they were teaching you a lesson."

Most of the V'Dan around them continued to talk, but all of the Terrans—and Li'eth—fell very still and very quiet. Jackie felt her face and her hands heating with rage.

"What. Did you. Say?" she repeated in V'Dan, clenching her hands into fists until her fingernails dug into her palms, just to keep them from tapping into Li'eth's pyromantic power.

"You dress too provocatively!"

"How do I dress 'too provocatively'?" Jackie demanded, so mad she was trembling.

"You know—showing off your body," the medic scorned. "Like an adult."

Hands clamped over her eyes, nose, and mouth. Startled by the unexpected attack, Jackie struggled to breathe. Her attacker shouted while she reached for his wrists. "Guards! Elite Guards! Arrest this medic!"

"—What? On what grounds?" the younger man demanded. "Your Highness, I haven't done *anything* wrong! I'm an emergency services doctor of the Third Tier, and I—"

"—And you will *be silent!*" Li'eth ordered. He released Jackie's nostrils as she struggled, but didn't uncover her mouth or her eyes. "Guards, detain this man for rest of the day—lock him up for as long as it takes, until I can find out the most remote, awful corner of the Empire to throw him away. *You*, meioa, are *not* going to treat *any* Terran from this point on. Take him away!"

(*Dammit, Li'eth!*) Jackie growled mentally, tugging at his wrists. She couldn't pull hard because that just made her body ache, warning her she was stressing her imperfectly healed injuries.

(*If* I *don't get to cause a diplomatic incident,* you *don't get to have a diplomatic incident,*) he told her. He released her eyes. "That goes for the rest of you. *Any* comment about these Terrans being *juveniles* will be treated as a formal diplomatic incident. You will treat them as adults, and you will take your orders from *their* medical chief of staff.

"Someone get Dr. de la Santoya on her way to the infirmary! *I* will be going with the Ambassador, every step of her treatment. I suggest you give her the *best* of care, as well as your *full respect*." Carefully, he helped her onto the padded bed that served as the hovercart's gurney.

"I'll go with you, too, Highness," Paea asserted. "A Squad Beta and Gamma, form up! Our Ambassador gets an honor guard wherever she goes . . . and for your information, meioas, that outfit she is wearing is called a *sari,* and it has been in fashion for over five and a half thousand years. That is a thousand years longer than *your* Empire has been around."

"You're an ignorant child! The V'Dan Empire has existed for nearly ten thousand years!" someone called back.

Jackie bristled again. Li'eth had to push her back down onto the pad. (*Lie still!*)

"Wrong, meioa!" Paea called back. "Your Empire started this nonsense of *jungen*-marks-means-adulthood with your War King during the so-called Reformation. According to your own history texts, the *original* Eternal Empress always stressed that the *unmarked* were just as mature as the marked. No insult to His Highness, who is mature enough to realize this, but most of the rest of you are the only immature idiots I see here. Now clean up this corridor and track down the attempted murderers responsible for this attack!"

Closing her eyes—once again feeling dizzy, thirsty, and hungry as her anger-fueled adrenaline spike fell and crashed— Jackie let Li'eth and the lieutenant take charge. She had been speed-healed before, but never by this much, and could only guess that she'd be bedridden and confined to very light duties for the next few weeks while her body caught up with all the biokinetic hurrying their combined efforts had just put it through.

. . . She was not, however, going to forget that medic's remarks. Or that Elite Guardsman's. Or any of the *other* remarks and acts from which she and her fellow Terrans were *still* suffering, despite their many, many attempts at pointing out how insulting and disrespectful such attitudes were.

CHAPTER 18

AUGUST 8, 2287 C.E.
AVRA 1, 9508 V.D.S.

There were just enough fully trained biokinetics on hand now to get Jackie on her feet and free to resume her duties far swifter than even the best combination of Terran and V'Dan medicine. Or rather, in conjunction with them. It required days of bed rest and gentle exercise, multiple psychic-healing sessions, and stuffing herself on carefully balanced meals practically every two hours, plus nutrient drips, and special creams rubbed into her healing skin at intervals. The massages felt a bit hedonistic but were actually important to prevent any lingering scar tissues from hardening.

It was just as well that she was on her feet, eyeing the new wardrobe the local V'Dan tailors had crafted for her to replace all her ruined clothes, when one of the embassy aides poked her head inside, calling out, "They caught 'em! Al-Fulan's hauling 'em downstairs for an interrogation right now!"

Confused, Jackie asked, "They caught *who*?"

"The ones who organized the attack on you! I don't know who it is, but it's one of us, and one of *them*," she reported to Jackie and her guests. "Sammy told me they just walked past the third-lift security checkpoint. I'm heading to second lift to see if they're still there!"

Pulling back quickly, the woman bustled down the hall. Jackie looked at the trio of clothing designers, the garments spread around her office, and grimaced. She gestured at the door, tired of wearing military fatigues since those were one of the few sets of garments that had been brought in enough quantities to share. "Excuse me—I have to go see who it is, too. I cannot let you stay in my office while I'm gone, but I shouldn't be gone long, so the clothes can stay here."

"We're coming with you, if that's alright, Ambassador," the eldest of the three stated. The other man and the woman nodded, quickly rising and joining him in following Jackie to the door.

"I want to see the idiots who think they can attempt to slaughter the Ambassador of our greatest ally," the woman added grimly.

The second-lift sector was crowded, but only with gawkers and the normal Marines who stood watch over everyone's comings and goings. Not with the captain or any prisoners. Seeing their Ambassador coming, the others quickly made way, letting her get into the lift the moment it arrived. Knowing the embassy detention area and its interrogation room were on a subfloor below the main level, Jackie pushed that button. Each of the four times the doors slid open on the way down, the Humans who peered inside quickly checked themselves and backed off, gesturing for her to continue down.

When they slid open on the right floor, Jackie didn't even have to ask. Every single person she passed pointed down the corridors toward the detention area, and the two Marines on guard came to attention. One of them opened the interrogation door for her. Not the observation door. Jackie made a mental note to praise him for his correct guesswork. She also made a mental note to praise the two guards for stopping the tailors trailing in her wake. This wasn't their business, even if they were interested in it for gossip's sake.

The two figures seated inside, their hands locked in cuffs, checked her stride. While Countess Shi'ol Nanu'oc sat in grim-faced silence, Captain al-Fulan argued with Lieutenant Colvers.

"—but I *didn't* intend to kill her!" Brad was saying. "I swear I didn't!"

"Camel shit!" Hamza snapped back. "You *deliberately* arranged to have those killer robots smuggled into *your own*

quarters. You arranged to slip them from *your* ventilation duct to *hers.* That is *Grand High Treason,* soldier, and you're going to *hang* for it!"

"They were only supposed to *humiliate* her! That was the plan! I *didn't* mean to kill her! I didn't—" Finally spotting Jackie, Brad choked on his words. He paled, flushed, paled again, and looked between her and Shi'ol, then held up his bound hands toward the Ambassador. "I *didn't* intend to kill you, I swear it! It was only supposed to be your clothes, and maybe your bed! I *didn't mean it!*"

His aura . . . was swirling too much in agitation for her to read it. Maybe Imperial Consort Te-los could—it turned out that His Highness *could* teach her people a trick or two about auramancy, particularly once he had a solid grounding in their precise training techniques—but Jackie could not read it. She folded her arms over her green-mottled chest. Green, because there were only a couple women her exact size in the Terran embassy zone, and the blue and the gray were in her laundry hamper today.

Seeing her skeptical pose, her scornfully arched brow, Colvers did something she did not expect. He begged. "Read my mind! Read it! Read the truth in my thoughts—I'm giving you *permission,* Jackie! *Read* me!"

She almost refused. Almost, because the moment she realized he was involved, she knew exactly how those robots had found her. Traces of her DNA, as sampled from the hairs *he* had plucked from her clothes. Not once, but several times over the intervening weeks they had been here on V'Dan. And all for . . . what? The *love* of Shi'ol?

"*Read* me," Brad begged, dropping his bound hands back onto the table, tears spilling onto his cheeks. "*Please . . .*"

She hated him so much . . . but he asked. *He* asked her to read his thoughts. *Her.* Dragging in a deep breath, she nodded sharply. Dragged in another. It took her five breaths, *after* she closed her eyes, to calm herself, center her mind and spirit, shield herself against negativity . . . She did not have to touch him to reach into his mind. If he had any natural shields, if they had been real walls, he would have detonated them with dynamite, his mind was so wide open to her.

Opening her eyes, Jackie spoke the truth. "Lieutenant

Colvers hates my guts. He deliberately chose to interact with Countess Nanu'oc to plot against me, using the excuse of a spurious relationship to cloak how often they got together to try to come up with some suitable ideas . . . but he only wanted to humiliate me. He did not want me directly harmed. And he did not intend to attempt to murder me. I do wonder, however; if I read *your* mind, Countess, what would I find?"

That provoked words out of the silently fuming woman. "I am a citizen of the Empire, and a Countess of the Second Tier! You have *no* right to hold me here, and *no* authority to accuse me!"

"*Wrong.* When we *established* this embassy, the V'Dan government granted us *all* Terran rights within its walls," al-Fulan told her coldly. "You broke the law within these walls. You're not going *anywhere.*"

"What evidence do you have, Captain?" Jackie asked. She could feel Li'eth reaching out to her and linked with him, letting her hear Hamza's report the moment she herself heard each word.

"We found squalene and its DNA on some of the robots, *some* of it from some of their hairs, both of the prisoners," he told Jackie. He did so without turning his head, still glaring at Shi'ol. "On a hunch, I coordinated with Grand Captain Tes'rin. We got the local equivalent of a *warrant* and sent a team of Peacekeepers, Marines, and Elite to her quarters here in the city this morning, as soon as she had gone out. They found programming equipment and two small stray parts from the kits she had used to construct the spider-bot things. They *also* found a V'Dan DNA sequencer, with a translation script for programming it into those robots . . . and *your* DNA sequence in its coding.

"She had tried to get rid of the evidence by dumping everything she could find in her suite's trash incinerator, but as it's been rather warm here these last few days, the thing never actually fired up to heat her place. On top of that, the analysis of the programming for the live 'bots we caged came back from the V'Dan computer-forensics teams assigned to study it. That happened midmorning, while we were still sifting through the incinerator. After that, the only thing we needed to do was to find the two of them. In *his* quarters.

"Shi'ol Nanu'oc has deliberately broken the V'Dan equivalent of the Three Laws of Robotics in those machines. That is a *capital* offense, back home. Capital means *death penalty*," the captain added, glaring at the green-spotted woman.

"We're *not* 'back home' on your squalid little planet," Shi'ol retorted. "We are on *V'Dan*, and the members of the Second Tier are *exempt* from any death penalty."

"Wrong." It was Jackie's turn to correct the arrogant, unrepentant woman. "There *is* one automatic death penalty. It applies even to the members of the Imperial Family themselves . . . and it is triggered whenever *any* attack threatens the life of a member of the Imperial Blood. Your robots moved to attack His Imperial Highness."

"He wasn't supposed to be with you!" Shi'ol snapped. "He was scheduled to be exercising!"

Jackie closed the meter or so between her and the table. She leaned on it, staring across the cold metal into Shi'ol's eyes. "He was. But as we are a *true* holy pairing, he *teleported* instantly to my side when he felt my life-threatened distress. Considering I kissed and *hugged* him just before he left to go exercise . . . while I was not wearing anything . . . he had a *lot* of my dead skin cells rubbed over his clothes. He might have been only a secondary target, but V'Dan law does not differentiate. *Any* attack on the members of the Imperial Tier by someone who is *not* of that Tier, nor authorized by that Tier, is automatically assigned the death penalty.

"Since the only person I know who hates me even a quarter as much as you do *might* be Crown Princess Vi'alla, there is a tiny, marginal chance that *she* ordered such a thing . . . but *she* knows her mother would never permit it. And even if she didn't care about that, she is far too enamored of her position as the Imperial Heir to commit political suicide by ordering such a thing." Jackie stared down at the rosette-marked noblewoman. "Be glad I do *not* have permission to scan your mind.

"Captain al-Fulan, you will hold the prisoners until I have arranged how to deal with them according to both Terran and V'Dan laws," she instructed al-Fulan. "This is our fourth major diplomatic incident." At the captain's frown, Jackie explained in an aside, "Li'eth prevented me from incinerating that idiot medic he ordered the Elite Guard to carry off; the other three were his trying to fry the prisoner in outrage, the prisoner exposing us to the K'Katta without mandatory psychological preparation, and Count Daachen's idiocy over giving a hyperrelay to the Nephrit System."

"Ah. In that case, sir, yes, sir. I'll make sure the prisoners cannot escape, and will only hand them over with your personal authorization to any appropriate V'Dan authorities," al-Fulan promised her.

". . . I *didn't* mean to kill you," Brad murmured, his blue eyes stark with fear, horror, and regret. "I didn't . . ."

Tightening her jaw, Jackie turned and strode out of the interrogation room. She barely even noticed the three tailors trailing in her wake until they reached her office. Only at the sight of the garments strewn across every available surface, awaiting her selection of what to wear until a new wardrobe could arrive from Earth, did she recall their presence.

Apologizing again, she had the trio wait in the reception room leading to her office while she made a few calls on her end. On his end, Li'eth murmured his excuses to the generals and admirals of the meeting he was attending, directed V'kol to take notes, and headed off to make some calls of his own. Shi'ol might not have *meant* to threaten his life, but Jackie could feel that her Gestalt partner was feeling about as forgiving over it as she did, right now.

Not in the least bit.

AUGUST 10, 2287 C.E.
AVRA 3, 9508 V.D.S.

Legal jurisdiction was a bit of a nightmare. Yes, the pair had begun their attack initially within the Terran zone of the North Embassy Wing. But the actual physical attack on both Jackie and Li'eth had taken place in the Guard Halls, a purely V'Dan location. The hyperrelays had been stress-tested by constant communications being sent between Earth and V'Dan. And those communications . . . had been hampered by the attitudes of the Imperial lawyers.

Their arguments had not just been over the fact that the actual blood-shedding had taken place in V'Dan territory, not

Terran; they wanted to apply V'Dan laws and V'Dan punishments to the criminals who had bloodied an offspring of their beloved Empress. But that was understandable. It was the condescending *dismissal* of any Terran legal rights, like the comment about her "provocative" and "too-adult" style of clothing, that became not only the last straw on Jackie's back, but the last straw on the entire Council's back.

The decision that the Council made, crafted in private away from V'Dan eyes, and with Jackie firmly shielded against even her Gestalt partner, was not a pleasant one. A downright painful one, from her own personal perspective. Not in the sense of her wounds, either; she wouldn't even scar, she had been speed-healed so carefully and so well by the psychics on her embassy staff. She still had a few faint pink lines here and there, but her own burgeoning biokinesis would get rid of that in a few more weeks even if she didn't exert herself any further.

The V'Dan lawyers had insisted against it, but Jackie had eventually gone straight to Hana'ka to make a bargain. Under Terran law, and willingly scanned by Heracles and Darian as well as herself, Brad's portion of the crime was not to be judged as attempted murder. Attempted manslaughter, perhaps, since he had tampered with equipment in ways that could put a person in danger, but not murder. His motive had been far more petty than that.

In the eyes of Terran law, that granted him more leniency, and so she had bartered with the Empress to have Lieutenant First Class Brad Colvers tried under Terran military law. The Empress, with some reluctance, had agreed to that, in exchange for trying Shi'ol Nanu'oc under Imperial law. She had even attended the solemn, grim ceremony in the Terran zone's modest auditorium, where the black-and-white-clad members of the Peacekeepers arranged for an angled platform, a mouthguard for the lieutenant, and a grim-faced fellow who precisely measured out the punishments one blow at a time to the man strapped to that angled platform.

Corporal punishment regulation number one. Committing a civilian crime. For a felony-level crime, the punishment was four strokes of the cane. Regulation number fifteen. Colluding with an enemy. Two strokes of the cane. Attacking a superior, regulation twenty-two—and Jackie *was* still his superior in the chain of command, even if she was no longer a commissioned colonel, since she was authorized to fill in for the Premiere and Secondaire in terms of their being commander-in-chief and lieutenant-in-chief—was four strokes of the cane. And finally, treason, the second regulation. For not only nearly killing Jackie, but nearly killing the eldest son of the V'Dan Empress. Five strokes of the cane.

A total of fifteen blows. There were limits in the Peace-keeper rules and regulations on corporal punishment for how many were to be delivered at one time, gauged on the physical fitness of the accused, but fifteen was deemed a bearable number in this case. And because it was now military law that every soldier had to witness at least one disciplinary caning, every Terran ship currently out there in space was ordered to stand down and watch, and the entire military complement of the embassy zone was ordered to either attend in person along-side Jackie and the Empress, or watch from any duty stations they could not in good conscience leave unattended.

It was not pleasant to watch. Or to listen to. Or to contemplate ever happening to oneself. It also took about as long as the actual trial and was over within a quarter of an hour. When it ended, Admiral Nayak pronounced the rest of Colvers' sentence: to be returned to Earth to be remanded into military custody for incarceration of no less than ten years even with parole for good behavior, and twenty years without it.

He would be attached to a particular gardening patch for those ten-to-twenty years, too, forced to slave away making food for the rest of the Terran population. Never again would Brad Colvers fly an OTL ship. He had achieved the fame of face that the precognitives back on Earth had predicted, and had associated with all those images of interacting with aliens . . . but not in any way Brad himself had predicted.

As soon as it ended, and the crying ex-lieutenant had been strapped onto a gurney and floated off, Jackie accompanied the Empress and her Elite Guards out of the North Embassy Wing and over to the Imperial Wing. Not to visit any private parlors, but because she was going to stand with them on the

Imperial Tier of the Inner Court—it was raining too hard outside to bother with a public trial in the Plazas—while Countess
Nanu'oc was dealt with under V'Dan law.

Caning Brad had been judged far more lenient and suitable
for his accidental manslaughter than letting him be tried under
Imperial law, where even accidental manslaughter ran the risk
of the death penalty when it came to the ruling bloodline.
Shi'ol . . . deserved what she was about to get, one way or another. Jackie had an idea about that "other."

The waiting area was more pleasant than all the fancifully
carved and gilded furniture should have suggested. Not that
Jackie's stomach could handle any of the food laid out buffet-
style on one of the tables, though she did drink a little juice.
Seeing her former crewmate screaming and writhing against his
bonds with each hard, precise stroke had spoiled her appetite.

As far as discipline measures went . . . from the pallid
faces of her fellow Terrans, it was going to be a very strong
incentive to keep their soldiers in line, enough officers or not.
Jackie made a mental note to suggest strongly to the Command Staff that they ensured the regulations insisting on
required viewings of corporal punishment have those viewings take place during Basic Training. That way, Terran soldiers would start out knowing exactly what would happen to
them. She suspected that, had Brad known in advance, he
would have been able to better resist Shi'ol's temptations leading him down the path of his prejudices to hatred's own hell.

Finally, a servant entered and announced that Master of
Ceremonies was ready to begin. Coached on where to sit—
between Hana'ka and Li'eth, once again at his father's insistence they not be parted—and where to stand, Jackie joined the
queue of red-and-gold-clad bodies. She herself was a sober
raven among the scarlet cardinals and gilded parakeets of the
Imperial Family. A foreigner in their midst.

As one of the persons who had been directly harmed alongside the Imperial Prince, she had a right to co-preside over the
sentencing. It was one of the few cases in V'Dan caste-
segregated culture where someone of even the Fifth Tier could
have the right to stand on the Imperial Tier without somehow
managing to marry into it or becoming a Consort Imperial.

To get there, they had to file through the temple-like room

with the actual sarcophagus-thing in it. The doorway to the
Plazas was sealed shut against the rain, a heavy blast-door
arrangement, but the interior was still well lit by that pool of
crystal-focused light. Jackie had been instructed not to touch
the giant stone block and not to break formation, but while the
line of people did not move at a shuffle, she did have enough
time to stare at the lettering carved into its ageworn surface.

Terranglo letters.

Ashes to ashes, dust to dust, the first line read. That line
was the same as the images Rosa had brought back from her
visit to the most holy site on all of V'Dan, the Necropolis of
Dawn, legendary entry point of the *d'aspra* of the original
V'Dan refugees escaping from the Before World of Earth to
this world.

The Necropolis of Dawn was a vast set of canyons in a
semiarid landscape. Most of those valleys had had their waters
rerouted because the ravines were filled with niches stuffed
with the bones of anyone and everyone who thought they
should have their ancestor's remains carted to the sacred
place. But the one point that irrefutably pointed to the legends
of the Immortal High One coming from the future had been
the exact same lettering carved into the vast archway that
V'Dan legend said was the site of the portal between the two
worlds, allowing those refugees to literally step from one
world to the other somehow.

Jackie didn't know if that meant the Immortal had used
Grey technology or something else. She did know, because
Rosa had showed her several pictures of the Arch of Dawn,
that this sarcophagus had a line the archway did not.

The first of my lives, the last if I must.

(*Legend has it there are bones inside, and that they are
those of the body of the Immortal's first beloved, from the
dawn of time itself. Or at least from roughly five thousand
years before the* d'aspra,) Li'eth murmured in her mind.
(*Mostly, the inscription—which is written in V'Dan as well,
though it does not rhyme in our tongue—was believed to be a
ritual the Immortal would undergo every two years to prove
her immortality to her followers, by literally stabbing herself
in the heart with a knife and dropping dead, only to somehow
burst back to life a few moments later.*)

Jackie nodded mentally since she did not want to confuse the somber quality of the moment physically. The Inner Court was crowded, with people on their feet as well as occupying every bench, padded stool, and seat. Even the Terran communications robots had been allowed to attend, so that the Terran government could witness Shi'ol's sentencing.

Standing long enough for everyone to be introduced, Jackie sat when Hana'ka gave the little hand signal that said they were allowed to sit, and listened to the opening rituals and protocols of the trial. Like the modern Terran version, the trial was succinct and to the point and not bogged down in procedural chicanery. Accusations were made and evidence presented. Witnesses were brought forth to make brief statements.

The accused was questioned and attempted to plead she had not meant to endanger any lives. The V'Dan chief prosecutor pointed out how their version of the Laws of Robotics—robots were not allowed by their programming to harm sentient lives through any action, nor to harm those lives through inaction if they could help it—had been deliberately circumvented. Shi'ol tried to protest that she hadn't thought the robots would shred clothing without those laws being broken, and the prosecutor stated that tests had proved that model of robot was quite capable of doing that while under the coding of those laws.

When she tried to protest again, Eternal Empress Hana'ka cut in. "*Enough.* You lie, and you lie again and again in my Court. You deliberately acted to harm an ally of the Empire in wartime. That is treason. Whether or not you meant His Imperial Highness to be a secondary target is immaterial. You attacked his holy partner, and *that* makes Grand High Ambassador Jacaranda Maq'Enzie a member of the Imperial Tier."

Out of the corner of her eye, Jackie noticed Vi'alla stiffening in her seat on the far side of her mother. Her fingers clenching on the armrests, she sat like a displeased statue. Li'eth's eldest sister did *not* like her mother claiming Jackie had the protection of her caste level.

Too bad. You're not in charge. Yet. That was a headache for a later moment.

"The attack on a member of the Imperial Tier was deliberate, even if the Grand High Ambassador is not of the Blood.

The damage done by those robots is irrefutable. The evidence linking Shi'ol Nanuoc, 373rd Countess S'Arrocan, to all of these crimes is undeniable. The only thing left is to sentence her. V'Daania, how do you vote?"

"Death," Balei'in stated from his seat to the far right. "The *Book of the Immortal* states that one should not permit a *sinjit* to make its nest in even the most remote corner of the grounds of the Temple of Eternity. Never mind within its actual walls."

Jackie almost laughed inappropriately, for in that exact same moment, she had spotted the face of a certain Dr. To-mi Kuna'mi. She clenched her fingers around her own carved and gilded armrests, stomach muscles tensing against that urge, to keep her expression calm.

"Death," Te-los declared flatly from his position on the far left. "Her schemes injured my son and nearly killed his future wife."

"Death," the next-eldest sister, Mah'nami, said. She spoke from her seat between her youngest brother and their eldest sister. "The evidence adds up flawlessly. Her intentions are clear."

"Death," Li'eth stated grimly. "She served under me as one of my officers. She *betrayed* the trust implicit in that."

"Death," Vi'alla said. "She has shamed the blood of her ancestors."

It was her turn to pronounce judgment. "*I* have a different punishment in mind. A far more cruel one."

That made every member of the family V'Daania twist and crane in their seats to look at Jackie. Empress Hana'ka blinked and frowned, but said, "Go on."

"Her actions are undeniable. Countess Shi'ol Nanu'oc deliberately sabotaged the safety programming of those robots so that they would destroy any *source* of the DNA they were ordered to seek out and rend. Not just the evidence shed onto my clothing, my carpets, my bedding, but *my own body*. But it is her *motive* I speak of punishing, not her actions," Jackie explained. "Death is too gentle. Too swift. It teaches her nothing.

"I'll admit even we Terrans admit that death as a punishment for certain crimes can serve a purpose. It is like cutting out a cancerous growth when that cancer resists treatment," she continued. "No matter how far medicine progresses, sometimes all you can do is remove an infected or excessively injured limb to save the rest of the patient. But in this case, Shi'ol would get off far too easily if her life was ended now.

"The Psi League trains its telepaths, its mind-speakers, in all manner of techniques," Jackie explained. "One of those is something we call a mind-block. It is the act of a highly skilled telepath deliberately going into someone's head and *altering* how their thought processes work. It is not done lightly, but my government has agreed that this situation does warrant its legal use. As the person most directly harmed by her deliberate, murderous attacks, as her *intended target* . . . I advocate the right to go into Shi'ol Nanu'oc's mind and remove her ability to see the *jungen* marks, of which she is so proud. Including her *own*."

Her words stirred a rustle of murmurs and whispers and questions throughout the Court. Vi'alla found her voice first. ". . . What kind of punishment is *that*?"

"One which even *you* could learn from, Your Highness. Shi'ol has consistently considered herself superior because of her spots," Jackie explained, looking past Vi'alla to her frowning mother. "She—and *most* V'Dan—have consistently considered we Terrans to be *inferior* because of our lack thereof. Including some *very* insulting remarks made by not only one of the medical professionals called in to tend my wounds in the aftermath of Shi'ol's deliberately plotted attack, but made by some of the *Elite Guards* who were supposed to be guarding us in the highest of respect.

"We Terrans will no longer put up with *any* disrespect over the matter of our lack of *jungen*," Jackie asserted, leaning forward in her seat to pin the whole audience with her glare. "My government has therefore authorized me to lay the following ultimatum upon the negotiation table: We demand the right to place mind-blocks upon *any* V'Dan from this point forward who continues to insult our sovereign and separate citizens as though we were markless V'Dan juveniles instead of treating us with the respect of the Terran adults we *are*."

"How *dare* you make that demand!" Vi'alla snapped. "Who do you think you are?"

"Premiere Callan?" Jackie called out.

The screens on the tops of the robot towers shifted from a

view of the sea of faces lining the Council Hall, to a close-up of Augustus Callan in his long white sleeveless robe and a somber black suit. Black like the one Jackie wore.

"Grand High Ambassador Jacaranda MacKenzie is correct," he stated in flawless V'Dan. Apparently he had been practicing it, perhaps with the aid of Ambassador Ah'nan. "Despite the gracious efforts of the Eternal Empress to see for herself how damaging that consistent disrespect has been, and despite her many commands that our people be given the respect we are due . . . the people of the V'Dan Empire do not take the people of the Terran United Planets seriously.

"You desperately want our toys to help you win your war," he added grimly, "but you *refuse* to 'play nicely' with us. We have not once asked to be exalted above any V'Dan citizen. We have simply asked to be treated as your equals. Yet you have *not bothered* as a nation. Our kindness, compassion, and generosity can only extend so far in the face of such repeated insults, discrimination, and blatant disrespect.

"If mere words cannot imprint this problem upon your minds and make you watch your ways and your words, if polite requests and even the most royal of commands cannot get you to treat us *as* your equals, with the full respect due *any* sort of ally regardless of their appearance . . . then the only resort we have left is to insist that *every* person—aliens as well as V'Dan—who wishes to benefit from our technologies be subjected to a mind-block," Callan stated firmly. "This mind-block will remove the subject's awareness of the very *jungen* marks that are *causing* your blatant, repeated, ongoing prejudices against those of us who—rightfully and *naturally*—have none."

This time, it was Hana'ka who clenched her fingers on the armrests of her throne. Whatever it was made from, it looked like a sort of giant, reddish-pink, hollowed-out pearl grown in the shape of a slightly overgrown, somewhat egg-shaped chair. Enough generations had clutched those armrests, wearing the nacreous material into the grooves cupping her fingers when she gripped it.

". . . And if we demand other options?" Her Eternal Majesty finally asked.

Callan's reply fell flatly from the tri-part screens and

speakers. "This is not a discussion, Eternity. It is *not* open to negotiation. If you want access to our technology, you and your people, and the entirety of the Alliance, will comply with our right to demand mind-blocks be placed upon anyone who attempts to interact in repeatedly disrespectful ways with our sovereign citizens. If you agree, those who refuse to comply will have only two choices. Compliance or incarceration. At *your* expense.

"If your nation refuses to accept and comply with our ultimatum, we will give you exactly what you deserve for your ongoing, free-willed disrespect. *Nothing,*" he stated coldly, his deep voice echoing the word against the hard stone walls and vaulted ceiling of the Inner Court. "Make up your mind, Empress. Our patience is at an end."

"You say this will affect the citizens of the other races," Hana'ka stated. She pointed into the First Tier audience at the aliens seated in the foremost rows. "The Solaricans, the Tlassians, and the rest. I cannot make a unilateral decision for their sovereign governments!"

"According to the Charter of the Alliance itself, as researched by my predecessor, Honorable Assistant Ambassador Rosa McCrary," Callan countered, "in cases where a ruling will affect *all* member states of the Alliance, the head of a particular state government may elect to make that ruling in the name of all member states, provided the ruling benefits *all* member citizens equally in whatever manner their citizens will be affected. You *do* have that right and that power . . . and whatever your answer is, it *will* affect the Alliance as a whole. Either positively, or advers—"

Sirens blared, loudly enough that most everyone clamped body parts over their auditory organs. They cut off after only a few seconds and were followed by a firm, neutral, female voice announcing. *"This is an Emergency Evacuation Alert. Incoming enemy attack. This is an Emergency Evactuation Alert. All personnel will evacuate to the emergency shelters immediately."*

Hidden strips of lights exploded into life, pulsing in shades of green and white toward doorways on either side of the Inner Court. The Terran tri-part screens flashed, and a markless face from on board what could only be one of the *Embassy* ships filled the screens. "Ambassador! Dozens of Salik missiles are headed straight for the Winter Palace!"

Startled screams accompanied a rush of hundreds of bodies bolting for those halls. Jackie snapped her gaze up at the ceiling, at the single layer of ceiling between her and those missiles, thinking hard and fast.

"Everyone, *evacuate*!" Hana'ka snapped, even as the Elite raced to grab her family and hustle them away. "Get the defense grids online!"

Jackie whipped around to face her. Somewhere outside, the shields snapped on, humming and crackling loudly enough to penetrate the stone ceiling and walls of the Inner Court. But it wouldn't be enough, she was dead certain of that. "Kill the positioning signals!"

"—What?"

"The global positioning signals! *Kill them*," Jackie ordered. "I can *save* this city, but *not* if those missiles have *your own positioning system* still active!"

"You heard the Ambassador!" Hana'ka yelled at her generals, who quickly grabbed for their personal comm units. "Get that system *down*!"

"Li'eth, Balei'in, Te-los! I *need* you—I need *every* psychic and priest, *now*!" Jackie hollered, projecting her voice through the hall. Her voice, and her thoughts. (*To-mi, I need you! Your* people *need you!*)

The markless, ageless woman was coming back from the corridor most people had taken in their escape route. She came dragging two priest-robed, protesting bodies by their arms. A few more trailed uncertainly, fearfully in her wake. (*On our way.*)

Heracles bounded up the steps, already grasping what Jackie had in mind. (*I'll go OOB to get the exact visuals ready—I have a very broad range, and an ability to view two or three places at once, so be prepared for a little bit of disorientation,*) he broadcast to everyone still in the hall. Even the Elite Guards gasped and fumbled midway through hustling the Empress out of the ancient throne room. (*Jackie, remember to shove the illusion past that temple-thing behind you! Everyone else, get your assets up here and concentrate on* giving your power *to the Ambassador!*)

"Te-los!" Hana'ka called out, struggling against the Guards. Both her husband and her two sons were ignoring the Guards' attempts to get them to leave—Li'eth was in fact holding them off telekinetically.

"I *have* to help!" the Imperial Consort shouted back. "Go! *Get her out of here!*"

(*To me!*) Jackie ordered, and dropped to her knees. Dropped everyone to their knees around her. With Li'eth at her side, shifting his telekinetic dome over their group of no more than a dozen and a half psis at most, Human and Solarican and Tlassian alike, and with Clees straining his mind upward, linking to Jackie an exact aerial view of the Winter City, Jackie threw her mind up and out, and *shifted* that image westward.

Her task was nearly impossible. Winter City was home to millions, sporting thousands of skyscraping buildings over two dozen kilometers to the north and south, and half a dozen east and west. Nearly impossible, indeed . . . until the woman who called herself To-mi Kuna'mi knelt at Li'eth and Jackie's backs, and placed her hands on both of them. Abruptly, dizzyingly abruptly, Jackie had enough power to cover *twice* as much terrain . . . and shoved the image of all of it westward by ten kilometers, stretching out the "wilderness" east of the capital with a patchwork illusion extending what was already there.

Li'eth reached up and out, too, but he shoved against actual matter, not reflected light. Most of the missiles swerved westward in a subtle diagonal as they came down. It meant, however, releasing his dome over the palace itself, because he still was not trained well enough to both protect *and* make scores of incoming warheads shift direction.

As it was, his efforts were almost too little, too late. Through one of the viewpoints Clees was feeding them, they could see a scorching line of laserfire stabbing down through the clouds. It sliced straight through the now-hard-humming shields outside, and the humming shut off a scant second before three explosions, two of them *very* close, rattled the heavy flagstones of the Winter Palace, while the third hit farther away. More explosions echoed faintly in the distance, a *lot* more, but they, too, receded and faded as the Salik weapons, forced to rely upon visual targets, shifted westward from their original impact sites, lured by that holokinetic city sprawling in solid-seeming comfort out over the actual bay.

How long they held the shield, Jackie could not have said. She and the others relied upon Heracles' real-time inner vision; with each impact, she blackened the city with smoke and fire and damaged structures, imperfectly envisioned, hurriedly sculpted and placed. It would not stand up to any close scrutiny, but it was far better than letting the "buildings" survive each impact visually unscathed.

They did hold it, until the Salik Fleet became fully engaged and could no longer spare the munitions to attack the surface of the planet. Terran ships, the size of wasps trying to sting horse-sized enemy warships, joined the fight as best they could, darting in and out, shooting lasers, slinging missiles, and making nuisances of themselves far out of proportion to their size and the power of their armaments. Particularly when Clees' now upward-turned vision spotted the huge white blasts of spare hyperrelay probes being sacrificed as hydrobombs, by being slung out of their cargo bays toward the enemy vessels.

That shook the enemy. Shook them hard and ripped giant holes in their ships. As Clees sent back to the others what he saw while he floated out of body in orbit over the capital, they could tell exactly when a relay probe was about to hit, by the abrupt shying-away of every V'Dan vessel near that target. The hydrobomb capabilities on those probes were strong enough even at a distance to blow holes that chewed off 12, even 20 percent of each of those five-lobed warships, and over half on a direct hit.

No, the Salik could no longer spare any attention for the surface of the V'Dan homeworld. Satisfied, Clees sank back into his body. Exhausted, Jackie stopped projecting the altered coastline. The moment she ended the mass Gestalt, almost everyone slumped flat on the floor around her. Li'eth leaned into her, his weight and hers counterbalancing each other. To-mi—the Immortal—gently removed her hands, and sent a private thought to the two of them.

(*Thank you for saving this palace. I was told you would. Just as I was told in my history lessons that things should turn out alright in the end, though not always in the clearest details of how,*) she added. (*But I need to get out of here before anyone thinks to question why an "ungifted" doctor was so eager to help a bunch of holy ones save the city.*)

Li'eth didn't bother to open his eyes. (*Because you are a doctor, a medical doctor. So do what a doctor does, and start checking over our vital signs. Even our own holy teachings have warned publicly about the overuse of gifts causing the holy users to collapse.*)

(*Don't sass your elder, young man. Even if it is a brilliant idea.*) Shifting her weight, she checked their pulses, then started moving around to the others, checking a wrist here, a throat there, and some spot on an inner leg joint for the one K'Katta who had joined them.

A few of the Elites came looking for them, but at Dr. Kuna'mi's insistent request, they ran off to fetch blankets and hot sweet drinks for the drained psis, to shelter them against any possible onset of shock while they recovered. One of the Guard murmured in regret-filled tones that one of the two nearest missile impacts had dropped a chunk of wall on top of the Empress; she had been rescued and rushed to the palace infirmary, but it didn't look good.

Te-los immediately lurched to his feet, demanding Elite assistance in getting to his mate. Li'eth chose to remain, as did Balei'in, just in case the enemy managed to start attacking the surface again. Jackie could tell that her Gestalt partner remained partly for her sake, and partly because both of them were so drained, he couldn't have summoned a scrap of biokinesis to save anything but his own life or hers, and only that much out of sheer survival instinct. Instead, she just hugged him close, giving her partner physical comfort as well as mental support, to cushion his deep fears about his mother's health.

The Elite weren't done with their report, however, and their other news was equally grim. The third explosion had struck the North Embassy Wing. The Elite giving them the information said sympathetically that the Guard were doing their best to organize search-and-rescue efforts, but that it probably would be best for Jackie and her Terran companions to wait right where they were while rescue crews searched for and dug out any of her people who had been trapped, injured, or rendered worse by the rubble.

One of the other blasts had short-circuited the power grid

just long enough to make the emergency shelters go into lock-down mode; the people down below were still quite safe—they had communications ability—but they were effectively trapped until the codes were reset, which would still take another hour.

Distressed, torn in his loyalties, Li'eth spoke quietly with Balei'in; his younger brother insisted on Li'eth's remaining with Jackie, while he went to go check on their parents after another half hour passed. A few Guards remained once the drinks and blankets came, but otherwise they were left alone while the fate of the invasion took place overhead.

Gradually, other people came back, Winter Palace staff who started cleaning up the scrambled mess of shoved benches and bits of fallen rubble from battle damage. Some of the impact from those first two explosions had damaged a bit of the Inner Court. Chunks of ceiling had fallen, and one of the two Terran communications bots had toppled. Clees joined them to help reprogram and right the fallen one so that they could continue with their work.

The Terran comm screens flicked to life after half an hour or so. The face that appeared was the same male as before, Captain Andu Li, she realized. The communications officer from the *Embassy 8*. She knew him, as she knew everyone in her embassy. Twisting where she sat on the dais step, Jackie brushed off her black pantsuit and faced the upright tower. "Captain Li, report."

He tipped his head to the side, his golden tanned face looking pale and exhausted. "Commodore Graves says that the last of the Salik are fleeing the system, Ambassador. He'd tell you himself, but some rubble fell on the *Embassy 1*'s nose as it sat in the bay, and they're still going over the damage millimeter by millimeter, repairing it. And . . . we lost the *10*, *13*, *21*, and *28*. There are half a dozen other ships in need of minor to major repairs, and the *25* and the *17* are badly damaged, but they are able to limp in under their own power. The *17* actually only lost its nose cone and a bit of hull integrity because of it. They're leaking air very slowly, but her crew got suited in plenty of time. Without the nose cone, the ship's unable to leave the system, but the commander says everything else can be used for spare parts for the other ships, so repair turn-around time will be pretty swift if she's the one dismantled.

"I, uh, can't get a signal from the surface, other than these towers and the *1* still in the North Hangar. How are things down there, sir?"

Jackie shook her head. "Bad. We don't know how badly the North Embassy Wing was hit. Just that it was hit after the Salik took out the palace shields. Just one missile's worth, but we've been asked to stay here, to keep us out of the way of the rescue efforts."

Off to the side, a group of red-and-gold-clad V'Dan reentered the Inner Court from the door behind her. Captain Li lifted his brows. "Why aren't you using your telekinesis to help with the rescue efforts, sir?"

"Yes, Grand High Ambassador," she heard Vi'alla state coldly. "Why *aren't* you using your vast holy powers to rescue your own people?"

Twisting so that she faced the other woman a bit more, Jackie replied just as coldly, "Because I have *exhausted* myself—I have exhausted *everyone* you see sitting here—to the point of being unable to even stand up, from rescuing your *entire* capital city. The *only* reason why this palace and its city were not bombed into blackened *shakk* is because—at great personal expense—I projected a holokinetic *lie* that the city was ten kilometers *west* of here. Out over the open sea.

"Your own eldest brother directed your youngest brother and father in *deflecting* most of those missiles westward to match my massive cloaking illusion," she continued, letting her anger give her some energy and heat to her reply. "He *would* have been advanced enough in his skills by now to have deflected *all* of them if we hadn't had to tread oh so *softly* around your squeamishness about our Gestalt bond. If your people hadn't been so *prejudiced* about the way *my people look*, we could have advanced our bond to the point where we could have *returned those missiles to their owners*.

". . . But no," Jackie finished, her anger draining out of her along with most of her energy. "The way we *look* has been too important to you and your people to see the damage your attitudes have been causing."

(*Jackie,*) Li'eth tried to soothe her. His sister cut that idea dead.

"You will *not* talk to me that way," Vi'alla growled. She

lifted the object in her hands, faced the temple-room behind the throne, and called out, "By the laws of V'Dan, I, Imperial Princess Vi'alla Sha-nu'en Tal'u-nakh Tuen-la V'Daania, duly acknowledged Heir to the Empire, take up the War Crown as Regent while Empress Hana'ka Iu'tua Has-natell Q'una-hash Mi'idenei V'Daania strives to recover from her injuries. Until the day she takes this from my head or her death bestows it permanently in place, I am Regent Princess Vi'alla V'Daania, rightful ruler in my mother's place!"

Her voice echoed through the not-quite-empty hall. The staff members who had been discreetly straightening and tidying had stilled during her strong-voiced speech. Now they all dropped to one knee, as did the Elite Guards, and thumped their fists over their hearts. In ragged unison, they shouted, "All hail Regent Princess Vi'alla V'Daania!"

Li'eth moved with them, twisting from sitting on one of the steps to half kneeling on it. Grimly, he lifted his fist to his heart as well, though he couldn't bring himself to speak in unison with the others. Jackie could feel how unhappy he was about this moment.

Jackie's response was a bit different. She waited to see if there was more to the ceremony, then snapped, "Captain Li! Connect us to Premiere Callan and get us a full broadcast to every V'Dan signal you can. I suspect the next few moments will either make or break the whole Alliance, and I want everyone to know *why*."

"Aye, sir," Captain Li confirmed. The transparent screens flashed blue and silver, displaying the logo of the United Planets.

Vi'alla, the War Crown now perched on her head—either the one that had been on her mother's head, or perhaps a duplicate—faced Jackie with a faint sneer. "What, exactly, do you think *you* are going to do about my regency? You have *no* say over what happens in the Empire."

The screens shifted from blue to an image of the Premiere's face. Behind him lay the Dome, the Premiere's office; the late-evening Council session had no doubt been canceled because of the local need to focus on surviving the Salik onslaught taking so long. They would still have to deal with the subject of Shi'ol's punishment and the Terran United Planets' demand to the V'Dan Empire on how to handle the prejudices behind her actions, but for now, the Premiere and the recording equipment on his end of the link were enough of a witness for what might come next. ". . . Ambassador MacKenzie? Is everything alright?"

Drawing upon the dregs of her reserves, Jackie pushed herself up onto her feet. (*I'm sorry, Li'eth.*) It was all she could afford to say to him. Shielding her mind tightly, bracing her legs so that she stood without wavering, she faced down the blond regent even as she bent metaphorically under the protocols of the situation. "Premiere Augustus Callan, I present to you Regent Princess Vi'alla V'Daania, who has taken up the War Crown in her mother's absence. The Salik invasion fleet has been sent running. Unfortunately, the Empress of V'Dan has been severely injured in the Salik attack, along with an unknown number of Terran and other personnel. We may not know for hours just who has been injured or killed . . . but we still have a very serious question in need of an answer."

Turning, she faced the Regent Princess.

"Think *carefully*, Vi'alla, about the needs of your people. Think *carefully*, Regent, about the *usefulness* of Terran strengths and Terran technologies in today's fight . . . and in all the fights that are yet to come. We grieve with you for the suffering of your mother and your people, for the injured and the dead . . . but we must still stand here and assert our right to be treated with respect and equality in the eyes of you and your people. We demand respect from your people. And we demand that those who continue to insult us, in the face of our right to be respected as peers, as equals, as allies—throughout *all* Tiers, even unto the Imperial Family—those who persist in insulting us must undergo a mind-block by a Terran psychic to remove the source of *your* pervasive cultural disrespect toward us: your overemphasis on your awareness of your precious, petty *jungen* marks.

"We will be kind in the light of today's tragedy, and will be willing to defer the final, permanent decision in this matter until your mother's health and recovery are known . . . but we demand that you treat us and our rights as sovereign adults with the respect we are due in the interim."

Vi'alla planted her fists on her golden-covered hips and

leaned in close enough that Jackie could feel the heat of her breath. "I will *never* allow your people to touch *my mind* . . . and I will *never* allow you to touch the minds of *my people!*"

Silence followed those low-growled words. Two seconds, four seconds . . .

Premiere Callan spoke. "Ambassador MacKenzie. I am Augustus Callan, Premiere of the Terran United Planets, Commander-in-Chief of the Terran United Planets Space Force . . . and I accept my responsibility in the consequences of the following command: Initiate Executive Order *Victor Delta Delta Zero*, authorization *Charlie-India-Charlie Alpha Charlie*. Every spare ship we have will be under way within the hour. Good luck, and Godspeed."

"Understood. Regent Princess Vi'alla," Jackie stated, her voice darkening with a mix of her anger, disappointment, and regret. On the Terran screens, the Premiere's face vanished, replaced by the exhausted and now-anxious, somber expression of Captain Li. "We thank you for your nation's hospitality. We will begin our evacuation efforts immediately. It will take some time, as there are still bodies, some injured, some probably slain, to be dug out of the rubble and accounted for. We also have ships that need to be repaired, and ships that need to reach V'Dan to aid in the evacuation. I trust you will be compassionate enough to allow us to do so in an orderly fashion.

"Be warned, however, that our patience and kindness, our *understanding* has ended. *Any* attempt to seize Terran property or personnel will be met as a declaration of war. Do not seek to detain us," Jackie added, while the Regent frowned in confusion. "I will remind you this once—since you seem so easily prone to forget such things—that *we* can coordinate both our attacks *and* our defenses . . . and you have *not* seen every weapon in our arsenal.

"You may keep the plans for hydrogenerators and so forth, as we shall keep the plans for artificial gravity . . . but we will *not* give you the secrets of making the catalyst for those generators. And yes, we *also* deny you *all* access to our hyper-relays. Captain Li? You heard the Premiere's orders and authorization?"

"Ambassador, yes, sir," the man on the robot tower screens replied.

"Please log this date and time, for following through on Executive Order *Victor Delta Delta Zero*."

"Time and date . . . logged, sir. Standing by to execute *Victor Delta Delta Zero* whenever you are ready, sir," Captain Li stated.

"Detonate, authorization *Juliett Mike*."

The images on the trio of screens held aloft by the two display towers immediately sparked with static and faded to clear. Vi'alla's frown deepened. "What . . . what just happened? What was that . . . executive order?"

"You now have a modestly small but very hot crater on the nearest side of your nearest moon," Jackie explained coldly. "Right where the *Terran* hyperrelay probe used to be. It, of course, has been obliterated as a warning of what will happen if you attempt to access any others. All of the other hyperrelays have been shut down and locked into countersabotage mode. They will no longer transmit *anything* until we send a very specific code to unlock their capabilities. Any attempt to move or open them will cause those probes to explode. Probes, I politely remind you, that were quite capable of vaporizing significant chunks of those rather large Salik warships that were attacking this world just a very short time ago."

"What . . . ?" Vi'alla leaned back in confused shock. "You can't . . ."

Jackie ignored her faint protest. The older woman was an idiot who needed to have things explained to her in painstaking detail. "The *only* hyperrelay communications equipment that still function in this system are the relays that are on board our ships. To rephrase more bluntly what I stated earlier, if your people even so much as *pat* the surface of one of our hulls without our clearly expressed and directly supervised permission from this moment onward . . . it will be taken as a declaration of war.

"In short, Regent Princess," Jackie bit out each word through her bared teeth, "respect for your allies is *everything*. Without it, your people—your whole Alliance!—will get *nothing* more from us." Turning, she strode down the shallow steps. Carefully, because she was still exhausted, and her balance threatened to wobble with each step. "I am going to go to the North Embassy Wing to see how my people are doing and to oversee our evacuation of this place."

"You cannot do that!" Vi'alla countermanded, anger and anxiety putting a stark edge into her demand.

Jackie swung around carefully, still mindful of how exhausted she was. "Oh yes, I can. You heard it from *my* emperor's lips. Executive Order *Victor Delta Delta Zero* instructed me to close this embassy, cut off all hyperrelay communications across the entire Alliance—not just the V'Dan Empire—and to evacuate my people as swiftly and safely as I can. Furthermore, it *also* instructs me—via the word *zero*, which means *nothing*—that the Terran government will *never* deal with you, personally. You violated the one thing a leader *must* always do: put the needs of his or her people *before* their own bruised feelings and arrogant attitudes.

"For your people's sake, Regent, I hope Her Eternal Majesty recovers swiftly and recovers well. When she does, or should anyone *else* take up the Eternal Throne and its responsibilities, we will consider dealing with them *if* they approach us in person to apologize and agree to our demand regarding the mind-blocks. But we will not deal with *you*. You, Vi'alla, have lost all respect in the eyes of my people. A very heavy price to pay, compared to the very tiny one of losing the ability to see a bunch of childish *blotches* on someone's skin."

She held the stunned regent's gaze a few seconds more, then swung around and started toward the door and hallway she remembered would take her back to the North Embassy Wing.

"What about Imperial Prince Kah'raman?" Vi'alla called out. "I guess your claims of the two of you being a holy pairing are a *lie* if you can so *easily abandon him*!"

Jackie stopped and turned once again. She faced Vi'alla, Li'eth, and the others. Clees, the only Terran still present, had risen and followed her. The others had fled to the bunkers, which meant the only ones left were the V'Dan psis who had helped them, who had been ordered to stay in place by the Elite for the time being. They looked like they either wanted to beg her to change her mind or wanted to be anywhere else. Every V'Dan but her Gestalt partner and the regent looked like they would rather have been anywhere else, right then.

Her mental walls were tissue-thin, since most of her strength was going into the physical effort of standing and moving, but she felt Li'eth restraining himself behind his own barriers so as not to influence her. For that much, he had her gratitude, for making this moment easier on her. For his sake—for both their sakes—she gave the truth.

"Imperial Prince Kah'raman Li'eth is free to stay if he wishes. He is also free to accompany us back to Earth if he wishes. But I *will not* remain." She saw his gray-and-burgundy gaze soften in relief that she would not deny him the right to accompany her—only his own kinswoman could *attempt* to do that—but did not respond to it. Shifting her gaze to his eldest sister, she stated, "It is crystal clear to me that *you*, Vi'alla, do not understand the responsibilities and prices a *true* leader must pay. In your case, you should have set aside your pride and your arrogance long enough to consider the long-term consequences of your overly proud insistence that you are automatically superior to us.

"In my case, the pain, suffering, and eventual decline and death each of us will undergo if he chooses to remain behind— or is *forced* to remain—will be nothing compared to the on-going suffering my entire *nation* would have had to endure at your people's prejudiced hands, without the threat of a mind-block to get them to look beyond mere skin color. I will *not* trade your arrogant disrespecting of billions of people for my own life and happiness . . . and my people sent me here knowing I will *always* choose the welfare and best interests of the Terran Empire over *anything* Li'eth could offer me in return. Gestalt bond or otherwise."

Facing away from the throne once more, Jackie resumed her slow, determined walk.

"You will not leave this hall! I command you to return!" The tone Vi'alla used was a double-edged sword, filled with both rising desperation and ongoing anger. "I will have you arrested!"

"Your threats are empty and hollow, Regent . . . because *my* people do not bow to the rantings of petty tyrants," Jackie dismissed coldly, stopping briefly, but without turning around this time. She spoke loudly, letting her words echo off the walls around them. "We are polite, and we are honorable, and we are stronger than the hardest of stones, the hottest of stars. My people will sacrifice me, and *every* member of our embassy, rather than cave in to your demands . . . and I knew this *before* I agreed to this post. So long as you are either regent *or* an Heir of the V'Dan Empire, *my* people will not have *anything* to do with you.

"Imperial Prince Kah'raman . . . you have until the last Terran ship leaves V'Dan to make up your mind. You may stay, or you may go with us. In the meantime, please convey my apologies to everyone in the Alliance with any sense of humility and compassion left in their heads. The rest of your people, including your eldest sibling, can rot in a Salik holding cell," she told the gaping staff, the Elite Guards, the exhausted psis, and the no-doubt-furious Regent Princess, given the insults Jackie was spouting. She wanted to say something about Vi'alla's giving the Salik as much indigestion as the Regent Princess had given her . . . but she could feel Li'eth's memory-seared pain at the mere mention of one of their holding cells. (*I'm sorry. That wasn't right of me. I should not have said that.*)

(*Thank you.*) He said nothing more, keeping his thoughts locked away from hers.

"You cannot go! You cannot take your communications gear from us!" Vi'alla demanded. "We *need* it!"

Jacaranda MacKenzie did not turn around. She forced herself to start moving again, and let the last of her hard-shouted words echo off the aging stone walls of the Inner Court, before she and the silent, grim-faced Heracles vanished into the hallway beyond.

"The Terran Embassy to V'Dan is now officially *closed*!"

READ ON FOR A SNEAK PEEK AT
THE NEXT BOOK IN JEAN JOHNSON'S
FIRST SALIK WAR SERIES

THE BLOCKADE

AVAILABLE IN JULY 2016 FROM ACE BOOKS!

"The Terran Embassy to V'Dan is now officially *closed*!"

Ambassador MacKenzie's final words echoed down the hall, stifling the right of anyone to make a sound in the wake of her departure. Seated on the top step of the highest dais of his mother's court, Li'eth felt that silence pressing down on him, squeezing his skin like some sort of congealing plastic film, for all he sat clad in comfortable silk and ballistics cloth.

His military uniform no longer fit him. It was still tailored perfectly to his figure, every crimson seam straight, every golden line neat . . . but the loyalty and pride with which Imperial Prince Kah'raman once wore it no longer fit the man whom Li'eth had become.

Li'eth loved his home nation. He loved his people. He loved his family. Mostly. Most of the time.

Right now . . . he wanted to smack his eldest sister repeatedly about the head and shoulders with the hardest, heaviest pillow he could find. Or something that would solidly bruise some sense back into her without actually killing or crippling her. Except the absurd idea of him smacking his sister—the Imperial Regent Princess Vi'alla V'Daania—about the head and shoulders with a pillow like some common Fifth Tier sibling did not cheer him out of his . . . grief? Regret? Ire? Despair? Desolation.

He had thought he knew Jacaranda MacKenzie, Grand High Ambassador of the Terran United Planets. No, he *did* know her. He had *known* Jackie would choose to serve and protect the needs and rights of her people over any personal inconvenience, pain, or peril. And she had chosen it, just now. They were bound in a holy pairing, a Gestalt of his and her psychically gifted minds entangled on a quantum level—the will of the Saints, pure random chance, or fate, he did not know. They were bound, and he could feel her subthoughts of pain and determination and anger just beyond his innermost walls.

She lived within his outermost mental shields, the very same shields she had taught him how to construct, support, and stabilize strong enough to keep her *out* of his head, even though he didn't want to do that. He did it right now, though, because Jackie was strong enough to do what was right for others, not what was best for herself. Li'eth—Imperial Prince Kah'raman, who had been raised from birth to heed his duty to the Eternal Throne—respected and honored that level of dedication.

Ambassador MacKenzie had chosen to refuse to allow his people to continue to insult hers over and over and over again, all due to a simple yet pervasive cultural difference that was literally just skin-deep. Their embassy was closed. His people had just lost their access to the only form of breathtakingly swift interstellar communication the entire Alliance knew, and he was going to lose personally one way or another, *because* the embassy was closed, his Gestalt partner was headed home . . . and either he would have to stay here and suffer without her, or abandon his people and go with her.

He didn't know what to do.

". . . An Imperial Prince does not sit on the steps of the Inner Court like a common Fifth Tier in a marketplace."

He twisted, looking up at his sister. Vi'alla's face looked tight with returning anger. The same anger that had caused her to refuse to even consider the Terrans' demands that they be either be treated with respect, or those who disrespected them be treated so that they could no longer see the cause of that disrespect via siomething called a mind-block. Her aura had broken into confusion when their Ambassador had closed the embassy, and panic when she discovered Jackie had ordered the nearest Terran hyperrelay unit destroyed. But now, that look on her face was the look of someone furious, hurt, and looking for a target.

She wanted one? He would give her one. Herself. Li'eth pinned his sister with a hard look. "An Imperial Regent does not treat her desperately needed allies like *u'v'shakk*."

Vi'alla stiffened, her gray eyes widening. "You dare talk to *me* that way?"

"You dared talk to *them* that way. Imperial Regent," Li'eth stated formally, pushing to his feet to face down his eldest sister. "Our people *need* what the Terrans can provide."

"Then they need to provide it!" Vi'alla snapped, frowning at him. "Instead of yanking it away like a child!"

"You don't even see it, do you?" Li'eth asked softly, more to himself than to her. *She* was trying to yank it away like a child. A child being deprived of a toy.

"See *what*?" his sister snapped.

Li'eth wracked his brain for a parable that could get her to understand. ". . . Do you remember the story of Saint Ba'nai?"

"A *story*?" she scorned.

"For once in your mind, will you *clear* it?" Li'eth demanded, gesturing at his head. "A *good* Empress listens to the counsel of her people! The story of Saint Ba'nai is about how she tried to get the people of a village she was visiting to listen to her warnings that they were going to be caught in a great fire because of a terrible drought that had plagued the land that year. They were stubborn and set in their ways, proud of their skill in cutting wood, trimming and shaping it, and sending it downriver. The river kept getting lower and lower until they could no longer pole their barges downstream to the cities that needed it, but the villagers kept cutti—"

"—The villagers kept cutting wood until a stray spark set fire to the forest, and only a third of the people managed to escape by heeding Ba'nai's warnings to go deep into the abandoned mines in the mountain while the firestorm raged through, *yes, yes, I know* the legend!" Vi'alla overrode him. "I've studied the *Book of Saints* far more often than you!"

"Did Nanny Ai-sha ever tell you *how* she got a third of the village to listen to her?" Li'eth asked her. "Because Nanny El'cor told *me* how she did it when I asked him." He waited to see if she would dismiss him. When his sister gave him an impatient look, but a silent, listening one, Li'eth said, "El'cor taught me that Ba'nai was of the Fifth Tier, the daughter of a herdsman. A pig herder. She had no training in eloquence, no ability to make fancy speeches, and no real grasp of etiquette, but she was smart, and she occasionally had dreams of the future, what the Terrans call precognition. Those dreams led her to that village.

"That village was filled with skilled laborers, lumberjacks and carpenters, Fourth and Third Tier, higher socially than her place in the Fifth. She was so worried about the firestorms in her dreams, she spoke bluntly, told everyone they had to stop working the lumber, stop leaving sawdust everywhere, stop piling up the bark against their wooden houses and the uncut trees. She demanded that they stop their livelihood, demanded that they leave the area to save their lives. She thought she was doing the right thing, trying to save lives, but *how* she went about it was wrong.

"El'cor taught me that because she was rude, because she did not *show* her respect, Ba'nai could not sway the hearts of the people—she tried urgency, she tried to describe the violence and horror of her visions, but they saw only someone being hysterical over nothing. Finally, one of the village elders spoke to her and reminded her that her words were like too much spice and soured wine in a dish. If she tried speaking sweetly, with respect, speaking of positive things—of gains instead of losses—the people would be more likely to listen to her. And so she went back to the people, and spoke gently, apologizing for her coarse ways, letting them know she understood how valuable their work was, how important their continued livelihoods.

"Saint Ba'nai pointed out how dry everything was, how many piles of dried limbs and sawdust there were, the layers of bark that had been stacked to provide them with fuel for winter fires, the cane poles stacked in bundles and set aside to dry out so they could be light enough to ship downriver when the water rose again and turned into pulp for paper . . . and how much hotter the days were growing. She asked them where they thought would be the safest place in the region to outwait a massive firestorm . . . and some finally listened. Some of the villagers, swayed by her politeness, her logic, told her that there was that abandoned mine in the river ravine.

"She asked them if they would be willing to help her store

water and a bit of food deep in those caves, some old rags and other supplies. Some of them actually helped her . . . and when the terrible fire started, she was able to get those people deep into those caves, cover their faces with wet cloths, and stay there while the world far above burned so hot and hard, they could not go near the entrance for three full days. Those whom she had turned into her friends with kind words were willing to cooperate, willing to go with her, and willing to understand that she meant the best for them. They grieved for those who felt too badly disrespected and who had perished, but rejoiced that she had managed to save at least *some* of their lives."

Vi'alla eyed him, her mouth tight, then lifted her chin toward the hall the Ambassador had taken. "Then *she* should have spoken sweetly to *me*, instead of with soured wine and too much spice!"

Li'eth felt his shoulders start to slump. She hadn't seen the analogy correctly. "Wrong person, Vi'alla. Ba'nai needed to be kind and respectful to those who had what she wanted, because she needed their cooperation. She was willing to come help save them, and she was willing to warn them of all the dangers, and she was willing to help them make a plan to survive . . . but she needed *their* cooperation. *Their* knowledge of the terrain. *Their* help in stockpiling resources.

"*We* need the *Terrans'* technology. Yet all we have done as a nation is be rude to them, like how Ba'nai treated those Third and Fourth Tiers like Fifth Tiers—we have been treating Terran *First* Tiers like Fifth Tiers," he emphasized, pointing at that hallway, where Jackie had vanished. "*All* non-V'Dan are to be treated like respected members of the Third Tier, as they are all *experts* in the knowledge of their ways and their people. More than that, their leadership is to be treated as equals of the First *and* Imperial Tiers. Yet we—the V'Dan Empire—consistently have treated them like *less* than Fifth Tiers.

"The irony in this, sister, is that without them, *we* are the villagers being burned alive by the Salik and their war," he told her, pointing upward. "The whole Empire is at stake! You don't get people willing to listen to your needs by being disrespectful to them. You don't encourage people to share what they have by demanding and grabbing and then *insulting* their hospitality and their generosity. You don't *close your ears* to their legitimate complaints about being disrespected, insulted, and treated as infants instead of as adult allies, and then *expect* them to still like you enough to *want* to stay and help you.

"And you, Imperial *Regent*," he emphasized, pointing at her, "have forgotten that it *is* my job as a member of the Imperial Tier to warn you when *you* are on a path that will destroy the Empire. *Which* is more important to you, Regent? Your personal pride? Or the survival of the Empire?"

"You *dare* ask me that?" Vi'alla demanded through clenched teeth, her hands tightening into fists at her sides.

"I am obliged to point out that your *pride* is busy making *enemies* of the *allies we need*," he reminded her fiercely. "You were free to be angry at them as a mere princess, yes, but you are now the Regent, and the needs of your people *must* come before everything else! Including your own feelings and opinions."

"If they weren't so stubborn—"

"That's the *jumax'a* flower calling the sky blue!" he retorted. "You have exactly two ways to get your hands on Terran technology, Vi'alla: You can *attempt* to steal it from them, turning them into our enemies . . . and they have *tens of thousands* of highly trained holy ones they can unleash upon us, never mind their ship hulls that cannot be deeply damaged by our energy weapons, and that can travel from system to system in mere moments.

"Or, you can swallow your pride, seek them out instead of demand they come to you, *apologize sincerely*, and try to make amends, to make *friends* of them." He stared at her, hoping she would understand. "Because the *third* option is to continue to abandon your duty to your people, and *prove* yourself unfit for the throne. Which is it, Vi'alla? Think *carefully*."

She glared back at him in anger, not saying a word. Li'eth knew he had backed his sister into a corner, though. Backing up a step, he bowed, then moved around her.

"I'm going to go check on Mother and Father. With luck, she will pull through and you won't have to choose between debasing yourself to do the right thing, or condemning the Empire to die out of pride. At the hands of one enemy *or* another."

It took her a few moments to find her voice. Just before he

reached the side exit on the uppermost dais, she asked, "You honestly think the Terrans can take on the might of the *Empire*? They don't even have any colonies outside their own star system!"

Swinging around to face her, Li'eth pointed at his sister. "Your arrogance and your pride are blinding you to reality, sister. If you do not reconsider your actions, your words, your beliefs, and your *responses* to all these events, then I am going to have to make a formal recommendation to the Imperial Cabinet that you be *reconsidered* as Regent. The War Crown is best worn by the most *competent* member of the Imperial Blood. *Not* necessarily the eldest-born . . . and your actions so far today are *not* that competent."

It was political suicide to say such things, but Li'eth was too angry. Turning back around, he headed for the hospital wing. He wanted to reach out to Jackie, to find out how she was doing, to learn who, if any, of her staff had been harmed in the attack . . . but her mental shields were tightly sealed at the moment. He couldn't bring himself to knock on that metaphysical wall, not when he didn't know what he could do to help the situation.

Footsteps approached. A familiar dark blond, almost brunette braided head streaked with hot pink came into view. V'kol looked up from the tablet in his hand, relief in his eyes. "Finally! Did you know my clearance to know your whereabouts as your military attaché doesn't cover when we're under attack? Who *invents* these rules?"

Li'eth rubbed at the bridge of his nose. "I'll see what I can do. What news do you have?"

"The palace is still on lockdown, but the admirals have confirmed that the Salik Fleet appears to have retreated from the system. They're at a bit of a loss to report more than that, though, because of the broadcasts the Terrans shared, before . . . ending transmission." V'kol gave him a grim, worried look. He glanced around, then moved in close and whispered, ". . . *Is your sister insane? Doing what she did?*"

"I don't know," Li'eth confessed out loud. "I honestly do not know. I am going to log a recommendation to the Imperial Cabinet that she be reconsidered as Regent. Her decisions so far have not been good ones for the Empire."

"Are you *crazy?"* V'kol hissed under his breath, turning to follow the prince as he kept walking. *"I am certain that* every- thing *that takes place in these halls is being recorded, and* that *is political suicide."*

His people had a saying: stealing a spoonful, stealing a barrel. If one was going to be caught for theft—under the old harsh penalties of his foremost ancestor—then one might as well go for a big score, rather than just a tiny fraction of it. "I *am* aware everything is being recorded. Including my sister's insistence upon alienating and chasing away the allies we need out of simple pride and arrogance. Her choices, made rashly out of anger and some aggrandized sense of self-importance, have cost us an *important* alliance.

"The rank of Imperial Regent is temporary. And it rests upon the requirement that the Regent consider and undertake whatever is *best* for the Empire during the period of the re- gency. Insulting our allies and disrespecting them to the point that they would rather leave than stay and help us survive is *not* good for the Empire at this point in time, let alone what is best," Li'eth told his fellow officer, cutting his hand through the air.

V'kol eyed his friend, but said nothing for several seconds. Li'eth started to turn to the left at the next junction, but the leftenant superior caught his elbow. "Not that way. The hall's a wreck, that way. That's where they pulled Her Eternity out of the rubble. We'll have to take one of the other lift clusters. I'd say take a stairwell, but it's seventeen floors down to the tram, and then another six back up to get to the palace infirmary."

Nodding, Li'eth turned to the right, and both men walked in silence. The next bank of lifts waited for them down a shal- low flight of stairs and at the far end of a long hallway. Two Imperial Elite Guards approached from a side hall just when they neared those lifts. Both gold-and-scarlet-clad men bore grim expressions, their attention focused on the prince.

Wary, Li'eth slowed. ". . . Is everything alright?"

"Imperial Prince Kah'raman. By order of the Imperial Re- gent, you are to report immediately to the *Dusk Army* for reas- signment back in space," the right-hand Elite told him.

Li'eth narrowed his eyes. "My assignment is liaison to the Terrans. While the Terrans are still here, I am still their liaison."

"Their embassy is closed," the Elite on the left stated. "That means your position as liaison has ended. We are to escort you straight to East Hangar Bay 2 where you will be flown to your next duty post."

This was not right. Something was very much not right. "I choose to exercise my right as Imper—"

"—Sorry," the Elite on the left apologized blandly, drawing a small hand-held device from his thigh pocket.

Li'eth recognized it instantly, a V'Dan version of a Salik stunner pistol. He had an instant in which to react, and flung out a telekinetic wall, shoving everyone back. Unfortunately, the Elite's aim was true . . . and a holy force that could move physical objects did absolutely nothing to stop an energy-based weapon . . . just as Master Sonam had once warned him, during his lessons on what telekinesis could, and could not do. Static snapped over his senses, dropping him out of consciousness.

From national bestselling author

JEAN JOHNSON

THE THEIRS NOT TO REASON WHY NOVELS

A SOLDIER'S DUTY

AN OFFICER'S DUTY

HELLFIRE

HARDSHIP

DAMNATION

PRAISE FOR THE SERIES

"Reminiscent of both *Starship Troopers* and *Dune*."
—*Publishers Weekly*

"An engrossing military SF series."
—*SF Signal*

jeanjohnson.net
facebook.com/AceRocBooks
penguin.com

M1662AS0415